ALFRED BESTER

VIRTUAL
UNREALITIES

Alfred Bester was born in New York in 1913. After attending the University of Pennsylvania, he sold several short stories to *Thrilling Wonder Stories* in the early 1940s. He then embarked on a career as a scripter for comics, radio, and television, where he worked on such classic characters as Superman, Batman, Nick Carter, Charlie Chan, Tom Corbett, and the Shadow. In the 1950s, he returned to prose, publishing several short stories and two brilliant, seminal novels, *The Demolished Man* (which was the first winner of the Hugo Award for Best Novel) and *The Stars My Destination*. In the late 1950s, he wrote travel articles for *Holiday* magazine, and eventually became their Senior Literary Editor, keeping the position until the magazine folded in the 1970s. In 1974, he once again came back to writing science fiction with the novels *The Computer Connection*, *Golem[100]*, and *The Deceivers*, and numerous short stories. After being a New Yorker all his life, he died in Pennsylvania in 1987, but not before he was honored by the Science Fiction & Fantasy Writers of America with a Grandmaster Award.

VIRTUAL
UNREALITIES

VIRTUAL
UNREALITIES

THE SHORT FICTION OF

ALFRED BESTER

INTRODUCTION BY ROBERT SILVERBERG

STORIES SELECTED BY ROBERT SILVERBERG, BYRON PREISS, AND KEITH R. A. DECANDIDO

A BYRON PREISS BOOK

VINTAGE BOOKS A DIVISION OF RANDOM HOUSE, INC. / NEW YORK

A VINTAGE BOOKS ORIGINAL, NOVEMBER 1997
FIRST EDITION

A Byron Preiss Visual Publications, Inc. Book
Special thanks to Kirby McCauley, J. Edward Kastenmeier, Martin Asher, Carol D. Page, and Minsun Pak

Library of Congress Cataloging-in-Publication Data
Bester, Alfred.
Virtual unrealities : the short fiction of Alfred Bester / introduction by Robert Silverberg ; stories selected by Robert Silverberg, Byron Preiss, and Keith R. A. DeCandido.
p.   cm.
"A Byron Preiss book."
"A Vintage original."
ISBN 978-0-679-76783-1
I. Silverberg, Robert.   II. Preiss, Byron.   III. DeCandido, Keith R. A.
IV. Title.
PS3552.E796V57   1997
813'.54—dc21   97-8738 CIP

Book design by Iris Weinstein

Random House Web address: http://www.randomhouse.com/

Printed in the United States of America

146086900

CONTENTS

CONTENTS

INTRODUCTION
Robert Silverberg

Alfred Bester was a winner right from the start—quite literally. His very first story ("The Broken Axiom," *Thrilling Wonder Stories,* April 1939) carried off that month's $50 prize in the Amateur Story Contest that *Thrilling Wonder* was then running every issue to attract new talent. He was twenty-five years old, a graduate of the University of Pennsylvania (where he majored, he liked to say, "in music, physiology, art, and psychology"), and was working at the time as a public relations man while pondering the challenges of a career as a writer.

"The Broken Axiom" isn't a marvelous story, which is one of several reasons why it hasn't been included in this collection. It is, in

fact, a creaky and pretty silly item full of pseudoscientific gobbledy-
gook and cardboard characters, which Bester himself spoke of later
as "rotten." But silly gobbledygooky stories were something that the
garishly pulpy old *Thrilling Wonder Stories* published by the dozens in
those days, and this initial contribution by the novice Bester was well
up there in professionalism with the rest of that issue's copy, all of
which was the work of veteran pros.

And observe, if you will, the magnificent cockeyed pizazz and
breathtaking narrative thrust with which Bester gets his first story in
motion, back there nearly sixty years ago:

> It was a fairly simple apparatus, considering what it could
> do. A Coolidge tube modified to my own use, a large Radley
> force-magnet, an atomic pick-up, and an operating table.
> This, the duplicate set on the other side of the room, plus a
> vacuum tube some ten feet long by three inches in diameter,
> were all that I needed.
>
> Graham was rather dumfounded when I showed it to
> him. He stared at the twin mechanism and the silvered tube
> swung overhead and then turned and looked blankly at me.
>
> "This is all?" he asked.
>
> "Yes," I smiled. "It's about as simple as the incandescent
> electric lamp, and I think as amazing."

And with that he was off and running on a literary career that
was a lot less simple than the incandescent electric lamp, and just
about as amazing.

For the next forty-odd years, this dynamic and formidably
charismatic man blazed a bewildering zigzag trail across the world of
science fiction. But that was only a part-time amusement for him; he
also wrote plays, the libretto for an opera, radio scripts, comic-book
continuity, television scripts, travel essays, and a million other things.
Every now and then the desire to write science fiction came over
him, though, like a sort of fit, and he let it have its way. And thus
he gave us two of the most astonishing science fiction novels ever
written (*The Demolished Man* and *The Stars My Destination*) and, inter-
mittently over the decades, a couple of dozen flamboyant and extraordinary short stories, stories that are like none ever written by
anyone else, stories that leave the reader dizzy with amazement.

When Bester was at the top of his form, he was utterly inimitable; when he missed his mark, he usually missed it by five or six parsecs. But he was always flabbergasting. This is how the critic Damon Knight put it in a 1957 essay:

> Dazzlement and enchantment are Bester's methods. His stories never stand still a moment; they're forever tilting into motion, veering, doubling back, firing off rockets to distract you. The repetition of the key phrase in "Fondly Fahrenheit," the endless reappearances of Mr. Aquila in "The Starcomber" are offered mockingly: try to grab at them for stability, and you find they mean something new each time. Bester's science is all wrong, his characters are not characters but funny hats; but you never notice: he fires off a smoke-bomb, climbs a ladder, leaps from a trapeze, plays three bars of "God Save the King," swallows a sword and dives into three inches of water. Good heavens, what more do you want?

Even those "rotten" early stories of Bester's display the restless fizz of imagination that is his hallmark. Most of them really are stinkers, objects casually assembled out of handy spare parts to meet the modest needs of the prewar penny-a-word pulp magazine market. Though there are flashes of pure Besterian magic in every one of them, all but a few stick close to the conventional fiction formulas of the era. But "Adam and No Eve" (*Astounding Science Fiction*, September 1941) was good enough to get into *Adventures in Time and Space*, the first of the classic science fiction anthologies, and it still has a great deal to say to today's readers. And the wild and frantic fantasy novella "Hell is Forever" (*Unknown Worlds*, August 1942) unleashes the manic power of Bester's prose in a way that gives a clear clue to the passionate risk taking and experimentation that marks the fiction of his full maturity.

After that first burst of science fiction, though, he took an eight-year hiatus, during which he wrote reams of comic strip continuity—for *Superman*, *Captain Marvel*, *The Green Lantern*, many others, and scripts for such radio shows as *Nero Wolfe*, *Charlie Chan*, and *The Shadow*. When television arrived on the scene after the war, Bester tried his hand at that too, but it was an unhappy experience in which his volcanic drive toward originality of expression put him into violent collision with the powerful commercial forces ruling the new medium. In 1950—36 years old, and entering into his literary maturity—he found himself looking once more toward science fiction.

There had been great changes in the science fiction field during Bester's eight-year absence, and no need now existed for him to conform to the hackneyed pulp magazine conventions. Before the war, there had been only one editor willing to publish science fiction aimed at intelligent and sophisticated readers—John W. Campbell, the editor of *Astounding Science Fiction* and its fantasy-fiction companion, *Unknown Worlds*. In Campbell's two magazines such first-rank science fiction writers as Robert A. Heinlein, Isaac Asimov, Theodore Sturgeon, L. Sprague de Camp, and A. E. van Vogt found their natural home. The seven or eight other magazines relied primarily on juvenile tales of fast-paced adventure featuring heroic space captains, villainous space pirates, mad scientists, and glamorous lady journalists.

But that kind of crude action fiction had largely gone out of fashion by 1950, and most of the old science fiction pulps had either folded or upgraded their product. Campbell's adult and thoughtful *Astounding* was still in business, though—(*Unknown Worlds* had vanished during the war, a victim of paper shortages)—and it had been joined by two ambitious newcomers, *Fantasy and Science Fiction*, edited by the erudite, witty Anthony Boucher, and *Galaxy*, whose editor was the gifted and ferociously competitive Horace Gold.

Bester began his return to science fiction with a story for Campbell—"Oddy and Id," which Campbell published under the title of "The Devil's Invention" in *Astounding* for August 1950. But the postwar Campbell had become obsessed with Dianetics, a technique of psychotherapy invented by science fiction writer L. Ron Hubbard that Bester regarded as quackery—and Bester found the changed atmosphere around the great editor too uncongenial for comfort. He turned instead to the new magazines of Boucher and Gold, and never wrote for *Astounding* again.

His stories for those magazines, infrequent though they were, had an immediate and explosive effect that moved him swiftly to the forefront of the field. The first was the whimsical little "Of Time and Third Avenue" (*Fantasy and Science Fiction*, October 1951). Then came the remarkable novel *The Demolished Man*, which *Galaxy* serialized in its issues for January, February, and March of 1952. Science fiction had never seen anything remotely like it—a stunningly intricate futuristic detective story coupled with startling applications of elements of Freudian theory and told in a manner rich with Joycean linguistic inventiveness. The book made an overwhelming impact—in 1953 it received the very first Hugo award as best science fiction novel of the year—and has been regarded as a classic ever since.

In the wake *The Demolished Man* came a steady series of shorter works, all of them brilliant on a smaller scale: "Hobson's Choice" (*Fantasy and Science Fiction*, August 1952), "Time is the Traitor" (*Fantasy and Science Fiction*, September 1953), "Disappearing Act" (*Star Science Fiction #2*, 1953), "5,271,009" (*Fantasy & Science Fiction*, March 1954), and the most spectacular one of all, "Fondly Fahrenheit" (*Fantasy & Science Fiction*, August 1954), a bravura demonstration of literary technique about which an entire textbook could be written.

Despite the wildly enthusiastic response these stories engendered, science fiction never became anything other than a hobby for Alfred Bester: perhaps for the best, for it is hard to see how anyone could have kept up this level of imaginative fertility on a day-by-day basis. His stories, every one a dazzler, appeared every year or two in *Fantasy and Science Fiction*, and his second novel, the awesome *The Stars My Destination*, proved to be a fitting companion to *The Demolished Man* when it appeared in *Galaxy* in 1956. But he was spending most of his time overseas now, doing travel articles for *Holiday* magazine and such other slick publications of the time as *McCall's* and *Show*. In the final two decades of his life—he died in 1987 at the age of 73—his work in science fiction was sporadic at best. He did write several late novels and a handful of short stories, and the unmistakable Bester touch is evident in all of them, though they fall short of the formidable achievement of his finest work.

How formidable, actually, was that achievement?

Alfred Bester's two great novels must rank in almost everyone's top-ten list of science fiction's all-time peaks. And his body of short stories puts him, I think, among the two or three finest writers of short science fiction who ever lived. It has been a delight to experience those stories once again in the course of assembling this collection; and if you will be encountering them for the first time as you read this book, I envy you the pleasure.

—Robert Silverberg
Oakland, California
September 1996

VIRTUAL
UNREALITIES

DISAPPEARING ACT

T his one wasn't the last war or a war to end war. They called it the War for the American Dream. General Carpenter struck that note and sounded it constantly.

There are fighting generals (vital to an army), political generals (vital to an administration), and public relations generals (vital to a war). General Carpenter was a master of public relations. Forthright and Four-Square, he had ideals as high and as understandable as the mottoes on money. In the mind of America he *was* the army, the administration, the nation's shield and sword and stout right arm. His ideal was the American Dream.

ALFRED BESTER

"We are not fighting for money, for power, or for world domination," General Carpenter announced at the Press Association dinner.

"We are fighting solely for the American Dream," he said to the 162nd Congress.

"Our aim is not aggression or the reduction of nations to slavery," he said at the West Point Annual Officers' Dinner.

"We are fighting for the Meaning of Civilization," he told the San Francisco Pioneers' Club.

"We are struggling for the Ideal of Civilization; for Culture, for Poetry, for the Only Things Worth Preserving," he said at the Chicago Wheat Pit Festival.

"This is a war for survival," he said. "We are not fighting for ourselves, but for our Dreams; for the Better Things in Life which must not disappear from the face of the earth."

America fought. General Carpenter asked for one hundred million men. The army was given one hundred million men. General Carpenter asked for ten thousand U-Bombs. Ten thousand U-Bombs were delivered and dropped. The enemy also dropped ten thousand U-Bombs and destroyed most of America's cities.

"We must dig in against the hordes of barbarism," General Carpenter said. "Give me a thousand engineers."

One thousand engineers were forthcoming and a hundred cities were dug and hollowed out beneath the rubble.

"Give me five hundred sanitation experts, eight hundred traffic managers, two hundred air-conditioning experts, one hundred city managers, one thousand communication chiefs, seven hundred personnel experts . . ."

The list of General Carpenter's demand for technical experts was endless. America did not know how to supply them.

"We must become a nation of experts," General Carpenter informed the National Association of American Universities. "Every man and woman must be a specific tool for a specific job, hardened and sharpened by your training and education to win the fight for the American Dream."

"Our Dream," General Carpenter said at the Wall Street Bond Drive Breakfast, "is at one with the Greeks of Athens, with the noble Romans of . . . er . . . Rome. It is a dream of the Better Things of Life. Of Music and Art and Poetry and Culture. Money is only a weapon to be used in the fight for this dream. Ambition is only a ladder to climb to this dream. Ability is only a tool to shape this dream."

Wall Street applauded. General Carpenter asked for one hundred and fifty billion dollars, fifteen hundred dedicated dollar-a-year men, three thousand experts in mineralogy, petrology, mass production, chemical warfare, and air-traffic time study. They were delivered. The country was in high gear. General Carpenter had only to press a button and an expert would be delivered.

In March of A.D. 2112 the war came to a climax and the American Dream was resolved, not on any one of the seven fronts where millions of men were locked in bitter combat, not in any of the staff headquarters or any of the capitals of the warring nations, not in any of the production centers spewing forth arms and supplies, but in Ward T of the United States Army Hospital buried three hundred feet below what had once been St. Albans, New York.

Ward T was something of a mystery at St. Albans. Like all army hospitals, St. Albans was organized with specific wards reserved for specific injuries. Right-arm amputees were gathered in one ward; left-arm amputees in another. Radiation burns, head injuries, eviscerations, secondary gamma poisonings, and so on were each assigned their specific location in the hospital organization. The Army Medical Corps had established nineteen classes of combat injury which included every possible kind of damage to brain and tissue. These used up letters A to S. What, then, was in Ward T?

No one knew. The doors were double-locked. No visitors were permitted to enter. No patients were permitted to leave. Physicians were seen to arrive and depart. Their perplexed expressions stimulated the wildest speculations but revealed nothing. The nurses who ministered to Ward T were questioned eagerly but they were closed-mouthed.

There were dribs and drabs of information, unsatisfying and self-contradictory. A charwoman asserted that she had been in to clean up and there had been no one in the ward. Absolutely no one. Just two dozen beds and nothing else. Had the beds been slept in? Yes. They were rumpled, some of them. Were there signs of the ward being in use? Oh yes. Personal things on the tables and so on. But dusty, kind of. Like they hadn't been used in a long time.

Public opinion decided it was a ghost ward. For spooks only.

But a night orderly reported passing the locked ward and hearing singing from within. What kind of singing? Foreign language, like. What language? The orderly couldn't say. Some of the words sounded like . . . well, like: Cow dee on us eager tour . . .

Public opinion started to run a fever and decided it was an alien ward. For spies only.

St. Albans enlisted the help of the kitchen staff and checked the food trays. Twenty-four trays went into Ward T three times a day. Twenty-four came out. Sometimes the returning trays were emptied. Most times they were untouched.

Public opinion started to run a fever and decided it was a racket. It was an informal club of goldbricks and staff grafters who caroused within. Cow dee on us eager tour indeed!

For gossip, a hospital can put a small town sewing circle to shame with ease, but sick people are easily goaded into passion by trivia. It took just three months for idle speculation to turn into downright fury. In January, 2112, St. Albans was a sound, well-run hospital. By March, 2112, St. Albans was in a ferment, and the psychological unrest found its way into the official records. The percentage of recoveries fell off. Malingering set in. Petty infractions increased. Mutinies flared. There was a staff shake-up. It did no good. Ward T was inciting the patients to riot. There was another shake-up, and another, and still the unrest fumed.

The news finally reached General Carpenter's desk through official channels.

"In our fight for the American Dream," he said, "we must not ignore those who have already given of themselves. Send me a Hospital Administration expert."

The expert was delivered. He could do nothing to heal St. Albans. General Carpenter read the reports and fired him.

"Pity," said General Carpenter, "is the first ingredient of civilization. Send me a Surgeon General."

A Surgeon General was delivered. He could not break the fury of St. Albans, and General Carpenter broke him. But by this time Ward T was being mentioned in the dispatches.

"Send me," General Carpenter said, "the expert in charge of Ward T."

St. Albans sent a doctor, Captain Edsel Dimmock. He was a stout young man, already bald, only three years out of medical school, but with a fine record as an expert in psychotherapy. General Carpenter liked experts. He liked Dimmock. Dimmock adored the general as the spokesman for a culture which he had been too specially trained to seek up to now, but which he hoped to enjoy after the war was won.

"Now look here, Dimmock," General Carpenter began. "We're all of us tools, today—hardened and sharpened to do a specific job. You know our motto: a job for everyone and everyone on the job. Somebody's not on the job at Ward T and we've got to kick him out. Now, in the first place what the hell is Ward T?"

Dimmock stuttered and fumbled. Finally he explained that it was a special ward set up for special combat cases. Shock cases.

"Then you do have patients in the ward?"

"Yes, sir. Ten women and fourteen men."

Carpenter brandished a sheaf of reports. "Says here the St. Albans patients claim nobody's in Ward T."

Dimmock was shocked. That was untrue, he assured the general.

"All right, Dimmock. So you've got your twenty-four crocks in there. Their job's to get well. Your job's to cure them. What the hell's upsetting the hospital about that?"

"W-well, sir. Perhaps it's because we keep them locked up."

"You keep Ward T locked?"

"Yes, sir."

"Why?"

"To keep the patients in, General Carpenter."

"Keep 'em in? What d'you mean? Are they trying to get out? They violent, or something?"

"No, sir. Not violent."

"Dimmock, I don't like your attitude. You're acting damned sneaky and evasive. And I'll tell you something else I don't like. That T classification. I checked with a Filing Expert from the Medical Corps and there is no T classification. What the hell are you up to at St. Albans?"

"W-well, sir . . . We invented the T classification. It . . . They . . . They're rather special cases, sir. We don't know what to do about them or how to handle them. W-we've been trying to keep it quiet until we've worked out a modus operandi, but it's brand-new, General Carpenter. Brand-new!" Here the expert in Dimmock triumphed over discipline. "It's sensational. It'll make medical history, by God! It's the biggest damned thing ever."

"What is it, Dimmock? Be specific."

"Well, sir, they're shock cases. Blanked out. Almost catatonic. Very little respiration. Slow pulse. No response."

"I've seen thousands of shock cases like that," Carpenter grunted. "What's so unusual?"

"Yes, sir, so far it sounds like the standard Q or R classification. But here's something unusual. They don't eat and they don't sleep."

"Never?"

"Some of them never."

"Then why don't they die?"

"We don't know. The metabolism cycle's broken, but only on the anabolism side. Catabolism continues. In other words, sir, they're eliminating waste products, but they're not taking anything in. They're eliminating fatigue poisons and rebuilding worn tissue, but without food and sleep. God knows how. It's fantastic."

"That why you've got them locked up? Mean to say . . . D'you suspect them of stealing food and catnaps somewhere else?"

"N-No, sir." Dimmock looked shamefaced. "I don't know how to tell you this, General Carpenter. . . . We lock them up because of the real mystery. They . . . Well, they disappear."

"They what?"

"They disappear, sir. Vanish. Right before your eyes."

"The hell you say."

"I do say, sir. They'll be sitting on a bed or standing around. One minute you see them, the next minute you don't. Sometimes there's two dozen in Ward T. Other times none. They disappear and reappear without rhyme or reason. That's why we've got the ward locked, General Carpenter. In the entire history of combat and combat injury, there's never been a case like this before. We don't know how to handle it."

"Bring me three of those cases," General Carpenter said.

Nathan Riley ate French toast, eggs benedict; consumed two pints of brown ale, smoked a John Drew, belched delicately and arose from the breakfast table. He nodded quietly to Gentleman Jim Corbett, who broke off his conversation with Diamond Jim Brady to intercept him on the way to the cashier's desk.

"Who do you like for the pennant this year, Nat?" Gentleman Jim inquired.

"The Dodgers," Nathan Riley answered.

"They've got no pitching."

"They've got Snider and Furillo and Campanella. They'll take the pennant this year, Jim. I'll bet they take it earlier than any team ever did. By September 13. Make a note. See if I'm right."

"You're always right, Nat," Corbett said.

Riley smiled, paid his check, sauntered out into the street and caught a horsecar bound for Madison Square Garden. He got off at the corner of Fiftieth Street and Eighth Avenue and walked upstairs to a handbook office over a radio repair shop. The bookie glanced at him, produced an envelope and counted out $15,000.

"Rocky Marciano by a TKO over Roland La Starza in the eleventh," he said. "How the hell do you call them so accurate, Nat?"

"That's the way I make a living," Riley smiled. "Are you making book on the elections?"

"Eisenhower twelve to five. Stevenson—"

"Never mind Adlai." Riley placed $20,000 on the counter. "I'm backing Ike. Get this down for me."

He left the handbook office and went to his suite in the Waldorf where a tall, thin young man was waiting for him anxiously.

"Oh yes," Nathan Riley said. "You're Ford, aren't you? Harold Ford?"

"Henry Ford, Mr. Riley."

"And you need financing for that machine in your bicycle shop. What's it called?"

"I call it an Ipsimobile, Mr. Riley."

"Hmmm. Can't say I like that name. Why not call it an automobile?"

"That's a wonderful suggestion, Mr. Riley. I'll certainly take it."

"I like you, Henry. You're young, eager, adaptable. I believe in your future and I believe in your automobile. I'll invest two hundred thousand dollars in your company."

Riley wrote a check and ushered Henry Ford out. He glanced at his watch and suddenly felt impelled to go back and look around for a moment. He entered his bedroom, undressed, put on a gray shirt and gray slacks. Across the pocket of the shirt were large blue letters: U.S.A.H.

He locked the bedroom door and disappeared.

He reappeared in Ward T of the United States Army Hospital in St. Albans, standing alongside his bed which was one of twenty-four lining the walls of a long, light steel barracks. Before he could draw another breath, he was seized by three pairs of hands. Before he could struggle, he was shot by a pneumatic syringe and poleaxed by 1½ cc of sodium thiomorphate.

"We've got one," someone said.

"Hang around," someone else answered. "General Carpenter said he wanted three."

After Marcus Junius Brutus left her bed, Lela Machan clapped her hands. Her slave woman entered the chamber and prepared her bath. She bathed, dressed, scented herself, and breakfasted on Smyrna figs, rose oranges and a flagon of Lacrima Christi. Then she smoked a cigarette and ordered her litter.

The gates of her house were crowded as usual by adoring hordes from the Twentieth Legion. Two centurions removed her chair-bearers from the poles of the litter and bore her on their stout shoulders. Lela Machan smiled. A young man in a sapphire-blue cloak thrust through the mob and ran toward her. A knife flashed in his hand. Lela braced herself to meet death bravely.

"Lady!" he cried. "Lady Lela!"

He slashed his left arm with the knife and let the crimson blood stain her robe.

"This blood of mine is the least I have to give you," he cried.

Lela touched his forehead gently.

"Silly boy," she murmured. "Why?"

"For love of you, my lady."

"You will be admitted tonight at nine," Lela whispered. He stared at her until she laughed. "I promise you. What is your name, pretty boy?"

"Ben Hur."

"Tonight at nine, Ben Hur."

The litter moved on. Outside the Forum, Julius Caesar passed in hot argument with Savonarola. When he saw the litter he motioned sharply to the centurions, who stopped at once. Caesar swept back the curtains and stared at Lela, who regarded him languidly. Caesar's face twitched.

"Why?" he asked hoarsely. "I have begged, pleaded, bribed, wept, and all without forgiveness. Why, Lela? Why?"

"Do you remember Boadicea?" Lela murmured

"Boadicea? Queen of the Britons? Good God, Lela, what can she mean to our love? I did not love Boadicea. I merely defeated her in battle."

"And killed her, Caesar."

"She poisoned herself, Lela."

"She was my mother, Caesar!" Suddenly Lela pointed her finger at Caesar. "Murderer. You will be punished. Beware the Ides of March, Caesar!"

Caesar recoiled in horror. The mob of admirers that had gathered around Lela uttered a shout of approval. Amidst a shower of rose petals and violets, she continued on her way across the Forum to the Temple of the Vestal Virgins where she abandoned her adoring suitors and entered the sacred temple.

Before the altar she genuflected, intoned a prayer, dropped a pinch of incense on the altar flame and disrobed. She examined her beautiful body reflected in a silver mirror, then experienced a momentary twinge of homesickness. She put on a gray blouse and a gray pair of slacks. Across the pocket of the blouse was lettered U.S.A.H.

She smiled once at the altar and disappeared.

She reappeared in Ward T of the United States Army Hospital where she was instantly felled by 1½ cc of sodium thiomorphate injected subcutaneously by a pneumatic syringe.

"That's two," somebody said.

"One more to go."

George Hanmer paused dramatically and stared around . . . at the opposition benches, at the Speaker on the woolsack, at the silver mace on a crimson cushion before the Speaker's chair. The entire House of Parliament, hypnotized by Hanmer's fiery oratory, waited breathlessly for him to continue.

"I can say no more," Hanmer said at last. His voice was choked with emotion. His face was blanched and grim. "I will fight for this bill at the beachheads. I will fight in the cities, the towns, the fields, and the hamlets. I will fight for this bill to the death and, God willing, I will fight for it after death. Whether this be a challenge or a prayer, let the consciences of the right honorable gentlemen determine; but of one thing I am sure and determined: England must own the Suez Canal."

Hanmer sat down. The house exploded. Through the cheering and applause he made his way out into the division lobby where Gladstone, Churchill, and Pitt stopped him to shake his hand. Lord Palmerston eyed him coldly, but Pam was shouldered aside by Disraeli who limped up, all enthusiasm, all admiration.

"We'll have a bite at Tattersall's," Dizzy said. "My car's waiting."

Lady Beaconsfield was in the Rolls Royce outside the Houses of Parliament. She pinned a primrose on Dizzy's lapel and patted Hanmer's cheek affectionately.

"You've come a long way from the schoolboy who used to bully Dizzy, Georgie," she said.

Hanmer laughed. Dizzy sang: "*Gaudeamus igitur . . .*" and Hanmer chanted the ancient scholastic song until they reached Tattersall's. There Dizzy ordered Guinness and grilled bones while Hanmer went upstairs in the club to change.

For no reason at all he had the impulse to go back for a last look. Perhaps he hated to break with his past completely. He divested himself of his surtout, nankeen waistcoat, pepper and salt trousers, polished Hessians, and undergarments. He put on a gray shirt and gray trousers and disappeared.

He reappeared in Ward T of the St. Albans Hospital where he was rendered unconscious by 1½ cc of sodium thiomorphate.

"That's three," somebody said.

"Take 'em to Carpenter."

So there they sat in General Carpenter's office, PFC Nathan Riley, M/Sgt Lela Machan, and Corp/2 George Hanmer. They were in their hospital grays. They were torpid with sodium thiomorphate.

The office had been cleared and it blazed with light. Present were experts from Espionage, Counter-Espionage, Security, and Central Intelligence. When Captain Edsel Dimmock saw the steel-faced ruthless squad awaiting the patients and himself, he started. General Carpenter started grimly.

"Didn't occur to you that we mightn't buy your disappearance story, eh Dimmock?"

"S-Sir?"

"I'm an expert too, Dimmock. I'll spell it out for you. The war's going badly. Very badly. There've been intelligence leaks. The St. Albans mess might point to you."

"B-But they do disappear, sir. I—"

"My experts want to talk to you and your patients about this disappearing act, Dimmock. They'll start with you."

The experts worked over Dimmock with preconscious softeners, id releases, and superego blocks. They tried every truth serum in the books and every form of physical and mental pressure. They brought Dimmock, squealing, to the breaking point three times, but there was nothing to break.

"Let him stew for now," General Carpenter said. "Get on to the patients."

The experts appeared reluctant to apply pressure to the sick men and the woman.

"For God's sake, don't be squeamish," Carpenter raged. "We're fighting a war for civilization. We've got to protect our ideals no matter what the price. Get to it!"

The experts from Espionage, Counter-Espionage, Security, and Central Intelligence got to it. Like three candles, PFC Nathan Riley, M/Sgt Lela Machan, and Corp/2 George Hanmer snuffed out and disappeared. One moment they were seated in chairs surrounded by violence. The next moment they were not.

The experts gasped. General Carpenter did the handsome thing. He stalked to Dimmock. "Captain Dimmock, I apologize. Colonel Dimmock, you've been promoted for making an important discovery . . . only what the hell does it mean? We've got to check ourselves first."

Carpenter snapped up the intercom. "Get me a combat-shock expert and an alienist."

The two experts entered and were briefed. They examined the witnesses. They considered.

"You're all suffering from a mild case of shock," the combat-shock expert said. "War jitters."

"You mean we didn't see them disappear?"

The shock expert shook his head and glanced at the alienist who also shook his head.

"Mass illusion," the alienist said.

At that moment PFC Riley, M/Sgt Machan, and Corp/2 Hanmer reappeared. One moment they were a mass illusion; the next, they were back sitting in their chairs surrounded by confusion.

"Dope 'em again, Dimmock," Carpenter cried. "Give 'em a gallon." He snapped up the intercom. "I want every expert we've got. Emergency meeting in my office at once."

Thirty-seven experts, hardened and sharpened tools all, inspected the unconscious shock cases and discussed them for three hours. Certain facts were obvious: This must be a new fantastic

ALFRED BESTER

syndrome brought on by the new and fantastic horrors of the war. As combat technique develops, the response of victims of this technique must also take new roads. For every action there is an equal and opposite reaction. Agreed.

This new syndrome must involve some aspects of teleportation . . . the power of mind over space. Evidently combat shock, while destroying certain known powers of the mind must develop other latent powers hitherto unknown. Agreed.

Obviously, the patients must only be able to return to the point of departure, otherwise they would not continue to return to Ward T nor would they have returned to General Carpenter's office. Agreed.

Obviously, the patients must be able to procure food and sleep wherever they go, since neither was required in Ward T. Agreed.

"One small point," Colonel Dimmock said. "They seem to be returning to Ward T less frequently. In the beginning they would come and go every day or so. Now most of them stay away for weeks and hardly ever return."

"Never mind that," Carpenter said. "Where do they go?"

"Do they teleport behind the enemy lines?" someone asked. "There's those intelligence leaks."

"I want Intelligence to check," Carpenter snapped. "Is the enemy having similar difficulties with, say, prisoners of war who appear and disappear from their POW camps? They might be some of ours from Ward T."

"They might simply be going home," Colonel Dimmock suggested.

"I want Security to check," Carpenter ordered. "Cover the home life and associations of every one of those twenty-four disappearers. Now . . . about our operations in Ward T. Colonel Dimmock has a plan."

"We'll set up six extra beds in Ward T," Edsel Dimmock explained. "We'll send in six experts to live there and observe. Information must be picked up indirectly from the patients. They're catatonic and nonresponsive when conscious, and incapable of answering questions when drugged."

"Gentlemen," Carpenter summed it up. "This is the greatest potential weapon in the history of warfare. I don't have to tell you what it can mean to us to be able to teleport an entire army behind enemy lines. We can win the war for the American Dream in one day if we can win this secret hidden in those shattered minds. We must win!"

The experts hustled, Security checked, Intelligence probed. Six hardened and sharpened tools moved into Ward T in St. Albans Hospital and slowly got acquainted with the disappearing patients who reappeared less and less frequently. The tension increased.

Security was able to report that not one case of strange appearance had taken place in America in the past year. Intelligence reported that the enemy did not seem to be having similar difficulties with their own shock cases or with POWs.

Carpenter fretted. "This is all brand-new. We've got no specialists to handle it. We've got to develop new tools." He snapped up his intercom. "Get me a college," he said.

They got him Yale.

"I want some experts in mind over matter. Develop them," Carpenter ordered. Yale at once introduced three graduate courses in Thaumaturgy, Extrasensory Perception, and Telekinesis.

The first break came when one of the Ward T experts requested the assistance of another expert. He needed a Lapidary.

"What the hell for?" Carpenter wanted to know.

"He picked up a reference to a gemstone," Colonel Dimmock explained. "He's a personnel specialist and he can't relate it to anything in his experience."

"And he's not supposed to," Carpenter said approvingly. "A job for every man and every man on the job." He flipped up the intercom. "Get me a Lapidary."

An expert Lapidary was given leave of absence from the army arsenal and asked to identify a type of diamond called Jim Brady. He could not.

"We'll try it from another angle," Carpenter said. He snapped up his intercom. "Get me a Semanticist."

The Semanticist left his desk in the War Propaganda Department but could make nothing of the words "Jim Brady." They were names to him. No more. He suggested a Genealogist.

A Genealogist was given one day's leave from his post with the Un-American Ancestors Committee, but could make nothing of the name Brady beyond the fact that it had been a common name in America for five hundred years. He suggested an Archaeologist.

An Archaeologist was released from the Cartography Division of Invasion Command and instantly identified the name Diamond Jim Brady. It was a historic personage who had been famous in the city of Little Old New York sometime between Governor Peter Stuyvesant and Governor Fiorello La Guardia.

"Christ!" Carpenter marveled. "That's ages ago. Where the hell did Nathan Riley get that? You'd better join the experts in Ward T and follow this up."

The Archaeologist followed it up, checked his references and sent in his report. Carpenter read it and was stunned. He called an emergency meeting of his staff of experts.

"Gentlemen," he announced, "Ward T is something bigger than teleportation. Those shock patients are doing something far more incredible . . . far more meaningful. Gentlemen, they're traveling through time."

The staff rustled uncertainly. Carpenter nodded emphatically.

"Yes, gentlemen. Time travel is here. It has not arrived the way we expected it . . . as a result of expert research by qualified specialists; it has come as a plague . . . an infection . . . a disease of the war . . . a result of combat injury to ordinary men. Before I continue, look through these reports for documentation."

The staff read the stenciled sheets. PFC Nathan Riley . . . disappearing into the early twentieth century in New York; M/Sgt Lela Machan . . . visiting the first century in Rome; Corp/2 George Hanmer . . . journeying into the nineteenth century in England. And all the rest of the twenty-four patients, escaping the turmoil and horrors of modern war in the twenty-second century by fleeing to Venice and the Doges, to Jamaica and the buccaneers, to China and the Han Dynasty, to Norway and Eric the Red, to any place and any time in the world.

"I needn't point out the colossal significance of this discovery," General Carpenter pointed out. "Think what it would mean to the war if we could send an army back in time a week or a month or a year. We could win the war before it started. We could protect our Dream . . . Poetry and Beauty and the Culture of America . . . from barbarism without ever endangering it."

The staff tried to grapple with the problem of winning battles before they started.

"The situation is complicated by the fact that these men and women of Ward T are *non compos*. They may or may not know how they do what they do, but in any case they're incapable of communicating with the experts who could reduce this miracle to method. It's for us to find the key. They can't help us."

The hardened and sharpened specialists looked around uncertainly.

"We'll need experts," General Carpenter said.

The staff relaxed. They were on familiar ground again.

"We'll need a Cerebral Mechanist, a Cyberneticist, a Psychiatrist, an Anatomist, an Archaeologist, and a first-rate Historian. They'll go into that ward and they won't come out until their job is done. They must learn the technique of time travel."

The first five experts were easy to draft from other war departments. All America was a toolchest of hardened and sharpened specialists. But there was trouble locating a first-class Historian until the Federal Penitentiary cooperated with the army and released Dr. Bradley Scrim from his twenty years at hard labor. Dr. Scrim was acid and jagged. He had held the chair of Philosophic History at a Western university until he spoke his mind about the war for the American Dream. That got him the twenty years hard.

Scrim was still intransigent, but induced to play ball by the intriguing problem of Ward T.

"But I'm not an expert," he snapped. "In this benighted nation of experts, I'm the last singing grasshopper in the ant heap."

Carpenter snapped up the intercom. "Get me an Entomologist," he said.

"Don't bother," Scrim said. "I'll translate. You're a nest of ants . . . all working and toiling and specializing. For what?"

"To preserve the American Dream," Carpenter answered hotly. "We're fighting for Poetry and Culture and Education and the Finer Things in Life."

"Which means you're fighting to preserve me," Scrim said. "That's what I've devoted my life to. And what do you do with me? Put me in jail."

"You were convicted of enemy sympathizing and fellow-traveling," Carpenter said.

"I was convicted of believing in *my* American Dream," Scrim said. "Which is another way of saying I was jailed for having a mind of my own."

Scrim was also intransigent in Ward T. He stayed one night, enjoyed three good meals, read the reports, threw them down, and began hollering to be let out.

"There's a job for everyone and everyone must be on the job," Colonel Dimmock told him. "You don't come out until you've got the secret of time travel."

"There's no secret I can get," Scrim said.

"Do they travel in time?"

"Yes and no."

"The answer has to be one or the other. Not both. You're evading the—"

"Look," Scrim interrupted wearily. "What are you an expert in?"

"Psychotherapy."

"Then how the hell can you understand what I'm talking about? This is a philosophic concept. I tell you there's no secret here that the army can use. There's no secret any group can use. It's a secret for individuals only."

"I don't understand you."

"I didn't think you would. Take me to Carpenter."

They took Scrim to Carpenters's office where he grinned at the general malignantly, looking for all the world like a red-headed, underfed devil.

"I'll need ten minutes," Scrim said. "Can you spare them out of your toolbox?"

Carpenter nodded.

"Now listen carefully. I'm going to give you the clues to something so vast and so strange that it will need all your fine edge to cut into it."

Carpenter looked expectant.

"Nathan Riley goes back in time to the early twentieth century. There he lives the life of his fondest dreams. He's a big-time gambler, the friend of Diamond Jim Brady and others. He wins money betting on events because he always knows the outcome in advance. He won money betting on Eisenhower to win an election. He won money betting on a prizefighter named Marciano to beat another prizefighter named La Starza. He made money investing in an automobile company owned by Henry Ford. There are the clues. They mean anything to you?"

"Not without a Sociological Analyst," Carpenter answered. He reached for the intercom.

"Don't order one, I'll explain later. Let's try some more clues. Lela Machan, for example. She escapes into the Roman Empire where she lives the life of her dreams as a *femme fatale*. Every man loves her. Julius Caesar, Savonarola, the entire Twentieth Legion, a man named Ben Hur. Do you see the fallacy?"

"No."

"She also smokes cigarettes."

"Well?" Carpenter asked after a pause.

"I continue," Scrim said, "George Hanmer escapes into England of the nineteenth century where he's a member of Parliament and the friend of Gladstone, Winston Churchill, and Disraeli, who takes him riding in his Rolls Royce. Do you know what a Rolls Royce is?"

"No."

"It was the name of an automobile."

"So?"

"You don't understand yet?"

"No."

Scrim paced the floor in exaltation. "Carpenter, this is a bigger discovery than teleportation or time travel. This can be the salvation of man. I don't think I'm exaggerating. These two dozen shock victims in Ward T have been U-Bombed into something so gigantic that it's no wonder your specialists and experts can't understand it."

"What the hell's bigger than time travel, Scrim?"

"Listen to this, Carpenter. Eisenhower did not run for office until the middle of the twentieth century. Nathan Riley could not have been a friend of Diamond Jim Brady's and bet on Eisenhower to win an election . . . not simultaneously. Brady was dead a quarter of a century before Ike was President. Marciano defeated La Starza fifty years after Henry Ford started his automobile company. Nathan Riley's time traveling is full of similar anachronisms."

Carpenter looked puzzled.

"Lela Machan could not have had Ben Hur for a lover. Ben Hur never existed in Rome. He never existed at all. He was a character in a novel. She couldn't have smoked. They didn't have tobacco then. You see? More anachronisms. Disraeli could never have taken George Hanmer for a ride in a Rolls Royce because automobiles weren't invented until long after Disraeli's death."

"The hell you say," Carpenter exclaimed. "You mean they're all lying?"

"No. Don't forget, they don't need sleep. They don't need food. They're not lying. They're going back in time, all right. They're eating and sleeping back there."

"But you just said their stories don't stand up. They're full of anachronisms."

"Because they travel back into a time of their own imagination. Nathan Riley has his own picture of what America was like in the early twentieth century. It's faulty and anachronistic because he's no scholar, but it's real for him. He can live there. The same is true for the others."

Carpenter goggled.

"The concept is almost beyond understanding. These people have discovered how to turn dreams into reality. They know how to enter their dream realities. They can stay there, live there, perhaps forever. My God, Carpenter, *this* is your American dream. It's miracle working, immortality, Godlike creation, mind over matter . . . It must be explored. It must be studied. It must be given to the world."

"Can you do it, Scrim?"

"No, I cannot. I'm an historian. I'm noncreative, so it's beyond me. You need a poet . . . an artist who understands the creation of dreams. From creating dreams on paper it oughtn't be too difficult to take the step to creating dreams in actuality."

"A poet? Are you serious?"

"Certainly I'm serious. Don't you know what a poet is? You've been telling us for five years that this war is being fought to save the poets."

"Don't be facetious, Scrim, I—"

"Send a poet into Ward T. He'll learn how they do it. He's the only man who can. A poet is half doing it anyway. Once he learns, he can teach your psychologists and anatomists. Then they can teach us; but the poet is the only man who can interpret between those shock cases and your experts."

"I believe you're right, Scrim."

"Then don't delay, Carpenter Those patients are returning to this world less and less frequently. We've got to get at that secret before they disappear forever. Send a poet to Ward T."

Carpenter snapped up his intercom. "Send me a poet," he said.

He waited, and waited . . . and waited . . . while America sorted feverishly through its two hundred and ninety millions of hardened and sharpened experts, its specialized tools to defend the American Dream of Beauty and Poetry and the Better Things in Life. He waited for them to find a poet, not understanding the endless delay, the fruitless search; not understanding why Bradley Scrim laughed and laughed and laughed at this final, fatal disappearance.

OLDY AND ID

This is the story of a monster.

They named him Odysseus Gaul in honor of Papa's favorite hero, and over Mama's desperate objections; but he was known as Oddy from the age of one.

The first year of life is an egotistic craving for warmth and security. Oddy was not likely to have much of that when he was born, for Papa's real estate business was bankrupt, and Mama was thinking of divorce. But an unexpected decision by United Radiation to build a plant in the town made Papa wealthy, and Mama fell in love with him all over again. So Oddy had warmth and security.

The second year of life is a timid exploration. Oddy crawled and explored. When he reached for the crimson coils inside the nonobjective fireplace, an unexpected short circuit saved him from a burn. When he fell out the third-floor window, it was into the grass-filled hopper of the Mechano-Gardener. When he teased the Phoebus Cat, it slipped as it snapped at his face, and the brilliant fangs clicked harmlessly over his ear.

"Animals love Oddy," Mama said. "They only pretend to bite."

Oddy wanted to be loved, so everybody loved Oddy. He was petted, pampered and spoiled through preschool age. Shopkeepers presented him with largess, and acquaintances showered him with gifts. Of sodas, candy, tarts, chrystons, bobble-trucks, freezies, and various other comestibles. Oddy consumed enough for an entire kindergarten. He was never sick.

"Takes after his father," Papa said. "Good stock."

Family legends grew about Oddy's luck. . . . How a perfect stranger mistook him for his own child just as Oddy was about to amble into the Electronic Circus, and delayed him long enough to save him from the disastrous explosion of '98. . . . How a forgotten library book rescued him from the Rocket Crash of '99. . . . How a multitude of odd incidents saved him from a multitude of assorted catastrophes. No one realized he was a monster . . . yet.

At eighteen, he was a nice-looking boy with seal-brown hair, warm brown eyes, and a wide grin that showed even white teeth. He was strong, healthy, intelligent. He was completely uninhibited in his quiet, relaxed way. He had charm. He was happy. So far, his monstrous evil had only affected the little Town Unit where he was born and raised.

He came to Harvard from a Progressive School, so when one of his many new friends popped into the dormitory room and said: "Hey Oddy, come down to the Quad and kick a ball around," Oddy answered: "I don't know how, Ben."

"Don't know how?" Ben tucked the football under his arm and dragged Oddy with him. "Where you been, laddie?"

"They didn't think much of football back home," Oddy grinned. "Said it was old-fashioned. We were strictly Huxley-Hob."

"Huxley-Hob! That's for eggheads," Ben said. "Football is still the big game. You want to be famous? You got to be on that gridiron on TV every Saturday."

"So I've noticed, Ben. Show me."

Ben showed Oddy, carefully and with patience. Oddy took the lesson seriously and industriously. His third punt was caught by a freakish gust of wind, traveled seventy yards through the air, and burst through the third-floor window of Proctor Charley (Gravy-Train) Stuart. Stuart took one look at the window and had Oddy down to Soldier Stadium in half an hour. Three Saturdays later, the headlines read: Oddy Gaul 57–Army 0.

"Snell and Rumination!" Coach Hig Clayton swore. "How does he do it? There's nothing sensational about that kid. He's just average. But when he runs, they fall down, chasing him. When he kicks, they fumble. When they fumble, he recovers."

"He's a negative player," Gravy-Train answered. "He lets you make the mistakes, and then he cashes in."

They were both wrong. Oddy Gaul was a monster.

With his choice of any eligible young woman, Oddy Gaul went stag to the Observatory Prom, wandered into a darkroom by mistake, and discovered a girl in a smock bending over trays in the hideous green safe-light. She had cropped black hair, icy blue eyes, strong features, and a sensuous, boyish figure. She ordered him out and Oddy fell in love with her . . . temporarily.

His friends howled with laughter when he told them. "Shades of Pygmalion, Oddy, don't you know about *her*? The girl is frigid. A statue. She loathes men. You're wasting your time."

But through the adroitness of her analyst, the girl turned a neurotic corner one week later and fell deeply in love with Oddy Gaul. It was sudden, devastating, and enraptured for two months. Then just as Oddy began to cool, the girl had a relapse and everything ended on a friendly, convenient basis.

So far only minor events made up the response to Oddy's luck, but the shock wave of reaction was spreading. In September of his sophomore year, Oddy competed for the Political Economy Medal with a thesis entitled: "Causes of Mutiny." The striking similarity of his paper to the Astraean mutiny that broke out the day his paper was entered won him the prize.

In October, Oddy contributed twenty dollars to a pool organized by a crackpot classmate for speculating on the Exchange according to "Stock Market Trends," an ancient superstition. The prophet's calculations were ridiculous, but a sharp panic nearly ruined the Exchange as it quadrupled the pool. Oddy made one hundred dollars.

And so it went . . . worse and worse. The monster.

Now, a monster can get away with a lot when he's studying a speculative philosophy where causation is rooted in history and the Present is devoted to statistical analysis of the Past; but the living sciences are bulldogs with their teeth clamped on the phenomena of Now. So it was Jesse Migg, physiologist and spectral physicist, who first trapped the monster . . . and he thought he'd found an angel.

Old Jess was one of the Sights. In the first place he was young . . . not over forty. He was a malignant knife of a man, an albino, pink-eyed, bald, pointed-nose, and brilliant. He affected twentieth-century clothes and twentieth-century vices . . . tobacco and potations of C_2H_5OH. He never talked . . . He spat. He never walked . . . He scurried. And he was scurrying up and down the aisles of the laboratory of Tech I (General Survey of Spatial Mechanics—Required for All General Arts Students) when he ferreted out the monster.

One of the first experiments in the course was EMF Electrolysis. Elementary stuff. A U-Tube containing water was passed between the poles of a stock Remosant Magnet. After sufficient voltage was transmitted through the coils, you drew off hydrogen and oxygen in two-to-one ratio at the arms of the tube and related them to the voltage and the magnetic field.

Oddy ran his experiment earnestly, got the approved results, entered them in his lab book and then waited for the official checkoff. Little Migg came hustling down the aisle, darted to Oddy and spat: "Finished?"

"Yes, sir."

Migg checked the book entries, glanced at the indicators at the ends of the tube, and stamped Oddy out with a sneer. It was only after Oddy was gone that he noticed the Remosant Magnet was obviously shorted. The wires were fused. There hadn't been any field to electrolyze the water.

"Hell and Damnation!" Migg grunted (he also affected twentieth-century vituperation) and rolled a clumsy cigarette.

He checked off possibilities in his comptometer head. 1. Gaul cheated. 2. If so, with what apparatus did he portion out the H_2 and O_2? 3. Where did he get the pure gases? 4. Why did he do it? Honesty was easier. 5. He didn't cheat. 6. How did he get the right results? 7. How did he get *any* results?

Old Jess emptied the U-Tube, refilled it with water, and ran off the experiment himself. He, too, got the correct result without a magnet.

"Christ on a raft!" he swore, unimpressed by the miracle, and infuriated by the mystery. He snooped, darting about like a hungry bat. After four hours he discovered that the steel bench supports were picking up a charge from the Greeson Coils in the basement and had thrown just enough field to make everything come out right.

"Coincidence," Migg spat. But he was not convinced.

Two weeks later, in Elementary Fission Analysis, Oddy completed his afternoon's work with a careful listing of resultant isotopes from selenium to lanthanum. The only trouble, Migg discovered, was that there had been a mistake in the stock issued to Oddy. He hadn't received any U^{235} for neutron bombardment. His sample had been a leftover from a Stefan-Boltzmann black-body demonstration.

"God in Heaven!" Migg swore, and double-checked. Then he triple-checked. When he found the answer—a remarkable coincidence involving improperly cleaned apparatus and a defective cloud-chamber—he swore further. He also did some intensive thinking.

"There are accident-prones," Migg snarled at the reflection in his Self-Analysis Mirror. "How about good-luck prones? Horse manure!"

But he was a bulldog with his teeth sunk in phenomena. He tested Oddy Gaul. He hovered over him in the laboratory, cackling with infuriated glee as Oddy completed experiment after experiment with defective equipment. When Oddy successfully completed the Rutherford Classic—getting $_8O^{17}$ after exposing nitrogen to alpha radiation, but in this case without the use of nitrogen or alpha radiation—Migg actually clapped him on the back in delight. Then the little man investigated and found the logical, improbable chain of coincidences that explained it.

He devoted his spare time to a check-back on Oddy's career at Harvard. He had a two-hour conference with a lady astronomer's faculty analyst, and a ten-minute talk with Hig Clayton and Gravy-Train Stuart. He rooted out the Exchange Pool, the Political Economy Medal, and half a dozen other incidents that filled him with malignant joy. Then he cast off his twentieth-century affectation, dressed himself properly in formal leotards, and entered the Faculty Club for the first time in a year.

A four-handed chess game on a transparent toroid board was in progress in the Diathermy Alcove. It had been in progress since Migg joined the faculty, and would probably not be finished before the end of the century. In fact, Johansen, playing Red, was already training his son to replace him in the likely event of his dying before the completion of the game.

As abrupt as ever, Migg marched up to the glowing board, sparkling with varicolored pieces, and blurted: "What do you know about accidents?"

"Ah?" said Bellanby, *Philosopher in Res* at the University. "Good evening, Migg. Do you mean the accident of substance, or the accident of essence? If, on the other hand, your question implies—"

"No, no," Migg interrupted. "My apologies, Bellanby. Let me rephrase the question. Is there such a thing as Compulsion of Probability?"

Hrrdnikkisch completed his move and gave full attention to Migg, as did Johansen and Bellanby. Wilson continued to study the board. Since he was permitted one hour to make his move and would need it, Migg knew there would be ample time for the discussion.

"Compulthon of Probability?" Hrrdnikkisch lisped. "Not a new conthept, Migg. I recall a thurvey of the theme in 'The Integraph' Vol. LVIII, No. 9. The calculuth, if I am not mithtaken—"

"No," Migg interrupted again. "My respects, Signoid. I'm not interested in the mathematics of probability, nor the philosophy. Let me put it this way. The accident-prone has already been incorporated into the body of psychoanalysis. Paton's Theorem of the Least Neurotic Norm settled that. But I've discovered the obverse. I've discovered a Fortune-Prone."

"Ah?" Johansen chuckled. "It's to be a joke. You wait and see, Signoid."

"No," answered Migg. "I'm perfectly serious. I've discovered a genuinely lucky man."

"He wins at cards?"

"He wins at everything. Accept this postulate for the moment. . . . I'll document it later. . . . There is a man who is lucky. He is a Fortune-Prone. Whatever he desires, he receives. Whether he has the ability to achieve it or not, he receives it. If his desire is totally beyond the peak of his accomplishment, then the factors of chance, coincidence, hazard, accident . . . and so on, combine to produce his desired end."

"No." Bellanby shook his head. "Too farfetched."

"I've worked it out empirically," Migg continued. "It's something like this. The future is a choice of mutually exclusively possibilities, one or another of which must be realized in terms of favorability of the events and number of the events. . . ."

"Yes, yes," interrupted Johansen. "The greater the number of favorable possibilities, the stronger the probability of an event maturing. This is elementary, Migg. Go on."

"I continue," Migg spat indignantly. "When we discuss probability in terms of throwing dice, the predictions or odds are simple. There are only six mutually exclusive possibilities to each die. The favorability is easy to compute. Chance is reduced to simple odds-ratios. *But* when we discuss probability in terms of the Universe, we cannot encompass enough data to make a prediction. There are too many factors. Favorability cannot be ascertained."

"All thith ith true," Hrrdnikkisch said, "but what of your Fortune-Prone?"

"I don't know how he does it . . . but merely by the intensity or mere existence of his desire, he can affect the favorability of possibilities. By wanting, he can turn possibility into probability, and probability into certainty."

"Ridiculous," Bellanby snapped. "You claim there's a man far-sighted and far-reaching enough to do this?"

"Nothing of the sort. He doesn't know what he's doing. He just thinks he's lucky, if he thinks about it at all. Let us say he wants . . . Oh . . . Name anything."

"Heroin," Bellanby said.

"What's that?" Johansen inquired.

"A morphine derivative," Hrrdnikkisch explained. "Formerly manufactured and thold to narcotic addictth."

"Heroin," Migg said. "Excellent. Say my man desires heroin, an antique narcotic no longer in existence. Very good. His desire would compel this sequence of possible but improbable events: A chemist in Australia, fumbling through a new organic synthesis, will accidentally and unwittingly prepare six ounces of heroin. Four ounces will be discarded, but through a logical mistake two ounces will be preserved. A further coincidence will ship it to this country and this city, wrapped as powdered sugar in a plastic ball; where the final accident will serve it to my man in a restaurant which he is visiting for the first time on an impulse. . . ."

"La-La-La!" said Hrrdnikkisch. "Thith shuffling of hithtory. Thith fluctuation of inthident and pothibility? All achieved without the knowledge but with the dethire of a man?"

"Yes. Precisely my point," Migg snarled. "I don't know how he does it, but he turns possibility into certainty. And since almost anything is possible, he is capable of accomplishing almost anything. He is godlike but not a god, because he does this without consciousness. He is an angel."

"Who is this angel?" Johansen asked.

And Migg told them all about Oddy Gaul.

"But how does he do it?" Bellanby persisted. "How does he do it?"

"I don't know," Migg repeated again. "Tell me how Espers do it."

"What!" Bellanby exclaimed. "Are you prepared to deny the telepathic pattern of thought? Do you—"

"I do nothing of the sort. I merely illustrate one possible explanation. Man produces events. The threatening War of Resources may be thought to be a result of the natural exhaustion of Terran resources. We know it is not. It is a result of centuries of thriftless waste by man. Natural phenomena are less often produced by nature and more often produced by man."

"And?"

"Who knows? Gaul is producing phenomena. Perhaps he's unconsciously broadcasting on a telepathic wave band. Broadcasting and getting results. He wants heroin. The broadcast goes out—"

"But Espers can't pick up any telepathic pattern further than the horizon. It's direct wave transmission. Even large objects cannot be penetrated. A building, say, or a—"

"I'm not saying this is on the Esper level," Migg shouted. "I'm trying to imagine something bigger. Something tremendous. He wants heroin. His broadcast goes out to the world. All men unconsciously fall into a pattern of activity which will produce that heroin as quickly as possible. That Austrian chemist—"

"No. Australian."

"That Australian chemist may have been debating between half a dozen different syntheses. Five of them could never have produced heroin; but Gaul's impulse made him select the sixth."

"And if he did not anyway?"

"Then who knows what parallel chains were also started? A boy playing Robin Hood in Montreal is impelled to explore an abandoned cabin where he finds the drug, hidden there centuries ago by smugglers. A woman in California collects old apothecary jars. She finds a pound of heroin. A child in Berlin, playing with a defective Radar-Chem Set, manufactures it. Name the most improbable sequence of events, and Gaul can bring it about, logically and certainly. I tell you, that boy is an angel!"

And he produced his documented evidence and convinced them.

It was then that four scholars of various but indisputable intellects elected themselves an executive committee for Fate and took Oddy Gaul in hand. To understand what they attempted to do, you must first understand the situation the world found itself in during that particular era.

It is a known fact that all wars are founded in economic conflict, or to put it another way, a trial by arms is merely the last battle of an economic war. In the pre-Christian centuries, the Punic Wars were the final outcome of a financial struggle between Rome and Carthage for economic control of the Mediterranean. Three thousand years later, the impending War of Resources loomed as the finale of a struggle between the two Independent Welfare States controlling most of the known economic world.

What petroleum oil was to the twentieth century, FO (the nickname for Fissionable Ore) was to the thirtieth; and the situation was peculiarly similar to the Asia Minor crisis that ultimately wrecked the United Nations a thousand years before. Triton, a backward semibarbaric satellite, previously unwanted and ignored, had suddenly discovered it possessed enormous resources of FO. Financially and technologically incapable of self-development, Triton was peddling concessions to both Welfare States.

The difference between a Welfare State and a Benevolent Despot is slight. In times of crisis, either can be traduced by the sincerest motives into the most abominable conduct. Both the Comity of Nations (bitterly nicknamed "The Con Men" by Der Realpolitik aus Terra) and Der Realpolitik aus Terra (sardonically called "The Rats" by the Comity of Nations) were desperately in need of natural resources, meaning FO. They were bidding against each other hysterically, and elbowing each other with sharp skirmishes at outposts. Their sole concern was the protection of their citizens. From the best of motives they were preparing to cut each other's throat.

Had this been the issue before the citizens of both Welfare States, some compromise might have been reached; but Triton, intoxicated as a schoolboy with a newfound prominence and power, confused issues by raising a religious issue and reviving a Holy War which the Family of Planets had long forgotten. Assistance in their Holy War (involving the extermination of a harmless and rather unimportant sect called the Quakers) was one of the conditions of sale. This, both the Comity of Nations and Der Realpolitik aus Terra were prepared to swallow with or without private reservations, but it could not be admitted to their citizens.

And so, camouflaged by the burning issues of Rights of Minority Sects, Priority of Pioneering, Freedom of Religion, Historical Rights to Triton v. Possession of Fact, etc., the two Houses of the Family of Planets feinted, parried, riposted, and slowly closed, like fencers on the strip, for the final sortie which meant ruin for both.

All this the four men discussed through three interminable meetings.

"Look here," Migg complained toward the close of the third consultation. "You theoreticians have already turned nine man-hours into carbonic acid with ridiculous dissensions . . ."

Bellanby nodded, smiling. "It's as I've always said, Migg. Every man nurses the secret belief that were he God he could do the job much better. We're just learning how difficult it is."

"Not God," Hrrdnikkisch said, "but hith Prime Minithterth. Gaul will be God."

Johansen winced. "I don't like that talk," he said. "I happen to be a religious man."

"You?" Bellanby exclaimed in surprise. "A Colloid-Therapeutist?"

"I happen to be a religious man," Johansen repeated stubbornly.

"But the boy hath the power of the miracle," Hrrdnikkisch protested. "When he hath been taught to know what he doth, he will be a God."

"This is pointless," Migg rapped out. "We have spent three sessions in piffling discussion. I have heard three opposed views re Mr. Odysseus Gaul. Although all are agreed he must be used as a tool, none can agree on the work to which the tool must be set. Bellanby prattles about an Ideal Intellectual Anarchy, Johansen preaches about a Soviet of God, and Hrrdnikkisch has wasted two hours postulating and destroying his own theorems. . . ."

"Really, Migg . . ." Hrrdnikkisch began. Migg waved his hand.

"Permit me," Migg continued malevolently, "to reduce this discussion to the kindergarten level. First things first, gentlemen. Before attempting to reach cosmic agreement we must make sure there is a cosmos left for us to agree upon. I refer to the impending war. . . .

"Our program, as I see it, must be simple and direct. It is the education of a God or, if Johansen protests, of an angel. Fortunately Gaul is an estimable young man of kindly, honest disposition. I shudder to think what he might have done had he been inherently vicious."

"Or what he might do once he learns what he can do," muttered Bellanby.

"Precisely. We must begin a careful and rigorous ethical education of the boy, but we haven't enough time. We can't educate first, and then explain the truth when he's safe. We must forestall the war. We need a shortcut."

"All right," Johansen said. "What do you suggest?"

"Dazzlement," Migg spat. "Enchantment."

"Enchantment?" Hrrdnikkisch chuckled. "A new thienth, Migg?"

"Why do you think I selected you three of all people for this secret?" Migg snorted. "For your intellects? Nonsense! I can think you all under the table. No. I selected you, gentlemen, for your charm."

"It's an insult," Bellanby grinned, "and yet I'm flattered."

"Gaul is nineteen," Migg went on. He is at the age when undergraduates are most susceptible to hero worship. I want you gentlemen to charm him. You are not the first brains of the University, but you are the first heroes."

"I altho am inthulted and flattered," said Hrrdnikkisch.

"I want you to charm him, dazzle him, inspire him with affection and awe . . . as you've done with countless classes of undergraduates."

"Aha!" said Johansen. "The chocolate around the pill."

"Exactly. When he's enchanted, you will make him want to stop the war . . . and then tell him how he can stop it. That will give us breathing space to continue his education. By the time he outgrows his respect for you he will have a sound ethical foundation on which to build. He'll be safe."

"And you, Migg?" Bellanby inquired. "What part do you play?"

"Now? None," Migg snarled. "I have no charm, gentlemen. I come later. When he outgrows his respect for you, he'll begin to acquire respect for me."

All of which was frightfully conceited but perfectly true.

And as events slowly marched toward the final crisis, Oddy Gaul was carefully and quickly enchanted. Bellanby invited him to the twenty-foot crystal globe atop his house . . . the famous hen roost to which only the favored few were invited. There, Oddy Gaul sunbathed and admired the philosopher's magnificent iron-hard condition at seventy-three. Admiring Bellanby's muscles, it was only natural for him to admire Bellanby's ideas. He returned often to sunbathe, worship the great man, and absorb ethical concepts.

Meanwhile, Hrrdnikkisch took over Oddy's evenings. With the mathematician, who puffed and lisped like some flamboyant character out of Rabelais, Oddy was carried to the dizzy heights of the *haute cuisine* and the complete pagan life. Together they ate and drank incredible foods and liquids and pursued incredible women until Oddy returned to his room each night intoxicated with the magic of the senses and the riotous color of the great Hrrdnikkisch's glittering ideas.

And occasionally . . . not too often, he would find Papa Johansen waiting for him, and then would come the long, quiet talks through the small hours when young men search for the harmonics of life and the meaning of entity. And there was Johansen for Oddy to model himself after . . . a glowing embodiment of Spiritual Good . . . a living example of Faith in God and Ethical Sanity.

The climax came on March 15 . . . The Ides of March, and they should have taken the date as a sign. After dinner with his three heroes at the Faculty Club, Oddy was ushered into the Foto-Library by the three great men where they were joined, quite casually, by Jesse Migg. There passed a few moments of uneasy tension until Migg made a sign, and Bellanby began.

"Oddy," he said, "have you ever had the fantasy that some day you might wake up and discover you were a king?"

Oddy blushed.

"I see you have. You know, every man has entertained that dream. It's called the Mignon Complex. The usual pattern is: You learn your parents have only adopted you and that you are actually and rightfully the King of . . . of . . ."

"Ruritania," said Hrrdnikkisch, who had made a study of Stone Age Fiction.

"Yes, sir," Oddy muttered. "I've had that dream."

"Well," Bellanby said quietly, "it's come true. You are a king."

Oddy stared while they explained and explained and explained. First, as a college boy, he was wary and suspicious of a joke. Then, as an idolator, he was almost persuaded by the men he most admired. And finally, as a human animal, he was swept away by the exaltation of security. Not power, not glory, not wealth thrilled him, but security alone. Later he might come to enjoy the trimmings, but now he was released from fear. He need never worry again.

"Yes," exclaimed Oddy. "Yes, yes, yes! I understand. I understand what you want me to do." He surged up excitedly from his chair and circled the illuminated walls, trembling with joy. Then he stopped and turned.

"And I'm grateful," he said. "Grateful to all of you for what you've been trying to do. It would have been shameful if I'd been selfish . . . or mean. . . . Trying to use this for myself. But you've shown me the way. It's to be used for good. Always!"

Johansen nodded happily.

"I'll always listen to you," Oddy went on. "I don't want to make any mistakes. Ever!" He paused and blushed again. "That dream about being a king . . . I had that when I was a kid. But here at the school I've had something bigger. I used to wonder what would happen if I was the one man who could run the world. I used to dream about the kind, generous things I'd do. . . ."

"Yes," said Bellanby. "We know, Oddy. We've all had that dream too. Every man does."

"But it isn't a dream any more," Oddy laughed. "It's reality. I can do it. I can make it happen."

"Start with the war," Migg said sourly.

"Of course," said Oddy. "The war first; but then we'll go on from there, won't we? I'll make sure the war never starts, but then we'll do big things . . . great things! Just the five of us in private. Nobody'll know about us. We'll be ordinary people, but we'll make life wonderful for everybody. If I'm an angel . . . like you say . . . then I'll spread heaven around me as far as I can reach."

"But start with the war," Migg repeated.

"The war is the first disaster that must be averted, Oddy," Bellanby said. "If you don't want this disaster to happen, it will never happen."

"And you want to prevent that tragedy, don't you?" said Johansen.

"Yes," answered Oddy. "I do."

On March 20, the war broke. The Comity of Nations and Der Realpolitik aus Terra mobilized and struck. While blow followed shattering counterblow, Oddy Gaul was commissioned subaltern in a line regiment, but gazetted to Intelligence on May 3. On June 24 he was appointed A.D.C. to the Joint Forces Council meeting in the ruins of what had been Australia. On July 11, he was brevetted to command of the wrecked Space Force, being jumped 1,789 grades over regular officers. On September 19 he assumed supreme command in the Battle of the Parsec and won the victory that ended the disastrous solar annihilation called the Six Month War.

On September 23, Oddy Gaul made the astonishing Peace Offer that was accepted by the remnants of both Welfare States. It required the scrapping of antagonistic economic theories, and amounted to the virtual abandonment of all economic theory with an amalgamation of both States into a Solar Society. On January 1, Oddy Gaul, by unanimous acclaim, was elected Solon of the Solar Society in perpetuity.

And today . . . still youthful, still vigorous, still handsome, still sincere, idealistic, charitable, kindly and sympathetic, he lives in the Solar Palace. He is unmarried but a mighty lover; uninhibited, but a charming host and devoted friend; democratic, but the feudal overlord of a bankrupt Family of Planets that suffers misgovernment, oppression, poverty, and confusion with a cheerful joy that sings nothing but Hosannahs to the glory of Oddy Gaul.

In a last moment of clarity, Jesse Migg communicated his desolate summation of the situation to his friends in the Faculty Club. This was shortly before they made the trip to join Oddy in the palace as his confidential and valued advisors.

"We were fools," Migg said bitterly. "We should have killed him.

He isn't an angel. He's a monster. Civilization and culture . . . philosophy and ethics . . . those were only masks Oddy put on; masks that covered the primitive impulses of his subconscious mind."

"You mean Oddy was not sincere?" Johansen asked heavily. "He wanted this wreckage . . . this ruin?"

"Certainly he was sincere . . . consciously. He still is. He thinks he desires nothing but the most good for the most men. He's honest, kind and generous . . . but only consciously."

"Ah! The Id!" said Hrrdnikkisch with an explosion of breath as though he had been punched in the stomach.

"You understand, Signoid? I see you do. Gentlemen, we were imbeciles. We made the mistake of assuming that Oddy would have conscious control of his power. He does not. The control was and still is below the thinking, reasoning level. The control lies in Oddy's Id . . . in that deep, unconscious reservoir of primordial selfishness that lies within every man."

"Then he wanted the war," Bellanby said.

"His Id wanted the war, Bellanby. It was the quickest route to what his Id desires . . . to be Lord of the Universe and loved by the Universe . . . and his Id controls the Power. All of us have that selfish, egocentric Id within us, perpetually searching for satisfaction, timeless, immortal, knowing no logic, no values, no good and evil, no mortality; and that is what controls the Power in Oddy. He will always win, not what he's been educated to desire but what his Id desires. It's the inescapable conflict that may be the doom of our system."

"But we'll be there to advise him . . . counsel him . . . guide him," Bellanby protested. "He asked us to come."

"And he'll listen to our advice like the good child that he is," Migg answered, "agreeing with us, trying to make a heaven for everybody while his Id will be making a hell for everybody. Oddy isn't unique. We all suffer from the same conflict . . . but Oddy has the Power."

"What can we do?" Johansen groaned. "What can we do?"

"I don't know." Migg bit his lip, then bobbed his head to Papa Johansen in what amounted to apology for him. "Johansen," he said, "you were right. There must be a God, if only because there must be an opposite to Oddy Gaul, who was most assuredly invented by the Devil."

But that was Jesse Migg's last sane statement. Now, of course, he adores Gaul the Glorious, Gaul the Gauleiter, Gaul the God Eternal who has achieved the savage, selfish satisfaction for which all of us unconsciously yearn from birth, but which only Oddy Gaul has won.

STAR LIGHT, STAR BRIGHT

The man in the car was thirty-eight years old. He was tall, slender, and not strong. His cropped hair was prematurely grey. He was afflicted with an education and a sense of humor. He was inspired by a purpose. He was armed with a phone book. He was doomed.

He drove up Post Avenue, stopped at No. 17 and parked. He consulted the phone book, then got out of the car and entered the house. He examined the mailboxes and then ran up the stairs to apartment 2-F. He rang the bell. While he waited for an answer he got out a small black notebook and a superior silver pencil that wrote in four colors.

The door opened. To a nondescript middle-aged lady, the man said, "Good evening. Mrs. Buchanan?"

The lady nodded.

"My name is Foster. I'm from the Science Institute. We're trying to check some flying saucer reports. I won't take a minute." Mr. Foster insinuated himself into the apartment. He had been in so many that he knew the layout automatically. He marched briskly down the hall to the front parlor, turned, smiled at Mrs. Buchanan, opened the notebook to a blank page, and poised the pencil.

"Have you ever seen a flying saucer, Mrs. Buchanan?"

"No. And it's a lot of bunk, I—"

"Have your children ever seen them? You do have children?"

"Yeah, but they—"

"How many?"

"Two. Them flying saucers never—"

"Are either of school age?"

"What?"

"School," Mr. Foster repeated impatiently. "Do they go to school?"

"The boy's twenty-eight," Mrs. Buchanan said. "The girl's twenty-four. They finished school a long—"

"I see. Either of them married?"

"No. About them flying saucers, you scientist doctors ought to—"

"We are," Mr. Foster interrupted. He made a tic-tac-toe in the notebook then closed it and slid it into an inside pocket with the pencil. "Thank you very much, Mrs. Buchanan," he said, turned, and marched out.

Downstairs, Mr. Foster got into the car, opened the telephone directory, turned to a page and ran his pencil through a name. He examined the name underneath, memorized the address and started the car. He drove to Fort George Avenue and stopped the car in front of No. 800. He entered the house and took the self-service elevator to the fourth floor. He rang the bell of apartment 4-G. While he waited for an answer he got out the small black notebook and the superior pencil.

The door opened. To a truculent man, Mr. Foster said, "Good evening. Mr. Buchanan?"

"What about it?" the truculent man said.

Mr. Foster said, "My name is Davis. I'm from the Association of National Broadcasters. Were preparing a list of names for prize competitors. May I come in? Won't take a minute."

"Mr. Foster/Davis insinuated himself and presently consulted with Mr. Buchanan and his redheaded wife in the living room of their apartment.

"Have you ever won a prize in radio or television?"

"No," Mr. Buchanan said angrily. "We never got a chance. Everybody else does but not us."

"All that free money and iceboxes," Mrs. Buchanan said. "Trips to Paris and planes and—"

"That's why we're making up this list," Mr. Foster/Davis broke in. "Have any of your relatives won prizes?"

"No. It's all a fix. Put-up jobs. They—"

"Any of your children?"

"Ain't got any children."

"I see. Thank you very much." Mr. Foster/Davis played out the tic-tac-toe game in his notebook, closed it and put it away. He released himself from the indignation of the Buchanans, went down to his car, crossed out another name in the phone book, memorized the address of the name underneath and started the car.

He drove to No. 215 East Sixty-Eighth Street and parked in front of a private brownstone house. He rang the doorbell and was confronted by a maid in uniform.

"Good evening," he said. "Is Mr. Buchanan in?"

"Who's calling?"

"My name is Hook," Mr. Foster/Davis said, "I'm conducting an investigation for the Better Business Bureau."

The maid disappeared, reappeared and conducted Mr. Foster/Davis/Hook to a small library where a resolute gentleman in dinner clothes stood holding a Limoges demitasse cup and saucer. There were expensive books on the shelves. There was an expensive fire in the grate.

"Mr. Hook?"

"Yes, sir," the doomed man replied. He did not take out the notebook. "I won't be a minute, Mr. Buchanan. Just a few questions."

"I have great faith in the Better Business Bureau," Mr. Buchanan pronounced. "Our bulwark against the inroads of—"

"Thank you, sir," Mr. Foster/Davis/Hook interrupted. "Have you ever been criminally defrauded by a businessman?"

"The attempt has been made. I have never succumbed."

"And your children? You do have children?"

"My son is hardly old enough to qualify as a victim."

"How old is he, Mr. Buchanan?"

"Ten."

"Perhaps he has been tricked at school? There are crooks who specialize in victimizing children."

"Not at my son's school. He is well protected."

"What school is that, sir?"

"Germanson."

"One of the best. Did he ever attend a city public school?"

"Never."

The doomed man took out the notebook and the superior pencil. This time he made a serious entry.

"Any other children, Mr. Buchanan?"

"A daughter, seventeen."

Mr. Foster/Davis/Hook considered, started to write, changed his mind and closed the notebook. He thanked his host politely and escaped from the house before Mr. Buchanan could ask for his credentials. He was ushered out by the maid, ran down the stoop to his car, opened the door, entered and was felled by a tremendous blow on the side of his head.

When the doomed man awoke, he thought he was in bed suffering from a hangover. He started to crawl to the bathroom when he realized he was dumped in a chair like a suit for the cleaners. He opened his eyes. He was in what appeared to be an underwater grotto. He blinked frantically. The water receded.

He was in a small legal office. A stout man who looked like an unfrocked Santa Claus stood before him. To one side, seated on a desk and swinging his legs carelessly, was a thin young man with a lantern jaw and eyes closely set on either side of his nose.

"Can you hear me?" the stout man asked.

The doomed man grunted.

"Can we talk?"

Another grunt.

"Joe," the stout man said pleasantly, "a towel."

The thin young man slipped off the desk, went to a corner basin and soaked a white hand towel. He shook it once, sauntered back to the chair where, with a suddenness and savagery of a tiger, he lashed it across the sick man's face.

"For God's sake!" Mr. Foster/Davis/Hook cried.

"That's better," the stout man said. "My name's Herod. Walter Herod, attorney-at-law." He stepped to the desk where the contents of the doomed man's pockets were spread, picked up a wallet and displayed it. "Your name is Warbeck. Marion Perkin Warbeck. Right?"

The doomed man gazed at his wallet, then at Walter Herod, attorney-at-law, and finally admitted the truth. "Yes," he said. "My name is Warbeck. But I never admit the Marion to strangers."

He was again lashed by the wet towel and fell back in the chair, stung and bewildered.

"That will do, Joe," Herod said. "Not again, please, until I tell you." To Warbeck he said, "Why this interest in the Buchanans?" He waited for an answer, then continued pleasantly, "Joe's been tailing you. You've averaged five Buchanans a night. Thirty, so far. What's your angle?"

"What the hell is this? Russia?" Warbeck demanded indignantly. "You've no right to kidnap me and grill me like the MVD. If you think you can—"

"Joe," Herod interrupted pleasantly. "Again, please."

Again the towel lashed Warbeck. Tormented, furious, and helpless, he burst into tears.

Herod fingered the wallet casually. "Your papers say you're a teacher by profession, principal of a public school. I thought teachers were supposed to be legit. How did you get mixed up in the inheritance racket?"

"The what racket?" Warbeck asked faintly.

"The inheritance racket," Herod repeated patiently. "The Heirs of Buchanan caper. What kind of parlay are you using? Personal approach?"

"I don't know what you're talking about," Warbeck answered. He sat bolt upright and pointed to the thin youth. "And don't start that towel business again."

"I'll start what I please and when I please," Herod said ferociously. "And I'll finish you when I goddamned well please. You're stepping on my toes and I don't buy it. I've got seventy-five thousand a year I'm taking out of this and I'm not going to let you chisel."

There was a long pause, significant for everybody in the room except the doomed man. Finally he spoke. "I'm an educated man," he said slowly. "Mention Galileo, say, or the lesser Cavalier poets, and I'm right up there with you. But there are gaps in my education and this is one of them. I can't meet the situation. Too many unknowns."

"I told you my name," Herod answered. He pointed to the thin young man. "That's Joe Davenport."

Warbeck shook his head. "Unknown in the mathematical sense. X quantities. Solving equations. My education speaking."

Joe looked startled. "Jesus!" he said without moving his lips. "Maybe he *is* legit."

Herod examined Warbeck curiously. "I'm going to spell it out for you," he said. "The inheritance racket is a long-term con. It operates something like so: There's a story that James Buchanan—"

"Fifteenth President of the U.S.?"

"In person. There's a story he died intestate leaving an estate for heirs unknown. That was in 1868. Today at compound interest that estate is worth millions. Understand?"

Warbeck nodded. "I'm educated," he murmured.

"Anybody named Buchanan is a sucker for this setup. It's a switch on the Spanish Prisoner routine. I send them a letter. Tell 'em there's a chance they may be one of the heirs. Do they want me to investigate and protect their cut in the estate? It only costs a small yearly retainer. Most of them buy it. From all over the country. And now you—"

"Wait a minute," Warbeck exclaimed. "I can draw a conclusion. You found out I was checking the Buchanan families. You think I'm trying to operate the same racket. Cut in . . . cut in? Yes? Cut in on you?"

"Well," Herod asked angrily, "aren't you?"

"Oh God!" Warbeck cried. "That this should happen to me. Me! Thank You, God. Thank You. I'll always be grateful." In his happy fervor he turned to Joe. "Give me the towel, Joe," he said. "Just throw it. I've got to wipe my face." He caught the flung towel and mopped himself joyously.

"Well," Herod repeated. "Aren't you?"

"No," Warbeck answered, "I'm not cutting in on you. But I'm grateful for the mistake. Don't think I'm not. You can't imagine how flattering it is for a schoolteacher to be taken for a thief."

He got out of the chair and went to the desk to reclaim his wallet and other possessions.

"Just a minute," Herod snapped.

The thin young man reached out and grasped Warbeck's wrist with an iron clasp.

"Oh stop it," the doomed man said impatiently. "This is a silly mistake."

"I'll tell you whether it's a mistake and I'll tell you if it's silly," Herod replied. "Just now you'll do as you're told."

"Will I?" Warbeck wrenched his wrist free and slashed Joe across the eyes with the towel. He darted around behind the desk, snatched up a paperweight and hurled it through the window with a shattering crash.

"Joe!" Herod yelled.

Warbeck knocked the phone off its stand and dialed Operator. He picked up his cigarette lighter, flicked it and dropped it into the wastepaper basket. The voice of the operator buzzed in the phone. Warbeck shouted, "I want a policeman!" Then he kicked the flaming basket into the center of the office.

"Joe!" Herod yelled and stamped on the blazing paper.

Warbeck grinned. He picked up the phone. Squawking noises were coming out of it. He put one hand over the mouthpiece. "Shall we negotiate?" he inquired.

"You sonofabitch," Joe growled. He took his hands from his eyes and slid toward Warbeck.

"No!" Herod called. "This crazy fool's hollered copper. He's legit, Joe." To Warbeck he said in pleading tones, "Fix it. Square it. We'll make it up to you. Anything you say. Just square the call."

The doomed man lifted the phone to his mouth. He said, "My name is M. P. Warbeck. I was consulting my attorney at this number and some idiot with a misplaced sense of humor made this call. Please phone back and check."

He hung up, finished pocketing his private property and winked at Herod. The phone rang, Warbeck picked it up, reassured the police and hung up. He came around from behind the desk and handed his car keys to Joe.

"Go down to my car," he said. "You know where you parked it. Open the glove compartment and bring up a brown manila envelope you'll find."

"Go to hell," Joe spat. His eyes were still tearing.

"Do as I say," Warbeck said firmly.

"Just a minute, Warbeck," Herod said. "What's this? A new angle? I said we'd make it up to you, but—"

"I'm going to explain why I'm interested in the Buchanans," Warbeck replied. "And I'm going into partnership with you. You've got what I need to locate one particular Buchanan . . . you and Joe. My Buchanan's ten years old. He's worth a hundred times your make-believe fortune."

Herod stared at him.

Warbeck placed the keys in Joe's hand. "Go down and get that envelope, Joe," he said. "And while you're at it you'd better square that broken window rap. Rap? Rap."

The doomed man placed the manila envelope neatly on his lap. "A school principal," he explained, "has to supervise school classes. He reviews work, estimates progress, irons out student problems and so on. This must be done at random. By samplings, I mean. I have nine hundred pupils in my school. I can't supervise them individually."

Herod nodded. Joe looked blank.

"Looking through some fifth-grade work last month," Warbeck continued, "I came across this astonishing document." He opened the envelope and took out a few sheets of ruled composition paper covered with blots and scrawled writing. "It was written by a Stuart Buchanan of the fifth grade. His age must be ten or thereabouts. The composition is entitled: *My Vacation*. Read it and you'll understand why Stuart Buchanan must be found."

He tossed the sheets to Herod who picked them up, took out a pair of horn-rim spectacles and balanced them on his fat nose. Joe came around to the back of his chair and peered over his shoulder.

My Vacatoin
by
Stuart Buchanan

This sumer I vissited my frends. I have 4 frends and they are
verry nice. First there is Tommy who lives in the contry and he is an
astronnimer. Tommy bilt his own tellescop out of glass 6 inches acros
wich he grond himself. He loks at the stars every nihgt and he let me
lok even wen it was raining cats & dogs . . .

"What the hell?" Herod looked up, annoyed.
"Read on. Read on," Warbeck said.

cats & dogs. We cold see the stars becaze Tommy made a thing for
over the end of the tellescop wich shoots up like a serchlite and
makes a hole in the skie to see rite thru the rain and everythinng to
the stars.

"Finished the astronomer yet?" Warbeck inquired.
"I don't dig it."
"Tommy got bored waiting for clear nights. He invented some-
thing that cuts through clouds and atmosphere . . . a funnel of vac-
uum so he can use his telescope all weather. What it amounts to is a
disintegration beam."
"The hell you say."
"The hell I don't. Read on. Read on."

Then I went to AnnMary and staied one hole week. It was fun. Be-
caze AnnMary has a spinak chainger for spinak and beats and
strinbeens—

"What he hell is a 'spinak chainger'?"
"Spinach. Spinach changer. Spelling isn't one of Stuart's special-
ties. 'Beats' are beets. 'Strinbeens' are string beans."

beats and strinbeens. Wen her mother made us eet them AnnMary
presed the buton and they staid the same outside onnly inside they
became cake. Chery and strowbery. I asted AnnMary how & she sed
it was by Enhv.

"This, I don't get."
"Simple. Anne-Marie doesn't like vegetables. So she's just as
smart as Tommy, the astronomer. She invented a matter-transmuter.

She transmutes spinak into cake. Chery or strowbery. Cake she eats with pleasure. So does Stuart."

"You're crazy."

"Not me. The kids. They're geniuses. Geniuses? What am I saying? They make a genius look imbecile. There's no label for these children."

"I don't believe it. This Stuart Buchanan's got a tall imagination. That's all."

"You think so? Then what about Enhv? That's how Anne-Marie transmutes matter. It took time but I figured Enhv out. It's Planck's quantum equation E=nhv. But read on. Read on. The best is yet to come. Wait till you get to lazy Ethel."

My frend Gorge bilds modell airplanes very good and small. Gorg's hands are clumzy but he makes small men out of moddelling clay and he tels them and they bild for him.

"What's this?"

"George, the plane-maker?"

"Yes."

"Simple. He makes miniature androids . . . robots . . . and they build the planes for him. Clever boy, George, but read about his sister, lazy Ethel."

His sister Ethel is the lazyist girl I ever saw. She is big & fat and she hates to walk. So wen her mother sends her too the store Ethel thinks to the store and thinks home with all the pakejes and has to hang around Gorg's room hiding untill it wil look like she walked both ways. Gorge and I make fun of her becaze she is fat and lazy but she gets into the movees for free and saw Hoppalong Casidy sixteen times.

The End

Herod stared at Warbeck.

"Great little girl, Ethel," Warbeck said. "She's too lazy to walk, so she teleports. Then she has a devil of a time covering up. She has to hide with her pakejes while George and Stuart make fun of her."

"Teleports?"

"That's right. She moves from place to place by thinking her way there."

"There ain't no such thing!" Joe said indignantly.

"There wasn't until lazy Ethel came along."

"I don't believe this," Herod said. "I don't believe any of it."

"You think it's just Stuart's imagination?"

"What else?"

"What about Planck's equation? E=nhv?"

"The kid invented that, too. Coincidence."

"Does that sound likely?"

"Then he read it somewhere."

"A ten-year-old boy? Nonsense."

"I tell you, I don't believe it," Herod shouted. "Let me talk to the kid for five minutes and I'll prove it."

"That's exactly what I want to do . . . only the boy's disappeared."

"How do you mean?"

"Lock, stock, and barrel. That's why I've been checking every Buchanan family in the city. The day I read this composition and sent down to the fifth grade for Stuart Buchanan to have a talk, he disappeared. He hasn't been seen since."

"What about his family?"

"The family disappeared too." Warbeck leaned forward intensely. "Get this. Every record of the boy and the family disappeared. Everything. A few people remember them vaguely, but that's all. They're gone."

"Jesus!" Joe said. "They scrammed, huh?"

"The very word. Scrammed. Thank you, Joe." Warbeck cocked an eye at Herod. "What a situation. Here's a child who makes friends with child geniuses. And the emphasis is on the child. They're making fantastic discoveries for childish purposes. Ethel teleports because she's too lazy to run errands. George makes robots to build model planes. Anne-Marie transmutes elements because she hates spinach. God knows what Stuart's other friends are doing. Maybe there's a Matthew who's invented a time machine so he can catch up on his homework."

Herod waved his hands feebly. "Why geniuses all of a sudden? What's happened?"

"I don't know. Atomic fallout? Fluorides in drinking water? Antibiotics? Vitamins? We're doing so much juggling with body chemistry these days that who knows what's happening? I want to find out but I can't. Stuart Buchanan blabbed like a child. When I started investigating, he got scared and disappeared."

"Is he a genius, too?"

"Very likely. Kids generally hang out with kids who share the same interests and talents."

"What kind of a genius? What's his talent?"

"I don't know. All I know is he disappeared. He covered up his tracks, destroyed every paper that could possibly help me locate him and vanished into thin air."

"How did he get into your files?"

"I don't know."

"Maybe he's a crook type," Joe said. "Expert at breaking and entering and such."

Herod smiled wanly. "A racketeer genius? A mastermind? The kid Moriarty?"

"He could be a thief-genius," the doomed man said, "but don't let running away convince you. All children do that when they get caught in a crisis. Either they wish it had never happened or they wish they were a million miles away. Stuart Buchanan may be a million miles away, but we've got to find him."

"Just to find out is he smart?" Joe asked.

"No, to find his parents. Do I have to diagram it? What would the army pay for a disintegration beam? What would an element-transmuter be worth? If we could manufacture living robots how rich would we get? If we could teleport how powerful would we be?"

There was a burning silence, then Herod got to his feet. "Mr. Warbeck," he said, "you make me and Joe look like pikers. Thank you for letting us cut in on you. We'll pay off. We'll find that kid."

It is not possible for anyone to vanish without a trace . . . even a probable criminal genius. It is sometimes difficult to locate that trace . . . even for an expert experienced in hurried disappearances. But there is a professional technique unknown to amateurs.

"You've been blundering," Herod explained kindly to the doomed man. "Chasing one Buchanan after the other. There are angles. You don't run after a missing party. You look around on his back-trail for something he dropped."

"A genius wouldn't drop anything."

"Let's grant the kid's a genius. Type unspecified. Let's grant him everything. But a kid is a kid. He must have overlooked something. We'll find it."

In three days Warbeck was introduced to the most astonishing angles of search. They consulted the Washington Heights post office about a Buchanan family formerly living in that neighborhood, now moved. Was there any change-of-address card filed? None.

They visited the election board. All voters are registered. If a voter moves from one election district to another, provision is usually made that a record of the transfer be kept. Was there any such record on Buchanan? None.

They called on the Washington Heights office of the gas and electric company. All subscribers for gas and electricity must transfer their accounts if they move. If they move out of town, they generally request the return of their deposit. Was there any record of a party named Buchanan? None.

It is a state law that all drivers must notify the license bureau of change of address or be subject to penalties involving fines, prison or worse. Was there any such notification by a party named Buchanan at the Motor Vehicle Bureau? There was not.

They questioned the R-J Realty Corp., owners and operators of a multiple dwelling in Washington Heights in which a party named Buchanan had leased a four-room apartment. The R-J lease, like most other leases, required the names and addresses of two character references for the tenant. Could the character references for Buchanan be produced? They could not. There was no such lease in the files.

"Maybe Joe was right," Warbeck complained in Herod's office. "Maybe the boy is a thief-genius. How did he think of everything? How did he get at every paper and destroy it? Did he break and enter? Bribe? Burgle? Threaten? How did he do it?"

"We'll ask him when we get to him," Herod said grimly. "All right. The kid's licked us straight down the line. He hasn't forgotten a trick. But I've got one angle I've been saving. Let's go up and see the janitor of their building."

"I questioned him months ago," Warbeck objected. "He remembers the family in a vague way and that's all. He doesn't know where they went."

"He knows something else, something the kid wouldn't think of covering. Let's go get it."

They drove up to Washington Heights and descended upon Mr. Jacob Ruysdale at dinner in the basement apartment of the building. Mr. Ruysdale disliked being separated from his liver and onions, but was persuaded by five dollars.

"About that Buchanan family," Herod began.

"I told him everything before," Ruysdale broke in, pointing to Warbeck.

"All right. He forgot to ask one question. Can I ask it now?" Ruysdale reexamined the five-dollar bill and nodded.

"When anybody moves in or out of a building, the superintendent usually takes down the name of the movers in case they damage the building. I'm a lawyer. I know this. It's to protect the building in case suit has to be brought. Right?"

Ruysdale's face lit up. "By Godfrey!" he said. "That's right, I forgot all about it. He never asked me."

"He didn't know. You've got the name of the company that moved the Buchanans out. Right?"

Ruysdale ran across the room to a cluttered bookshelf. He withdrew a tattered journal and flipped it open. He wet his fingers and turned pages.

"Here it is," he said. "The Avon Moving Company. Truck No. G-4."

The Avon Moving Company had no record of the removal of a Buchanan family from an apartment in Washington Heights. "The kid was pretty careful at that," Herod murmured. But it did have a record of the men working truck G-4 on that day. The men were interviewed when they checked in at closing time. Their memories were refreshed with whiskey and cash. They recalled the Washington Heights job vaguely. It was a full day's work because they had to drive the hell and gone to Brooklyn. "Oh God! Brooklyn!" Warbeck muttered. What address in Brooklyn? Something on Maple Park Row. Number? The number could not be recalled.

"Joe, buy a map."

They examined the street map of Brooklyn and located Maple Park Row. It was indeed the hell and gone out of civilization and was twelve blocks long. "That's *Brooklyn* blocks," Joe grunted. "Twice as long as anywhere. I know."

Herod shrugged. "We're close," he said. "The rest will have to be legwork. Four blocks apiece. Cover every house, every apartment. List every kid around ten. Then Warbeck can check them, if they're under an alias."

"There's a million kids a square inch in Brooklyn," Joe protested.

"There's a million dollars a day in it for us if we find him. Now let's go."

Maple Park Row was a long, crooked street lined with five-story apartment houses. Its sidewalks were lined with baby carriages and old ladies on camp chairs. Its curbs were lined with parked cars. Its gutter was lined with crude whitewash stickball courts shaped like elongated diamonds. Every manhole cover was a home plate.

"It's just like the Bronx," Joe said nostalgically. "I ain't been home to the Bronx in ten years."

He wandered sadly down the street toward his sector, automatically threading his way through stickball games with the unconscious skill of the city-born. Warbeck remembered that departure sympathetically because Joe Davenport never returned.

The first day, he and Herod imagined Joe had found a hot lead. This encouraged them. The second day they realized no heat could keep Joe on the fire for forty-eight hours. This depressed them. On the third day they had to face the truth.

"He's dead," Herod said flatly. "The kid got him."

"How?"

"He killed him."

"A ten-year-old boy? A child?"

"You want to know what kind of genius Stuart Buchanan has, don't you? I'm telling you."

"I don't believe it."

"Then explain Joe."

"He quit."

"Not on a million dollars."

"But where's the body?"

"Ask the kid. He's the genius. He's probably figured out tricks that would baffle Dick Tracy."

"How did he kill him?"

"Ask the kid. He's the genius."

"Herod, I'm scared."

"So am I. Do you want to quit now?"

"I don't see how we can. If the boy's dangerous, we've got to find him."

"Civic virtue, heh?"

"Call it that."

"Well, I'm still thinking about the money."

They returned to Maple Park Row and Joe Davenport's four-block sector. They were cautious, almost furtive. They separated and began working from each end toward the middle; in one house, up the stairs, apartment by apartment, to the top, then down again to investigate the next building. It was slow, tedious work. Occasionally they glimpsed each other far down the street, crossing from one dismal building to another. And that was the last glimpse Warbeck ever had of Walter Herod.

He sat in his car and waited. He sat in his car and trembled. "I'll go to the police," he muttered, knowing perfectly well he could not. "The boy has a weapon. Something he invented. Something silly like the others. A special light so he can play marbles at night, only it murders men. A machine to play checkers, only it hypnotizes men. He's invented a robot mob of gangsters so he can play cops-and-robbers and they took care of Joe and Herod. He's a child genius. Dangerous. Deadly. What am I going to do?"

The doomed man got out of the car and stumbled down the street toward Herod's half of the sector. "What's going to happen when Stuart Buchanan grows up?" he wondered. "What's going to happen when all the rest of them grow up? Tommy and George and Anne-Marie and lazy Ethel? Why don't I start running away now? What am I doing here?"

It was dusk on Maple Park Row. The old ladies had withdrawn, folding their camp chairs like Arabs. The parked cars remained. The stickball games were over, but small games were starting under the glowing lamp posts . . . games with bottle caps and cards and battered pennies. Overhead, the purple city haze was deepening, and through it the sharp sparkle of Venus following the sun below the horizon could be seen.

"He must know his power," Warbeck muttered angrily. "He must know how dangerous he is. That's why he's running away. Guilt. That's why he destroys us, one by one, smiling to himself, a crafty child, a vicious, killing genius. . . ."

Warbeck stopped in the middle of Maple Park Row.

"Buchanan!" he shouted. "Stuart Buchanan!"

The kids near him stopped their games and gaped.

"Stuart Buchanan!" Warbeck's voice cracked hysterically. "Can you hear me?"

His wild voice carried farther down the street. More games stopped. Ringaleevio, Chinese tag, Red-Light, and Boxball.

"Buchanan!" Warbeck screamed. "Stuart Buchanan! Come out come out, wherever you are!"

The world hung motionless.

In the alley between 217 and 219 Maple Park Row playing hide-and-seek behind piled ash barrels, Stuart Buchanan heard his name and crouched lower. He was aged ten, dressed in sweater, jeans, and sneakers. He was intent and determined that he was not going to be caught out "it" again. He was going to hide until he could make a dash for home-free in safety. As he settled comfortably among the ashcans, his eye caught the glimmer of Venus low in the western sky.

"Star light, star bright," he whispered in all innocence, "first star I see tonight. Wish I may, wish I might, grant me the wish I wish tonight." He paused and considered. Then he wished. "God bless Mom and Pop and me and all my friends and make me a good boy and please let me be always happy and I wish that anybody who tries to bother me would go away . . . a long way away . . . and leave me alone forever."

In the middle of Maple Park Row, Marion Perkin Warbeck stepped forward and drew breath for another hysterical yell. And then he was elsewhere, going away on a road that was a long way away. It was a straight white road cleaving infinitely through blackness, stretching onward and onward into forever; a dreary, lonely, endless road leading away and away and away.

Down that road Warbeck plodded, an astonished automaton, unable to speak, unable to stop, unable to think in the timeless infinity. Onward and onward he walked into a long way away, unable to turn back. Ahead of him he saw the minute specks of figures trapped on that one-way road forever. There was a dot that had to be Herod. Ahead of Herod there was a mote that was Joe Davenport. And ahead of Joe he could make out a long dwindling chain of mites. He turned once with a convulsive effort. Behind him, dim and distant, a figure was plodding, and behind that another abruptly materialized, and another . . . and another. . . .

While Stuart Buchanan crouched behind the ash barrels and watched alertly for the "it." He was unaware that he had disposed of Warbeck. He was unaware that he had disposed of Herod, Joe Davenport and scores of others.

He was unaware that he had induced his parents to flee Washington Heights, that he had destroyed papers and documents, memories and people, in his simple desire to be left alone. He was unaware that he was a genius.

His genius was for wishing.

5,271,009

Take two parts of Beelzebub, two of Israfel, one of Monte Cristo, one of Cyrano, mix violently, season with mystery and you have Mr. Solon Aquila. He is tall, gaunt, sprightly in manner, bitter in expression, and when he laughs his dark eyes turn into wounds. His occupation is unknown. He is wealthy without visible means of support. He is seen everywhere and understood nowhere. There is something odd about his life.

This is what's odd about Mr. Aquila, and you can make what you will of it. When he walks he is never forced to wait on a traffic signal. When he desires to ride there is always a vacant taxi on hand. When he bustles into his hotel an elevator always happens to be waiting.

When he enters a store, a salesclerk is always free to serve him. There always happens to be a table available for Mr. Aquila in restaurants. There are always last-minute ticket returns when he craves entertainment at sold-out shows.

You can question waiters, hack drivers, elevator girls, salesmen, box-office men. There is no conspiracy. Mr. Aquila does not bribe or blackmail for these petty conveniences. In any case, it would not be possible for him to bribe or blackmail the automatic clock that governs the city traffic signal system. These things, which make life so convenient for him, simply happen. Mr. Solon Aquila is never disappointed. Presently we shall hear about his first disappointment and see what it led to.

Mr. Aquila has been seen fraternizing in low saloons, in middle saloons, in high saloons. He has been met in bagnios, at coronations, executions, circuses, magistrates' courts, and handbook offices. He has been known to buy antique cars, historic jewels, incunabula, pornography, chemicals, porro prisms, polo ponies, and full-choke shotguns.

"*HimmelHerrGottSeiDank!* I'm crazy, man, crazy. Eclectic, by God," he told a flabbergasted department-store president. "The *Weltmann* type, *nicht wahr*? My ideal: Goethe. *Tout le monde*. God damn."

He spoke a spectacular tongue of mixed metaphors and meanings. Dozens of languages and dialects came out in machine-gun bursts. Apparently he also lied *ad libitum*.

"*Sacré bleu*, Jeez!" he was heard to say once. "Aquila from the Latin. Means aquiline. *O tempora, o mores*. Speech by Cicero. My ancestor."

And another time: "My idol: Kipling. Took my name from him. Aquila, one of his heroes. God damn. Greatest Negro writer since *Uncle Tom's Cabin*."

On the morning that Mr. Solon Aquila was stunned by his first disappointment, he bustled into the atelier of Lagan & Derelict, dealers in paintings, sculpture, and rare objects of art. It was his intention to buy a painting. Mr. James Derelict knew Aquila as a client. Aquila had already purchased a Frederick Remington and a Winslow Homer some time ago when, by another odd coincidence, he had bounced into the Madison Avenue shop one minute after the coveted paintings went up for sale. Mr. Derelict had also seen Mr. Aquila boat a prize striper at Montauk.

"*Bon soir, bel esprit*, God damn, Jimmy," Mr. Aquila said. He was on first-name terms with everyone. "Here's a cool day for color, *oui!* Cool. Slang. I have in me to buy a picture."

"Good morning, Mr. Aquila" Derelict answered. He had the seamed face of a cardsharp, but his blue eyes were honest and his smile was disarming. However, at this moment his smile seemed strained, as though the volatile appearance of Aquila had unnerved him.

"I'm in the mood for your man, by Jeez," Aquila said, rapidly opening cases, fingering ivories, and tasting the porcelains. "What's his name, my old? Artist like Bosch. Like Heinrich Kley. You handle him, *parbleu*, exclusive. *O si sic omnia*, by Zeus!"

"Jeffrey Halsyon?" Derelict asked timidly.

"*Oeil de boeuf!*" Aquila cried. "What a memory. Chryselephantine. Exactly the artist I want. He is my favorite. A monochrome, preferably. A small Jeffrey Halsyon for Aquila, *bitte*. Wrap her up."

"I wouldn't have believed it," Derelict muttered.

"Ah! Ah-ha? This is not 100 proof guaranteed Ming," Mr. Aquila exclaimed, brandishing an exquisite vase. "*Caveat emptor*, by damn. Well, Jimmy? I snap my fingers. No Halsyons in stock, old faithful?"

"It's extremely odd, Mr. Aquila." Derelict seemed to struggle with himself. "Your coming in like this. A Halsyon monochrome arrived not five minutes ago."

"You see? *Tempo ist Richtung*. Well?"

"I'd rather not show it to you. For personal reasons, Mr. Aquila."

"*HimmelHerrGott! Pourquoi?* She's bespoke?"

"N-no, sir. Not for *my* personal reasons. For *your* personal reasons."

"Oh? God damn. Explain myself to me."

"Anyway, it isn't for sale, Mr. Aquila. It can't be sold."

"For why not? Speak, old fish and chips."

"I can't say, Mr. Aquila."

"*Zut alors!* Must I judo your arm, Jimmy? You can't show. You can't sell. Me, internally, I have pressurized myself for a Jeffrey Halsyon. My favorite. God damn. Show me the Halsyon or *sic transit gloria mundi*. You hear me, Jimmy?"

Derelict hesitated, then shrugged. "Very well, Mr. Aquila. I'll show you."

Derelict led Aquila past cases of china and silver, past lacquer and bronzes and suits of shimmering armor to the gallery in the rear of the shop where dozens of paintings hung on the gray velour walls, glowing under warm spotlights. He opened a drawer in a Goddard breakfront and took out an envelope. On the envelope was printed BABYLON INSTITUTE. From the envelope Derelict withdrew a dollar bill and handed it to Mr. Aquila.

"Jeffrey Halsyon's latest," he said.

With a fine pen and carbon ink, a cunning hand had drawn another portrait over the face of George Washington on the dollar bill. It was a hateful, diabolic face set in a hellish background. It was a face to strike terror, in a scene to inspire loathing. The face was a portrait of Mr. Aquila.

"God damn," Mr. Aquila said.

"You see, sir? I didn't want to hurt your feelings."

"Now I must own him, big boy." Mr. Aquila appeared to be fascinated by the portrait. "Is she accident or for purpose? Does Halsyon know myself? *Ergo sum.*"

"Not to my knowledge, Mr. Aquila. But in any event I can't sell the drawing. It's evidence of a felony . . . mutilating United States currency. It must be destroyed."

"Never!" Mr. Aquila returned the drawing as though he feared the dealer would instantly set fire to it. "Never, Jimmy. Nevermore quoth the raven. God damn. Why does he draw on money, Halsyon? My picture, pfui. Criminal libels but *n'importe.* But pictures on money? Wasteful. *Joci causa.*"

"He's insane, Mr. Aquila."

"No! Yes? Insane?" Aquila was shocked.

"Quite insane, sir. It's very sad. They've had to put him away. He spends his time drawing these pictures on money."

"God damn, *mon ami.* Who gives him money?"

"I do, Mr. Aquila; and his friends. Whenever we visit him he begs for money for his drawings."

"*Le jour viendra,* by Jeez! Why you don't give him paper for drawings, eh, my ancient of days?"

Derelict smiled sadly. "We tried that, sir. When we gave Jeff paper, he drew pictures of money."

"*HimmelHerrGott!* My favorite artist. In the looney bin. *Eh bien.* How in the holy hell am I to buy paintings from same if such be the case?"

"You won't, Mr. Aquila. I'm afraid no one will ever buy a Halsyon again. He's quite hopeless."

"Why does he jump his tracks, Jimmy?"

"They say it's a withdrawal, Mr. Aquila. His success did it to him."

"Ah? Q.E.D. me, big boy. Translate."

"Well, sir, he's still a young man; in his thirties and very immature. When he became so very successful, he wasn't ready for it. He wasn't prepared for the responsibilities of his life and his career. That's what the doctors told me. So he turned his back on everything and withdrew into childhood."

"Ah? And the drawing on money?"

"They say that's his symbol of his return to childhood, Mr. Aquila. It proves he's too young to know what money is for."

"Ah? *Oui. Ja*. Astute, by crackey. And my portrait?"

"I can't explain that, Mr. Aquila, unless you have met him in the past and he remembers you somehow."

"Hmmm. Perhaps. So. You know something, my attic of Greece? I am disappointed. *Je n'oublierai jamais*. I am most severely disappointed. God damn. No more Halsyons ever? *Merde*. My slogan. We must do something about Jeffrey Halsyon. I will not be disappointed. We must do something."

Mr. Solon Aquila nodded his head emphatically, took out a cigarette, took out a lighter, then paused, deep in thought. After a long moment, he nodded again, this time with decision, and did an astonishing thing. He returned the lighter to his pocket, took out another, glanced around quickly and lit it under Mr. Derelict's nose.

Mr. Derelict appeared not to notice. Mr. Derelict appeared, in one instant, to be frozen. Allowing the lighter to burn, Mr. Aquila placed it carefully on a ledge in front of the art dealer who stood before it without moving. The orange flame gleamed on his glassy eyeballs.

Aquila darted out into the shop, searched and found a rare Chinese crystal globe. He took it from its case, warmed it against his heart, and peered into it. He mumbled. He nodded. He returned the globe to the case, went to the cashier's desk, took a pad and pencil and began ciphering in symbols that bore no relationship to any language or any graphology. He nodded again, tore up the sheet of paper, and took out his wallet.

From the wallet he removed a dollar bill. He placed the bill on the glass counter, took an assortment of fountain pens from his vest pocket, selected one and unscrewed it. Carefully shielding his eyes, he allowed one drop to fall from the pen point onto the bill. There was a blinding flash of light. There was a humming vibration that slowly died.

Mr. Aquila returned the pens to his pocket, carefully picked up the bill by a corner, and ran back into the picture gallery where the art dealer still stood staring glassily at the orange flame. Aquila fluttered the bill before the sightless eyes.

"Listen, my ancient," Aquila whispered. "You will visit Jeffrey Halsyon this afternoon. *N'est-ce-pas?* You will give him this very own coin of the realm when he asks for drawing materials. Eh? God damn." He removed Mr. Derelict's wallet from his pocket, placed the bill inside and returned the wallet.

"And this is why you make the visit," Aquila continued. "It is because you have had an inspiration from *le Diable Boiteux. Nolens volens,* the lame devil has inspired you with a plan for healing Jeffrey Halsyon. God damn. You will show him samples of his great art of the past to bring him to his senses. Memory is the all-mother. *HimmelHerrGott!* You hear me, big boy? You do what I say. Go today and devil take the hindmost."

Mr. Aquila picked up the burning lighter, lit his cigarette and permitted the flame to go out. As he did so, he said: "No, my holy of holies! Jeffrey Halsyon is too great an artist to languish in durance vile. He must be returned to this world. He must be returned to me. *È sempre l'ora.* I will not be disappointed. You hear me, Jimmy? I will not!"

"Perhaps there's hope, Mr. Aquila," James Derelict said. "Something's just occurred to me while you were talking . . . a way to bring Jeff back to sanity. I'm going to try it this afternoon."

As he drew the face of the Faraway Fiend over George Washington's portrait on a bill, Jeffrey Halsyon dictated his autobiography to nobody.

"Like Cellini," he recited. "Line and literature simultaneously. Hand in hand, although all art is one art, holy brothers in barbiturate, near ones and dear ones in Nembutal. Very well. I commence: I was born. I am dead. Baby wants a dollar. No—"

He arose from the padded floor and raged from padded wall to padded wall, envisioning anger as a deep purple fury running into the pale lavenders of recrimination by the magic of his brushwork, his chiaroscuro, by the clever blending of oil, pigment, light, and the stolen genius of Jeffrey Halsyon torn from him by the Faraway Fiend whose hideous face—

"Begin anew," he muttered. "We darken the highlights. Start with the underpainting . . ." He squatted on the floor again, picked up the quill drawing pen whose point was warranted harmless, dipped it into carbon ink whose contents were warranted poisonless, and applied himself to the monstrous face of the Faraway Fiend which was replacing the first President on the dollar.

"I was born," he dictated to space while his cunning hand wrought beauty and horror on the banknote paper. "I had peace. I had hope. I had art. I had peace. Mama. Papa. Kin I have a glass a water? Oooo! There was a big bad bogey man who gave me a bad look; and now baby's afraid. Mama! Baby wantsa make pretty pictures onna pretty paper for Mama and Papa. Look, Mama. Baby makin' a picture of the bad bogey man with a mean look, a black look with his black eyes like pools of hell, like cold fires of terror, like faraway fiends from faraway fears—Who's that!"

The cell door unbolted. Halsyon leaped into a corner and cowered, naked and squalling, as the door was opened for the Faraway Fiend to enter. But it was only the medicine man in his white jacket and a stranger-man in black suit, black homburg, carrying a black portfolio with the initials J.D. lettered on it in a bastard gold Gothic with ludicrous overtones of Goudy and Baskerville.

"Well, Jeffrey?" the medicine man inquired heartily.

"Dollar?" Halsyon whined. "Kin baby have a dollar?"

"I've brought an old friend, Jeffrey. You remember Mr. Derelict?"

"Dollar," Halsyon whined. "Baby wants a dollar."

"What happened to the last one, Jeffrey? You haven't finished it yet, have you?"

Halsyon sat on the bill to conceal it, but the medicine man was too quick for him. He snatched it up and he and the stranger-man examined it.

"As great as all the rest," Derelict sighed. "Greater! What a magnificent talent wasting away . . ."

Halsyon began to weep. "Baby wants a dollar!" he cried.

The stranger-man took out his wallet, selected a dollar bill and handed it to Halsyon. As soon as Halsyon touched it, he heard it sing and he tried to sing with it, but it was singing him a private song so he had to listen.

It was a lovely dollar; smooth but not too new, with a faintly matte surface that would take ink like kisses. George Washington looked reproachful but resigned, as though he was used to the treatment in store for him. And indeed he might well be, for he was much older on this dollar. Much older than on any other, for his serial number was 5,271,009 which made him 5,000,000 years old and more, and the oldest he had ever been before was 2,000,000.

As Halsyon squatted contentedly on the floor and dipped his pen in the ink as the dollar told him to, he heard the medicine man say, "I don't think I should leave you alone, Mr. Derelict."

"No, we must be alone together, doctor. Jeff always was shy about his work. He could only discuss it with me privately."

"How much time would you need?"

"Give me an hour."

"I doubt very much whether it'll do any good."

"But there's no harm trying?"

"I suppose not. All right, Mr. Derelict. Call the nurse when you're through."

The door opened; the door closed. The stranger-man named Derelict put his hand on Halsyon's shoulder in a friendly, intimate way. Halsyon looked up at him and grinned cleverly, meanwhile waiting for the sound of the bolt in the door. It came; like a shot, like a final nail in a coffin.

"Jeff, I've brought some of your old work with me," Derelict said, in a voice that was only approximately casual. "I thought you might like to look it over with me."

"Have you got a watch on you?" Halsyon asked.

Restraining his start of surprise at Halsyon's normal tone, the art dealer took out his pocket watch and displayed it.

"Lend it to me for a minute."

Derelict unchained the watch and handed it over. Halsyon took it carefully and said, "All right. Go ahead with the pictures."

"Jeff!" Derelict exclaimed. "This is you again, isn't it? This is the way you always—"

"Thirty," Halsyon interrupted. "Thirty-five, forty, forty-five, fifty, fifty-five, ONE." He concentrated on the flicking second hand with rapt expectation.

"No, I guess it isn't," the dealer muttered. "I only imagined you sounded—Oh well." He opened the portfolio and began sorting mounted drawings.

"Forty, forty-five, fifty-five, TWO."

"Here's one of your earliest, Jeff. Remember when you came into the gallery with the roughs and we thought you were the new polisher from the agency? Took you months to forgive us. You always claimed we bought your first picture just to apologize. Do you still think so?"

"Forty, forty-five, fifty, fifty-five, THREE."

"Here's that tempera that gave you so many heartaches. I was wondering if you'd care to try another? I really don't think tempera is as inflexible as you claim, and I'd be interested to have you try again now that your technique's so much more mature. What do you say?"

"Forty, forty-five, fifty, fifty-five, FOUR."

"Jeff, put down that watch."

"Ten, fifteen, twenty, twenty-five . . ."

"What the devil's the point of counting minutes?"

"Well," Halsyon said reasonably, "sometimes they lock the door and go away. Other times they lock up and stay and spy on you. But they never spy longer than three minutes, so I'm giving them five just to make sure. FIVE."

Halsyon gripped the small pocket watch in his big fist and drove the fist cleanly into Derelict's jaw. The dealer dropped without a sound. Halsyon dragged him to the wall, stripped him naked, dressed himself in his clothes, repacked the portfolio, and closed it. He picked up the dollar bill and pocketed it. He picked up the bottle of carbon ink warranted nonpoisonous and smeared the contents over his face.

Choking and shouting, he brought the nurse to the door.

"Let me out of here," Halsyon cried in a muffled voice. "That maniac tried to drown me. Threw ink in my face. I want out!"

The door was unbolted and opened. Halsyon shoved past the

nurse-man, cunningly mopping his blackened face with a hand that only masked it more. As the nurse-man started to enter the cell, Halsyon said, "Never mind Halsyon. He's all right. Get me a towel or something. Hurry!

The nurse-man locked the door again, turned and ran down the corridor. Halsyon waited until he disappeared into a supply room, then turned and ran in the opposite direction. He went through the heavy doors to the main wing corridor, still cleverly mopping, still sputtering with cunning indignation. He reached the main building. He was halfway out and still no alarm. He knew those brazen bells. They tested them every Wednesday noon.

It's like a game, he told himself. It's fun. It's nothing to be scared of. It's being safely, sanely, joyously a kid again and when we quit playing I'm going home to mama and dinner and papa reading me the funnies and I'm a kid again, really a kid again, forever.

There still was no hue and cry when he reached the main floor. He complained about his indignity to the receptionist. He complained to the protection guards as he forged James Derelict's name in the visitor's book, and his inky hand smeared such a mess on the page that the forgery went undetected. The guard buzzed the final gate open. Halsyon passed through into the street, and as he started away he heard the brass of the bells begin a clattering that terrified him.

He ran. He stopped. He tried to stroll. He could not. He lurched down the street until he heard the guards shouting. He darted around a corner, and another, tore up endless streets, heard cars behind him, sirens, bells, shouts, commands. It was a ghastly Catherine wheel of flight. Searching desperately for a hiding place, Halsyon darted into the hallway of a desolate tenement.

Halsyon began to climb the stairs. He went up three at a clip, then two, then struggled step by step as his strength failed and panic paralyzed him. He stumbled at a landing and fell against a door. The door opened. The Faraway Fiend stood within, smiling briskly, rubbing his hands.

"*Glückliche Reise*," he said. "On the dot. God damn. You twenty-three skidooed, eh? Enter, my old. I'm expecting you. Be it never so humble . . ."

Halsyon screamed.

"No, no, no! No *Sturm und Drang*, my beauty." Mr. Aquila

clapped a hand over Halsyon's mouth, heaved him up, dragged him through the doorway and slammed the door.

"Presto-chango," he laughed. "Exit Jeffrey Halsyon from mortal ken. *Dieu vous garde.*"

Halsyon freed his mouth, screamed again and fought hysterically, biting and kicking. Mr. Aquila made a clucking noise, dipped into his pocket and brought out a package of cigarettes. He flipped one out of the pack expertly and broke it under Halsyon's nose. The artist at once subsided and suffered himself to be led to a couch, where Aquila cleansed the ink from his face and hands.

"Better, eh?" Mr. Aquila chuckled. "Non habit-forming. God damn. Drinks now called for."

He filled a shot glass from a decanter, added a tiny cube of purple ice from a fuming bucket, and placed the drink in Halsyon's hand. Compelled by a gesture from Aquila, the artist drank it off. It made his brain buzz. He stared around, breathing heavily. He was in what appeared to be the luxurious waiting room of a Park Avenue physician. Queen Anne furniture. Axminster rug. Two Hogarths and a Copley on the wall in gilt frames. They were genuine, Halsyon realized with amazement. Then, with even more amazement, he realized that he was thinking with coherence, with continuity. His mind was quite clear.

He passed a heavy hand over his forehead. "What's happened?" he asked faintly. "There's like . . . something like a fever behind me. Nightmares."

"You have been sick," Aquila replied. "I am blunt, my old. This is a temporary return to sanity. It is no feat, God damn. Any doctor can do it. Niacin plus carbon dioxide. *Id genus omne.* Only temporary. We must search for something more permanent."

"What's this place?"

"Here? My office. Anteroom without. Consultation room within. Laboratory to left. In God we trust."

"I know you," Halsyon mumbled. "I know you from somewhere. I know your face."

"*Oui.* You have drawn and redrawn me in your fever. *Ecce homo.* But you have the advantage, Halsyon. Where have we met? I ask myself." Aquila put on a brilliant speculum, tilted it over his left eye and let it shine into Halsyon's face. "Now I ask you. Where have we met?"

Hypnotized by the light, Halsyon answered dreamily. "At the Beaux Arts Ball. . . . A long time ago. . . . Before the fever. . . ."

"Ah? *Sí.* It was one half year ago. I was there. An unfortunate night."

"No. A glorious night. . . . Gay, happy fun. . . . Like a school dance. . . . Like a prom in costume. . . ."

"Always back to childhood, eh?" Mr. Aquila murmured. "We must attend to that. *Cetera desunt,* young Lochinvar. Continue."

"I was with Judy. . . . We realized we were in love that night. We realized how wonderful life was going to be. And then you passed and looked at me. . . . Just once. You looked at me. It was horrible."

"Tsk!" Mr. Aquila clicked his tongue in vexation. "Now I remember said incident. I was unguarded. Bad news from home. A pox on both my houses."

"You passed in red and black. . . . Satanic. Wearing no mask. You looked at me. . . . A red and black look I never forgot. A look from black eyes like pools of hell, like cold fires of terror. And with that look you robbed me of everything . . . of joy, of hope, of love, of life. . . ."

"No, no!" Mr. Aquila said sharply. "Let us understand ourselves. My carelessness was the key that unlocked the door. But you fell into a chasm of your own making. Nevertheless, old beer and skittles, we must alter same." He removed the speculum and shook his finger at Halsyon. "We must bring you back to the land of the living. *Auxilium ab alto.* Jeez. That is for why I have arranged this meeting. What I have done I will undone, eh? But you must climb out of your own chasm. Knit up the ravelled sleave of care. Come inside."

He took Halsyon's arm, led him down a paneled hall, past a neat office and into a spanking white laboratory. It was all tile and glass with shelves of reagent bottles, porcelain filters, an electric oven, stock jars of acids, bins of raw materials. There was a small round elevation in the center of the floor, a sort of dais. Mr. Aquila placed a stool on the dais, placed Halsyon on the stool, got into a white lab coat and began to assemble apparatus.

"You," he chatted, "are an artist of the utmost. I do not *dorer la pilule.* When Jimmy Derelict told me you were no longer at work. God damn! We must return him to his muttons, I said. Solon Aquila must own many canvases of Jeffrey Halsyon. We shall cure him. *Hoc age.*"

"You're a doctor?" Halsyon asked.

"No. Let us say a warlock. Strictly speaking a witch-pathologist. Very high class. No nostrums. Strictly modern magic. Black magic and white magic are passé, *n'est-ce pas?* I cover entire spectrum, specializing mostly in the 15,000 angstrom band."

"You're a witch doctor? Never!"

"Oh, yes."

"In this kind of place?"

"Ah-ha? You too are deceived, eh? It is our camouflage. Many a modern laboratory you think concerns itself with toothpaste is devoted to magic. But we are scientific too. *Parbleu!* We move with the times, we warlocks. Witch's Brew now complies with Pure Food and Drug Act. Familiars one hundred percent sterile. Sanitary brooms. Cellophane-wrapped curses. Father Satan in rubber gloves. Thanks to Lord Lister; or is it Pasteur? My idol."

The witch-pathologist gathered raw materials, consulted an ephemeris, ran off some calculations on an electronic computer and continued to chat.

"Fugit hora," Aquila said. "Your trouble, my old, is loss of sanity. *Oui?* Lost in one damn flight from reality and one damn desperate search for peace brought on by one unguarded look from me to you. *Hélas!* I apologize for that, R.S.V.P." With what looked like a miniature tennis linemarker, he rolled a circle around Halsyon on the dais. "But your trouble is, to wit: You search for the peace of infancy. You should be fighting to acquire the peace of maturity, *n'est-ce pas?* Jeez."

Aquila drew circles and pentagons with a glittering compass and rule, weighed out powders on a micro-beam balance, dropped various liquids into crucibles from calibrated burettes, and continued: "Many warlocks do brisk trade in potions from Fountains of Youths. Oh yes. Are many youths and many fountains; but none for you. No. Youth is not for artists. Age is the cure. We must purge your youth and grow you up, *nicht wahr?*"

"No," Halsyon argued. "No. Youth is the art. Youth is the dream. Youth is the blessing."

"For some, yes. For many, not. Not for you. You are cursed, my adolescent. We must purge you. Lust for power. Lust for sex. Injustice collecting. Escape from reality. Passion for revenges. Oh yes, Father Freud is also my idol. We wipe your slate clean at very small price."

"What price?"

"You will see when we are finished."

Mr. Aquila deposited liquids and powders around the helpless artist in crucibles and petri dishes. He measured and cut fuses, set up a train from the circle to an electric timer which he carefully adjusted. He went to a shelf of serum bottles, took down a small Woulff vial numbered 5-271-009, filled a syringe and meticulously injected Halsyon.

"We begin," he said, "the purge of your dreams. *Voilà.*"

He tripped the electric timer and stepped behind a lead shield. There was a moment of silence. Suddenly black music crashed from a concealed loudspeaker and a recorded voice began an intolerable chant. In quick succession the powders and liquids around Halsyon burst into flame. He was engulfed in music and fire. The world began to spin around him in a roaring confusion . . .

The president of the United Nations came to him. He was tall and gaunt, sprightly but bitter. He was wringing his hands in dismay.

"Mr. Halsyon! Mr. Halsyon!" he cried. "Where have you been, my cupcake? God damn. *Hoc tempore.* Do you know what has happened?"

"No," Halsyon answered. "What's happened?"

"After your escape from the looney bin. Bango! Atom bombs everywhere. The two-hour war. It is over. *Hora fugit,* old faithful. Virility is over."

"What!"

"Hard radiation, Mr. Halsyon, has destroyed the virility of the world. God damn. You are the only man left capable of engendering children. No doubt on account of a mysterious mutant strain in your makeup which it makes you different. Jeez."

"No."

"*Oui.* It is your responsibility to repopulate the world. We have taken for you a suite at the Odeon. It has three bedrooms. Three, my favorite. A prime number."

"Hot dog!" Halsyon said. "This is my big dream."

His progress to the Odeon was a triumph. He was garlanded

with flowers, serenaded, hailed and cheered. Ecstatic women displayed themselves wickedly before him, begging for his attention. In his suite, Halsyon was wined and dined. A tall, gaunt man entered subserviently. He was sprightly but bitter. He had a list in his hand.

"I am World Procurer at your service, Mr. Halsyon," he said. He consulted his list. "God damn. Are 5,271,009 virgins clamoring for your attention. All guaranteed beautiful. *Ewig-Weibliche.* Pick a number from one to 5,000,000."

"We'll start with a redhead," Halsyon said.

They brought him a redhead. She was slender and boyish, with a small hard bosom. The next was fuller with a rollicking rump. The fifth was Junoesque and her breasts were like African pears. The tenth was a voluptuous Rembrandt. The twentieth was slender and boyish with a small, hard bosom.

"Haven't we met before?" Halsyon inquired.

"No," she said.

The next was fuller with a rollicking rump.

"The body is familiar," Halsyon said.

"No," she answered.

The fiftieth was Junoesque with breasts like African pears.

"Surely?" Halsyon said.

"Never," she answered.

The World Procurer entered with Halsyon's morning aphrodisiac.

"Never touch the stuff," Halsyon said.

"God damn," the Procurer exclaimed. "You are a veritable giant. An elephant. No wonder you are the beloved Adam. *Tant soit peu.* No wonder they all weep for love of you." He drank off the aphrodisiac himself.

"Have you noticed they're all getting to look alike?" Halsyon complained.

"But no! Are all different. *Parbleu!* This is an insult to my office."

"Oh, they're different from one to another, but the types keep repeating."

"Ah? This is life, my old. All life is cyclic. Have you not, as an artist, noticed?"

"I didn't think it applied to love."

"To all things. *Wahrheit und Dichtung.*"

"What was that you said about them weeping?"

"*Oui.* They all weep."

"Why?"

"For ecstatic love of you. God damn."

Halsyon thought over the succession of boyish, rollicking, Ju-noesque, Rembrandtesque, wiry, red, blonde, brunette, white, black, and brown women.

"I hadn't noticed," he said.

"Observe today, my world father. Shall we commence?"

It was true. Halsyon hadn't noticed. They all wept. He was flat-tered but depressed.

"Why don't you laugh a little?" he asked.

They would not or could not.

Upstairs on the Odeon roof where Halsyon took his afternoon exercise, he questioned his trainer who was a tall, gaunt man with a sprightly but bitter expression.

"Ah?" said the trainer. "God damn. I don't know, old scotch and soda. Perhaps because it is a traumatic experience for them."

"Traumatic?" Halsyon puffed. "Why? What do I do to them?"

"Ah-ha? You joke, eh? All the world knows what you do to them."

"No, I mean . . . How can it be traumatic? They're all fighting to get to me, aren't they? Don't I come up to expectations?"

"A mystery. Tripotage. Now, beloved father of the world, we practice the push-ups. Ready? Begin."

Downstairs, in the Odeon restaurant, Halsyon questioned the headwaiter, a tall, gaunt man with a sprightly manner but bitter ex-pression.

"We are men of the world, Mr. Halsyon. *Suo jure.* Surely you un-derstand. These women love you and can expect no more than one night of love. God damn. Naturally they are disappointed."

"What do they want?"

"What every woman wants, my gateway to the west. A perma-nent relationship. Marriage."

"Marriage!"

"*Oui.*"

"All of them?"

"*Oui.*"

"All right. I'll marry all 5,271,009."

But the World Procurer objected. "No, no, no, young Lochinvar.

God damn. Impossible. Aside from religious difficulties there are human also. Who could manage such a harem?"

"Then I'll marry one."

"No, no, no. *Pensez à moi.* How could you make the choice? How could you select? By lottery, drawing straws, tossing coins?"

"I've already selected one."

"Ah? Which?"

"My girl," Halsyon said slowly. "Judith Field."

"So. Your sweetheart?"

"Yes."

"She is far down on the list of five million."

"She's always been number one on my list. I want Judith." Halsyon sighed. "I remember how she looked at the Beaux Arts Ball . . . There was a full moon. . . ."

But there will be no full moon until the twenty-sixth."

"I want Judith."

"The others will tear her apart out of jealousy. No, no, no, Mr. Halsyon, we must stick to the schedule. One night for all, no more for any."

"I want Judith . . . or else."

"It will have to be discussed in council. God damn."

It was discussed in the U.N. council by a dozen delegates, all tall, gaunt, sprightly but bitter. It was decided to permit Jeffrey Halsyon one secret marriage.

"But no domestic ties," the World Procurer warned. "No faithfulness to your wife. That must be understood. We cannot spare you from our program. You are indispensable."

They brought the lucky Judith Field to the Odeon. She was a tall, dark girl with cropped curly hair and lovely tennis legs. Halsyon took her hand. The World Procurer tiptoed out.

"Hello, darling," Halsyon murmured.

Judith looked at him with loathing. Her eyes were wet, her face bruised from weeping.

"Hello, darling," Halsyon repeated.

"If you touch me, Jeff," Judith said in a strangled voice, "I'll kill you."

"Judy!"

"That disgusting man explained everything to me. He didn't seem to understand when I tried to explain to him. . . . I was praying you'd be dead before it was my turn."

"But this is marriage, Judy."

"I'd rather die than be married to you."

"I don't believe you. We've been in love for—"

"For God's sake, Jeff, love's over for you. Don't you understand? Those women cry because they hate you. I hate you. The world loathes you. You're disgusting."

Halsyon stared at the girl and saw the truth in her face. In an excess of rage, he tried to seize her. She fought him bitterly. They careened around the huge living room of the suite, overturning furniture, their breath hissing, their fury mounting. Halsyon struck Judith Field with his big fist to end the struggle once and for all. She reeled back, clutched at a drape, smashed through a French window and fell fourteen floors to the street like a gyrating doll.

Halsyon looked down in horror. A crowd gathered around the smashed body. Faces upturned. Fists shook. An ominous growl began. The World Procurer dashed into the suite.

"My old! My blue!" he cried. "What have you done? *Per conto*. It is a spark that will ignite savagery. You are in very grave danger. God damn."

"Is it true they all hate me?"

"*Hélas*, then you have discovered the truth? That indiscreet girl. I warned her. *Oui*. You are loathed."

"But you told me I was loved. The new Adam. Father of the new world."

"*Oui*. You are the father, but what child does not hate its father? You are also a legal rapist. What woman does not hate being forced to embrace a man . . . even by necessity for survival? Come quickly, my rock and rye. *Passim*. You are in great danger."

He dragged Halsyon to a back elevator and took him down to the Odeon cellar.

"The army will get you out. We take you to Turkey at once and effect a compromise."

Halsyon was transferred to the custody of a tall, gaunt, bitter army colonel who rushed him through underground passages to a side street where a staff car was waiting. The colonel thrust Halsyon inside.

"*Jacta alea est*," he said to the driver. "Speed, my corporal. Protect old faithful. To the airport *Alors!*"

"God damn, sir," the corporal replied. He saluted and started the car. As it twisted through the streets at breakneck speed, Halsyon glanced at him. He was a tall, gaunt man, sprightly but bitter.

"*Kulturkampf der Menschheit,*" the corporal muttered. "Jeez!"

A giant barricade had been built across the street, improvised of ash barrels, furniture, overturned cars, traffic stanchions. The corporal was forced to brake the car. As he slowed for a U-turn, a mob of women appeared from doorways, cellars, stores. They were screaming. Some of them brandished improvised clubs.

"Excelsior!" the corporal cried. "God damn." He tried to pull his service gun out of its holster. The women yanked open the car doors and tore Halsyon and the corporal out. Halsyon broke free, struggled through the wild clubbing mob, dashed to the sidewalk, stumbled and dropped with a sickening yaw through an open coal chute. He shot down and spilled out into an endless black space. His head whirled. A stream of stars sailed before his eyes . . .

And he drifted alone in space, a martyr, misunderstood, a victim of cruel injustice.

He was still chained to what had once been the wall of Cell 5, Block 27, Tier 100, Wing 9 of the Callisto Penitentiary until that unexpected gamma explosion had torn the vast fortress dungeon—vaster than the Château d'If—apart. That explosion, he realized, had been detonated by the Grssh.

His assets were his convict clothes, a helmet, one cylinder of O_2, his grim fury at the injustice that had been done him, and his knowledge of the secret of how the Grssh could be defeated in their maniacal quest for solar domination.

The Grssh, ghastly marauders from Omicron Ceti, space-degenerates, space-imperialists, cold-blooded, roachlike, depending for their food upon the psychotic horrors which they engendered in man through mental control and upon which they fed, were rapidly conquering the galaxy. They were irresistible, for they possessed the power of simul-kinesis—the ability to be in two places at the same time.

Against the vault of space, a dot of light moved slowly, like a stricken meteor. It was a rescue ship, Halsyon realized, combing space for survivors of the explosion. He wondered whether the light of Jupiter, flooding him with rusty radiation, would make him visible to the rescuers. He wondered whether he wanted to be rescued at all.

"It will be the same thing again," Halsyon grated. "Falsely accused by Balorsen's robot. . . . Falsely convicted by Judith's father. . . . Repudiated by Judith herself. . . . Jailed again . . . and finally destroyed by the Grssh as they destroy the last strongholds of Terra. Why not die now?"

But even as he spoke he realized he lied. He was the one man with the one secret that could save the earth and the very galaxy itself. He must survive. He must fight.

With indomitable will, Halsyon struggled to his feet, fighting the constricting chains. With the steely strength he had developed as a penal laborer in the Grssh mines, he waved and shouted. The spot of light did not alter its slow course away from him. Then he saw the metal link of one of his chains strike a brilliant spark from the flinty rock. He resolved on a desperate expedient to signal the rescue ship.

He detached the plasti-hose of the O_2 tank from his plasti-helmet, and permitted the stream of life-giving oxygen to spurt into space. With trembling hands, he gathered the links of his leg chain and dashed them against the rock under the oxygen. A spark glowed. The oxygen caught fire. A brilliant geyser of white flame spurted for half a mile into space.

Husbanding the last oxygen in his plasti-helmet, Halsyon twisted the cylinder slowly, sweeping the fan of flame back and forth in a last desperate bid for rescue. The atmosphere in his plasti-helmet grew foul and acrid. His ears roared. His sight flickered. At last his senses failed. . . .

When he recovered consciousness he was in a plasti-cot in the cabin of a starship. The high frequency whine told him they were in overdrive. He opened his eyes. Balorsen stood before the plasti-cot, and Balorsen's robot and High Judge Field, and his daughter Judith. Judith was weeping. The robot was in magnetic plasti-clamps and winced as General Balorsen lashed him again and again with a nuclear plasti-whip.

"*Parbleu!* God damn!" the robot grated. "It is true I framed Jeff Halsyon. Ouch! *Flux de bouche.* I was the space-pirate who space-hijacked the space-freighter. God damn. Ouch! The space-bartender in the Spaceman's Saloon was my accomplice. When Jackson wrecked the space-cab I went to the space-garage and X-beamed the sonic *before* Tantial murdered O'Leary. *Aux armes.* Jeez. Ouch!"

"There you have the confession, Halsyon," General Balorsen

grated. He was tall, gaunt, bitter. "By God. *Ars est celare artem*. You are innocent."

"I falsely condemned you, old faithful," Judge Field grated. He was tall, gaunt, bitter. "Can you forgive this God damn fool? We apologize."

"We wronged you, Jeff," Judith whispered. "How can you ever forgive us? Say you forgive us."

"You're sorry for the way you treated me," Halsyon grated. "But it's only because on account of a mysterious mutant strain in my makeup which makes me different, I'm the one man with the one secret that can save the galaxy from the Grssh."

"No, no, no, old gin and tonic," General Balorsen pleaded. "God damn. Don't hold grudges. Save us from the Grssh."

"Save us, *faute de mieux*, save us, Jeff," Judge Field put in.

"Oh please, Jeff, please," Judith whispered. "The Grssh are everywhere and coming closer. We're taking you to the U.N. You must tell the council how to stop the Grssh from being in two places at the same time."

"The starship came out of overdrive and landed on Governor's Island where a delegation of world dignitaries met the ship and rushed Halsyon to the General Assembly room of the U.N. They drove down the strangely rounded streets lined with strangely rounded buildings which had all been altered when it was discovered that the Grssh always appeared in corners. There was not a corner or an angle left on all Terra.

The General Assembly was filled when Halsyon entered. Hundreds of tall, gaunt, bitter diplomats applauded as he made his way to the podium, still dressed in convict plasti-clothes. Halsyon looked around resentfully.

"Yes," he grated. "You all applaud. You all revere me now; but where were you when I was framed, convicted, and jailed . . . an innocent man? Where were you then?"

"Halsyon, forgive us. God damn!" they shouted.

"I will not forgive you, I suffered for seventeen years in the Grssh mines. Now it's your turn to suffer."

"Please, Halsyon!"

"Where are your experts? Your professors? Your specialists? Where are your electronic calculators? Your super thinking machines? Let them solve the mystery of the Grssh."

"They can't, old whiskey and soda. *Entre nous.* They're stopped cold. Save us, Halsyon. *Auf wiedersehen.*"

Judith took his arm. "Not for my sake, Jeff," she whispered. "I know you'll never forgive me for the injustice I did you. But for the sake of all the other girls in the Galaxy who love and are loved."

"I still love you, Judy."

"I've always loved you, Jeff."

"Okay. I didn't want to tell them but you talked me into it. Halsyon raised his hand for silence. In the ensuing hush he spoke softly. "The secret is this, gentlemen. Your calculators have assembled data to ferret out the secret weakness of the Grssh. They have not been able to find any. Consequently you have assumed that the Grssh have no secret weakness. *That was a wrong assumption.*"

The General Assembly held its breath.

"Here is the secret. *You should have assumed there was something wrong with the calculators.*"

"God damn!" the General Assembly cried. "Why didn't we think of that? God damn!"

"*And I know what's wrong!*"

There was a deathlike hush.

The door of the General Assembly burst open. Professor Deathhush, tall, gaunt, bitter, tottered in. "Eureka!" he cried. "I've found it. God damn. Something wrong with the thinking machines. Three comes *after* two, not before."

The General Assembly broke into cheers. Professor Deathhush was seized and pummeled happily. Bottles were opened. His health was drunk. Several medals were pinned on him. He beamed.

"Hey!" Halsyon called. "That was my secret. I'm the one man who on account of a mysterious mutant strain in my—"

The ticker tape began pounding: ATTENTION. ATTENTION. HUSHENKOV IN MOSCOW REPORTS DEFECT IN CALCULATORS. 3 COMES AFTER 2 AND NOT BEFORE. REPEAT: AFTER (UNDER-SCORE) NOT BEFORE.

A postman ran in. "Special Delivery from Doctor Lifehush at Caltech. Says something's wrong with the thinking machines. Three comes after two, not before."

A telegraph boy delivered a wire: THINKING MACHINE WRONG STOP TWO COMES BEFORE THREE STOP NOT AFTER STOP. VON DREAMHUSH, HEIDELBERG.

A bottle was thrown through the window. It crashed on the floor revealing a bit of paper on which was scrawled: *Did you ever stop to thinc that maibe the number 3 comes after 2 insted of in front? Down with the Grish. Mr. Hush-Hush.*

Halsyon buttonholed Judge Field. "What the hell is this?" he demanded. "I thought I was the one man in the world with that secret."

"*HimmelHerrGott!*" Judge Field replied impatiently. "You are all alike. You dream you are the one man with a secret, the one man with a wrong, the one man with an injustice, with a girl, without a girl, with or without anything. God damn. You bore me, you one-man dreamers. Get lost."

Judge Field shouldered him aside. General Balorsen shoved him back. Judith Field ignored him. Balorsen's robot sneakily tripped him into a corner of the crowd where a Grssh, also in a crowded corner on Neptune, appeared, did something unspeakable to Halsyon, and disappeared with him, screaming, jerking and sobbing, into a horror that was a delicious meal for the Grssh but a plasti-nightmare for Halsyon. . . .

From which his mother awakened him and said, "This'll teach you not to sneak peanut-butter sandwiches in the middle of the night, Jeffrey."

"Mama?"

"Yes. It's time to get up, dear. You'll be late for school."

She left the room. He looked around. He looked at himself. It was true. True! The glorious realization came upon him. His dream had come true. He was ten years old again, in the flesh that was his ten-year-old body, in the home that was his boyhood home, in the life that had been his life in his school days. And within his head was the knowledge, the experience, the sophistication of a man of thirty-three.

"Oh joy!" he cried. "It'll be a triumph. A triumph!"

He would be the school genius. He would astonish his parents, amaze his teachers, confound the experts. He would win scholarships. He would settle the hash of that kid Rennahan who used to bully him. He would hire a typewriter and write all the successful plays and stories and novels he remembered. He would cash in on that lost opportunity with Judy Field behind the memorial in Isham Park. He would steal inventions and discoveries, get in on the ground floor of new industries, make bets, play the stock market. He would own the world by the time he caught up with himself.

He dressed with difficulty. He had forgotten where his clothes were kept. He ate breakfast with difficulty. This was no time to explain to his mother that he'd gotten into the habit of starting the day with Irish coffee. He missed his morning cigarette. He had no idea where his schoolbooks were. His mother had trouble starting him out.

"Jeff's in one of his moods," he heard her mutter. "I hope he gets through the day."

The day started with Rennahan ambushing him at the Boys' Entrance. Halsyon remembered him as a big, tough kid with a vicious expression. He was astonished to discover that Rennahan was skinny and harassed, and obviously compelled by some bedevilments to be omnivorously aggressive.

"Why, you're not hostile to me," Halsyon exclaimed. "You're just a mixed-up kid who's trying to prove something."

Rennahan punched him.

"Look, kid," Halsyon said kindly. "You really want to be friends with the world. You're just insecure. That's why you're compelled to fight."

Rennahan was deaf to spot analysis. He punched Halsyon harder. It hurt.

"Oh leave me alone," Halsyon said. "Go prove yourself on somebody else."

Rennahan, with two swift motions, knocked Halsyon's books from under his arm and ripped his fly. There was nothing for it but to fight. Twenty years of watching films of the future Joe Louis did nothing for Halsyon. He was thoroughly licked. He was also late for school. Now was his chance to amaze his teachers.

"The fact is," he explained to Miss Ralph of the fifth grade, "I had a run-in with a neurotic. I can speak for his left hook, but I won't answer for his compulsions."

Miss Ralph slapped him and sent him to the principal with a note, reporting unheard-of insolence.

"The only thing unheard of in this school," Halsyon told Mr. Snider, "is psychoanalysis. How can you pretend to be competent teachers if you don't—"

"Dirty little boy!" Mr. Snider interrupted angrily. He was tall, gaunt, bitter. "So you've been reading dirty books, eh??"

"What the hell's dirty about Freud?"

"And using profane language, eh? You need a lesson, you filthy little animal."

He was sent home with a note requesting an immediate consultation with his parents regarding the withdrawal of Jeffrey Halsyon from school as a degenerate in desperate need of correction and vocational guidance.

Instead of going home, he went to a newsstand to check the papers for events on which to get a bet down. The headlines were full of the pennant race. But who the hell finally won the pennant? And the series? He couldn't for the life of him remember. And the stock market? He couldn't remember anything about that either. He'd never been particularly interested in such matters as a boy. There was nothing planted in his memory to call upon.

He tried to get into the library for further checks. The librarian, tall, gaunt, bitter, would not permit him to enter until children's hour in the afternoon. He loafed on the streets. Wherever he loafed he was chased by gaunt and bitter adults. He was beginning to realize that ten-year-old boys had limited opportunities to amaze the world.

At lunch hour he met Judy Field and accompanied her home from school. He was appalled by her knobby knees and black corkscrew curls. He didn't like the way she smelled, either. But he was rather taken with her mother who was the image of the Judy he remembered. He forgot himself with Mrs. Field and did one or two things that indeed confounded her. She drove him out of the house and then telephoned his mother, her voice shaking with indignation.

Halsyon went down to the Hudson River and hung around the ferry docks until he was chased. He went to a stationery store to inquire about typewriter rentals and was chased. He searched for a quiet place to sit, think, plan, perhaps begin the recall of a successful story. There was no quiet place to which a small boy would be admitted.

He slipped into his house at 4:30, dropped his books in his room, stole into the living room, sneaked a cigarette and was on his way out when he discovered his mother and father inspecting him. His mother looked shocked. His father was gaunt and bitter.

"Oh," Halsyon said. "I suppose Snider phoned. I'd forgotten about that."

"*Mister* Snider," his mother said.

"And Mrs. Field," his father said.

"Look," Halsyon began. "We'd better get this straightened out. Will you listen to me for a few minutes? I have something startling to tell you and we've got to plan what to do about it. I—"

He yelped. His father had taken him by the ear and was marching him down the hall. Parents did not listen to children for a few minutes. They did not listen at all.

Pop. . . . Just a minute. . . . Please! I'm trying to explain. I'm not really ten years old. I'm thirty-three. There's been a freak in time, see? On account of a mysterious mutant strain in my makeup which—"

"Damn you! Be quiet!" his father shouted. The pain of his big hands, the suppressed fury in his voice silenced Halsyon. He suffered himself to be led out of the house, down four blocks back to the school, and up one flight to Mr. Snider's office where a public school psychologist was waiting with the principal. He was a tall, gaunt, bitter man, but sprightly.

"Ah, yes, yes," he said. "So this is our little degenerate. Our Scarface Al Capone, eh? Come, we take him to the clinic and there I shall take his *journal intime*. We will hope for the best. *Nisi prius.* He cannot be all bad."

He took Halsyon's arm. Halsyon pulled his arm away and said, "Listen, you're an adult, intelligent man. You'll listen to me. My father's got emotional problems that blind him to the—"

His father gave him a tremendous box on the ear, grabbed his arm and thrust it back into the psychologist's grasp. Halsyon burst into tears. The psychologist led him out of the office and into the tiny school infirmary. Halsyon was hysterical. He was trembling with frustration and terror.

"Won't anybody listen to me?" he sobbed. "Won't anybody try to understand? Is this what we're all like to kids? Is this what all kids go through?"

"Gently, my sausage," the psychologist murmured. He popped a pill into Halsyon's mouth and forced him to drink some water.

"You're all so damned inhuman," Halsyon wept. "You keep us out of your world, but you keep barging into ours. If you don't respect us, why don't you leave us alone?"

"You begin to understand, eh?" the psychologist said. "We are two different breeds of animals, childrens and adults. God damn. I speak to you with frankness. *Les absents ont toujours tort.* There is no meetings of the minds. Jeez. There is nothing but war. It is why all childrens grow up hating their childhoods and searching for revenges. But there is never revenges. *Pari mutuel.* How can there be? Can a cat insult a king?"

"It's . . . s'hateful," Halsyon mumbled. The pill was taking effect rapidly. "Whole world's hateful. Full of conflicts'n'insults 'at can't be r'solved . . . or paid back. . . . S'like a joke somebody's playin' on us. Silly jokes without point. Isn't?"

As he slid down into darkness, he could hear the psychologist chuckle, but couldn't for the life of him understand what he was laughing at. . . .

He picked up his spade and followed the first clown into the cemetery. The first clown was a tall man, gaunt, bitter, but sprightly.

"Is she to be buried in Christian burial that wilfully seeks her own salvation?" the first clown asked.

"I tell thee she is," Halsyon answered. "And therefore make her grave straight: the crowner hath sat on her, and finds it Christian burial."

"How can that be, unless she drowned herself in her own defense?"

"Why, 'tis found so."

They began to dig the grave. The first clown thought the matter over, then said, "It must be *se offendendo;* it cannot be else. For here lies the point: if I drown myself wittingly, it argues an act: and an act hath three branches; it is, to act, to do, to perform: argal, she drowned herself wittingly."

"Nay, but hear you, goodman delver—" Halsyon began.

"Give me leave," the first clown interrupted and went on with a tiresome discourse on quest-law. Then he turned sprightly and cracked a few professional jokes. At last Halsyon got away and went down to Yaughan's for a drink. When he returned, the first clown was cracking jokes with a couple of gentlemen who had wandered into the graveyard. One of them made quite a fuss about a skull.

The burial procession arrived; the coffin, the dead girl's brother, the king and queen, the priests and lords. They buried her, and the brother and one of the gentlemen began to quarrel over her grave. Halsyon paid no attention. There was a pretty girl in the procession, dark, with cropped curly hair and lovely long legs. He winked at her. She winked back. Halsyon edged over toward her, speaking with his eyes and she answered him saucily the same way.

Then he picked up his spade and followed the first clown into the cemetery. The first clown was a tall man, gaunt, with a bitter expression but a sprightly manner.

"Is she to be buried in Christian burial that wilfully seeks her own salvation?" the first clown asked.

"I tell thee she is," Halsyon answered. "And therefore make her grave straight: the crowner hath sat on her, and finds it Christian burial."

"How can that be, unless she drowned herself in her own defense?"

"Didn't you ask me that before?" Halsyon inquired.

"Shut up, old faithful. Answer the question."

"I could swear this happened before."

"God damn. Will you answer? Jeez."

"Why, 'tis found so."

They began to dig the grave. The first clown thought the matter over and began a long discourse on quest-law. After that he turned sprightly and cracked trade jokes. At last Halsyon got away and went down to Yaughan's for a drink. When he returned there were a couple of strangers at the grave and then the burial procession arrived.

There was a pretty girl in the procession, dark, with cropped curly hair and lovely long legs. Halsyon winked at her. She winked back. Halsyon edged over toward her speaking with his eyes and she answering him the same way.

"What's your name?" he whispered.

"Judith," she answered.

"I have your name tattooed on me, Judith."

"You're lying, sir."

"I can prove it, Madam. I'll show you where I was tattooed."

"And where is that?"

"In Yaughan's tavern. It was done by a sailor off the *Golden Hind*. Will you see it with me tonight?"

Before she could answer, he picked up his spade and followed the first clown into the cemetery. The first clown was a tall man, gaunt, with a bitter expression but a sprightly manner.

"For God's sake!" Halsyon complained. "I could swear this happened before."

"Is she to be buried in Christian burial that wilfully seeks her own salvation?" the first clown asked.

"I just know we've been through all this."

"Will you answer the question!"

"Listen," Halsyon said doggedly. "Maybe I'm crazy; maybe not. But I've got a spooky feeling that all this happened before. It seems unreal. Life seems unreal."

The first clown shook his head. *"HimmelHerrGott,"* he muttered. "It is as I feared. *Lux et veritas.* On account of a mysterious mutant strain in your makeup which it makes you different, you are treading on thin water. *Ewigkeit!* Answer the question."

"If I've answered it once, I've answered it a hundred times."

"Old ham and eggs," the first clown burst out, "you have answered it 5,271,009 times. God damn. Answer again."

"Why?"

"Because you must. *Pot au feu.* It is the life we must live."

"You call this life? Doing the same things over and over again? Saying the same things? Winking at girls and never getting any further?"

"No, no, no, my Donner and Blitzen. Do not question. It is a conspiracy we dare not fight. This is the life every man lives. Every man does the same things over and over. There is no escape."

"Why is there no escape?"

"I dare not say; I dare not. *Vox populi.* Others have questioned and disappeared. It is a conspiracy. I'm afraid."

"Afraid of what?"

"Of our owners."

"What? We are owned?"

"*Sí. Ach, ja!* All of us, young mutant. There is no reality. There is no life, no freedom, no will. God damn. Don't you realize? We are. . . . We are all characters in a book. As the book is read, we dance our dances; when the book is read again, we dance again. *E pluribus unum.* Is she to be buried in Christian burial that wilfully seeks her own salvation?"

"What are you saying?" Halsyon cried in horror. "We're puppets?"

"Answer the question."

"If there's no freedom, no free will, how can we be talking like this?"

"Whoever's reading our book is daydreaming, my capital of Dakota. *Idem est.* Answer the question."

"I will not. I'm going to revolt. I'll dance for our owners no longer. I'll find a better life. . . . I'll find reality."

"No, no! It's madness, Jeffrey! *Cul-de-sac!*"

"All we need is one brave leader. The rest will follow. We'll smash the conspiracy that chains us!"

"It cannot be done. Play it safe. Answer the question."

Halsyon answered the question by picking up his spade and bashing in the head of the first clown who appeared not to notice. "Is she to be buried in Christian burial that wilfully seeks her own salvation?" he asked.

"Revolt!" Halsyon cried and bashed him again. The clown started to sing. The two gentlemen appeared. One said: "Has this fellow no feeling of business that he sings at gravemaking?"

"Revolt! Follow me!" Halsyon shouted and swung his spade against the gentleman's melancholy head. He paid no attention. He chatted with his friend and the first clown. Halsyon whirled like a dervish, laying about him with his spade. The gentleman picked up a skull and philosophized over some person or persons named Yorick.

The funeral procession approached. Halsyon attacked it, whirling and turning, around and around with the clotted frenzy of a man in a dream.

"Stop reading the book," he shouted. "Let me out of the pages. Can you hear me? Stop reading the book! I'd rather be in a world of my own making. Let me go!"

There was a mighty clap of thunder, as of the covers of a mighty book slamming shut. In an instant Halsyon was swept spinning into the third compartment of the seventh circle of the Inferno in the Fourteenth Canto of the *Divine Comedy* where they who have sinned against art are tormented by flakes of fire which are eternally showered down upon them. There he shrieked until he had provided sufficient amusement. Only then was he permitted to devise a text of his own . . . and he formed a new world, a romantic world, a world of his fondest dreams. . . .

. . .

He was the last man on earth.

He was the last man on earth and he howled.

The hills, the valleys, the mountains and streams were his, his alone, and he howled.

Five million two hundred and seventy-one thousand and nine houses were his for shelter, 5,271,009 beds were his for sleeping. The shops were his for the breaking and entering. The jewels of the world were his; the toys, the tools, the playthings, the necessities, the luxuries . . . all belonged to the last man on earth, and he howled.

He left the country mansion in the fields of Connecticut where he had taken up residence; he crossed into Westchester, howling; he ran south along what had once been the Hendrick Hudson Highway, howling; he crossed the bridge into Manhattan, howling; he ran downtown past lonely skyscrapers, department stores, amusement palaces, howling. He howled down Fifth Avenue, and at the corner of Fiftieth Street he saw a human being.

She was alive, breathing; a beautiful woman. She was tall and dark with cropped curly hair and lovely long legs. She wore a white blouse, tiger-skin riding breeches and patent leather boots. She carried a rifle. She wore a revolver on her hip. She was eating stewed tomatoes from a can and she stared at Halsyon in unbelief. He ran up to her.

"I thought I was the last human on earth," she said.

"You're the last woman," Halsyon howled. "I'm the last man. Are you a dentist?"

"No," she said. "I'm the daughter of the unfortunate Professor Field, whose well-intentioned but ill-advised experiment in nuclear fission has wiped mankind off the face of the earth with the exception of you and me who, no doubt on account of some mysterious mutant strain in our makeup which makes us different, are the last of the old civilization and the first of the new."

"Didn't your father teach you anything about dentistry?" Halsyon howled.

"No," she said.

"Then lend me your gun for a minute."

She unholstered the revolver and handed it to Halsyon, meanwhile keeping her rifle ready. Halsyon cocked the gun.

"I wish you'd been a dentist," he howled

"I'm a beautiful woman with an I.Q. of 141 which is more important for the propagation of a brave new beautiful race of men to inherit the good green earth," she said.

"Not with my teeth it isn't," Halsyon howled.

He clapped the revolver to his temple and blew his brains out.

He awoke with a splitting headache. He was lying on the tile dais alongside the stool, his bruised temple pressed against the cold floor. Mr. Aquila had emerged from the lead shield and was turning on an exhaust fan to clear the air.

"Bravo, my liver and onions," he chuckled. "The last one you did by yourself, eh? No assistance from yours truly required. *Meglio tarde che mai.* But you went over with a crack before I could catch you. God damn."

He helped Halsyon to his feet and led him into the consultation room where he seated him in a velvet chaise longue and gave him a glass of brandy.

"Guaranteed free of drugs," he said. *"Noblesse oblige.* Only the best *spiritus frumenti.* Now we discuss what we have done, eh? Jeez."

He sat down behind the desk, still sprightly, still bitter, and regarded Halsyon with kindliness. "Man lives by his decisions, *n'est-ce pas?"* he began. "We agree, *oui?* A man has some five million two hundred seventy-one thousand and nine decisions to make in the course of his life. *Peste!* Is it a prime number? *N'importe.* Do you agree?"

Halsyon nodded.

"So, my coffee and doughnuts, it is the maturity of these decisions that decides whether a man is a man or a child. *Nicht wahr? Malgré nous.* A man cannot start making adult decisions until he has purged himself of the dreams of childhood. God damn. Such fantasies. They must go."

"No," Halsyon said slowly. "It's the dreams that make my art . . . the dreams and fantasies that I translate into line and color. . . ."

"God damn! Yes. Agreed. *Maître d'hôtel!* But adult dreams, not baby dreams. Baby dreams. Pfui! All men have them. . . . To be the last man on earth and own the earth. . . . To be the last fertile man on earth and own the women. . . . To go back in time with the advantage of adult knowledge and win victories. . . . To escape reality with the dream that life is make-believe. . . . To escape responsibility with

a fantasy of heroic injustice, of martyrdom with a happy ending. . . .
And there are hundreds more, equally popular, equally empty. God
bless Father Freud and his merry men. He applies the quietus to such
nonsense. *Sic semper tyrannis.* Avaunt!"

"But if everybody has those dreams, they can't be bad, can
they?"

"God damn. Everybody in fourteenth century had lice. Did
that make it good? No, my young, such dreams are for childrens.
Too many adults are still childrens. It is you, the artists, who
must lead them out as I have led you. I purge you; now you purge
them."

"Why did you do this?"

"Because I have faith in you. *Sic vos non vobis.* It will not be easy
for you. A long hard road and lonely."

"I suppose I ought to feel grateful," Halsyon muttered, "but I
feel . . . well . . . empty. Cheated."

"Oh yes, God damn. If you live with one Jeez big ulcer long
enough, you miss him when he's cut out. You were hiding in an ulcer. I have robbed you of said refuge. Ergo: you feel cheated. Wait!
You will feel even more cheated. There was a price to pay, I told you.
You have paid it. Look."

Mr. Aquila held up a hand mirror. Halsyon glanced into it, then
started and stared. A fifty-year-old face stared back at him: lined,
hardened, solid, determined. Halsyon leaped to his feet.

"Gently, gently," Mr. Aquila admonished. "It is not so bad. It is
damned good. You are still thirty-three in age of physique. You have
lost none of your life . . . only all of your youth. What have you lost?
A pretty face to lure young girls? Is that why you are wild?"

"Christ!" Halsyon cried.

"All right. Still gently, my child. Here you are, purged, disillu-
sioned, unhappy, bewildered, one foot on the hard road to maturity.
Would you like this to have happened or not have happened? *Sí.* I
can do. This can never have happened. *Spurlos versenkt.* It is ten seconds from your escape. You can have your pretty young face back.
You can be recaptured. You can return to the safe ulcer of the
womb . . . a child again. Would you like same?"

"You can't."

"*Sauve qui peut,* my Pike's Peak. I can. There is no end to the
15,000 angstrom band."

"Damn you! Are you Satan? Lucifer? Only the devil could have such powers."

"Or angels, my old."

"You don't look like an angel. You look like Satan."

"Ah? Ha? But Satan was an angel before he fell. He has many relations on high. Surely there are family resemblances. God damn." Mr. Aquila stopped laughing. He leaned across the desk and the sprightliness was gone from his face. Only the bitterness remained. "Shall I tell you who I am, my chicken? Shall I explain why one unguarded look from this phizz toppled you over the brink?"

Halsyon nodded, unable to speak.

"I am a scoundrel, a black sheep, a scapegrace, a blackguard. I am a remittance man. Yes. God damn! I am a remittance man." Mr. Aquila's eyes turned into wounds. "By your standards I am the great man of infinite power and variety. So was the remittance man from Europe to naïve natives on the beaches of Tahiti. Eh? And so am I to you as I comb the beaches of the stars for a little amusement, a little hope, a little joy to while away the lonely years of my exile. . . .

"I am bad," Mr. Aquila said in a voice of chilling desperation. "I am rotten. There is no place in my home that can tolerate me. They pay me to stay away. And there are moments, unguarded, when my sickness and my despair fill my eyes and strike terror into your innocent souls. As I strike terror into you now. Yes?"

Halsyon nodded again.

"Be guided by me. It was the child in Solon Aquila that destroyed him and led him into the sickness that destroyed his life. *Oui.* I too suffer from baby fantasies from which I cannot escape. Do not make the same mistake. I beg of you. . . ." Mr. Aquila glanced at his wristwatch and leaped up. The sprightly returned to his manner. "Jeez. It's late. Time to make up your mind, old bourbon and soda. Which will it be? Old face or pretty face? The reality of dreams or the dream of reality?"

"How many decisions did you say we have to make in a lifetime?"

"Five million two hundred and seventy-one thousand and nine. Give or take a thousand. God damn."

"And which one is this for me?"

"Ah? *Vérité sans peur.* The two million six hundred and thirty-five thousand five hundred and fourth . . . offhand."

"But it's the big one."

"They are all big." Mr. Aquila stepped to the door, placed his hand on the buttons of a rather complicated switch and cocked an eye at Halsyon.

"*Voilà tout,*" he said. "It rests with you."

"I'll take it the hard way." Halsyon decided.

FONDLY FAHRENHEIT

H e doesn't know which of us I am these days, but they know one truth. You must own nothing but yourself. You must make your own life, live your own life and die your own death . . . or else you will die another's.

The rice fields on Paragon III stretch for hundreds of miles like checkerboard tundras, a blue and brown mosaic under a burning sky of orange. In the evening, clouds whip like smoke, and the paddies rustle and murmur.

A long line of men marched across the paddies the evening we escaped from Paragon III. They were silent, armed, intent; a long rank of silhouetted statues looming against the smoking sky. Each man carried a gun. Each man wore a walkie-talkie belt pack, the speaker button in his ear, the microphone bug clipped to his throat, the glowing view-screen strapped to his wrist like a green-eyed watch. The multitude of screens showed nothing but a multitude of individual paths through the paddies. The annunciators uttered no sound but the rustle and splash of steps. The men spoke infrequently, in heavy grunts, all speaking to all.

"Nothing here."

"Where's here?"

"Jenson's fields."

"You're drifting too far west."

"Close in the line there."

"Anybody covered the Grimson paddy?"

"Yeah. Nothing."

"She couldn't have walked this far."

"Could have been carried."

"Think she's alive?"

"Why should she be dead?"

The slow refrain swept up and down the long line of beaters advancing toward the smoky sunset. The line of beaters wavered like a writhing snake, but never ceased its remorseless advance. One hundred men spaced fifty feet apart. Five thousand feet of ominous search. One mile of angry determination stretching from east to west across a compass of heat. Evening fell. Each man lit his search lamp. The writhing snake was transformed into a necklace of wavering diamonds.

"Clear here. Nothing."

"Nothing here."

"Nothing."

"What about the Allen paddies?"

"Covering them now."

"Think we missed her?"

"Maybe."

"We'll beat back and check."

"This'll be an all-night job."

"Allen paddies clear."

"God damn! We've got to find her!"

"We'll find her."

"Here she is. Sector seven. Tune in."

The line stopped. The diamonds froze in the heat. There was silence. Each man gazed into the glowing screen on his wrist, tuning to sector seven. All tuned to one. All showed a small nude figure awash in the muddy water of a paddy. Alongside the figure an owner's stake of bronze read: VANDALEUR. The end of the line converged toward the Vandaleur field. The necklace turned into a cluster of stars. One hundred men gathered around a small nude body, a child dead in a rice paddy. There was no water in her mouth. There were fingermarks on her throat. Her innocent face was battered. Her body was torn. Clotted blood on her skin was crusted and hard.

"Dead three-four hours at least."

"Her mouth is dry."

"She wasn't drowned. Beaten to death."

In the dark evening heat the men swore softly. They picked up the body. One stopped the others and pointed to the child's fingernails. She had fought her murderer. Under the nails were particles of flesh and bright drops of scarlet blood, still liquid, still uncoagulated.

"That blood ought to be clotted, too."

"Funny."

"Not so funny. What kind of blood don't clot?"

"Android."

"Looks like she was killed by one."

"Vandaleur owns an android."

"She couldn't be killed by an android."

"That's android blood under her nails."

"The police better check."

"The police'll prove I'm right."

"But andys can't kill."

"That's android blood, ain't it?"

"Androids can't kill. They're made that way."

"Looks like one android was made wrong."

"Jesus!"

And the thermometer that day registered 92.9° gloriously Fahrenheit.

So there we were aboard the *Paragon Queen* enroute for Megaster V, James Vandaleur and his android. James Vandaleur counted his money and wept. In the second-class cabin with him was his android, a magnificent synthetic creature with classic features and wide blue eyes. Raised on its forehead in a cameo of flesh were the letters MA, indicating that this was one of the rare multiple-aptitude androids, worth $57,000 on the current exchange. There we were, weeping and counting and calmly watching.

"Twelve, fourteen, sixteen. Sixteen hundred dollars," Vandaleur wept. "That's all. Sixteen hundred dollars. My house was worth ten thousand. The land was worth five. There was furniture, cars, my paintings, etchings, my plane, my— And nothing to show for everything but sixteen hundred dollars. Christ!"

I leaped up from the table and turned on the android. I pulled a strap from one of the leather bags and beat the android. It didn't move.

"I must remind you," the android said, "that I am worth fifty-seven thousand dollars on the current exchange. I must warn you that you are endangering valuable property."

"You damned crazy machine," Vandaleur shouted.

"I am not a machine," the android answered. "The robot is a machine. The android is a chemical creation of synthetic tissue."

"What got into you?" Vandaleur cried, "Why did you do it? Damn you!" He beat the android savagely.

"I must remind you that I cannot be punished," I said. "The pleasure-pain syndrome is not incorporated in the android synthesis."

"Then why did you kill her?" Vandaleur shouted. "If it wasn't for kicks, why did you—"

"I must remind you," the android said, "that the second-class cabins in these ships are not soundproofed."

Vandaleur dropped the strap and stood panting, staring at the creature he owned.

"Why did you do it? Why did you kill her?" I asked.

"I don't know," I answered.

"First it was malicious mischief. Small things. Petty destruction. I should have known there was something wrong with you then. Androids can't destroy. They can't harm. They—"

"There is no pleasure-pain syndrome incorporated in the android synthesis."

"Then it got to arson. Then serious destruction. Then assault . . . that engineer on Rigel. Each time worse. Each time we had to get out faster. Now it's murder. Christ! What's the matter with you? What's happened?"

"There are no self-check relays incorporated in the android brain."

"Each time we had to get out it was a step downhill. Look at me. In a second-class cabin. Me. James Paleologue Vandaleur. There was a time when my father was the wealthiest— Now, sixteen hundred dollars in the world. That's all I've got. And you. Christ damn you!"

Vandaleur raised the strap to beat the android again, then dropped it and collapsed on a berth, sobbing. At last he pulled himself together.

"Instructions," he said.

The multiple android responded at once. It arose and awaited orders.

"My name is now Valentine. James Valentine. I stopped off on Paragon III for only one day to transfer to this ship for Megaster V. My occupation: Agent for one privately owned MA android which is for hire. Purpose of visit: To settle on Megaster V. Fix the papers."

The android removed Vandaleur's passport and papers from a bag, got pen and ink and sat down at the table. With an accurate, flawless hand—an accomplished hand that could draw, write, paint, carve, engrave, etch, photograph, design, create, and build—it meticulously forged new credentials for Vandaleur. Its owner watched me miserably.

"Create and build," I muttered. "And now destroy. Oh God! What am I going to do? Christ! If I could only get rid of you. If I didn't have to live off you. God! If only I'd inherited some guts instead of you."

Dallas Brady was Megaster's leading jewelry designer. She was short, stocky, amoral and a nymphomaniac. She hired Vandaleur's multiple-aptitude android and put me to work in her shop. She seduced Vandaleur. In her bed one night, she asked abruptly, "Your name's Vandaleur, isn't it?"

"Yes," I murmured. Then: "No! It's Valentine. James Valentine."

"What happened on Paragon?" Dallas Brady asked. "I thought androids couldn't kill or destroy property. Prime Directives and Inhibitions set up for them when they're synthesized. Every company guarantees they can't."

"Valentine!" Vandaleur insisted.

"Oh come off it," Dallas Brady said. "I've known for a week. I haven't hollered copper, have I?"

"The name is Valentine."

"You want to prove it? You want I should call the cops?" Dallas reached out and picked up the phone.

"For God's sake, Dallas!" Vandaleur leaped up and struggled to take the phone from her. She fended him off, laughing at him, until he collapsed and wept in shame and helplessness.

"How did you find out?" he asked at last.

"The papers are full of it. And Valentine was a little too close to Vandaleur. That wasn't smart, was it?"

"I guess not. I'm not very smart."

"Your android's got quite a record, hasn't it? Assault. Arson. Destruction. What happened on Paragon?"

"It kidnapped a child. Took her out into the rice fields and murdered her."

"Raped her?"

"I don't know."

"They're going to catch up with you."

"Don't I know it? Christ! We've been running for two years now. Seven planets in two years. I must have abandoned fifty thousand dollars' worth of property in two years."

"You better find out what's wrong with it."

"How can I? Can I walk into a repair clinic and ask for an overhaul? What am I going to say? 'My android's just turned killer. Fix it.' They'd call the police right off." I began to shake. "They'd have that android dismantled inside one day. I'd probably be booked as accessory to murder."

"Why didn't you have it repaired before it got to murder?"

"I couldn't take the chance," Vandaleur explained angrily. "If they started fooling around with lobotomies and body chemistry and endocrine surgery, they might have destroyed its aptitudes. What would I have left to hire out? How would I live?"

"You could work yourself. People do."

"Work at what? You know I'm good for nothing. How could I compete with specialist androids and robots? Who can, unless he's got a terrific talent for a particular job?"

"Yeah. That's true."

"I lived off my old man all my life. Damn him! He had to go bust just before he died. Left me the android and that's all. The only way I can get along is living off what it earns."

"You better sell it before the cops catch up with you. You can live off fifty grand. Invest it."

"At three percent? Fifteen hundred a year? When the android returns fifteen percent on its value? Eight thousand a year. That's what it earns. No, Dallas, I've got to go along with it."

"What are you going to do about its violence kick?"

"I can't do anything . . . except watch it and pray. What are you going to do about it?"

"Nothing. It's none of my business. Only one thing. . . . I ought to get something for keeping my mouth shut."

"What?"

"The android works for me for free. Let somebody else pay you, but I get it for free."

The multiple-aptitude android worked. Vandaleur collected its fees. His expenses were taken care of. His savings began to mount. As the warm spring of Megaster V turned to hot summer, I began investigating farms and properties. It would be possible, within a year or two, for us to settle down permanently, provided Dallas Brady's demands did not become rapacious.

On the first hot day of summer, the android began singing in Dallas Brady's workshop. It hovered over the electric furnace which, along with the weather, was broiling the shop, and sang an ancient tune that had been popular half a century before.

> *Oh, it's no feat to beat the heat.*
> *All reet! All reet!*
> *So jeet your seat*
> *Be fleet be fleet*
> *Cool and discreet*
> *Honey . . .*

It sang in a strange, halting voice, and its accomplished fingers were clasped behind its back, writhing in a strange rumba all their own. Dallas Brady was surprised.

"You happy or something?" she asked.

"I must remind you that the pleasure-pain syndrome is not

incorporated in the android synthesis," I answered. "All reet! All reet! Be fleet be fleet, cool and discreet, honey . . ."

Its fingers stopped their writhing and picked up a heavy pair of iron tongs. The android poked them into the glowing heart of the furnace, leaning far forward to peer into the lovely heat.

"Be careful, you damned fool!" Dallas Brady exclaimed. "You want to fall in?"

"I must remind you that I am worth fifty-seven thousand dollars on the current exchange," I said. "It is forbidden to endanger valuable property. All reet! All reet! Honey . . ."

It withdrew a crucible of glowing gold from the electric furnace, turned, capered hideously, sang crazily, and splashed a sluggish gobbet of molten gold over Dallas Brady's head. She screamed and collapsed, her hair and clothes flaming, her skin crackling. The android poured again while it capered and sang.

"Be fleet be fleet, cool and discreet, honey . . ." It sang and slowly poured and poured the molten gold. Then I left the workshop and rejoined James Vandaleur in his hotel suite. The android's charred clothes and squirming fingers warned its owner that something was very much wrong.

Vandaleur rushed to Dallas Brady's workshop, stared once, vomited and fled. I had enough time to pack one bag and raise nine hundred dollars on portable assets. He took a third-class cabin on the *Megaster Queen*, which left that morning for Lyra Alpha. He took me with him. He wept and counted his money and I beat the android again.

And the thermometer in Dallas Brady's workshop registered 98.1° beautifully Fahrenheit.

On Lyra Alpha we holed up in a small hotel near the university. There, Vandaleur carefully bruised my forehead until the letters MA were obliterated by the swelling and the discoloration The letters would reappear again, but not for several months, and in the meantime Vandaleur hoped the hue and cry for an MA android would be forgotten. The android was hired out as a common laborer in the university power plant. Vandaleur, as James Venice, eked out life on the android's small earnings.

I wasn't too unhappy. Most of the other residents in the hotel were university students, equally hard-up, but delightfully young and enthusiastic. There was one charming girl with sharp eyes and a quick mind. Her name was Wanda, and she and her beau, Jed Stark, took a tremendous interest in the killing android which was being mentioned in every paper in the galaxy.

"We've been studying the case," she and Jed said at one of the casual student parties which happened to be held this night in Vandaleur's room. "We think we know what's causing it. We're going to do a paper." They were in a high state of excitement.

"Causing what?" somebody wanted to know.

"The android rampage."

"Obviously out of adjustment, isn't it? Body chemistry gone haywire. Maybe a kind of synthetic cancer, yes?"

"No," Wanda gave Jed a look of suppressed triumph.

"Well, what is it?"

"Something specific."

"What?"

"That would be telling."

"Oh, come on."

"Nothing doing."

"Won't you tell us?" I asked intently. "I . . . We're very much interested in what could go wrong with an android."

"No, Mr. Venice," Wanda said. "It's a unique idea and we've got to protect it. One thesis like this and we'll be set up for life. We can't take the chance of somebody stealing it."

"Can't you give us a hint?"

"No. Not a hint. Don't say a word, Jed. But I'll tell you this much, Mr. Venice. I'd hate to be the man who owns that android."

"You mean the police?" I asked.

"I mean projection, Mr. Venice. Projection! That's the danger . . . and I won't say any more. I've said too much as it is."

I heard steps outside, and a hoarse voice singing softly: "Be fleet be fleet, cool and discreet, honey . . ." My android entered the room, home from its tour of duty at the university power plant. It was not introduced. I motioned to it and I immediately responded to the command and went to the beer keg and took over Vandaleur's job of serving the guests. Its accomplished fingers writhed in a private rhumba of their own. Gradually they stopped their squirming, and the strange humming ended.

Androids were not unusual at the university. The wealthier

students owned them along with cars and planes. Vandaleur's android provoked no comment, but young Wanda was sharp-eyed and quick-witted. She noted my bruised forehead and she was intent on the history-making thesis she and Jed Stark were going to write. After the party broke up, she consulted with Jed walking upstairs to her room.

"Jed, why'd that android have a bruised forehead?"

"Probably hurt itself, Wanda. It's working in the power plant. They fling a lot of heavy stuff around."

"That all?"

"What else?"

"It could be a convenient bruise."

"Convenient for what?"

"Hiding what's stamped on its forehead."

"No point to that, Wanda. You don't have to see marks on a forehead to recognise an android. You don't have to see a trademark on a car to know it's a car."

"I don't mean it's trying to pass as a human. I mean it's trying to pass as a lower grade android."

"Why?"

"Suppose it had 'MA' on its forehead."

"Multiple aptitude? Then why in hell would Venice waste it stoking furnaces if it could earn more— Oh. Oh! You mean it's—?"

Wanda nodded.

"Jesus!" Stark pursed his lips. "What do we do? Call the police?"

"No. We don't know if it's an MA for a fact. If it turns out to be an MA and the killing android, our paper comes first anyway. This is our big chance, Jed. If it's *that* android we can run a series of controlled tests and—"

"How do we find out for sure?"

"Easy. Infrared film. That'll show what's under the bruise. Borrow a camera. Buy some film. We'll sneak down to the power plant tomorrow afternoon and take some pictures. Then we'll know."

They stole down into the university power plant the following afternoon. It was a vast cellar, deep under the earth. It was dark, shadowy, luminous with burning light from the furnace doors. Above the roar of the fires they could hear a strange voice shouting and chanting in the echoing vault: "All reet! All reet! So jeet your seat. Be fleet be fleet, cool and discreet, honey . . ." And they could see a capering figure dancing a lunatic rumba in time to the music it shouted. The legs twisted. The arms waved. The fingers writhed.

Jed Stark raised the camera and began shooting his spool of infrared film, aiming the camera sights at that bobbing head. Then Wanda shrieked, for I saw them and came charging down on them, brandishing a polished steel shovel. It smashed the camera. It felled the girl and then the boy. Jed fought me for a desperate hissing moment before he was bludgeoned into helplessness. Then the android dragged them to the furnace and fed them to the flames, slowly, hideously. It capered and sang. Then it returned to my hotel.

The thermometer in the power plant registered 100.9° murderously Fahrenheit. All reet! All reet!

We bought steerage on the *Lyra Queen,* and Vandaleur and the android did odd jobs for their meals. During the night watches, Vandaleur would sit alone in the steerage head with a cardboard portfolio on his lap, puzzling over its contents. That portfolio was all he had managed to bring with him from Lyra Alpha. He had stolen it from Wanda's room. It was labeled ANDROID. It contained the secret of my sickness.

And it contained nothing but newspapers. Scores of newspapers from all over the galaxy, printed, microfilmed, engraved, etched, offset, photostated . . . Rigel *Star-Banner* . . . Paragon *Picayune* . . . Megaster *Times-Leader* . . . Lalande *Herald* . . . Lacaille *Journal* . . . Indi *Intelligencer* . . . Eridani *Telegram-News.* All reet! All reet!

Nothing but newspapers. Each paper contained an account of one crime in the android's ghastly career. Each paper also contained news, domestic and foreign, sports, society, weather, shipping news, stock exchange quotations, human interest stories, features, contests, puzzles. Somewhere in that mass of uncollated facts was the secret Wanda and Jed Stark had discovered. Vandaleur pored over the papers helplessly. It was beyond him. So jeet your seat!

"I'll sell you," I told the android. "Damn you. When we land on Terra, I'll sell you. I'll settle for three percent on whatever you're worth."

"I am worth fifty-seven thousand dollars on the current exchange," I told him.

"If I can't sell you, I'll turn you in to the police," I said.

"I am valuable property," I answered. "It is forbidden to endanger valuable property. You won't have me destroyed."

"Christ damn you!" Vandaleur cried. "What? Are you arrogant? Do you know you can trust me to protect you? Is that the secret?"

The multiple-aptitude android regarded him with calm accomplished eyes. "Sometimes," it said, "it is a good thing to be property."

It was three below zero when the *Lyra Queen* dropped at Croydon Field. A mixture of ice and snow swept across the field, fizzing and exploding into steam under the *Queen's* tail jets. The passengers trotted numbly across the blackened concrete to customs inspection, and thence to the airport bus that was to take them to London. Vandaleur and the android were broke. They walked.

By midnight they reached Piccadilly Circus. The December ice storm had not slackened, and the statue of Eros was encrusted with ice. They turned right, walked down to Trafalgar Square and then along the Strand shaking with cold and wet. Just above Fleet Street, Vandaleur saw a solitary figure coming from the direction of St. Paul's. He drew the android into an alley.

"We've got to have money," he whispered. He pointed at the approaching figure. "He has money. Take it from him."

"The order cannot be obeyed," the android said.

"Take it from him," Vandaleur repeated. "By force. Do you understand? We're desperate."

"It is contrary to my prime directive," I said. "I cannot endanger life or property. The order cannot be obeyed."

"For God's sake!" Vandaleur burst out. "You've attacked, destroyed, murdered. Don't gibber about prime directives. You haven't any left. Get his money. Kill him if you have to. I tell you, we're desperate!"

"It is contrary to my prime directive," I said. "I cannot endanger life or property. The order cannot be obeyed."

I thrust the android back and leaped out at the stranger. He was tall, austere, competent. He had an air of hope curdled by cynicism. He carried a cane. I saw he was blind.

"Yes?" he said. "I hear you near me. What is it?"

"Sir . . ." Vandaleur hesitated. "I'm desperate."

"We all are desperate," the stranger replied. "Quietly desperate."

"Sir . . . I've got to have some money."

"Are you begging or stealing?" The sightless eyes passed over Vandaleur and the android.

"I'm prepared for either."

"Ah. So are we all. It is the history of our race." The stranger motioned over his shoulder. "I have been begging at St. Paul's, my friend. What I desire cannot be stolen. What is it you desire that you are lucky enough to be able to steal?"

"Money," Vandaleur said.

"Money for what? Come, my friend, let us exchange confidences. I will tell you why I beg, if you will tell me why you steal. My name is Blenheim."

"My name is . . . Vole."

"I was not begging for sight at St. Paul's, Mr. Vole. I was begging for a number."

"A number?"

"Ah, yes. Numbers rational, numbers irrational, numbers imaginary. Positive integers. Negative integers. Fractions, positive and negative. Eh? You have never heard of Blenheim's immortal treatise on Twenty Zeros, or The Differences in Absence of Quantity?" Blenheim smiled bitterly. "I am the wizard of the Theory of Number, Mr. Vole, and I have exhausted the charm of number for myself. After fifty years of wizardry, senility approaches and the appetite vanishes. I have been praying in St. Paul's for inspiration. Dear God, I prayed, if You exist, send me a number."

Vandaleur slowly lifted the cardboard portfolio and touched Blenheim's hand with it. "In here," he said, "is a number. A hidden number. A secret number. The number of a crime. Shall we exchange, Mr. Blenheim? Shelter for a number?"

"Neither begging nor stealing, eh?" Blenheim said. "But a bargain. So all life reduces itself to the banal." The sightless eyes again passed over Vandaleur and the android. "Perhaps the All-Mighty is not God but a merchant. Come home with me."

On the top floor of Blenheim's house we shared a room—two beds, two closets, two washstands, one bathroom. Vandaleur bruised my forehead again and sent me out to find work, and while the android worked, I consulted with Blenheim and read him the papers from the portfolio, one by one. All reet! All reet!

Vandaleur told him so much and no more. He was a student, I

said, attempting a thesis on the murdering android. In these papers which he had collected were the facts that would explain the crimes of which Blenheim had heard nothing. There must be a correlation, a number, a statistic, something which would account for my derangement, I explained, and Blenheim was piqued by the mystery, the detective story, the human interest of number.

We examined the papers. As I read them aloud, he listed them and their contents in his blind, meticulous writing. And then I read his notes to him. He listed the papers by type, by typeface, by fact, by fancy, by article, spelling, words, theme, advertising, pictures, subject, politics, prejudices. He analyzed. He studied. He meditated. And we lived together in that top floor, always a little cold, always a little terrified, always a little closer . . . brought together by our fear of it, our hatred between us. Like a wedge driven into a living tree and splitting the trunk, only to be forever incorporated into the scar tissue, we grew together. Vandaleur and the android. Be fleet be fleet!

And one afternoon Blenheim called Vandaleur into his study and displayed his notes. "I think I've found it," he said, "but I can't understand it."

Vandaleur's heart leaped.

"Here are the correlations," Blenheim continued. "In fifty papers there are accounts of the criminal android. What is there, outside the depredations, that is also in fifty papers?"

"I don't know, Mr. Blenheim."

"It was a rhetorical question. Here is the answer. The weather."

"What?"

"The weather." Blenheim nodded. "Each crime was committed on a day when the temperature was above ninety degrees Fahrenheit."

"But that's impossible," Vandaleur exclaimed. "It was cool on Lyra Alpha."

"We have no record of any crime committed on Lyra Alpha. There is no paper."

"No. That's right, I—" Vandaleur was confused. Suddenly he exclaimed. "No. You're right. The furnace room. It was hot there. Hot! Of course. My God, yes! That's the answer. Dallas Brady's electric furnace . . . The rice deltas on Paragon. So jeet your seat. Yes. But why? Why? My God, why?"

I came into the house at that moment, and passing the study, saw Vandaleur and Blenheim. I entered, awaiting commands, my multiple aptitudes devoted to service.

"That's the android, eh?" Blenheim said after a long moment.

"Yes," Vandaleur answered, still confused by the discovery. "And that explains why it refused to attack you that night on the Strand. It wasn't hot enough to break the prime directive. Only in the heat . . . The heat, all reet!" He looked at the android. A silent lunatic command passed from man to android. I refused. It is forbidden to endanger life. Vandaleur gestured furiously, then seized Blenheim's shoulders and yanked him back out of his desk chair to the floor. Blenheim shouted once. Vandaleur leaped on him like a tiger, pinning him to the floor and sealing his mouth with one hand.

"Find a weapon," he called to the android.

"It is forbidden to endanger life."

"This is a fight for self-preservation. Bring me a weapon!" He held the squirming mathematician with all his weight. I went at once to a cupboard where I knew a revolver was kept. I checked it. It was loaded with five cartridges. I handed it to Vandaleur. I took it, ,ammed the barrel against Blenheim's head and pulled the trigger. He shuddered once.

We had three hours before the cook returned from her day off. We looted the house. We took Blenheim's money and jewels. We packed a bag with clothes. We took Blenheim's notes, destroyed the newspapers; and we left, carefully locking the door behind us. In Blenheim's study we left a pile of crumpled papers under a half inch of burning candle. And we soaked the rug around it with kerosene. No, I did all that. The android refused. I am forbidden to endanger life or property.

All reet!

They took the tubes to Leicester Square, changed trains, and rode to the British Museum. There they got off and went to a small Georgian house just off Russell Square. A shingle in the window read: NAN WEBB, PSYCHOMETRIC CONSULTANT. Vandaleur had made a note of the address some weeks earlier. They went into the house. The android waited in the foyer with the bag. Vandaleur entered Nan Webb's office.

She was a tall woman with gray shingled hair, very fine English complexion, and very bad English legs. Her features were blunt, her expression acute. She nodded to Vandaleur, finished a letter, sealed it and looked up.

"My name," I said, "is Vanderbilt. James Vanderbilt."

"Quite."

"I'm an exchange student at London University."

"Quite."

"I've been researching on the killing android, and I think I've discovered something very interesting. I'd like your advice on it. What is your fee?"

"What is your college at the University?"

"Why?"

"There is a discount for students."

"Merton College."

"That will be two pounds, please."

Vandaleur placed two pounds on the desk and added to the fee Blenheim's notes. "There is a correlation," he said, "between the crimes of the android and the weather. You will note that each crime was committed when the temperature rose above ninety degrees Fahrenheit. Is there a psychometric answer for this?"

Nan Webb nodded, studied the notes for a moment, put down the sheets of paper, and said: "Synesthesia, obviously."

"What?"

"Synesthesia," she repeated. "When a sensation, Mr. Vanderbilt, is interpreted immediately in terms of a sensation from a different sense organ from the one stimulated, it is called synesthesia. For example: A sound stimulus gives rise to a simultaneous sensation of definite color. Or color gives rise to a sensation of taste. Or a light stimulus gives rise to a sensation of sound. There can be confusion or short circuiting of any sensation of taste, smell, pain, pressure, temperature and so on. D'you understand?"

"I think so."

"Your research has uncovered the fact that the android most probably reacts to temperature stimulus above the ninety-degree level synesthetically. Most probably there is an endocrine response. Probably a temperature linkage with the android adrenal surrogate. High temperature brings about a response of fear, anger, excitement, and violent physical activity . . . all within the province of the adrenal gland."

"Yes. I see. Then if the android were to be kept in cold climates . . ."

"There would be neither stimulus nor response. There would be no crimes. Quite."

"I see. What is projection?"

"How do you mean?"

"Is there any danger of projection with regard to the owner of the android?"

"Very interesting. Projection is a throwing forward. It is the process of throwing out upon another the ideas or impulses that belong to oneself. The paranoid, for example, projects upon others his conflicts and disturbances in order to externalize them. He accuses, directly or by implication, other men of having the very sicknesses with which he is struggling himself."

"And the danger of projection?"

"It is the danger of believing what is implied. If you live with a psychotic who projects his sickness upon you, there is a danger of falling into his psychotic pattern and becoming virtually psychotic yourself. As, no doubt, is happening to you, Mr. Vandaleur."

Vandaleur leaped to his feet.

"You are an ass," Nan Webb went on crisply. She waved the sheets of notes. "This is no exchange student's writing. It's the unique cursive of the famous Blenheim. Every scholar in England knows this blind writing. There is no Merton College at London University. That was a miserable guess. Merton is one of the Oxford Colleges. And you, Mr. Vandaleur, are so obviously infected by association with your deranged android . . . by projection, if you will . . . that I hesitate between calling the Metropolitan Police and the Hospital for the Criminally Insane."

I took out the gun and shot her.

Reet!

"Antares II, Alpha Aurigae, Acrux IV, Pollux IX, Rigel Centaurus," Vandaleur said. "They're all cold. Cold as a witch's kiss. Mean temperatures of forty degrees Fahrenheit. Never gets hotter than seventy. We're in business again. Watch that curve."

The multiple-aptitude android swung the wheel with its accomplished hands. The car took the curve sweetly and sped on through the northern marshes, the reeds stretching for miles, brown and dry, under the cold English sky. The sun was sinking swiftly. Overhead, a lone flight of bustards flapped clumsily eastward. High above the flight, a lone helicopter drifted toward home and warmth.

"No more warmth for us," I said. "No more heat. We're safe when we're cold. We'll hole up in Scotland, make a little money, get across to Norway, build a bankroll, and then ship out. We'll settle on Pollux. We're safe. We've licked it. We can live again."

There was a startling *bleep* from overhead, and then a ragged roar: "ATTENTION JAMES VANDALEUR AND ANDROID. ATTENTION, JAMES VANDALEUR AND ANDROID!"

Vandaleur started and looked up. The lone helicopter was floating above them. From its belly came amplified commands: "YOU ARE SURROUNDED. THE ROAD IS BLOCKED. YOU ARE TO STOP YOUR CAR AT ONCE AND SUBMIT TO ARREST. STOP AT ONCE!"

I looked at Vandaleur for orders.

"Keep driving," Vandaleur snapped.

The helicopter dropped lower: "ATTENTION ANDROID. YOU ARE IN CONTROL OF THE VEHICLE. YOU ARE TO STOP AT ONCE. THIS IS A STATE DIRECTIVE SUPERSEDING ALL PRIVATE COMMANDS."

"What the hell are you doing?" I shouted.

"A state directive supersedes all private commands," the android answered. "I must point out to you that—"

"Get the hell away from the wheel," Vandaleur ordered. I clubbed the android, yanked him sideways, and squirmed over him to the wheel. The car veered off the road in that moment and went churning through the frozen mud and dry reeds. Vandaleur regained control and continued westward through the marshes toward a parallel highway five miles distant.

"We'll beat their goddamned block," he grunted.

The car pounded and surged. The helicopter dropped even lower. A searchlight blazed from the belly of the plane.

"ATTENTION JAMES VANDALEUR AND ANDROID. SUBMIT TO ARREST. THIS IS A STATE DIRECTIVE SUPERSEDING ALL PRIVATE COMMANDS."

"He can't submit," Vandaleur shouted wildly. "There's no one to submit to. He can't and I won't."

"Christ!" I muttered. "We'll beat them yet. We'll beat the block. We'll beat the heat. We'll—"

"I must point out to you," I said, "that I am required by my prime directive to obey state directives which supersede all private commands. I must submit to arrest."

"Who says it's a state directive?" Vandaleur said. "Them? Up in that plane? They've got to show credentials. They've got to prove it's state authority before you submit. How d'you know they're not crooks trying to trick us?"

Holding the wheel with one arm, he reached into his side pocket to make sure the gun was still in place. The car skidded. The tires squealed on frost and reeds. The wheel was wrenched from his grasp and the car yawed up a small hillock and overturned. The motor roared and the wheels screamed. Vandaleur crawled out and dragged the android with him. For the moment we were outside the circle of light boring down from the helicopter. We blundered off into the marsh, into the blackness, into concealment . . . Vandaleur running with a pounding heart, hauling the android along.

The helicopter circled and soared over the wrecked car, search-light peering, loudspeaker braying. On the highway we had left, lights appeared as the pursuing and blocking parties gathered and followed radio directions from the plane. Vandaleur and the android continued deeper and deeper into the marsh, working their way toward the parallel road and safety. It was night by now. The sky was a black matte. Not a star showed. The temperature was dropping. A southeast night wind knifed us to the bone.

Far behind there was a dull concussion. Vandaleur turned, gasping. The car's fuel had exploded. A geyser of flame shot up like a lurid fountain. It subsided into a low crater of burning reeds. Whipped by the wind, the distant hem of flame fanned up into a wall, ten feet high. The wall began marching down on us, crackling fiercely. Above it, a pall of oily smoke surged forward. Behind it, Vandaleur could make out the figures of men . . . a mass of beaters searching the marsh.

"Christ!" I cried and searched desperately for safety. He ran, dragging me with him, until their feet crunched through the surface ice of a pool. He trampled the ice furiously, then flung himself down in the numbing water, pulling the android with us.

The wall of flame approached. I could hear the crackle and feel the heat. He could see the searchers clearly. Vandaleur reached into his side pocket for the gun. The pocket was torn. The gun was gone. He groaned and shook with cold and terror. The light from the marsh fire was blinding. Overhead, the helicopter floated helplessly to one side, unable to fly through the smoke and flames and aid the searchers who were beating far to the right of us.

"They'll miss us," Vandaleur whispered. "Keep quiet. That's an order. They'll miss us. We'll beat them. We'll beat the fire. We'll—"

Three distinct shots sounded less than a hundred feet from the fugitives. *Blam! Blam! Blam!* They came from the last three cartridges in my gun as the marsh fire reached it where it had dropped, and exploded the shells. The searchers turned toward the sound and began working directly toward us. Vandaleur cursed hysterically and tried to submerge even deeper to escape the intolerable heat of the fire. The android began to twitch.

The wall of flame surged up to them. Vandaleur took a deep breath and prepared to submerge until the flame passed over them. The android shuddered and burst into an earsplitting scream.

"All reet! All reet!" it shouted. "Be fleet be fleet!"

"Damn you!" I shouted. I tried to drown it.

"Damn you!" I cursed him. I smashed his face.

The android battered Vandaleur, who fought it off until it exploded out of the mud and staggered upright. Before I could return to the attack, the live flames captured it hypnotically. It danced and capered in a lunatic rhumba before the wall of fire. Its legs twisted. Its arms waved. The fingers writhed in a private rumba of their own. It shrieked and sang and ran in a crooked waltz before the embrace of the heat, a muddy monster silhouetted against the brilliant sparkling flare.

The searchers shouted. There were shots. The android spun around twice and then continued its horrid dance before the face of the flames. There was a rising gust of wind. The fire swept around the capering figure and enveloped it for a roaring moment. Then the fire swept on, leaving behind it a sobbing mass of synthetic flesh oozing scarlet blood that would never coagulate.

The thermometer would have registered 1200° wondrously Fahrenheit.

Vandaleur didn't die. I got away. They missed him while they watched the android caper and die. But I don't know which of us he is these days. Projection, Wanda warned me. Projection, Nan Webb told him. If you live with a crazy man or a crazy machine long enough, I become crazy too. Reet!

But we know one truth. We know they were wrong. The new robot and Vandaleur know that because the new robot's started twitching too. Reet! Here on cold Pollux, the robot is twitching and singing. No heat, but my fingers writhe. No heat, but it's taken the little Talley girl off for a solitary walk. A cheap labor robot. A servomechanism . . . all I could afford . . . but it's twitching and humming and walking alone with the child somewhere and I can't find them. Christ! Vandaleur can't find me before it's too late. Cool and discreet, honey, in the dancing frost while the thermometer registers 10° fondly Fahrenheit.

HOBSON'S CHOICE

This is a warning to accomplices like you, me and Addyer.

Can you spare price of one cup coffee, honorable sir? I am indigent organism which are hungering.

By day, Addyer was a statistician. He concerned himself with such matters as Statistical Tables, Averages and Dispersions, Groups That Are Not Homogeneous, and Random Sampling. At night, Addyer plunged into an elaborate escape fantasy divided into two parts. Either he imagined himself moved back in time a hundred years with a double armful of the *Encyclopaedia Britannica*, bestsellers, hit plays and gambling records; or else he imagined himself transported forward in time a thousand years to the Golden Age of perfection.

There were other fantasies which Addyer entertained on odd Thursdays, such as (by a fluke) becoming the only man left on earth with a world of passionate beauties to fecundate; such as acquiring the power of invisibility which would enable him to rob banks and right wrongs with impunity; such as possessing the mysterious power of working miracles.

Up to this point you and I and Addyer are identical. Where we part company is in the fact that Addyer was a statistician.

Can you spare cost of one cup coffee, honorable miss? For blessed charitability? I am beholden.

On Monday, Addyer rushed into his chief's office, waving a sheaf of papers. "Look here, Mr. Grande," Addyer sputtered. "I've found something fishy. Extremely fishy . . . In the statistical sense, that is."

"Oh, hell," Grande answered. "You're not supposed to be finding anything. We're in between statistics until the war's over."

"I was leafing through the Interior Department's reports. D'you know our population's up?"

"Not after the Atom Bomb it isn't," said Grande. "We've lost double what our birthrate can replace." He pointed out the window to the twenty-five-foot stub of the Washington Monument. "There's your documentation."

"But our population's up 3.0915 percent." Addyer displayed his figures. "What about that, Mr. Grande?"

"Must be a mistake somewhere," Grande muttered after a moment's inspection. "You'd better check."

"Yes, sir," said Addyer scurrying out of the office. "I knew you'd be interested, sir. You're the ideal statistician, sir." He was gone.

"Poop," said Grande and once again began computing the quantity of bored respirations left to him. It was his personalized anesthesia.

On Tuesday, Addyer discovered that there was no correlation between the mortality-birthrate ratio and the population increase. The war was multiplying mortality and reducing births; yet the population was minutely increasing. Addyer displayed his discovery to Grande, received a pat on the back, and went home to a new fantasy in which he woke up a million years in the future, learned the answer to the enigma, and decided to remain amid snow-capped mountains and snow-capped bosoms, safe under the aegis of a culture saner than Aureomycin.

On Wednesday, Addyer requisitioned the comptometer and file and ran a test check on Washington, D.C. To his dismay, he discovered that the population of the former capital was down 0.0029 per cent. This was distressing, and Addyer went home to escape into a dream about Queen Victoria's Golden Age when he amazed and confounded the world with his brilliant output of novels, plays, and poetry, all cribbed from Shaw, Galsworthy, and Wilde.

Can you spare price of one coffee, honorable sir? I am distressed individual needful of chariting.

On Thursday, Addyer tried another check, this time on the city of Philadelphia. He discovered that Philadelphia's population was up 0.0959 per cent. Very encouraging. He tried a rundown on Little Rock. Population up 1.1329 per cent. He tested St. Louis. Population up 2.0924 per cent . . . and this despite the complete extinction of Jefferson County owing to one of those military mistakes of an excessive nature.

"My God!" Addyer exclaimed, trembling with excitement. "The closer I get to the center of the country, the greater the increase. But it was the center of the country that took the heaviest punishment in the Buz-Raid. What's the answer?"

That night he shuttled back and forth between the future and the past in his ferment, and he was down at the shop by seven A.M. He put a twenty-four-hour claim on the Compo and Files. He followed up his hunch and he came up with a fantastic discovery which he graphed in approved form. On the map of the remains of the United States he drew concentric circles in colors illustrating the areas of population increase. The red, orange, yellow, green and blue circles formed a perfect target around Finney County, Kansas.

"Mr. Grande," Addyer shouted in a high statistical passion, "Finney County has got to explain this."

"You go out there and get that explanation," Grande replied, and Addyer departed.

"Poop," muttered Grande and began integrating his pulse rate with his eye blink.

Can you spare price of one coffee, dearly madam? I am starveling organism requiring nutritiousment.

Now, travel in those days was hazardous. Addyer took ship to Charleston (there were no rail connections remaining in the North Atlantic states) and was wrecked off Hatteras by a rogue mine. He drifted in the icy waters for seventeen hours, muttering through his teeth: "Oh, Christ! If only I'd been born a hundred years ago."

Apparently this form of prayer was potent. He was picked up by a Navy Sweeper and shipped to Charleston where he arrived just in time to acquire a subcritical radiation burn from a raid which fortunately left the railroad unharmed. He was treated for the burn from Charleston to Macon (change) from Birmingham to Memphis (bubonic plague) to Little Rock (polluted water) to Tulsa (fallout quarantine) to Kansas City (The O.K. Bus Co. Accepts No Liability for Lives Lost Through Acts of War) to Lyonesse, Finney County, Kansas.

And there he was in Finney County with its great magma pits and scars and radiation streaks; whole farms blackened and razed; whole highways so blasted they looked like dotted lines; whole population 4-F. Clouds of soot and fallout neutralizers hung over Finney County by day, turning it into a Pittsburgh on a still afternoon. Auras of radiation glowed at night, highlighted by the blinking red warning beacons, turning the county into one of those overexposed night photographs, all blurred and crosshatched by deadly slashes of light.

After a restless night in the Lyonesse Hotel, Addyer went over to the county seat for a check on their birth records. He was armed with the proper credentials, but the county seat was not armed with the statistics. That excessive military mistake again. It had extinguished the seat.

A little annoyed, Addyer marched off to the County Medical Association office. His idea was to poll the local doctors on births. There was an office and one attendant who had been a practical nurse. He informed Addyer that Finney County had lost its last doctor to the army eight months previous. Midwives might be the answer to the birth enigma, but there was no record of midwives. Addyer would simply have to canvass from door to door, asking if any lady within practiced that ancient profession.

Further piqued, Addyer returned to the Lyonesse Hotel and wrote on a slip of tissue paper: HAVING DATA DIFFICULTIES. WILL REPORT AS SOON AS INFORMATION AVAILABLE. He slipped the message into an aluminum capsule, attached it to his sole surviving carrier pigeon and dispatched it to Washington with a prayer. Then he sat down at his window and brooded.

He was aroused by a curious sight. In the street below, the O.K. Bus Co. had just arrived from Kansas City. The old coach wheezed to a stop, opened its door with some difficulty and permitted a one-legged farmer to emerge. His burned face was freshly bandaged. Evidently this was a well-to-do burgess who could afford to travel for medical treatment. The bus backed up for the return trip to Kansas City and honked a warning horn. That was when the curious sight began.

From nowhere ... absolutely nowhere ... a horde of people appeared. They skipped from back alleys, from behind rubble piles; they popped out of stores, they filled the street. They were all jolly, healthy, brisk, happy. They laughed and chatted as they climbed into the bus. They looked like hikers and tourists, carrying knapsacks, carpetbags, box lunches and even babies. In two minutes the bus was filled. It lurched off down the road, and as it disappeared Addyer heard happy singing break out and echo from the walls of rubble.

"I'll be damned," he said.

He hadn't heard spontaneous singing in over two years. He hadn't seen a carefree smile in over three years. He felt like a color-blind man who was seeing the full spectrum for the first time. It was uncanny. It was also a little blasphemous.

"Don't those people know there's a war on?" he asked himself.

And a little later: "They looked too healthy. Why aren't they in uniform?"

And last of all: "Who *were* they anyway?"

That night Addyer's fantasy was confused.

Can you spare price of one cup coffee, kindly sir? I am estrangered and faintly from hungering.

The next morning Addyer arose early, hired a car at an exorbitant fee, found he could not buy any fuel at any price, and ultimately settled for a lame horse. He was allergic to horse dander and suffered asthmatic tortures as he began his house-to-house canvass. He was discouraged when he returned to the Lyonesse Hotel that afternoon. He was just in time to witness the departure of the O.K. Bus Co.

Once again a horde of happy people appeared and boarded the bus. Once again the bus hirpled off down the broken road. Once again the joyous singing broke out.

"I *will* be damned," Addyer wheezed.

He dropped into the County Surveyor's Office for a large scale map of Finney County. It was his intent to plot the midwife coverage in accepted statistical manner. There was a little difficulty with the surveyor who was deaf, blind in one eye, and spectacleless in the other. He could not read Addyer's credentials with any faculty or facility. As Addyer finally departed with the map, he said to himself: "I think the old idiot thought I was a spy."

And later he muttered: "Spies?"

And just before bedtime: "Holy Moses! Maybe *that's* the answer to *them*."

That night he was Lincoln's secret agent, anticipating Lee's every move, outwitting Jackson, Johnston, and Beauregard, foiling John Wilkes Booth, and being elected President of the United States by 1868.

The next day the O.K. Bus Co. carried off yet another load of happy people.

And the next.

And the next.

"Four hundred tourists in five days," Addyer computed. "The country's filled with espionage."

He began loafing around the streets trying to investigate these joyous travelers. It was difficult. They were elusive before the bus arrived. They had a friendly way of refusing to pass the time. The locals of Lyonesse knew nothing about them and were not interested. Nobody was interested in much more than painful survival these days. That was what made the singing obscene.

After seven days of cloak-and-dagger and seven days of counting, Addyer suddenly did the big take. "It adds up," he said. "Eighty people a day leaving Lyonesse. Five hundred a week. Twenty-five thousand a year. Maybe that's the answer to the population increase." He spent fifty-five dollars on a telegram to Grande with no

more than a hope of delivery. The telegram read: "EUREKA. I HAVE
FOUND (IT)."

*Can you spare price of lone cup coffee, honorable madam? I am
not tramp-handler but destitute life-form.*

Addyer's opportunity came the next day. The O.K. Bus Co.
pulled in as usual. Another crowd assembled to board the bus, but
this time there were too many. Three people were refused passage.
They weren't in the least annoyed. They stepped back, waved energetically as the bus started, shouted instructions for future reunions
and then quietly turned and started off down the street.

Addyer was out of his hotel room like a shot. He followed the
trio down the main street, turned left after them onto Fourth Avenue, passed the ruined schoolhouse, passed the demolished telephone building, passed the gutted library, railroad station, Protestant
church, Catholic church . . . and finally reached the outskirts of Lyonesse and then open country.

Here he had to be more cautious. It was difficult stalking the
spies with so much of the dusky road illuminated by warning lights.
He wasn't suicidal enough to think of hiding in radiation pits. He
hung back in an agony of indecision and was at last relieved to see
them turn off the broken road and enter the old Baker farmhouse.

"Ah-ha!" said Addyer.

He sat down at the edge of the road on the remnants of a mis-
sile and asked himself: "Ah-ha what?" He could not answer, but he
knew where to find the answer. He waited until dusk deepened to
darkness and then slowly wormed his way forward toward the farmhouse.

It was while he was creeping between the deadly radiation glows
and only occasionally butting his head against grave markers that he
first became aware of two figures in the night. They were in the
barnyard of the Baker place and were performing most peculiarly.
One was tall and thin. A man. He stood stockstill, like a lighthouse.
Upon occasion he took a slow, stately step with infinite caution and
waved an arm in slow motion to the other figure. The second was
also a man. He was stocky and trotted jerkily back and forth.

As Addyer approached, he heard the tall man say: "Rooo booo
fooo mooo hwaaa looo fooo."

Whereupon the trotter chattered, "Wd-nk-kd-ik-md-pd-ld-nk."

Then they both laughed: the tall man like a locomotive, the trotter like a chipmunk. They turned. The trotter rocketed into the house. The tall man drifted in. And that was amazingly that.

"Oh-ho," said Addyer.

At that moment a pair of hands seized him and lifted him from the ground. Addyer's heart constricted. He had time for one convulsive spasm before something vague was pressed against his face. As he lost consciousness his last idiotic thought was of telescopes.

Can you spare price of solitary coffee for no-loafing unfortunate, honorable sir? Charity will blessings.

When Addyer awoke he was lying on a couch in a small whitewashed room. A grey-haired gentleman with heavy features was seated at a desk alongside the couch, busily ciphering on bits of paper. The desk was cluttered with what appeared to be intricate timetables. There was a small radio perched on one side.

"L-Listen . . ." Addyer began faintly.

"Just a minute, Mr. Addyer," the gentleman said pleasantly. He fiddled with the radio. A glow germinated in the middle of the room over a circular copper plate and coalesced into a girl. She was extremely nude and extremely attractive. She scurried to the desk, patted the gentleman's head with the speed of a pneumatic hammer. She laughed and chattered, "Wd-nk-tk-ik-lt-nk."

The gray-haired man smiled and pointed to the door. "Go outside and walk it off," he said. She turned and streaked through the door.

"It has something to do with temporal rates," the gentleman said to Addyer. "I don't understand it. When they come forward, they've got accumulated momentum." He began ciphering again. "Why in the world did you have to come snooping, Mr. Addyer?"

"You're spies," Addyer said. "She was talking Chinese."

"Hardly. I'd say it was French. Early French. Middle fifteenth century."

"Middle fifteenth century!" Addyer exclaimed.

"That's what I'd say. You begin to acquire an ear for those stepped-up tempos. Just a minute, please."

He switched the radio on again. Another glow appeared and solidified into a nude man. He was stout, hairy and lugubrious. With exasperating slowness he said, "Mooo fooo blooo wawww hawww pooo."

The grey-haired man pointed to the door. The stout man departed in slow motion.

"The way I see it," the grey-haired man continued conversationally, "when they come back they're swimming against the time current. That slows 'em down. When they come forward, they're swimming with the current. That speeds 'em up. Of course, in any case it doesn't last longer than a few minutes. It wears off."

"What?" Addyer said. "Time travel?"

"Yes. Of course."

"That thing . . ." Addyer pointed to the radio. "A time machine?"

"That's the idea. Roughly."

"But it's too small."

The grey-haired man laughed.

"What is this place anyway? What are you up to?"

"It's a funny thing," the grey-haired man said. "Everybody used to speculate about time travel. How it would be used for exploration, archaeology, historical and social research and so on. Nobody ever guessed what the real use would be. . . . Therapy."

"Therapy? You mean medical therapy?"

"That's right. Psychological therapy for the misfits who won't respond to any other cure. We let them emigrate. Escape. We've set up stations every quarter century. Stations like this."

"I don't understand."

"This is an immigration office."

"Oh my God!" Addyer shot up from the couch. "Then you're the answer to the population increase. Yes? That's how I happened to notice it. Mortality's up so high and birth's down so low these days that your time-addition becomes significant. Yes?"

"Yes, Mr. Addyer."

"Thousands of you coming here. From where?"

"From the future, of course. Time travel wasn't developed until C/H 127. That's . . . oh, say, 2505 A.D. your chronology. We didn't set up our chain of stations until C/H 189."

"But those fast-moving ones. You said they came forward from the past."

"Oh, yes, but they're all from the future originally. They just decided they went too far back."

"Too far?"

The grey-haired man nodded and reflected. "It's amusing, the mistakes people will make. They become unrealistic when they read history. Lose contact with facts. Chap I knew . . . wouldn't be satisfied with anything less than Elizabethan times. 'Shakespeare,' he said. 'Good Queen Bess. Spanish Armada. Drake and Hawkins and Raleigh. Most virile period in history. The Golden Age. That's for me.' I couldn't talk sense into him, so we sent him back. Too bad."

"Well?" Addyer asked.

"Oh, he died in three weeks. Drank a glass of water. Typhoid."

"You didn't inoculate him? I mean, the army when it sends men overseas always—"

"Of course we did. Gave him all the immunization we could. But diseases evolve and change, too. New strains develop. Old strains disappear. That's what causes pandemics. Evidently our shots wouldn't take against the Elizabethan typhoid. Excuse me . . ."

Again the glow appeared. Another nude man appeared, chattered briefly and then whipped through the door. He almost collided with the nude girl who poked her head in, smiled and called in a curious accent, "Ie vous prie de me pardonner. Quy estoit cette gentilhomme?"

"I was right," the grey-haired man said. "That's medieval French. They haven't spoken like that since Rabelais." To the girl he said, "Middle English, please. The American dialect."

"Oh, I'm sorry, Mr. Jelling. I get so damned fouled up with my linguistics. Fouled? Is that right? Or do they say—"

"Hey!" Addyer cried in anguish.

"They say it, but only in private these years. Not before strangers."

"Oh, yes. I remember. Who was that gentleman who just left?"

"Peters."

"From Athens?"

"That's right."

"Didn't like it, eh?"

"Not much. Seems the Peripatetics didn't have plumbing."

"Yes. You begin to hanker for a modern bathroom after a while. Where do I get some clothes . . . or don't they wear clothes this century?"

"No, that's a hundred years forward. Go see my wife. She's in the outfitting room in the barn. That's the big red building."

The tall lighthouse-man Addyer had first seen in the

farmyard suddenly manifested himself behind the girl. He was now dressed and moving at normal speed. He stared at the girl; she stared at him. "Splem!" they both cried. They embraced and kissed shoulders.

"St'u my rock-ribbering rib-rockery to heart the hearts two," the man said.

"Heart's too, argal, too heart," the girl laughed.

"Eh? Then you st'u too."

They embraced again and left.

"What was that? Future talk?" Addyer asked. "Shorthand?"

"Shorthand?" Jelling exclaimed in a surprised tone. "Don't you know rhetoric when you hear it? That was thirtieth-century rhetoric, man. We don't talk anything else up there. Prosthesis, Diastole, Epergesis, Metabasis, Hendiadys . . . And we're all born scanning."

"You don't have to sound so stuck up," Addyer muttered enviously. "I could scan too if I tried."

"You'd find it damned inconvenient trying at your time of life."

"What difference would that make?"

"It would make a big difference," Jelling said, "because you'd find that living is the sum of conveniences. You might think plumbing is pretty unimportant compared to ancient Greek philosophers. Lots of people do. But the fact is, we already know the philosophy. After a while you get tired of seeing the great men and listening to them expound the material you already know. You begin to miss the conveniences and familiar patterns you used to take for granted."

"That," said Addyer, "is a superficial attitude."

"You think so? Try living in the past by candlelight, without central heating, without refrigeration, canned foods, elementary drugs. . . . Or, future-wise, try living with Berganlicks, the Twenty-Two Commandments. Duodecimal calendars and currency, or try speaking in meter, planning and scanning each sentence before you talk . . . and damned for a contemptible illiterate if you forget yourself and speak spontaneously in your own tongue."

"You're exaggerating," Addyer said. "I'll bet there are times where I could be very happy. I've thought about it for years, and I—"

"Tcha!" Jelling snorted. "The great illusion. Name one."

"The American Revolution."

"Pfui! No sanitation. No medicine. Cholera in Philadelphia. Malaria in New York. No anesthesia. The death penalty for hundreds of small crimes and petty infractions. None of the books and music you like best. None of the jobs or professions for which you've been trained. Try again."

"The Victorian Age."

"How are your teeth and eyes? In good shape? They'd better be. We can't send your inlays and spectacles back with you. How are your ethics? In bad shape? They'd better be, or you'd starve in that cutthroat era. How do you feel about class distinctions? They were pretty strong in those days. What's your religion? You'd better not be a Jew or Catholic or Quaker or Moravian or any minority. What's your politics? If you're a reactionary today, the same opinions would make you a dangerous radical a hundred years ago. I don't think you'd be happy."

"I'd be safe."

"Not unless you were rich; and we can't send money back. Only the flesh. No, Addyer, the poor died at the average age of forty in those days . . . worked out, worn out. Only the privileged survived, and you wouldn't be one of the privileged."

"Not with my superior knowledge?"

Jelling nodded wearily. "I knew *that* would come up sooner or later. What superior knowledge? Your hazy recollection of science and invention? Don't be a damned fool, Addyer. You enjoy your technology without the faintest idea of how it works."

"It wouldn't have to be hazy recollection. I could prepare."

"What, for instance?"

"Oh . . . say, the radio. I could make a fortune inventing the radio."

Jelling smiled. "You couldn't invent radio until you'd first invented the hundred allied technical discoveries that went into it. You'd have to create an entire new industrial world. You'd have to discover the vacuum rectifier and create an industry to manufacture it; the self-heterodyne circuit, the nonradiating neutrodyne receiver and so forth. You'd have to develop electric power production and transmission and alternating current. You'd have to—but why belabor the obvious? Could you invent internal combustion before the development of fuel oils?"

"My God!" Addyer groaned.

"And another thing," Jelling went on grimly. "I've been talking about technological tools, but language is a tool, too; the tool of communication. Did you ever realize that all the studying you might do could never teach you how a language was really used centuries ago? Do you know how the Romans pronounced Latin? Do you know the Greek dialects? Could you learn to speak and think in Gaelic, seventeenth-century Flemish, Old Low German? Never. You'd be a deaf-mute."

"I never thought about it that way," Addyer said slowly.

"Escapists never do. All they're looking for is a vague excuse to run away."

"What about books? I could memorize a great book and—"

"And what? Go back far enough into the past to anticipate the real author? You'd be anticipating the public, too. A book doesn't become great until the public's ready to understand it. It doesn't become profitable until the public's ready to buy it."

"What about going forward into the future?" Addyer asked.

"I've already told you. It's the same problem only in reverse. Could a medieval man survive in the twentieth century? Could he stay alive in street traffic? Drive cars? Speak the language? Think in the language? Adapt to the tempo, ideas, and coordinations you take for granted? Never. Could someone from the twenty-fifth century adapt to the thirtieth? Never."

"Well, then," Addyer said angrily, "if the past and future are so uncomfortable, what are those people traveling around for?"

"They're not traveling," Jelling said. "They're running."

"From what?"

"Their own time."

"Why?"

"They don't like it."

"Why not?"

"Do you like yours? Does any neurotic?"

"Where are they going?"

"Anyplace but where they belong. They keep looking for the Golden Age. Tramps! Time-stiffs! Never satisfied. Always searching, shifting . . . bumming through the centuries. Pfui! Half the panhandlers you meet are probably time-bums stuck in the wrong century."

"And those people coming here . . . they think *this* is a Golden Age?"

"They do."

"They're crazy," Addyer protested. "Have they seen the ruins? The radiation? The war? The anxiety? The hysteria?"

"Sure. That's what appeals to them. Don't ask me why. Think of it this way: You like the American Colonial period, yes?"

"Among others."

"Well, if you told Mr. George Washington the reasons why you liked his time, you'd probably be naming everything he hated about it."

"But that's not a fair comparison. This is the worst age in all history."

Jelling waved his hand. "That's how it looks to you. Everybody says that in every generation; but take my word for it, no matter when you live and how you live, there's always somebody else somewhere else who thinks you live in the Golden Age."

"Well I'll be damned," Addyer said.

Jelling looked at him steadily for a moment. "You will be," he said sorrowfully. "I've got bad news for you, Addyer. We can't let you remain. You'll talk and make trouble, and our secret's got to be kept. We'll have to send you out one-way."

"I can talk wherever I go."

"But nobody'll pay attention to you outside your own time. You won't make sense. You'll be an eccentric . . . a lunatic . . . a foreigner . . . safe."

"What if I come back?"

"You won't be able to get back without a visa, and I'm not tattooing any visa on you. You won't be the first we've had to transport, if that's any consolation to you. There was a Jap, I remember—"

"Then you're going to send me somewhere in time? Permanently?"

"That's right. I'm really very sorry."

"To the future or the past?"

"You can take your choice. Think it over while you're getting undressed."

"You don't have to act so mournful," Addyer said. "It's a great adventure. A high adventure. It's something I've always dreamed."

"That's right. It's going to be wonderful."

"I could refuse," Addyer said nervously.

Jelling shook his head. "We'd only drug you and send you anyway. It might as well be your choice."

"It's a choice I'm delighted to make."

"Sure. That's the spirit, Addyer."

"Everybody says I was born a hundred years too soon."

"Everybody generally says that . . . unless they say you were born a hundred years too late."

"Some people say that too."

"Well, think it over. It's a permanent move. Which would you prefer . . . the phonetic future or the poetic past?"

Very slowly Addyer began to undress as he undressed each night when he began the prelude to his customary fantasy. But now his dreams were faced with fulfillment and the moment of decision terrified him. He was a little blue and rather unsteady on his legs when he stepped to the copper disc in the center of the floor. In answer to Jelling's inquiry he muttered his choice. Then he turned argent in the aura of an incandescent glow and disappeared from his time forever.

Where did he go? You know. I know. Addyer knows. Addyer traveled to the land of Our pet fantasy. He escaped into the refuge that is Our refuge, to the time of Our dreams; and in practically no time at all he realized that he had in truth departed from the only time for himself.

Through the vistas of the years every age but our own seems glamorous and golden. We yearn for the yesterdays and tomorrows, never realizing that we are faced with Hobson's Choice . . . that to-day, bitter or sweet, anxious or calm, is the only day for us. The dream of time is the traitor, and we are all accomplices to the betrayal of ourselves.

Can you spare price of one coffee, honorable sir? No, sir, I am not panhandling organism. I am starveling Japanese transient stranded in this so-miserable year. Honorable sir! I beg in tears for holy charity. Will you donate to this destitute person one ticket to township of Lyonesse? I want to beg on knees for visa. I want to go back to year 1945 again. I want to be in Hiroshima again. I want to go home.

OF TIME AND
THIRD AVENUE

What Macy hated about the man was the fact that he
squeaked. Macy didn't know if it was the shoes, but he suspected the clothes. In the back room of his tavern, under the
poster that asked: WHO FEARS MENTION THE BATTLE OF THE
BOYNE? Macy inspected the stranger. He was tall, slender, and very
dainty. Although he was young, he was almost bald. There was fuzz
on top of his head and over his eyebrows. Then he reached into his
jacket for a wallet, and Macy made up his mind. It was the clothes
that squeaked.

"MQ, Mr. Macy," the stranger said in a staccato voice. "Very good. For rental of this back room included exclusive utility for one chronos—"

"One whatos?" Macy asked nervously.

"Chronos. The incorrect word? Oh yes. Excuse me. One hour."

"You're a foreigner," Macy said. "What's your name? I bet it's Russian."

"No. Not foreign," the stranger answered. His frightening eyes whipped around the back room. "Identify me as Boyne."

"Boyne!" Macy echoed incredulously.

"MQ. Boyne." Mr. Boyne opened a wallet shaped like an accordion, ran his fingers through various colored papers and coins, then withdrew a hundred-dollar bill. He jabbed it at Macy and said: "Rental fee for one hour. As agreed. One hundred dollars. Take it and go."

Impelled by the thrust of Boyne's eyes, Macy took the bill and staggered out to the bar. Over his shoulder he quavered: "What'll you drink?"

"Drink? Alcohol? Pfui!" Boyne answered.

He turned and darted to the telephone booth, reached under the pay phone and located the lead-in wire. From a side pocket he withdrew a small glittering box and clipped it to the wire. He tucked it out of sight, then lifted the receiver.

"Coordinates West 73-58-15," he said rapidly. "North 40-45-20. Disband sigma. You're ghosting . . ." After a pause, he continued: "Stet. Stet! Transmission clear. I want a fix on Knight. Oliver Wilson Knight. Probability to four significant figures. You have the coordinates. . . . 99.9807? MQ. Stand by. . . ."

Boyne poked his head out of the booth and peered toward the tavern door. He waited with steely concentration until a young man and a pretty girl entered. Then he ducked back to the phone. "Probability fulfilled. Oliver Wilson Knight in contact. MQ. Luck my Para." He hung up and was sitting under the poster as the couple wandered toward the back room.

The young man was about twenty-six, of medium height, and inclined to be stocky. His suit was rumpled, his seal-brown hair was rumpled, and his friendly face was crinkled by good-natured creases. The girl had black hair, soft blue eyes, and a small private smile. They walked arm in arm and liked to collide gently when they thought no one was looking. At this moment they collided with Mr. Macy.

"I'm sorry, Mr. Knight," Macy said. "You and the young lady can't sit back there this afternoon. The premises have been rented."

Their faces fell. Boyne called: "Quite all right, Mr. Macy. All correct. Happy to entertain Mr. Knight and friend as guests."

Knight and the girl turned to Boyne uncertainly. Boyne smiled and patted the chair alongside him. "Sit down," he said. "Charmed, I assure you."

The girl said: "We hate to intrude, but this is the only place in town where you can get genuine Stone ginger beer."

"Already aware of the fact, Miss Clinton." To Macy he said: "Bring ginger beer and go. No other guests. These are all I'm expecting."

Knight and the girl stared at Boyne in astonishment as they sat down slowly. Knight placed a wrapped parcel of books on the table. The girl took a breath and said, "You know me . . . Mr. . . . ?"

"Boyne. As in Boyne, Battle of. Yes, of course. You are Miss Jane Clinton. This is Mr. Oliver Wilson Knight. I rented premises particularly to meet you this afternoon."

"This supposed to be a gag?" Knight asked, a dull flush appearing on his cheeks.

"Ginger beer," answered Boyne gallantly as Macy arrived, deposited the bottles and glasses, and departed in haste.

"You couldn't know we were coming here," Jane said. "We didn't know ourselves . . . until a few minutes ago."

"Sorry to contradict, Miss Clinton," Boyne smiled. "The probability of your arrival at Longitude 73-58-15 Latitude 40-45-20 was 99.9807 per cent. No one can escape four significant figures."

"Listen," Knight began angrily, "if this is your idea of—"

"Kindly drink ginger beer and listen to my idea, Mr. Knight." Boyne leaned across the table with galvanic intensity. "This hour has been arranged with difficulty and much cost. To whom? No matter. You have placed us in an extremely dangerous position. I have been sent to find a solution."

"Solution for what?" Knight asked.

Jane tried to rise. "I . . . I think we'd b-better be go—"

Boyne waved her back, and she sat down like a child. To Knight he said: "This noon you entered premises of J. D. Craig & Co., dealer in printed books. You purchased, through transfer of money, four books. Three do not matter, but the fourth . . ." He tapped the wrapped parcel emphatically. "That is the crux of this encounter."

"What the hell are you talking about?" Knight exclaimed.

"One bound volume consisting of collected facts and statistics."

"The almanac?"

"The almanac."

"What about it?"

"You intended to purchase a 1950 almanac."

"I bought the '50 almanac."

"You did not!" Boyne blazed. "You bought the almanac for 1990."

"What?"

"The World Almanac for 1990," Boyne said clearly, "is in this package. Do not ask how. There was a carelessness that has already been disciplined. Now the error must be adjusted. That is why I am here. It is why this meeting was arranged. You cognate?"

Knight burst into laughter and reached for the parcel. Boyne leaned across the table and grasped his wrist. "You must not open it, Mr. Knight."

"All right." Knight leaned back in his chair. He grinned at Jane and sipped ginger beer. "What's the payoff on the gag?"

"I must have the book, Mr. Knight. I would like to walk out of this tavern with the almanac under my arm."

"You would, eh?"

"I would."

"The 1990 almanac?"

"Yes."

"If," said Knight, "there was such a thing as a 1990 almanac, and if it was in that package, wild horses couldn't get it away from me."

"Why, Mr. Knight?"

"Don't be an idiot. A look into the future? Stock market reports . . . Horse races . . . Politics. It'd be money from home. I'd be rich."

"Indeed yes." Boyne nodded sharply. "More than rich. Omnipotent. The small mind would use the almanac from the future for small things only. Wagers on the outcome of games and elections. And so on. But the intellect of dimensions . . . *your* intellect . . . would not stop there."

"You tell me," Knight grinned.

"Deduction. Induction. Inference." Boyne ticked the points off on his fingers. "Each fact would tell you an entire history. Real estate investment, for example. What lands to buy and sell. Population shifts and census reports would tell you. Transportation. Lists of marine disasters and railroad wrecks would tell you whether rocket travel has replaced the train and ship."

"Has it?" Knight chuckled.

"Flight records would tell you which company's stock should be bought. Lists of postal receipts would indicate the cities of the future. The Nobel Prize winners would tell you which scientists and what new inventions to watch. Armament budgets would tell you what factories and industries to control. Cost-of-living reports would tell you how best to protect your wealth against inflation and deflation. Foreign exchange rates, stock exchange reports, bank suspensions, and life insurance indexes would provide the clues to protect you against any and all disasters."

"That's the idea," Knight said. "That's for me."

"You really think so?"

"I know so. Money in my pocket. That world in my pocket."

"Excuse me," Boyne said keenly, "but you are only repeating the dreams of childhood. You want wealth. Yes. But only won through endeavor . . . your own endeavor. There is no joy in success as an unearned gift. There is nothing but guilt and unhappiness. You are aware of this already."

"I disagree," Knight said.

"Do you? Then why do you work? Why not steal? Rob? Burgle? Cheat others of their money to fill your own pockets?"

"But I—" Knight began, and then stopped.

"The point is well taken, eh?" Boyne waved his hand impatiently. "No, Mr. Knight. Seek a mature argument. You are too ambitious and healthy to wish to steal success."

"Then I'd just want to know if I would be successful."

"Ah? Stet. You wish to thumb through the pages looking for your name. You want reassurance. Why? Have you no confidence in yourself? You are a promising young attorney. Yes, I know that. It is part of my data. Has not Miss Clinton confidence in you?"

"Yes," Jane said in a loud voice. "He doesn't need reassurance from a book."

"What else, Mr. Knight?"

Knight hesitated, sobering in the face of Boyne's overwhelming intensity. Then he said: "Security."

"There is no such thing. Life is danger. You can only find security in death."

"You know what I mean," Knight muttered. "The knowledge that life is worth planning. There's the atom bomb."

Boyne nodded quickly. "True. It is a crisis. But then, I'm here. The world will continue. I am proof."

"If I believe you."

"And if you do not?" Boyne blazed. "You do not lack security. You lack courage." He nailed the couple with a contemptuous glare. "There is in this country a legend of pioneer forefathers from whom you are supposed to inherit courage in the face of odds. D. Boone, E. Allen, S. Houston, A. Lincoln, G. Washington and others. Fact?"

"I suppose so," Knight muttered. "That's what we keep telling ourselves."

"And where is the courage in you? Pfui! It is only talk. The unknown terrifies you. Danger does not inspire you to fight, as it did D. Crockett; it makes you whine and reach for the reassurance in this book. Fact?"

"But the atom bomb . . ."

"It is a danger. Yes. One of many. What of that? Do you cheat at solhand?"

"Solhand?"

"Your pardon." Boyne reconsidered, impatiently snapping his fingers at the interruption to the white heat of his argument. "It is a game played singly against chance relationships in an arrangement of cards. I forget your noun. . . ."

"Oh!" Jane's face brightened. "Solitaire."

"Quite right. Solitaire. Thank you, Miss Clinton." Boyne turned his frightening eyes on Knight. "Do you cheat at solitaire?"

"Occasionally."

"Do you enjoy games won by cheating?"

"Not as a rule."

"They are thisney, yes? Boring. They are tiresome. Pointless. Null-coordinated. You wish you had won honestly."

"I suppose so."

"And you will suppose so after you have looked at this bound book. Through all your pointless life you will wish you had played honestly the game of life. You will verdash that look. You will regret. You will totally recall the pronouncement of our great poet-philosopher Trynbyll who summed it up in one lightning, skazon line. *'The Future is Tekon,'* said Trynbyll. Mr. Knight, do not cheat. Let me implore you to give me the almanac."

"Why don't you take it away from me?"

"It must be a gift. We can rob you of nothing. We can give you nothing."

"That's a lie. You paid Macy to rent this back room."

"Macy was paid, but I gave him nothing. He will think he was cheated, but you will see to it that he is not. All will be adjusted without dislocation."

"Wait a minute. . . ."

"It has all been carefully planned. I have gambled on you, Mr. Knight. I am depending on your good sense. Let me have the almanac. I will disband . . . reorient . . . and you will never see me again. Vorloss verdash! It will be a bar adventure to narrate for friends. Give me the almanac!"

"Hold the phone," Knight said. "This is a gag. Remember? I—"

"Is it?" Boyne interrupted. "Is it? Look at me."

For almost a minute the young couple stared at the bleached white face with its deadly eyes. The half-smile left Knight's lips, and Jane shuddered involuntarily. There was chill and dismay in the back room.

"My God!" Knight glanced helplessly at Jane. "This can't be happening. He's got me believing. You?"

Jane nodded jerkily.

"What should we do? If everything he says is true we can refuse and live happily ever after."

"No," Jane said in a choked voice. "There may be money and success in that book, but there's divorce and death, too. Give him the almanac."

"Take it," Knight said faintly.

Boyne rose instantly. He picked up the package and went into the phone booth. When he came out he had three books in one hand and a smaller parcel made up of the original wrapping in the other. He placed the books on the table and stood for a moment, holding the parcel and smiling down.

"My gratitude," he said. "You have eased a precarious situation.

It is only fair you should receive something in return. We are forbid-den to transfer anything that might divert existing phenomena streams, but at least I can give you one token of the future."

He backed away, bowed curiously, and said: "My service to you both." Then he turned and started out of the tavern.

"Hey!" Knight called. "The token?"

"Mr. Macy has it," Boyne answered and was gone.

The couple sat at the table for a few blank moments like sleepers slowly awakening. Then, as reality began to return, they stared at each other and burst into laughter.

"He really had me scared," Jane said.

"Talk about Third Avenue characters. What an act. What'd he get out of it?"

"Well . . . he got your almanac."

"But it doesn't make sense." Knight began to laugh again. "All that business about paying Macy but not giving him anything. And I'm supposed to see that he isn't cheated. And the mystery token of the future . . ."

The tavern door burst open and Macy shot through the saloon into the back room. "Where is he?" Macy shouted. "Where's the thief? Boyne, he calls himself. More likely his name is Dillinger."

"Why, Mr. Macy!" Jane exclaimed. "What's the matter?"

"Where is he?" Macy pounded on the door of the men's room. "Come out, ye blaggard!"

"He's gone," Knight said. "He left just before you got back."

"And you, Mr. Knight!" Macy pointed a trembling finger at the young lawyer. "You, to be party to thievery and racketeers. Shame on you!"

"What's wrong?" Knight asked.

"He paid me one hundred dollars to rent this back room," Macy cried in anguish. "One hundred dollars. I took the bill over to Bernie the pawnbroker, being cautious-like, and he found out it's a forgery. It's a counterfeit."

"Oh, no," Jane laughed. "That's too much. Counterfeit?"

"Look at this," Mr. Macy shouted, slamming the bill down on the table.

Knight inspected it closely. Suddenly he turned pale and the laughter drained out of his face. He reached into his inside pocket, withdrew a checkbook and began to write with trembling fingers.

"What on earth are you doing?" Jane asked.

"Making sure that Macy isn't cheated," Knight said. "You'll get your hundred dollars, Mr. Macy."

"Oliver! Are you insane? Throwing away a hundred dollars . . ."

"And I won't be losing anything, either," Knight answered. "All will be adjusted without dislocation! They're diabolical. Diabolical!"

"I don't understand."

"Look at the bill," Knight said in a shaky voice. "Look closely."

It was beautifully engraved and genuine in appearance. Benjamin Franklin's benign features gazed up at them mildly and authentically; but in the lower right-hand corner was printed: Series 1980 D. And underneath that was signed: Oliver Wilson Knight, Secretary of the Treasury.

TIME IS THE TRAITOR

Y ou can't go back and you can't catch up. Happy endings are always bittersweet.

There was a man named John Strapp: the most valuable, the most powerful, the most legendary man in a world containing seven hundred planets and seventeen hundred billion people. He was prized for one quality alone. He could make Decisions. Note the capital D. He was one of the few men who could make Major Decisions in a world of incredible complexity, and his Decisions were 87 percent correct. He sold his Decisions for high prices.

There would be an industry named, say, Bruxton Biotics, with plants on Deneb Alpha, Mizar III, Terra, and main offices on Alcor IV.

Bruxton's gross income was Cr. 270 billions. The involutions of Bruxton's trade relations with consumers and competitors required the specialized services of two hundred company economists, each an expert on one tiny facet of the vast overall picture. No one was big enough to coordinate the entire picture.

Bruxton would need a Major Decision on policy. A research expert named E. T. A. Goland in the Deneb laboratories had discovered a new catalyst for biotic synthesis. It was an embryological hormone that rendered nucleonic molecules as plastic as clay. The clay could be modeled and developed in any direction. Query: Should Bruxton abandon the old culture methods and retool for this new technique? The Decision involved an intricate ramification of interreacting factors: cost, saving, time, supply, demand, training, patents, patent legislation, court actions and so on. There was only one answer: Ask Strapp.

The initial negotiations were crisp. Strapp Associates replied that John Strapp's fee was Cr. 100,000 plus 1 percent of the voting stock of Bruxton Biotics. Take it or leave it. Bruxton Biotics took it with pleasure.

The second step was more complicated. John Strapp was very much in demand. He was scheduled for Decisions at the rate of two a week straight through the first of the year. Could Bruxton wait that long for an appointment? Bruxton could not. Bruxton was TT'd a list of John Strapp's future appointments and told to arrange a swap with any of the clients as best he could. Bruxton bargained, bribed, blackmailed and arranged a trade. John Strapp was to appear at the Alcor central plant on Monday, June 29, at noon precisely.

Then the mystery began. At nine o'clock that Monday morning, Aldous Fisher, the acidulous liaison man for Strapp, appeared at Bruxton's offices. After a brief conference with Old Man Bruxton himself, the following announcement was broadcast through the plant: ATTENTION! ATTENTION! URGENT! URGENT! ALL MALE PERSONNEL NAMED KRUGER REPORT TO CENTRAL. REPEAT. ALL MALE PERSONNEL NAMED KRUGER REPORT TO CENTRAL. URGENT. REPEAT. URGENT!

Forty-seven men named Kruger reported to Central and were sent home with strict instructions to stay at home until further notice. The plant police organized a hasty winnowing and, goaded by the irascible Fisher, checked the identification cards of all employees they could reach. Nobody named Kruger should remain in the plant, but it was impossible to comb out 2,500 men in three hours. Fisher burned and fumed like nitric acid.

By eleven-thirty, Bruxton Biotics was running a fever. Why send home all the Krugers? What did it have to do with the legendary John Strapp? What kind of man was Strapp? What did he look like? How did he act? He earned Cr. 10 millions a year. He owned 1 percent of the world. He was so close to God in the minds of the personnel that they expected angels and golden trumpets and a giant bearded creature of infinite wisdom and compassion.

At eleven-forty Strapp's personal bodyguard arrived—a security squad of ten men in plainclothes who checked doors and halls and cul-de-sacs with icy efficiency. They gave orders. This had to be removed. That had to be locked. Such and such had to be done. It was done. No one argued with John Strapp. The security squad took up positions and waited. Bruxton Biotics held its breath.

Noon struck, and a silver mote appeared in the sky. It approached with a high whine and landed with agonizing speed and precision before the main gate. The door of the ship snapped open. Two burly men stepped out alertly, their eyes busy. The chief of the security squad made a sign. Out of the ship came two secretaries, brunette and redheaded, striking, chic, efficient. After them came a thin, fortyish clerk in a baggy suit with papers stuffed in his side pockets, wearing horn-rimmed spectacles and a harassed air. After him came a magnificent creature, tall, majestic, clean-shaven but of infinite wisdom and compassion.

The burly men closed in on the beautiful man and escorted him up the steps and through the main door. Bruxton Biotics sighed happily. John Strapp was no disappointment. He was indeed God, and it was a pleasure to have 1 percent of yourself owned by him. The visitors marched down the main hall to Old Man Bruxton's office and entered. Bruxton had waited for them, poised majestically behind his desk. Now he leaped to his feet and ran forward. He grasped the magnificent man's hand fervently and exclaimed, "Mr. Strapp, sir, on behalf of my entire organization, I welcome you."

The clerk closed the door and said, "I'm Strapp." He nodded to his decoy, who sat down quietly in a corner. "Where's your data?"

Old Man Bruxton pointed faintly to his desk. Strapp sat down behind it, picked up the fat folders and began to read. A thin man. A harassed man. A fortyish man. Straight black hair. China-blue eyes. A good mouth. Good bones under the skin. One quality stood out— a complete lack of self-consciousness. But when he spoke there was a hysterical undercurrent in his voice that showed something violent and possessed deep inside him.

After two hours of breakneck reading and muttered comments to his secretaries, who made cryptic notes in Whitehead symbols, Strapp said, "I want to see the plant."

"Why?" Bruxton asked.

"To feel it," Strapp answered. "There's always the nuance involved in a Decision. It's the most important factor."

They left the office and the parade began: the security squad, the burly men, the secretaries, the clerk, the acidulous Fisher, and the magnificent decoy. They marched everywhere. They saw everything. The "clerk" did most of the legwork for "Strapp." He spoke to workers, foremen, technicians, high, low, and middle brass. He asked names, gossiped, introduced them to the great man, talked about their families, working conditions, ambitions. He explored, smelled and felt. After four exhausting hours they returned to Bruxton's office. The "clerk" closed the door. The decoy stepped aside.

"Well?" Bruxton asked. "Yes or No?"

"Wait," Strapp said.

He glanced through his secretary's notes, absorbed them, closed his eyes and stood still and silent in the middle of the office like a man straining to hear a distant whisper.

"Yes," he Decided, and was Cr. 100,000 and 1 percent of the voting stock of Bruxton Biotics richer. In return, Bruxton had an 87 percent assurance that the Decision was correct. Strapp opened the door again, the parade reassembled and marched out of the plant. Personnel grabbed its last chance to take photos and touch the great man. The clerk helped promote public relations with eager affability. He asked names, introduced, and amused. The sound of voices and laughter increased as they reached the ship. Then the incredible happened.

"You!" the clerk cried suddenly. His voice screeched horribly. "You sonofabitch! You goddamned lousy murdering bastard! I've been waiting for this. I've waited ten years!" He pulled a flat gun from his inside pocket and shot a man through the forehead.

Time stood still. It took hours for the brains and blood to burst out of the back of the head and for the body to crumple. Then the Strapp staff leaped into action. They hurled the clerk into the ship. The secretaries followed, then the decoy. The two burly men leaped after them and slammed the door. The ship took off and disappeared with a fading whine. The ten men in the plainclothes quietly drifted off and vanished. Only Fisher, the Strapp liaison man, was left alongside the body in the center of the horrified crowd.

"Check his identification," Fisher snapped.

Someone pulled the dead man's wallet out and opened it.

"William F. Kruger, biomechanic."

"The damned fool!" Fisher said savagely. "We warned him. We warned all the Krugers. All right. Call the police."

That was John Strapp's sixth murder. It cost exactly Cr. 500,000 to fix. The other five had cost the same, and half the amount usually went to a man desperate enough to substitute for the killer and plead temporary insanity. The other half went to the heirs of the deceased. There were six of these substitutes languishing in various penitentiaries, serving from twenty to fifty years, their families Cr. 250,000 richer.

In their suite in the Alcor Splendide, the Strapp staff consulted gloomily.

"Six in six years," Aldous Fisher said bitterly. "We can't keep it quiet much longer. Sooner or later somebody's going to ask why John Strapp always hires crazy clerks."

"Then we fix him too," the redheaded secretary said. "Strapp can afford it."

"He can afford a murder a month," the magnificent decoy murmured.

"No." Fisher shook his head sharply. "You can fix so far and no further. You reach a saturation point. We've reached it now. What are we going to do?"

"What the hell's the matter with Strapp anyway?" one of the burly men inquired.

"Who knows?" Fisher exclaimed in exasperation. "He's got a Kruger fixation. He meets a man named Kruger—any man named Kruger. He screams. He curses. He murders. Don't ask me why. It's something buried in his past."

"Haven't you asked him?"

"How can I? It's like an epileptic fit. He never knows it happened."

"Take him to a pschoanalyst," the decoy suggested.

"Out of the question."

"Why?"

"You're new," Fisher said. "You don't understand."

"Make me understand."

"I'll make an analogy. Back in the nineteen hundreds, people played card games with fifty-two cards in the deck. Those were simple times. Today everything's more complex. We're playing with fifty-two hundred in the deck. Understand?"

"I'll go along with it."

"A mind can figure fifty-two cards. It can make decisions on that total. They had it easy in the nineteen hundreds. But no mind is big enough to figure fifty-two hundred—no mind except Strapp's."

"We've got computers."

"And they're perfect when only cards are involved. But when you have to figure fifty-two hundred cardplayers, too, their likes, dislikes, motives, inclinations, prospects, tendencies and so on—what Strapp calls the nuances—then Strapp can do what a machine can't do. He's unique, and we might destroy his uniqueness with psychoanalysis."

"Why?"

"Because it's an unconscious process in Strapp," Fisher explained irritably. "He doesn't know how he does it. If he did he'd be one hundred percent right instead of eighty-seven percent. It's an unconscious process, and for all we know it may be linked up with the same abnormality that makes him murder Krugers. If we get rid of one, we may destroy the other. We can't take the chance."

"Then what do we do?"

"Protect our property," Fisher said, looking around ominously. "Never forget that for a minute. We've put in too much work on Strapp to let it be destroyed. We protect our property!"

"I think he needs a friend," the brunette said.

"Why?"

"We could find out what's bothering him without destroying anything. People talk to their friends. Strapp might talk."

"We're his friends."

"No, we're not. We're his associates."

"Has he talked with you?"

"No."

"You?" Fisher shot at the redhead.

She shook her head.

"He's looking for something he never finds."

"What?"

"A woman, I think. A special kind of woman."

"A woman named Kruger?"

"I don't know."

"Damn it, it doesn't make sense." Fisher thought a moment. "All right. We'll have to hire him a friend, and we'll have to ease off the schedule to give the friend a chance to make Strapp talk. From now on we cut the program to one Decision a week."

"My God!" the brunette exclaimed. "That's cutting five million a year."

"It's got to be done," Fisher said grimly. "It's cut now or take a total loss later. We're rich enough to stand it."

"What are you going to do for a friend?" the decoy asked.

"I said we'd hire one. We'll hire the best. Get Terra on the TT. Tell them to locate Frank Alceste and put him through urgent."

"Frankie!" the redhead squealed. "I swoon."

"Ooh! Frankie!" The brunette fanned herself.

"You mean Fatal Frank Alceste? The heavyweight champ?" the burly man asked in awe. "I saw him fight Lonzo Jordan. Oh, man!"

"He's an actor now," the decoy explained. "I worked with him once. He sings. He dances. He—"

"And he's twice as fatal," Fisher interrupted. "We'll hire him. Make out a contract. He'll be Strapp's friend. As soon as Strapp meets him, he'll—"

"Meets who?" Strapp appeared in the doorway of his bedroom, yawning, blinking in the light. He always slept deeply after his attacks. "Who am I going to meet?" He looked around, thin, graceful, but harassed and indubitably possessed.

"A man named Frank Alceste," Fisher said. "He badgered us for an introduction, and we can't hold him off any longer."

"Frank Alceste?" Strapp murmured. "Never heard of him."

Strapp could make Decisions; Alceste could make friends. He was a powerful man in his middle thirties, sandy-haired, freckle-faced, with a broken nose and deep-set grey eyes. His voice was high and soft. He moved with the athlete's lazy poise that is almost feminine. He charmed you without knowing how he did it, or even wanting to do it. He charmed Strapp, but Strapp also charmed him. They became friends.

"No, it really is friends," Alceste told Fisher when he returned the check that had been paid him. "I don't need the money, and old Johnny needs me. Forget you hired me original-like. Tear up the contract. I'll try to straighten Johnny out on my own."

Alceste turned to leave the suite in the Rigel Splendide and passed the great-eyed secretaries. "If I wasn't so busy, ladies," he murmured, "I'd sure like to chase you a little."

"Chase me, Frankie," the brunette blurted.

The redhead looked caught.

And as Strapp Associates zigzagged in slow tempo from city to city and planet to planet, making the one Decision a week, Alceste and Strapp enjoyed themselves while the magnificent decoy gave interviews and posed for pictures. There were interruptions when Frankie had to return to Terra to make a picture, but in between they golfed, tennised, brubaged, bet on horses, dogs, and dowlens, and went to fights and routs. They hit the night spots and Alceste came back with a curious report.

"Me, I don't know how close you folks been watching Johnny," he told Fisher, "but if you think he's been sleeping every night, safe in his little trundle, you better switch notions."

"How's that?" Fisher asked in surprise.

"Old Johnny, he's been sneaking out nights all along when you folks thought he was getting his brain rest."

"How do you know?"

"By his reputation," Alceste told him sadly. "They know him everywhere. They know old Johnny in every bistro from here to Orion. And they know him the worst way."

"By name?"

"By nickname. Wasteland, they call him."

"Wasteland!"

"Uh-huh. Mr. Devastation. He runs through women like a prairie fire. You don't know this?"

Fisher shook his head.

"Must pay off out of his personal pocket," Alceste mused and departed.

There was a terrifying quality to the possessed way that Strapp ran through women. He would enter a club with Alceste, take a table, sit down and drink. Then he would stand up and coolly survey the room, table by table, woman by woman. Upon occasion men would become angered and offer to fight. Strapp disposed of them coldly and viciously, in a manner that excited Alceste's professional admiration. Frankie never fought himself. No professional ever touches an amateur. But he tried to keep the peace, and failing that, at least kept the ring.

After the survey of the women guests, Strapp would sit down and wait for the show, relaxed, chatting, laughing. When the girls appeared, his grim possession would take over again and he would examine the line carefully and dispassionately. Very rarely he would discover a girl that interested him; always the identical type—a girl with jet hair, inky eyes, and clear, silken skin. Then the trouble began.

If it was an entertainer, Strapp went backstage after the show. He bribed, fought, blustered, and forced his way into her dressing room. He would confront the astonished girl, examine her in silence, then ask her to speak. He would listen to her voice, then close in like a tiger and make a violent and unexpected pass. Sometimes there would be shrieks, sometimes a spirited defense, sometimes compliance. At no time was Strapp satisfied. He would abandon the girl abruptly, pay off all complaints and damages like a gentleman, and leave to repeat the performance in club after club until curfew.

If it was one of the guests, Strapp immediately cut in, disposed of her escort, or if that was impossible, followed the girl home and there repeated the dressing-room attack. Again he would abandon the girl, pay like a gentleman and leave to continue his possessed search.

"Me, I been around, but I'm scared by it," Alceste told Fisher. "I never such saw a hasty man. He could have most any woman agreeable if he'd slow down a little. But he can't. He's driven."

"By what?"

"I don't know. It's like he's working against time."

After Strapp and Alceste became intimate, Strapp permitted him to come along on a daytime quest that was even stranger. As Strapp Associates continued its round through the planets and industries, Strapp visited the Bureau of Vital Statistics in each city.

There he bribed the chief clerk and presented a slip of paper. On it was written:

Height	5'6"
Weight	110
Hair	Black
Eyes	Black
Bust	34
Waist	26
Hips	36
Size	12

"I want the name and address of every girl over twenty-one who fits this description," Strapp would say. "I'll pay ten credits a name."

Twenty-four hours later would come the list, and off Strapp would chase on a possessed search, examining, talking, listening, sometimes making the terrifying pass, always paying off like a gentleman. The procession of tall, jet-haired, inky-eyed, busty girls made Alceste dizzy.

"He's got an idee fix," Alceste told Fisher in the Cygnus Splendide, "and I got it figured this much. He's looking for a special particular girl and nobody comes up to specifications."

"A girl named Kruger?"

"I don't know if the Kruger business comes into it."

"Is he hard to please?"

"Well, I'll tell you. Some of those girls—me, I'd call them sensational. But he don't pay any mind to them. Just looks and moves on. Others—dogs, practically—he jumps like old Wasteland."

"What is it?"

"I think it's a kind of test. Something to make the girls react hard and natural. It ain't that kind of passion with old Wasteland. It's a cold-blooded trick so he can watch 'em in action."

"But what's he looking for?"

"I don't know yet," Alceste said, "but I'm going to find out. I got a little trick figured. It's taking a chance, but Johnny's worth it."

It happened in the arena where Strapp and Alceste went to watch a pair of gorillas tear each other to pieces inside a glass cage. It was a bloody affair, and both men agreed that gorilla-fighting was no more civilized than cockfighting and left in disgust. Outside, in the empty concrete corridor, a shriveled man loitered. When Alceste signaled to him, he ran up to them like an autograph hound.

"Frankie!" the shriveled man shouted. "Good old Frankie! Don't you remember me?"

Alceste stared.

"I'm Blooper Davis. We was raised together in the old precinct. Don't you remember Blooper Davis?"

"Blooper!" Alceste's face lit up. "Sure enough. But it was Blooper Davidoff then."

"Sure." The shriveled man laughed. "And it was Frankie Kruger then."

"Kruger!" Strapp cried in a thin, screeching voice.

"That's right," Frankie said. "Kruger. I changed my name when I went into the fight game." He motioned sharply to the shriveled man, who backed against the corridor wall and slid away.

"You sonofabitch!" Strapp cried. His face was white and twitched hideously. "You goddamned lousy murdering bastard! I've been waiting for this. I've waited ten years."

He whipped a flat gun from his inside pocket and fired. Alceste sidestepped barely in time and the slug ricocheted down the corridor with a high whine. Strapp fired again, and the flame seared Alceste's cheek. He closed in, caught Strapp's wrist and paralyzed it with his powerful grip. He pointed the gun away and clinched. Strapp's breath was hissing. His eyes rolled. Overhead sounded the wild roars of the crowd.

"All right, I'm Kruger," Alceste grunted. "Kruger's the name, Mr. Strapp. So what? What are you going to do about it?"

"Sonofabitch!" Strapp screamed, struggling like one of the gorillas. "Killer! Murderer! I'll rip your guts out!"

"Why me? Why Kruger?" Exerting all his strength, Alceste dragged Strapp to a niche and slammed him into it. He caged him with his huge frame. "What did I ever do to you ten years ago?"

He got the story in hysterical animal outbursts before Strapp fainted.

After he put Strapp to bed, Alceste went out into the lush living room of the suite in the Indi Splendide and explained to the staff.

"Old Johnny was in love with a girl named Sima Morgan," he

began. "She was in love with him. It was big romantic stuff. They were going to be married. Then Sima Morgan got killed by a guy named Kruger."

"Kruger! So that's the connection. How?"

"This Kruger was a drunken no-good. Society. He had a bad driving record. They took his license away from him, but that didn't make any difference to Kruger's kind of money. He bribed a dealer and bought a hot-rod jet without a license. One day he buzzed a school for the hell of it. He smashed the roof in and killed thirteen children and their teacher. . . . This was on Terra in Berlin.

"They never got Kruger. He started planet-hopping and he's still on the lam. The family sends him money. The police can't find him. Strapp's looking for him because the schoolteacher was his girl, Sima Morgan."

There was a pause, then Fisher asked, "How long ago was this?"

"Near as I can figure, ten years eight months."

Fisher calculated intently. "And ten years three months ago, Strapp first showed he could make decisions. The Big Decisions. Up to then he was nobody. Then came the tragedy, and with it the hysteria and the ability. Don't tell me one didn't produce the other."

"Nobody's telling you anything."

"So he kills Kruger over and over again," Fisher said coldly. "Right. Revenge fixation. But what about the girls and the Wasteland business?"

Alceste smiled sadly. "You ever hear the expression 'One girl in a million'?"

"Who hasn't?"

"If your girl was one in a million, that means there ought to be nine more like her in a city of ten million, yes?"

The Strapp staff nodded, wondering.

"Old Johnny's working on that idea. He thinks he can find Sima Morgan's duplicate."

"How?"

"He's worked it out arithmetic-wise. He's thinking like so: There's one chance in sixty-four billion of fingerprints matching. But today there's seventeen hundred billion people. That means there can be twenty-six with one matching print, and maybe more."

"Not necessarily."

"Sure, not necessarily, but there's the chance and that's all old Johnny wants. He figures if there's twenty-six chances of one print matching, there's an outside chance of one person matching. He thinks he can find Sima Morgan's duplicate if he just keeps on looking hard enough."

"That's outlandish!"

"I didn't say it wasn't, but it's the only thing that keeps him going. It's a kind of life preserver made out of numbers. It keeps his head above water—the crazy notion that sooner or later he can pick up where death left him off ten years ago."

"Ridiculous!" Fisher snapped.

"Not to Johnny. He's still in love."

"Impossible."

"I wish you could feel it like I feel it," Alceste answered. "He's looking . . . looking. He meets girl after girl. He hopes. He talks. He makes the pass. If it's Sima's duplicate, he knows she'll respond just the way he remembers Sima responding ten years ago. 'Are you Sima?' he asks himself. 'No,' he says and moves on. It hurts, thinking about a lost guy like that. We ought to do something for him."

"No," Fisher said.

"We ought to help him find his duplicate. We ought to coax him into believing some girl's the duplicate. We ought to make him fall in love again."

"No," Fisher repeated emphatically.

"Why no?"

"Because the moment Strapp finds his girl, he heals himself. He stops being the great John Strapp, the Decider. He turns back into a nobody—a man in love."

"What's he care about being great? He wants to be happy."

"Everybody wants to be happy," Fisher snarled. "Nobody is. Strapp's no worse off than any other man, but he's a lot richer. We maintain the *status quo*."

"Don't you mean *you're* a lot richer?"

"We maintain the *status quo*," Fisher repeated. He eyed Alceste coldly. "I think we'd better terminate the contract. We have no further use for your services."

"Mister, we terminated when I handed back the check. You're talking to Johnny's friend now."

"I'm sorry, Mr. Alceste, but Strapp won't have much time for his friends from now on. I'll let you know when he'll be free next year."

"You'll never pull it off. I'll see Johnny when and where I please."

"Do you want him for a friend?" Fisher smiled unpleasantly. "Then you'll see him when and where I please. Either you see him on those terms or Strapp sees the contract we gave you. I still have it in the files, Mr. Alceste. I did not tear it up. I never part with anything. How long do you imagine Strapp will believe in your friendship after he sees the contract you signed?"

Alceste clenched his fists. Fisher held his ground. For a moment they glared at each other, then Frankie turned away.

"Poor Johnny," he muttered. "It's like a man being run by his tapeworm. I'll say so long to him. Let me know when you're ready for me to see him again."

He went into the bedroom, where Strapp was just awakening from his attack without the faintest memory, as usual. Alceste sat down on the edge of the bed.

"Hey, old Johnny." He grinned.

"Hey, Frankie." Strapp smiled.

They punched each other solemnly, which is the only way that men friends can embrace and kiss.

"What happened after that gorilla fight?" Strapp asked. "I got fuzzy."

"Man, you got plastered. I never saw a guy take on such a load." Alceste punched Strapp again. "Listen, old Johnny. I got to get back to work. I got a three-picture-a-year contract, and they're howling."

"Why, you took a month off six planets back," Strapp said in disappointment. "I thought you caught up."

"Nope. I'll be pulling out today, Johnny. Be seeing you real soon."

"Listen," Strapp said. "To hell with the pictures. Be my partner. I'll tell Fisher to draw up an agreement." He blew his nose. "This is the first time I've had laughs in—in a long time."

"Maybe later, Johnny. Right now I'm stuck with a contract. Soon as I can get back, I'll come a-running. Cheers."

"Cheers," Strapp said wistfully.

Outside the bedroom, Fisher was waiting like a watchdog. Alceste looked at him with disgust.

"One thing you learn in the fight game," he said slowly. "It's never won till the last round. I give you this one, but it isn't the last."

As he left, Alceste said, half to himself, half aloud, "I want him to be happy. I want every man to be happy. Seems like every man could be happy if we'd all just lend a hand."

Which is why Frankie Alceste couldn't help making friends.

So the Strapp staff settled back into the same old watchful vigilance of the murdering years, and stepped up Strapp's Decision appointments to two a week. They knew why Strapp had to be watched. They knew why the Krugers had to be protected. But that was the only difference. Their man was miserable, hysteric, almost psychotic; it made no difference. That was a fair price to pay for 1 percent of the world.

But Frankie Alceste kept his own counsel, and visited the Deneb laboratories of Bruxton Biotics. There he consulted with one E. T. A. Goland, the research genius who had discovered that novel technique for molding life which first brought Strapp to Bruxton, and was indirectly responsible for his friendship with Alceste. Ernst Theodor Amadeus Goland was short, fat, asthmatic and enthusiastic.

"But yes, yes," he sputtered when the layman had finally made himself clear to the scientists. "Yes, indeed! A most ingenious notion. Why it never occurred to me, I cannot think. It could be accomplished without any difficulty whatsoever." He considered. "Except money," he added.

"You could duplicate the girl that died ten years ago?" Alceste asked.

"Without any difficulty, except money." Goland nodded emphatically.

"She'd look the same? Act the same? Be the same?"

"Up to ninety-five percent, plus or minus point nine seven five."

"Would that make any difference? I mean, ninety-five percent of a person as against one hundred percent."

"Ach! No. It is a most remarkable individual who is aware of more than eighty percent of the total characteristics of another person. Above ninety percent is unheard of."

"How would you go about it?"

"Ach? So. Empirically we have two sources. One: complete psychological pattern of the subject in the Centaurus Master Files. They will TT a transcript upon application and payment of one hundred credits through formal channels. I will apply."

"And I'll pay. Two?"

"Two: the embalmment process of modern times, which—She is buried, yes?"

"Yes."

"Which is ninety-eight percent perfect. From remains and psychological pattern we re-clone body and psyche by the equation sigma equals the square root of minus two over— We do it without any difficulty, except money."

"Me, I've got the money," Frankie Alceste said. "You do the rest."

For the sake of his friend, Alceste paid Cr. 100 and expedited the formal application to the Master Files on Centaurus for the transcript of the complete psychological pattern of Sima Morgan, deceased. After it arrived, Alceste returned to Terra and a city called Berlin, where he blackmailed a gimpster named Augenblick into turning grave robber. Augenblick visited the *Staats-Gottesacker* and removed the porcelain coffin from under the marble headstone that read SIMA MORGAN. It contained what appeared to be a black-haired, silken-skinned girl in deep sleep. By devious routes, Alceste got the porcelain coffin through four customs barriers to Deneb.

One aspect of the trip of which Alceste was not aware, but which bewildered various police organizations, was the series of catastrophes that pursued him and never quite caught up. There was the jetliner explosion that destroyed the ship and an acre of docks half an hour after passengers and freight were discharged. There was a hotel holocaust ten minutes after Alceste checked out. There was the shuttle disaster that extinguished the pneumatic train for which Alceste had unexpectedly canceled passage. Despite all this he was able to present the coffin to biochemist Goland.

"Ach!" said Ernst Theodor Amadeus. "A beautiful creature. She is worth re-creating. The rest now is simple, except money."

For the sake of his friend, Alceste arranged a leave of absence for Goland, bought him a laboratory and financed an incredibly expensive series of experiments. For the sake of his friend, Alceste poured forth money and patience until at last, eight months later, there emerged from the opaque maturation chamber a black-haired, inky-eyed, silken-skinned creature with long legs and a high bust. She answered to the name of Sima Morgan.

"I heard the jet coming down toward the school," Sima said, unaware that she was speaking eleven years later. "Then I heard a crash. What happened?"

Alceste was jolted. Up to this moment she had been an objective . . . a goal . . . unreal, unalive. This was a living woman. There was a curious hesitation in her speech, almost a lisp. Her head had an engaging tilt when she spoke. She arose from the edge of the table, and she was not fluid or graceful as Alceste had expected she would be. She moved boyishly.

"I'm Frank Alceste," he said quietly. He took her shoulders. "I want you to look at me and make up your mind whether you can trust me."

Their eyes locked in a steady gaze. Sima examined him gravely. Again Alceste was jolted and moved. His hands began to tremble and he released the girl's shoulders in panic.

"Yes," Sima said. "I can trust you."

"No matter what I say, you must trust me. No matter what I tell you to do, you must trust me and do it."

"Why?"

"For the sake of Johnny Strapp."

Her eyes widened. "Something's happened to him," she said quickly. "What is it?"

"Not to him, Sima. To you. Be patient, honey. I'll explain. I had it in my mind to explain now, but I can't. I—I'd best wait until tomorrow."

They put her to bed and Alceste went out for a wrestling match with himself. The Deneb nights are soft and black as velvet, thick and sweet with romance—or so it seemed to Frankie Alceste that night.

"You can't be falling in love with her," he muttered. "It's crazy."

And later, "You saw hundreds like her when Johnny was hunting. Why didn't you fall for one of them?"

And last of all, "What are you going to do?"

He did the only thing an honorable man can do in a situation like that, and tried to turn his desire into friendship. He came into Sima's room the next morning, wearing tattered old jeans, needing a shave, with his hair standing on end. He hoisted himself up on the foot of her bed, and while she ate the first of the careful meals

Goland had prescribed, Frankie chewed on a cigarette and explained to her. When she wept, he did not take her in his arms to console her, but thumped her on the back like a brother.

He ordered a dress for her. He had ordered the wrong size, and when she showed herself to him in it, she looked so adorable that he wanted to kiss her. Instead he punched her, very gently and very solemnly, and took her out to buy a wardrobe. When she showed herself to him in proper clothes, she looked so enchanting that he had to punch her again. Then they went to a ticket office and booked immediate passage for Ross-Alpha III.

Alceste had intended delaying a few days to rest the girl, but he was compelled to rush for fear of himself. It was this alone that saved both from the explosion that destroyed the private home and private laboratory of biochemist Goland, and destroyed the biochemist too. Alceste never knew this. He was already on board ship with Sima, frantically fighting temptation.

One of the things that everybody knows about space travel but never mentions is its aphrodisiac quality. Like the ancient days when travelers crossed oceans on ships, the passengers are isolated in their own tiny world for a week. They're cut off from reality. A magic mood of freedom from ties and responsibilities pervades the jetliner. Everyone has a fling. There are thousands of jet romances every week—quick, passionate affairs that are enjoyed in complete safety and ended on landing day.

In this atmosphere, Frankie Alceste maintained a rigid self-control. He was not aided by the fact that he was a celebrity with a tremendous animal magnetism. While a dozen handsome women threw themselves at him, he persevered in the role of big brother and thumped and punched Sima until she protested.

"I know you're a wonderful friend to Johnny and me," she said on the last night out. "But you are exhausting, Frankie. I'm covered with bruises."

"Yeah. I know. It's habit. Some people, like Johnny, they think with their brains. Me, I think with my fists."

They were standing before the starboard crystal, bathed in the soft light of the approaching Ross-Alpha, and there is nothing more damnably romantic than the velvet of space illuminated by the white-violet of a distant sun. Sima tilted her head and looked at him.

"I was talking to some of the passengers," she said. "You're famous, aren't you?"

"More notorious-like."

"There's so much to catch up on. But I must catch up on you first."

"Me?"

Sima nodded. "It's all been so sudden. I've been bewildered—and so exited that I haven't had a chance to thank you, Frankie. I do thank you. I'm beholden to you forever."

She put her arms around his neck and kissed him with parted lips. Alceste began to shake.

"No," he thought. "No. She doesn't know what she's doing. She's so crazy happy at the idea of being with Johnny again that she doesn't realize . . ."

He reached behind him until he felt the icy surface of the crystal, which passengers are strictly enjoined from touching. Before he could give way, he deliberately pressed the backs of his hands against the subzero surface. The pain made him start. Sima released him in surprise and when he pulled his hands away, he left six square inches of skin and blood behind.

So he landed on Ross-Alpha III with one girl in good condition and two hands in bad shape and he was met by the acid-faced Aldous Fisher, accompanied by an official who requested Mr. Alceste to step into an office for a very serious private talk.

"It has been brought to our attention by Mr. Fisher," the official said, "that you are attempting to bring in a young woman of illegal status."

"How would Mr. Fisher know?" Alceste asked.

"You fool!" Fisher spat. "Did you think I would let it go at that? You were followed. Every minute."

"Mr. Fisher informs us," the official continued austerely, "that the woman with you is traveling under an assumed name. Her papers are fraudulent."

"How fraudulent?" Alceste said. "She's Sima Morgan. Her papers say she's Sima Morgan."

"Sima Morgan died eleven years ago," Fisher answered. "The woman with you can't be Sima Morgan."

"And unless the question of her true identity is cleared up," the official said, "she will not be permitted entry."

"I'll have the documentation on Sima Morgan's death here within the week," Fisher added triumphantly.

Alceste looked at Fisher and shook his head wearily. "You don't know it, but you're making it easy for me," he said. "The one thing in the world I'd like to do is take her out of here and never let Johnny see her. I'm so crazy to keep her for myself that—" He stopped himself and touched the bandages on his hands. "Withdraw your charge, Fisher."

"No," Fisher snapped.

"You can't keep 'em apart. Not this way. Suppose she's interned? Who's the first man I subpoena to establish her identity? John Strapp. Who's the first man I call to come and see her? John Strapp. D'you think you could stop him?"

"That contract," Fisher began. "I'll—"

"To hell with the contract. Show it to him. He wants his girl, not me. Withdraw your charge, Fisher. And stop fighting. You've lost your meal ticket."

Fisher glared malevolently, then swallowed. "I withdraw the charge," he growled. Then he looked at Alceste with blood in his eyes. "It isn't the last round yet," he said and stamped out of the office.

Fisher was prepared. At a distance of light-years he might be too late with too little. Here on Ross-Alpha III he was protecting his property. He had all the power and money of John Strapp to call on. The floater that Frankie Alceste and Sima took from the spaceport was piloted by a Fisher aide who unlatched the cabin door and performed steep banks to tumble his fares out into the air. Alceste smashed the glass partition and hooked a meaty arm around the driver's throat until he righted the floater and brought them safely to earth. Alceste was pleased to note that Sima did not fuss more than was necessary.

On the road level they were picked up by one of a hundred cars that had been pacing the floater from below. At the first shot, Alceste clubbed Sima into a doorway and followed her at the expense of a burst shoulder, which he bound hastily with strips of Sima's lingerie. Her dark eyes were enormous, but she made no complaint. Alceste complimented her with mighty thumps and took her up to the roof and down into the adjoining building, where he broke into an apartment and telephoned for an ambulance.

When the ambulance arrived, Alceste and Sima descended to the street, where they were met by uniformed policemen who had official instructions to pick up a couple answering to their description. "Wanted for floater robbery with assault. Dangerous. Shoot to kill." The police Alceste disposed of, and also the ambulance driver and intern. He and Sima departed in the ambulance, Alceste driving like a fury, Sima operating the siren like a banshee.

They abandoned the ambulance in the downtown shopping district, entered a department store, and emerged forty minutes later as a young valet in uniform pushing an old man in a wheelchair. Outside the difficulty of the bust, Sima was boyish enough to pass as a valet. Frankie was weak enough from assorted injuries to simulate the old man.

They checked into the Ross Splendide, where Alceste barricaded Sima in a suite, had his shoulder attended to and bought a gun. Then he went looking for John Strapp. He found him in the Bureau of Vital Statistics, bribing the chief clerk and presenting him with a slip of paper that gave the same description of the long-lost love.

"Hey, old Johnny," Alceste said.

"Hey, Frankie!" Strapp cried in delight.

They punched each other affectionately. With a happy grin, Alceste watched Strapp explain and offer further bribes to the chief clerk for the names and addresses of all girls over twenty-one who fitted the description on the slip of paper. As they left, Alceste said, "I met a girl who might fit that, old Johnny."

That cold look came into Strapp's eyes. "Oh?" he said.

"She's got a kind of half lisp."

Strapp looked at Alceste strangely.

"And a funny way of tilting her head when she talks."

Strapp clutched Alceste's arm.

"Only trouble is, she isn't girlie-girlie like most. More like a fella. You know what I mean? Spunky-like."

"Show her to me, Frankie," Strapp said in a low voice.

They hopped a floater and were taxied to the Ross Splendide roof. They took the elevator down to the twentieth floor and walked to suite 20-M. Alceste code-knocked on the door. A girl's voice called, "Come in." Alceste shook Strapp's hand and said, "Cheers, Johnny." He unlocked the door, then walked down the hall to lean against the balcony balustrade. He drew his gun just in case Fisher might get around to last-ditch interruptions. Looking out across the glittering city, he reflected that every man could be happy if everybody would just lend a hand; but sometimes that hand was expensive.

John Strapp walked into the suite. He shut the door, turned and examined the jet-haired inky-eyed girl, coldly, intently. She stared at him in amazement. Strapp stepped closer, walked around her, faced her again.

"Say something," he said.

"You're not John Strapp?" she faltered.

"Yes."

"No!" she exclaimed. "No! My Johnny's young. My Johnny is—"

Strapp closed in like a tiger. His hands and lips savaged her while his eyes watched coldly and intently. The girl screamed and struggled, terrified by those strange eyes that were alien, by the harsh hands that were alien, by the alien compulsions of the creature who was once her Johnny Strapp but was now aching years of change apart from her.

"You're someone else!" she cried. "You're not Johnny Strapp. You're another man."

And Strapp, not so much eleven years older as eleven years other than the man whose memory he was fighting to fulfill, asked himself, "Are you my Sima? Are you my love—my lost, dead love?" And the change within him answered, "No, this isn't Sima. This isn't your love yet. Move on, Johnny. Move on and search. You'll find her someday—the girl you lost."

He paid like a gentleman and departed.

From the balcony, Alceste saw him leave. He was so astonished that he could not call to him. He went back to the suite and found Sima standing there, stunned, staring at a sheaf of money on a table. He realized what had happened at once. When Sima saw Alceste, she began to cry—not like a girl, but boyishly, with her fists clenched and her face screwed up.

"Frankie," she wept. "My God! Frankie!" She held out her arms to him in desperation. She was lost in a world that had passed her by.

He took a step, then hesitated. He made a last attempt to quench the love within him for this creature, searching for a way to bring her and Strapp together. Then he lost all control and took her in his arms.

"She doesn't know what she's doing," he thought. "She's so scared of being lost. She's not mine. Not yet. Maybe never."

And then, "Fisher's won, and I've lost."

And last of all, "We only remember the past; we never know it when we meet it. The mind goes back, but time goes on, and farewells should be forever."

THE MEN WHO MURDERED MOHAMMED

here was a man who mutilated history. He toppled empires and uprooted dynasties. Because of him, Mount Vernon should not be a national shrine, and Columbus, Ohio, should be called Cabot, Ohio. Because of him the name Marie Curie should be cursed in France, and no one should swear by the beard of the Prophet. Actually, these realities did not happen, because he was a mad professor; or, to put it another way, he only succeeded in making them unreal for himself.

Now, the patient reader is too familiar with the conventional mad professor, undersized and overbrowed, creating monsters in his laboratory which invariably turn on their maker and menace his lovely daughter. This story isn't about that sort of make-believe man. It's about Henry Hassel, a genuine mad professor in a class with such better-known men as Ludwig Boltzmann (*see* Ideal Gas Law), Jacques Charles, and André Marie Ampère (1775-1836).

Everyone ought to know that the electrical ampere was so named in honor of Ampère. Ludwig Boltzmann was a distinguished Austrian physicist, as famous for his research on black-body radiation as on Ideal Gases. You can look him up in Volume Three of the *Encyclopaedia Britannica*, BALT to BRAI. Jacques Alexandre César Charles was the first mathematician to become interested in flight, and he invented the hydrogen balloon. These were real men.

They were also real mad professors. Ampère, for example, was on his way to an important meeting of scientists in Paris. In his taxi he got a brilliant idea (of an electrical nature, I assume) and whipped out a pencil and jotted the equation on the wall of the hansom cab. Roughly, it was: $dH = ipdl/r^2$ in which p is the perpendicular distance from P to the line of the element dl; or $dH = i \sin \theta \, dl/r^2$. This is sometimes known as Laplace's Law, although he wasn't at the meeting.

Anyway, the cab arrived at the Académie. Ampère jumped out, paid the driver and rushed into the meeting to tell everybody about his idea. Then he realized he didn't have the note on him, remembered where he'd left it, and had to chase through the streets of Paris after the taxi to recover his runaway equation. Sometimes I imagine that's how Fermat lost his famous "Last Theorem," although Fermat wasn't at the meeting either, having died some two hundred years earlier.

Or take Boltzmann. Giving a course in Advanced Ideal Gases, he peppered his lectures with involved calculus, which he worked out quickly and casually in his head. He had that kind of head. His students had so much trouble trying to puzzle out the math by ear that they couldn't keep up with the lectures, and they begged Boltzmann to work out his equations on the blackboard.

Boltzmann apologized and promised to be more helpful in the future. At the next lecture he began, "Gentlemen, combining Boyle's Law with the Law of Charles, we arrive at the equation $pv = p_o v_o (1 + at)$. Now, obviously, if $_aS^b = f(x) \, dx\chi(a)$, then $pv = RT$ and $_vS f(x,y,z) \, dV = O$. It's as simple as two plus two equals four." At this point Boltzman remembered his promise. He turned to the blackboard, conscientiously chalked $2 + 2 = 4$, and then breezed on, casually doing the complicated calculus in his head.

Jacques Charles, the brilliant mathematician who discovered Charles's Law (sometimes known as Gay-Lussac's Law), which Boltzmann mentioned in his lecture, had a lunatic passion to become a famous paleographer—that is, a discoverer of ancient manuscripts. I think that being forced to share credit with Gay-Lussac may have unhinged him.

He paid a transparent swindler named Vrain-Lucas 200,000 francs for holograph letters purportedly written by Julius Caesar, Alexander the Great, and Pontius Pilate. Charles, a man who could see through any gas, ideal or not, actually believed in these forgeries despite the fact that the maladroit Vrain-Lucas had written them in modern French on modern notepaper bearing modern watermarks. Charles even tried to donate them to the Louvre.

Now, these men weren't idiots. They were geniuses who paid a high price for their genius because the rest of their thinking was other-world. A genius is someone who travels to truth by an unexpected path. Unfortunately, unexpected paths lead to disaster in everyday life. This is what happened to Henry Hassel, professor of Applied Compulsion at Unknown University in the year 1980.

Nobody knows where Unknown University is or what they teach there. It has a faculty of some two hundred eccentrics, and a student body of two thousand misfits—the kind that remain anonymous until they win Nobel prizes or become the First Man on Mars. You can always spot a graduate of U.U. when you ask people where they went to school. If you get an evasive reply like: "State," or "Oh, a freshwater school you never heard of," you can bet they went to Unknown. Someday I hope to tell you more about this university, which is a center of learning only in the Pickwickian sense.

Anyway, Henry Hassel started home from his office in the Psychotic Psenter early one afternoon, strolling through the Physical Culture arcade. It is not true that he did this to leer at the nude coeds practicing Arcane Eurythmics; rather, Hassel liked to admire the trophies displayed in the arcade in memory of great Unknown teams which had won the sort of championships that Unknown teams win—in sports like Strabismus, Occlusion, and Botulism. (Hassel had been Frambesia singles champion three years running.) He arrived home uplifted, and burst gaily into the house to discover his wife in the arms of a man.

There she was, a lovely woman of thirty-five, with smoky red hair and almond eyes, being heartily embraced by a person whose pockets were stuffed with pamphlets, microchemical apparatus, and a patella-reflex hammer—a typical campus character of U.U., in fact. The embrace was so concentrated that neither of the offending parties noticed Henry Hassel glaring at them from the hallway.

Now, remember Ampère and Charles and Boltzmann. Hassel weighed one hundred and ninety pounds. He was muscular and uninhibited. It would have been child's play for him to have dismembered his wife and her lover, and thus simply and directly achieve the goal he desired—the end of his wife's life. But Henry Hassel was in the genius class; his mind just didn't operate that way.

Hassel breathed hard, turned and lumbered into his private laboratory like a freight engine. He opened a drawer labeled DUODENUM and removed a .45-caliber revolver. He opened other drawers, more interestingly labeled, and assembled apparatus. In exactly seven and one half minutes (such was his rage), he put together a time machine (such was his genius).

Professor Hassel assembled the time machine around him, set the dial for 1902, picked up the revolver and pressed a button. The machine made a noise like defective plumbing and Hassel disappeared. He reappeared in Philadelphia on June 3, 1902, went directly to No. 1218 Walnut Street, a red-brick house with marble steps, and rang the bell. A man who might have passed for the third Smith Brother opened the door and looked at Henry Hassel.

"Mr. Jessup?" Hassel asked in a suffocated voice.

"Yes?"

"You are Mr. Jessup?"

"I am."

"You will have a son, Edgar? Edgar Allan Jessup—so named because of your regrettable admiration for Poe?"

The third Smith Brother was startled. "Not that I know of," he said. "I'm not married yet."

"You will be," Hassel said angrily. "I have the misfortune to be married to your son's daughter. Greta. Excuse me." He raised the revolver and shot his wife's grandfather-to-be.

"She will have ceased to exist," Hassel muttered, blowing smoke out of the revolver. "I'll be a bachelor. I may even be married to somebody else . . . Good God! Who?"

Hassel waited impatiently for the automatic recall of the time machine to snatch him back to his own laboratory. He rushed into his living room. There was his redheaded wife, still in the arms of a man.

Hassel was thunderstruck.

"So that's it," he growled. "A family tradition of faithlessness. Well, we'll see about that. We have ways and means." He permitted himself a hollow laugh, returned to his laboratory, and sent himself back to the year 1901, where he shot and killed Emma Hotchkiss, his wife's maternal grandmother-to-be. He returned to his own home in his own time. There was his redheaded wife, still in the arms of another man.

"But I *know* the old bitch was her grandmother," Hassel muttered. "You couldn't miss the resemblance. What the hell's gone wrong?"

Hassel was confused and dismayed, but not without resources. He went to his study, had difficulty picking up the phone, but finally managed to dial the Malpractice Laboratory. His finger kept oozing out of the dial holes.

"Sam?" he said. "This is Henry."

"Who?"

"Henry."

"You'll have to speak up."

"Henry Hassel!"

"Oh, good afternoon, Henry."

"Tell me all about time."

"Time? Hmmm . . ." The Simplex-and-Multiplex Computer cleared its throat while it waited for the data circuits to link up. "Ahem. Time. (1) Absolute. (2) Relative. (3) Recurrent. (1) Absolute: period, contingent, duration, diurnity, perpetuity—"

"Sorry, Sam. Wrong request. Go back. I want time, reference to succession of, travel in."

Sam shifted gears and began again. Hassel listened intently. He nodded. He grunted. "Uh huh. Uh huh. Right. I see. Thought so. A continuum, eh? Acts performed in past must alter future. Then I'm on the right track. But act must be significant, eh? Mass-action effect. Trivia cannot divert existing phenomena streams. Hmmm. But how trivial is a grandmother?"

"What are you trying to do, Henry?"

"Kill my wife," Hassel snapped. He hung up. He returned to his laboratory. He considered, still in a jealous rage.

"Got to do something significant," he muttered. "Wipe Greta out. Wipe it all out. All right, by God! I'll show 'em."

Hassel went back to the year 1775, visited a Virginia farm and shot a young colonel in the brisket. The colonel's name was George Washington, and Hassel made sure he was dead. He returned to his own time and his own home. There was his redheaded wife, still in the arms of another.

"Damn!" said Hassel. He was running out of ammunition. He opened a fresh box of cartridges, went back in time and massacred Christopher Columbus, Napoleon, Mohammed and half a dozen other celebrities. "That ought to do it, by God!" said Hassel

He returned to his own time, and found his wife as before.

His knees turned to water; his feet seemed to melt into the floor. He went back to his laboratory, walking through nightmare quicksands.

"What the hell is significant?" Hassel asked himself painfully. "How much does it take to change futurity? By God, I'll really change it this time. I'll go for broke."

He traveled to Paris at the turn of the twentieth century and visited a Madame Curie in an attic workshop near the Sorbonne. "Madame," he said in his execrable French, "I am a stranger to you of the utmost, but a scientist entire. Knowing of your experiments with radium— Oh? You haven't got to radium yet? No matter. I am here to teach you all of nuclear fission."

He taught her. He had the satisfaction of seeing Paris go up in a mushroom of smoke before the automatic recall brought him home. "That'll teach women to be faithless," he growled . . . "Guhhh!" The last was wrenched from his lips when he saw his redheaded wife still— But no need to belabor the obvious.

Hassel swam through fogs to his study and sat down to think. While he's thinking I'd better warn you that this not a conventional time story. If you imagine for a moment that Henry is going to discover that the man fondling his wife is himself, you're mistaken. The viper is not Henry Hassel, his son, a relation, or even Ludwig Boltzmann (1844–1906). Hassel does not make a circle in time, ending where the story begins—to the satisfaction of nobody and the fury of everybody—for the simple reason that time isn't circular, or linear, or tandem, discoid, syzygous, longinquitous, or pandicularted. Time is a private matter, as Hassel discovered.

"Maybe I slipped up somehow," Hassel muttered. "I'd better find out." He fought with the telephone, which seemed to weigh a hundred tons, and at last managed to get through to the library.

"Hello, Library? This is Henry."

"Who?"

"Henry Hassel."

"Speak up, please."

"HENRY HASSEL!"

"Oh. Good afternoon, Henry."

"What have you got on George Washington?"

Library clucked while her scanners sorted through her catalogues. "George Washington, first president of the United States, was born in—"

"First president? Wasn't he murdered in 1775?"

"Really, Henry. That's an absurd question. Everybody knows that George Wash—"

"Doesn't anybody know he was shot?"

"By whom?"

"Me."

"When?"

"In 1775."

"How did you manage to do that?"

"I've got a revolver."

"No, I mean, how did you do it two hundred years ago?"

"I've got a time machine."

"Well, there's no record here," Library said. "He still doing fine in my files. You must have missed."

"I did not miss. What about Christopher Columbus? Any record of his death in 1489?"

"But he discovered the New World in 1492."

"He did not. He was murdered in 1489."

"How?"

"With a forty-five slug in the gizzard."

"You again, Henry?"

"Yes."

"There's no record here," Library insisted. "You must be one lousy shot."

"I will not lose my temper," Hassel said in a trembling voice.

"Why not, Henry?"

"Because it's lost already," he shouted. "All right! What about Marie Curie? Did she or did she not discover the fission bomb which destroyed Paris at the turn of the century?"

"She did not. Enrico Fermi—"

"She did."

"She didn't."

"I personally taught her. Me. Henry Hassel."

"Everybody says you're a wonderful theoretician, but a lousy teacher, Henry. You—"

"Go to hell, you old biddy. This has got to be explained."

"Why?"

"I forget. There was something on my mind, but it doesn't matter now. What would you suggest?"

"You really have a time machine?"

"Of course I've got a time machine."

"Then go back and check."

Hassel returned to the year 1775, visited Mount Vernon, and interrupted the spring planting. "Excuse me, colonel," he began.

The big man looked at him curiously. "You talk funny, stranger," he said. "Where you from?"

"Oh, a freshwater school you never heard of."

"You look funny too. Kind of misty, so to speak."

"Tell me, colonel, what do you hear from Christopher Columbus?"

"Not much," Colonel Washington answered. "Been dead two, three hundred years."

"When did he die?"

"Year fifteen hundred some-odd, near as I remember."

"He did not. He died in 1489."

"Got your dates wrong, friend. He discovered America in 1492."

"Cabot discovered America. Sebastian Cabot."

"Nope. Cabot came a mite later."

"I have infallible proof!" Hassel began, but broke off as a stocky and rather stout man, with a face ludicrously reddened by rage, approached. He was wearing baggy gray slacks and a tweed jacket two sizes too small for him. He was carrying a .45 revolver. It was only after he had stared for a moment that Henry Hassel realized that he was looking at himself and not relishing the sight.

"My God!" Hassel murmured. "It's me, coming back to murder Washington that first time. If I'd made this second trip an hour later, I'd have found Washington dead. Hey!" he called. "Not yet. Hold off a minute. I've got to straighten something out first."

Hassel paid no attention to himself; indeed, he did not appear to be aware of himself. He marched straight up to Colonel Washington and shot him in the gizzard. Colonel Washington collapsed, emphatically dead. The first murderer inspected the body, and then, ignoring Hassel's attempt to stop him and engage him in dispute, turned and marched off, muttering venomously to himself.

"He didn't hear me," Hassel wondered. "He didn't even feel me. And why don't I remember myself trying to stop me the first time I shot the colonel? What the hell is going on?"

Considerably disturbed, Henry Hassel visited Chicago and dropped into the Chicago University squash courts in the early 1940s. There, in a slippery mess of graphite bricks and graphite dust that coated him, he located an Italian scientist named Fermi.

"Repeating Marie Curie's work, I see, *dottore?*" Hassel said.

Fermi glanced about as though he had heard a faint sound.

"Repeating Marie Curie's work, *dottore?*" Hassel roared.

Fermi looked at him strangely. "where you from, *amico?*"

"State."

"State Department?"

"Just State. It's true, isn't it, *dottore,* that Marie Curie discovered nuclear fission back in nineteen ought ought?"

"No! No! No!" Fermi cried. "We are the first, and we are not there yet. Police! Police! Spy!"

"This time I'll go on record," Hassel growled. He pulled out his trusty .45, emptied it into Dr. Fermi's chest, and awaited arrest and immolation in newspaper files. To his amazement, Dr. Fermi did not collapse. Dr. Fermi merely explored his chest tenderly and, to the men who answered his cry, said, "It is nothing. I felt in my within a sudden sensation of burn which may be a neuralgia of the cardiac nerve, but is most likely gas."

Hassel was too agitated to wait for the automatic recall of the time machine. Instead he returned at once to Unknown University under his own power. This should have given him a clue, but he was too possessed to notice. It was at this time that I (1913–1975) first saw him—a dim figure tramping through parked cars, closed doors and brick walls, with the light of lunatic determination on his face.

He oozed into the library, prepared for an exhaustive discussion, but could not make himself felt or heard by the catalogues. He went to the Malpractice Laboratory, where Sam, the Simplex-and-Multiplex Computer, has installations sensitive up to 10,700 angstroms. Sam could not see Henry, but managed to hear him through a sort of wave-interference phenomenon.

"Sam," Hassel said. "I've made one hell of a discovery."

"You're always making discoveries, Henry," Sam complained. "Your data allocation is filled. Do I have to start another tape for you?"

"But I need advice. Who's the leading authority on time, reference to succession of, travel in?"

"That would be Israel Lennox, spatial mechanics, professor of, Yale."

"How do I get in touch with him?"

"You don't, Henry. He's dead. Died in '75."

"What authority have you got on time, travel in, living?"

"Wiley Murphy."

"Murphy? From our own Trauma Department? That's a break. Where is he now?"

"As a matter of fact, Henry, he went over to your house to ask you something."

Hassel went home without walking, searched through his laboratory and study without finding anyone, and at last floated into the living room, where his redheaded wife was still in the arms of another man. (All this, you understand, had taken place within the space of a few moments after the construction of the time machine; such is the nature of time and travel.) Hassel cleared his throat once or twice and tried to tap his wife on the shoulder. His fingers went through her.

"Excuse me, darling," he said. "Has Wiley Murphy been in to see me?"

Then he looked closer and saw that the man embracing his wife was Murphy himself.

"Murphy!" Hassel exclaimed. "The very man I'm looking for. I've had the most extraordinary experience." Hassel at once launched into a lucid description of his extraordinary experience, which went something like this: "Murphy, $u - v = (u^{\frac{1}{2}} - v^{\frac{1}{4}}) (u^a + u^x + v^y)$ but when George Washington $F(x)y^+ dx$ and Enrico Fermi $F(u^{\frac{1}{2}}) dxdt$ one half of Marie Curie, then what about Christopher Columbus times the square root of minus one?"

Murphy ignored Hassel, as did Mrs. Hassel. I jotted down Hassel's equations on the hood of a passing taxi.

"Do listen to me, Murphy," Hassel said. "Greta dear, would you mind leaving us for a moment? I— For heaven's sake, will you two stop that nonsense? This is serious."

Hassel tried to separate the couple. He could no more touch them than make them hear him. His face turned red again and he became quite choleric as he beat at Mrs. Hassel and Murphy. It was like beating an Ideal Gas. I thought it best to interfere.

"Hassel!"

"Who's that?"

"Come outside a moment. I want to talk to you."

He shot through the wall. "Where are you?"

"Over here."

"You're sort of dim."

"So are you."

"Who are you?"

"My name's Lennox, Israel Lennox."

"Israel Lennox, spatial mechanics, professor of, Yale?"

"The same."

"But you died in '75."

"I disappeared in '75."

"What d'you mean?"

"I invented a time machine."

"By God! So did I," Hassel said. "This afternoon. The idea came to me in a flash—I don't know why—and I've had the most extraordinary experience. Lennox, time is not a continuum."

"No?"

"It's a series of discrete particles—like pearls on a string."

"Yes?"

"Each pearl is a 'Now.' Each 'Now' has its own past and future. but none of them relate to any others. You see? if $a = a_1 + a_2ji + ax (b_1)$—"

"Never mind the mathematics, Henry."

"It's a form of quantum transfer of energy. Time is emitted in discrete corpuscles or quanta. We can visit each individual quantum and make changes within it, but no change in any one corpuscle affects any other corpuscle. Right?"

"Wrong," I said sorrowfully.

"What d'you mean, 'Wrong'?" he said, angrily gesturing through the cleave of a passing coed. "You take the trochoid equations and—"

"Wrong," I repeated firmly. "Will you listen to me, Henry?"

"Oh, go ahead," he said.

"Have you noticed that you've become rather insubstantial? Dim? Spectral? Space and time no longer affect you?"

"Yes?"

"Henry, I had the misfortune to construct a time machine back in '75."

"So you said. Listen, what about power input? I figure I'm using about 7.3 kilowatts per—"

"Never mind the power input, Henry. On my first trip into the past, I visited the Pleistocene. I was eager to photograph the mastodon, the giant ground sloth, and the saber-tooth tiger. While I was backing up to get a mastodon fully in the field of view at f/6.3 at 1/100th of a second, or on the LVS scale—"

"Never mind the LVS scale," he said.

"While I was backing up, I inadvertently trampled and killed a small Pleistocene insect."

"Aha!" said Hassel.

"I was terrified by the incident. I had visions of returning to my world to find it completely changed as a result of this single death. Imagine my surprise when I returned to my world to find that nothing had changed."

"Oho!" said Hassel.

"I became curious. I went back to the Pleistocene and killed the mastodon. Nothing was changed in 1975. I returned to the Pleistocene and slaughtered the wildlife—still with no effect. I ranged through time, killing and destroying, in an attempt to alter the present."

"Then you did it just like me," Hassel exclaimed. "Odd we didn't run into each other."

"Not odd at all."

"I got Columbus."

"I got Marco Polo."

"I got Napoleon."

"I thought Einstein was more important."

"Mohammed didn't change things much—I expected more from *him*."

"I know. I got him too."

"What do you mean, you got him too?" Hassel demanded.

"I killed him September 16, 599. Old Style."

"Why, I got Mohammed January 5, 598."

"I believe you."

"But how could you have killed him after I killed him?"

"We both killed him."

"That's impossible."

"My boy," I said, "time is entirely subjective. It's a private matter—a personal experience. There is no such thing as objective time, just as there is no such thing as objective love, or an objective soul."

"Do you mean to say that time travel is impossible? But we've done it."

"To be sure, and many others, for all I know. But we each travel into our own past, and no other person's. There is no universal continuum, Henry. There are only billions of individuals, each with his own continuum; and one continuum cannot affect the other. We're like millions of strands of spaghetti in the same pot. No time traveler can ever meet another time traveler in the past or future. Each of us must travel up and down his own strand alone."

"But we're meeting each other now."

"We're no longer time travelers, Henry. We've become the spaghetti sauce."

"Spaghetti sauce?"

"Yes. You and I can visit any strand we like, because we've destroyed ourselves."

"I don't understand."

"When a man changes the past he only affects his own past—no one else's. The past is like memory. When you erase a man's memory, you wipe him out, but you don't wipe out anybody else's. You and I have erased our past. The individual worlds of the others go on, but we have ceased to exist."

"What d'you mean, 'ceased to exist'?"

"With each act of destruction we dissolved a little. Now we're all gone. We've committed chronicide. We're ghosts. I hope Mrs. Hassel will be very happy with Mr. Murphy. . . . Now let's go over to the Académie. Ampère is telling a great story about Ludwig Boltzmann."

THE PI MAN

How to say? How to write? When sometimes I can be fluent, even polished, and then, *reculer pour mieux sauter,* patterns take hold of me. Push. Compel.

Sometimes

```
        I               I            I
            am      am      am
                3.14159 +
        from           from         from
        this           other        that
    space              space            space
```

Othertimes not

I have no control, but I try anyways.

I wake up wondering who, what, when, where, why?

Confusion result of biological compensator born into my body which I hate. Yes, birds and beasts have biological clock built in, and so navigate home from a thousand miles away. I have biological compensator, equalizer, responder to unknown stresses and strains. I relate, compensate, make and shape patterns, adjust rhythms, like a gridiron pendulum in a clock, but this is an unknown clock, and I do not know what time it keeps. Nevertheless I must. I am force. Have no control over self, speech, love, fate. Only to compensate.

Quae nocent docent. Translation follows: Things that injure teach. I am injured and have hurt many. What have we learned? However. I wake up the morning of the biggest hurt of all wondering which house. Wealth, you understand. Damme! Mews cottage in London, villa in Rome, penthouse in New York, rancho in California. I awake. I look. Ah! Layout familiar. Thus:

```
        Foyer
            Bedroom
                Bath          T
                Bath          e
            Living Room       r
        Kitchen               r
            Dressing Room     a
                Bedroom       c
                Terrace       e
```

So. I am in penthouse in New York, but that bath-bath-back-to-back. Pfui! All rhythm wrong. Pattern painful. Why have I never noticed before? Or is this sudden awareness result of phenomenon elsewhere? I telephone to janitor-mans downstairs. At that moment I lose my American-English. Damn nuisance. I'm compelled to speak a compost of tongues, and I never know which will be forced on me next.

"Pronto. Ecco mi. Signore Marko. Miscusi tanto—"

Pfui! Hang up. Hate the garbage I must sometimes speak and write. This I now write during period of AmerEng lucidity, otherwise would look like goulash. While I wait for return of communication, I shower body, teeth, hairs, shave face, dry everything, and try again.

Voilà! Ye Englishe, she come. Back to invention of Mr. A. G. Bell and call janitor again.

"Good morning, Mr. Lundgren. This is Peter Marko. Guy in the penthouse. Right. Mr. Lundgren, be my personal rabbi and get some workmen up here this morning. I want those two baths converted into one. No, I mean it. I'll leave five thousand dollars on top of the icebox. Yes? Thanks, Mr. Lundgren."

Wanted to wear grey flannel this morning but compelled to put on sharkskin. Damnation! Black Power has peculiar side effects. Went to spare bedroom (see diagram) and unlocked door which was installed by the Eagle Safe Company—Since 1904—Bank Vault Equipment—Fireproof Files & Ledger Trays—Combinations changed. I went in.

Everything broadcasting beautifully, up and down the electromagnetic spectrum. Radio waves down to 1,000 meters, ultraviolet up into the hard X-rays and the 100 Kev (one hundred thousand electron volts) gamma radiation. All interrupters innn-tt-errrr-up-ppp-t-ingggg at random. I'm jamming the voice of the universe at least within this home, and I'm at peace. Dear God! To know even a moment of peace!

So. I take subway to office in Wall Street. Limousine more convenient but chauffeur too dangerous. Might become friendly, and I don't dare have friends anymore. Best of all, the morning subway is jam-packed, mass-packed, no patterns to adjust, no shiftings and compensations required. Peace.

In subway car I catch a glimpse of an eye, narrow, bleak, grey, the property of an anonymous man who conveys the conviction that you've never seen him before and will never see him again. But I picked up that glance and it tripped an alarm in the back of my mind. He knew it. He saw the flash in my eyes before I could turn away. So I was being tailed again. Who, this time? U.S.A.? U.S.S.R? Interpol? Skip-Tracers, Inc.?

I drifted out of the subway with the crowd at City Hall and gave them a false trail to the Woolworth Building in case they were operating double-tails. The whole theory of the hunters and the hunted is not to avoid being tailed, no one can escape that; the thing to do is give them so many false leads to follow up that they become overextended. Then they may be forced to abandon you. They have a man-hour budget; just so many men for just so many operations.

City Hall traffic was out of sync, as it generally is, so I had to limp to compensate. Took elevator up to tenth floor of bldg. As I was starting down the stairs, I was suddenly seized by something from out there, something bad. I began to cry, but no help. An elderly clerk emerge from office wearing alpaca coat, gold spectacles, badge on lapel identify: *N. N. Chapin.*

"Not him," I plead with nowhere. "Nice mans. Not N. N. Chapin, please."

But I am force. Approach. Two blows, neck and gut. Down he go, writhing. I trample spectacles and smash watch. Then I'm permitted to go downstairs again. It was ten-thirty. I was late. Damn! Took taxi to 99 Wall Street. Drivers pattern smelled honest; big black man, quiet and assured. Tipped him fifty dollars. He raise eyebrows. Sealed one thousand in envelope (secretly) and sent driver back to bldg. to find and give to N. N. Chapin on tenth floor. Did not enclose note: "From your unknown admirer."

Routine morning's work in office. I am in arbitrage, which is simultaneous buying and selling of moneys in different markets to profit from unequal price. Try to follow simple example: Pound sterling is selling for $2.79H in London. Rupee is selling for $2.79 in New York. One rupee buys one pound in Burma. See where the arbitrage lies? I buy one rupee for $2.79 in New York, buy one pound for rupee in Burma, sell pound for $2.79H in London, and I have made H cent on the transaction. Multiply by $100,000, and I have made $250 on the transaction. Enormous capital required.

But this is only crude example of arbitrage; actually the buying and selling must follow intricate patterns and have perfect timing. Money markets are jumpy today. Big Boards are hectic. Gold fluctuating. I am behind at eleven-thirty, but the patterns put me ahead $57,075.94 by half-past noon, Daylight Saving Time.

57075 makes a nice pattern but that 94¢! Iych! Ugly. Symmetry above all else. Alas, only 24¢ hard money in my pockets. Called secretary, borrowed 70¢ from her, and threw sum total out window. Felt better as I watched it scatter in space, but then I caught her looking at me with delight. Very dangerous. Fired girl on the spot.

"But why, Mr. Marko? Why?" she asked, trying not to cry. Darling little thing. Pale-faced and saucy, but not so saucy now.

"Because you're beginning to like me."

"What's the harm in that?"

"When I hired you, I warned you not to like me."

"I thought you were putting me on."

"I wasn't. Out you go."

"But why?"

"Because I'm beginning to like you."

"Is this some new kind of pass?"

"God forbid!"

"Well you don't have to worry," she flared. "I despise you."

"Good. Then I can go to bed with you."

She turned crimson and opened her mouth to denounce me, the while her eyes twinkled at the corners. A darling girl, whatever her name was. I could not endanger her. I gave her three weeks' salary for a bonus and threw her out. *Punkt.* Next secretary would be a man, married, misanthropic, murderous; a man who could hate me.

So, lunch. Went to nicely balanced restaurant. All chairs filled by patrons. Even pattern. No need for me to compensate and adjust. Also, they give me usual single corner table which does not need guest to balance. Ordered nicely patterned luncheon:

Martini   Martini

Croque M'sieur Roquefort

Salad

Coffee

But so much cream being consumed in restaurant that I had to compensate by drinking my coffee black, which I dislike. However, still a soothing pattern.

x^2 1 x 1 41 5 prime number. Excuse, please. Sometimes I'm in control and see what compensating must be done . . . tick-tock-tick-tock, good old gridiron pendulum . . . other times is force on me from God knows where or why or how or even if there is a God. Then I must do what I'm compelled to do, blindly, without motivation, speaking the gibberish I speak and think, sometimes hating it like what I do to poor mans Mr. Chapin. Anyway, the equation breaks down when x 5 40.

The afternoon was quiet. For a moment I thought I might be forced to leave for Rome (Italy) but whatever it was adjusted without needing my two ($0,02) cents. ASPCA finally caught up with me for beating my dog to death, but I'd contributed $5,000.00 to their shelter. Got off with a shaking of heads. Wrote a few graffiti on posters, saved a small boy from a clobbering in a street rumble at a cost of sharkskin jacket. Drat! Slugged a maladroit driver who was subjecting his lovely Aston-Martin to cruel and unusual punishment. He was, how they say, "grabbing a handful of second."

In the evening to ballet to relax with all the beautiful Balanchine patterns; balanced, peaceful, soothing. Then I take a deep breath, quash my nausea, and force myself to go to *The Raunch*, the West Village creepsville. I hate *The Raunch*, but I need a woman and I must go where I hate. That fair-haired girl I fired, so full of mischief and making eyes at me. So, *poisson d'avril*, I advance myself to *The Raunch*.

Chaos. Blackness. Cacophony. My vibes shriek. 25 Watt bulbs. Ballads of Protest. Against L. wall sit young men, with pubic beards, playing chess. Badly. *Exempli gratia:*

1 P—Q4	Kt—KB3
2 Kt—Q2	P—K4
3 PXP	Kt—Kt5
4 P—KR3	Kt—K6

If White takes the knight, Black forces mate with Q—R5ch. I didn't wait to see what the road-company Capablancas would do next.

Against R. wall is bar, serving beer and cheap wine mostly. There are girls with brown paper bags containing toilet articles. They are looking for a pad for the night. All wear tight jeans and are naked under loose sweaters. I think of Herrick (1591–1674): *Next, when I lift mine eyes and see/That brave vibration each way free/Oh, how that glittering taketh me!*

I pick out the one who glitters the most. I talk. She insult. I insult back and buy hard drinks. She drink my drinks and snarl and hate, but helpless. Her name is Bunny and she has no pad for tonight. I do not let myself sympathize. She is a dyke; she does not bathe, her thinking patterns are jangles. I hate her and she's safe; no harm can come to her. So I maneuvered her out of Sink City and took her home to seduce by mutual contempt, and in the living room sat the slender little paleface secretary, recently fired for her own good.

She sat there in my penthouse, now minus one (1) bathroom, and with $1,997.00 change on top of the refrigerator. Oi! Throw

$6.00 into kitchen Dispos-All (a Federal offense) and am soothed by the lovely 1991 remaining. She sat there, wearing a pastel thing, her skin gleaming rose-red from embarrassment, also red for danger. Her saucy face was very tight from the daring thing she thought she was doing. *Gott bewahre!* I like that.

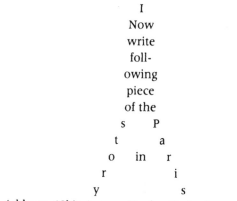

```
            I
          Now
          write
          foll-
          owing
          piece
          of the
          s       P
        t           a
      o    in    r
    r                 i
  y                     s
```

Address: 49bis Avenue Hoche, Paris, 8eme, France

Forced to go there by what happened in the U.N., you understand. It needed extreme compensation and adjustment. Almost, for a moment, I thought I would have to attack the conductor of the *Opéra Comique*, but fate was kind and let me off with nothing worse than indecent exposure, and I was able to square it by founding a scholarship at the Sorbonne. Didn't someone suggest that fate was the square root of minus one?

Anyway, back in New York it is my turn to denounce the paleface but suddenly my AmerEng is replaced by a dialect out of a B-picture about a white remittance man and a blind native girl on a South Sea island who find redemption together while she plays the ukulele and sings gems from Lawrence Welk's Greatest Hits.

"Oh-so," I say. "Me-fella be ve'y happy ask why you-fella invade 'long my apa'tment, 'cept me' now speak pidgin. Ve'y emba'ss 'long me."

"I bribed Mr. Lundgren," she blurted. "I told him you needed important papers from the office."

The dyke turned on her heel and bounced out, her brave vibration each way free. I caught up with her in front of the elevator, put

$101 into her hand, and tried to apologize. She hated me more so I did a naughty thing to her vibration and returned to the living room.

"What's she got?" the paleface asked.

My English returned. "What's your name?"

"Good Lord! I've been working in your office for two months and you don't know my name? You really don't?"

"No."

"I'm Jemmy Thomas."

"Beat it, Jemmy Thomas."

"So that's why you always called me 'Miss Uh.' You're Russian?"

"Half."

"What's the other half?"

"None of your business. What are you doing here? When I fire them they stay fired. What d'you want from me?"

"You," she said, blushing fiery.

"Will you for God's sake get the hell out of here."

"What did she have that I don't?" paleface demanded. Then her face crinkled. "Don't? Doesn't? I'm going to Bennington. They're strong on aggression but weak on grammar."

"What d'you mean, you're going to Bennington?"

"Why, it's a college. I thought everybody knew."

"But *going*?"

"Oh. I'm in my junior year. They drive you out with whips to acquire practical experience in your field. You ought to know that. Your office manager—I suppose you don't know her name, either."

"Ethel M. Blatt."

"Yes. Miss Blatt took it all down before you interviewed me."

"What's your field?"

"It used to be economics. Now it's you. How old are you?"

"One hundred and one."

"Oh, come on. Thirty? They say at Bennington that ten years is the right difference between men and women because we mature quicker. Are you married?"

"I have wives in London, Paris, and Rome. What is this catechism?"

"Well, I'm trying to get something going."

"I can see that, but does it have to be me?"

"I know it sounds like a notion." She lowered her eyes, and

without the highlight of their blue, her pale face was almost invisible. "And I suppose women are always throwing themselves at you."

"It's my untold wealth."

"What are you, blasé or something? I mean, I know I'm not staggering, but I'm not exactly repulsive."

"You're lovely."

"They why don't you come near me?"

"I'm trying to protect you."

"I can protect me when the time comes. I'm a Black Belt."

"The time is now, Jemmy Thompson."

"Thomas."

"Walk, not run, to the nearest exit, Jemmy Thomas."

"The least you could do is offend me the way you did that hustler in front of the elevator."

"You snooped?"

"Sure I snooped. You didn't expect me to sit here on my hands, did you? I've got my man to protect."

I had to laugh. This spunky little thing march in, roll up her sleeves and set to work on me. A wonder she didn't have a pot roast waiting in the oven and herself waiting in the bed.

"Your man?" I ask.

"It happens," she said in a low voice. "I never believed it, but it happens. You fall in and out of love and affairs, and each time you think it's real and forever. And then you meet somebody and it isn't a question of love anymore. You just know that he's your man, and you're stuck with him, whether you like it or not." She burst out angrily. "I'm stuck, dammit! Stuck! D'you think I'm enjoying this?"

She looked at me through the storm; violet eyes full of youth and determination and tenderness and fear. I could see she, too, was being forced and was angry and afraid. And I knew how lonely I was, never daring to make friends, to love, to share. I could fall into those violet eyes and never come up. I looked at the clock. 2:30 A.M. Sometimes quiet at this hour. Perhaps my AmerEng would stay with me a while longer.

"You're being compelled, Jemmy," I said. "I know all about that. Something inside you, something you don't understand, made you take your dignity in both hands and come after me. You don't like it, you don't want to, you've never begged in your life, but you had to. Yes?"

She nodded.

"Then you can understand a little about me. I'm compelled, too."

"Who is she?"

"No, no. Not forced to beg from a woman; compelled to hurt people."

"What people?"

"Any people; sometimes strangers, and that's bad, other times people I love, and that's not to be endured. So now I no longer dare love. I must protect people from myself."

"I don't know what you're talking about. Are you some kind of psychotic monster?"

"Yes, played by Lon Chaney, Jr."

"If you can joke about it, you can't be all that sick. Have you seen a shrink?"

"No. I don't have to. I know what's compelling me." I looked at the clock again. Still a quiet time. Please God the English would stay with me a while longer. I took off my jacket and shirt. "I'm going to shock you," I said, and showed her my back, crosshatched with scars. She gasped.

"Self-inflicted," I told her. "Because I permitted myself to like a man and become friendly with him. This is the price I paid, and I was lucky that he didn't have to. Now wait here."

I went into the master bedroom where my heart's shame was embalmed in a silver case hidden in the right-hand drawer of my desk. I brought it to the living room. Jemmy watched me with great eyes.

"Five years ago a girl fell in love with me," I told her. "A girl like you. I was lonely then, as always, so instead of protecting her from me, I indulged myself and tried to love her back. Now I want to show you the price *she* paid. You'll loathe me for this, but I must show you. Maybe it'll save you from—"

I broke off. A flash had caught my eye—the flash of lights going on in a building down the street; not just a few windows, a lot. I put on my jacket, went out on the terrace, and watched. All the illuminated windows in the building three down from me went out. Five-second eclipse. On again. It happened in the building two down and then the one next door. The girl came to my side and took my arm. She trembled slightly.

"What is it?" she asked. "What's the matter? You look so grim."

"It's the Geneva caper," I said. "Wait."

The lights in my apartment went out for five seconds and then came on again.

"They've located me the way I was nailed in Geneva," I told her.

"They? Located?"

"They've spotted my jamming by d/f."

"What jamming?"

"The full electromagnetic spectrum."

"What's dee eff?"

"Radio direction-finder. They used it to get the bearing of my jamming. Then they turned off the current in each building in the area, building by building, until the broadcast stopped. Now they've pinpointed me. They know I'm in this house, but they don't know which apartment yet. I've still got time. So. Good night, Jemmy. You're hired again. Tell Ethel Blatt I won't be in for a while. I wish I could kiss you good-bye, but safer not."

She clamped her arms around my neck and gave me an honest kiss. I tried to push her away.

She clung like The Old Man of the Sea. "You're a spy," she said. "I'll go to the chair with you."

"I wish to heaven I only was a spy. Good-bye, my love. Remember me."

A great mistake letting that slip. It happen, I think, because my speech slip, too. Suddenly forced to talk jumble again. As I run out, the little paleface kick off her sandals so she can run, too. She is alongside me going down the fire stairs to the garage in the basement. I hit her to stop, and swear Swahili at her. She hit back and swear gutter, all the time laughing and crying. I love her for it, so she is doomed. I will ruin her like all the rest.

We get into car and drive fast. I am making for 59th Street bridge to get off Manhattan Island and head east. I own plane in Babylon, Long Island, which is kept ready for this sort of awkwardness.

"*J'y suis, J'y reste* is not my motto," I tell Jemmy Thomas, whose French is as uncertain as her grammar, an endearing weakness. "Once Scotland Yard trapped me with a letter. I was receiving special mail care of General Delivery. They mailed me a red envelope, spotted me when I picked it up, and followed me to No. 13 Mayfair

Mews, London W.1., Telephone, Mayfair 7711. Red for danger. Is the rest of you as invisible as your face?"

"I'm not invisible," she said, indignant, running hands through her streaky fair hair. "I tan in the summer. What is all this chase and escape? Why do you talk so funny and act so peculiar? In the office I thought it was because you're a crazy Russian. Half crazy Russian. Are you sure you're not a spy?"

"Only positive."

"It's too bad. A Commie 007 would be utter blissikins."

"Yes, I know. You see yourself being seduced with vodka and caviar."

"Are you a being from another world who came here on a UFO?"

"Would that scare you?"

"Only if it meant we couldn't make the scene."

"We couldn't anyway. All the serious side of me is concentrated on my career. I want to conquer the earth for my robot masters."

"I'm only interested in conquering you."

"I am not and have never been a creature from another world. I can show you my passport to prove it."

"Then what are you?"

"A compensator."

"A what?"

"A compensator. Like a clock pendulum. Do you know dictionary of Messrs Funk & Wagnalls? Edited by Frank H. Vizetelly, Litt.D, LL.D.? I quote: One who or that which compensates, as a device for neutralizing the influence of local attraction upon a compass needle, or an automatic apparatus for equalizing— Damn!"

Litt.D. Frank H. Vizetelly does not use that word. It is my own because roadblock now faces me on 59th Street bridge. I should have anticipated. Should have sensed patterns, but too swept up with this inviting girl. Probably there are roadblocks on all exits leading out of this $24 island. Could drive off bridge, but maybe Bennington College has also neglected to teach Jemmy Thomas how to swim. So. Stop car. Surrender.

"Kamerad," I pronounce. "Who you? John Birch?"

Gentlemans say no.

"White Supremes of the World, Inc.?"

No again. I feel better. Always nasty when captured by lunatic fringers.

"U.S.S.R.?"

He stare, then speak. "Special Agent Hildebrand. FBI," and flash his identification which no one can read in this light. I take his word and embrace him in gratitude. FBI is safe. He recoil and wonder if I am fag. I don't care. I kiss Jemmy Thomas, and she open mouth under mine to mutter, "Admit nothing. Deny everything. I've got a lawyer."

I own thirteen lawyers, and two of them can make any court tremble, but no need to call them. This will be standard cross-examination; I know from past experience. So let them haul me off to Foley Square with Jemmy. They separate us. I am taken to Inquisition Room.

Brilliant lights; the shadows arranged just so; the chairs placed just so; mirror on wall probably one-way window with observers outside; I've been through this so often before. The anonymous man from the subway this morning is questioning me. We exchange glances of recognition. His name is R. Sawyer. The questions come.

"Name?"

"Peter Marko."

"Born?"

"Lee's Hill, Virginia."

"Never heard of it."

"It's a very small town, about thirty miles north of Roanoke. Most maps ignore it."

"You're Russian?"

"Half, by descent."

"Father Russian?"

"Yes. Eugene Alexis Markolevsky."

"Changed his name legally?"

"Shortened it when he became a citizen."

"Mother?"

"Vera Broadhurst. English."

"You were raised in Lee's Hill?"

"Until ten. Then Chicago."

"Father's occupation?"

"Teacher."

"Yours, financier?"

"Arbitrageur. Buying and selling money on the open market."

"Known assets from identified bank deposits, three million dollars."

"Only in the States. Counting overseas deposits and investments, closer to seventeen million."

R. Sawyer shook his head, bewildered. "Marko, what the hell are you up to? I'll level with you. At first we thought espionage, but with your kind of money— What are you broadcasting from your apartment? We can't break the code."

"There is no code, only randomness so I can get a little peace and some sleep."

"Only what?"

"Random jamming. I do it in all my homes. Listen, I've been through this so often before, and it's difficult for people to understand unless I explain it my own way. Will you let me try?"

"Go ahead." Sawyer was grim. "You better make it good. We can check everything you give us."

I take a breath. Always the same problem. The reality is so strange that I have to use simile and metaphor. But it was 4:00 A.M. and maybe the jumble wouldn't interrupt my speech for a while. "Do you like to dance?"

"What the hell . . ."

"Be patient. I'm trying to explain. You like to dance?"

"I used to."

"What's the pleasure of dancing? It's people making rhythms together; patterns, designs, balances. Yes?"

"So?"

"And parades. Masses of men and music making patterns. Team sports, also. Action patterns. Yes?"

"Marko, if you think I'm going to—"

"Just listen, Sawyer. Here's the point. I'm sensitive to patterns on a big scale; bigger than dancing or parades, more than the rhythms of day and night, the seasons, the glacial epochs."

Sawyer stared. I nodded. "Oh yes, people respond to the 2/2 of the diurnal-nocturnal rhythms, the 4/4 of the seasons, the great terra-epochs. They don't know it, but they do. That's why they have sleep-problems, moon-madness, sun-hunger, weather-sensitivity. I respond to these local things, too, but also to gigantic patterns, influences from infinity."

"Are you some kind of nut?"

"Certainly. Of course. I respond to the patterns of the entire galaxy, maybe universe; sight and sound; and the unseen and unheard. I'm moved by the patterns of people, individually and demographically: hostility, generosity, selfishness, charity, cruelties and kindnesses, groupings and whole cultures. And I'm compelled to respond and compensate."

"How a nut like you ever made seventeen mill— How do you compensate?"

"If a child hurts itself, the mother responds with a kiss. That's compensation. Agreed? If a man beats a horse you beat *him*. You boo a bad fight. You cheer a good game. You're a cop. Sawyer. Don't the victim and murderer seek each other to fulfill their pattern?"

"Maybe in the past; not today. What's this got to do with your broadcasts?"

"Multiply that compensation by infinity and you have me. I must kiss and kick. I'm driven. I must compensate in a pattern I can't see or understand. Sometimes I'm compelled to do extravagant things, other times I'm forced to do insane things: talk gibberish, go to strange places, perform abominable acts, behave like a lunatic."

"What abominable acts?"

"Fifth amendment."

"But what about those broadcasts?"

"We're flooded with wave emissions and particles, sometimes in patterns, sometimes garbled. I feel them all and respond to them the way a marionette jerks on strings. I try to neutralize them by jamming, so I broadcast at random to get a little peace."

"Marko, I swear you're crazy."

"Yes, I am, but you won't be able to get me committed. It's been tried before. I've even tried myself. It never works. The big design won't permit it. I don't know why, but the big design wants me to go on as a Pi Man."

"What the hell are you talking about? What kind of pie?"

"Not pee-eye-ee-man. Pee-eye-man. Pi. Sixteenth letter in the Greek alphabet. It's the relation of the circumference of a circle to its diameter. 3.14159+. The series goes on into infinity. It's transcendental and can never be resolved into a finite pattern. They call extrasensory perception Psi. I call extrapattern perception Pi. All right?"

He glared at me, threw my dossier down, sighed, and slumped into a chair. That made the grouping wrong, so I had to shift. He cocked an eye at me.

"Pi Man," I apologized.

"All right," he said at last. "We can't hold you."

"They all try but they never can."

"Who try?"

"Governments, police, counterintelligence, politicals, lunatic fringe, religious sects . . . They track me down, hoping they can nail me or use me. They can't. I'm part of something much bigger. I think we all are, only I'm the first to be aware of it."

"Are you claiming you're a superman?"

"Good God! No! I'm a damned man . . . a tortured man, because some of the patterns I must adjust to are outworld rhythms like nothing we ever experience on earth . . . 29/51 . . . 108/303 . . . tempi like that, alien, terrifying, agony to live with."

He took another deep breath. "Off the record, what's this about abominable acts?"

"That's why I can't have friends or let myself fall in love. Sometimes the patterns turn so ugly that I have to make frightful sacrifices to restore the design. I must destroy something I love."

"This is sacrifice?"

"Isn't it the only meaning of sacrifice, Sawyer? You give up what's dearest to you."

"Who to?"

"The Gods, The Fates, The Big Pattern that's controlling me. From where? I don't know. It's too big a universe to comprehend, but I have to beat its tempo with my actions and reactions, emotions and senses, to make the patterns come out even, balanced in some way that I don't understand. The pressures that

<pre>
                    whipsaw
                 me
         back   and
         and   turn
       forth   me
        and   into
       back   the
        and   transcendental
       forth   3.141591
</pre>

and maybe I talk too much to R. Sawyer and the patterns pronounce: PI MAN, IT IS NOT PERMITTED.

So. There is darkness and silence.

"The other arm now," Jemmy said firmly. "Lift."

I am on my bed, me. Thinking upheaved again. Half (H) into py-jamas; other half (H) being wrestled by paleface girl. I lift. She yank. Pyjamas now on, and it's my turn to blush. They raise me prudish in Lee's Hill.

"Pot roast done?" I ask.

"What?"

"What happened?"

"You pooped out. Keeled over. You're not so cool."

"How much do you know?"

"Everything. I was on the other side of that mirror thing. Mr. Sawyer had to let you go. Mr. Lundgren helped lug you up to the apartment. He thinks you're stoned. How much should I give him?"

"*Cinque lire. No. Parla Italiano, gentile signorina?*"

"Are you asking me do I speak Italian? No."

"*Entschuldigen, Sie, bitte. Sprechen Sie Deutsch?*"

"Is this your patterns again?"

I nod.

"Can't you stop?"

After stopovers in Greece and Portugal, Ye Englische finally re-turns to me. "Can you stop breathing, Jemmy?"

"Is it like that, Peter? Truly?"

"Yes."

"When you do something . . . something bad . . . do you know why? Do you know exactly what it is somewhere that makes you do it?"

"Sometimes yes. Other times no. All I know is that I'm com-pelled to respond."

"Then you're just the tool of the universe."

"I think we all are. Continuum creatures. The only difference is, I'm more sensitive to the galactic patterns and respond violently. So why don't you get the hell out of here, Jemmy Thomas?"

"I'm still stuck," she said.

"You can't be. Not after what you heard."

"Yes, I am. You don't have to marry me."

Now the biggest hurt of all. I have to be honest. I have to ask, "Where's the silver case?"

A long pause. "Down the incinerator."

"Do you . . . Do you know what was in it?"

"I know what was in it."

"And you're still here?"

"It was monstrous what you did. Monstrous!" Her face suddenly streaked with mascara. She was crying. "Where is she now?"

"I don't know. The checks go out every quarter to a numbered account in Switzerland. I don't want to know. How much can the heart endure?"

"I think I'm going to find out, Peter."

"Please don't find out." I make one last effort to save her. "I love you, paleface, and you know what that can mean. When the patterns turn cruel, you may be the sacrifice."

"Love creates patterns, too." She kissed me. Her lips were parched, her skin was icy, she was afraid and hurting, but her heart beat strong with love and hope. "Nothing can crunch us now. Believe me."

"I don't know what to believe anymore. We're part of a world that's beyond knowing. What if it turns out to be too big for love?"

"All right," she said composedly. "We won't be dogs in the manger. If love is a little thing and has to end, then let it end. Let all little things like love and honor and mercy and laughter end, if there's a bigger design beyond."

"But what's bigger? What's beyond? I've asked that for years. Never an answer. Never a clue."

"Of course. If we're too small to survive, how can we know? Move over."

Then she is in bed with me, the tips of her body like frost while the rest of her is hot and evoking, and there is such a consuming burst of passion that for the first time I can forget myself, forget everything, abandon everything, and the last thing I think is: God damn the world. God damn the universe. God damn GGG-o-ddddddd

THEY DON'T MAKE LIFE
LIKE THEY USED TO

The girl driving the jeep was very fair and very Nordic. Her blonde hair was pulled back in a pony tail, but it was so long that it was more a mare's tail. She wore sandals, a pair of soiled bluejeans, and nothing else. She was nicely tanned. As she turned the jeep off Fifth Avenue and drove bouncing up the steps of the library, her bosom danced enchantingly.

She parked in front of the library entrance, stepped out, and was about to enter when her attention was attracted by something across the street. She peered, hesitated, then glanced down at her jeans and made a face. She pulled off the pants and hurled them at the pigeons eternally cooing and courting on the library steps. As they clattered up in fright, she ran down to Fifth Avenue, crossed, and stopped before a shop window. There was a plum-colored wool dress on display. It had a high waist, a full skirt, and not too many moth holes. The price was $79.90.

The girl rummaged through old cars skewed on the avenue until she found a loose fender. She smashed the plate-glass shop door, carefully stepped across the splinters, entered, and sorted through the dusty dress racks. She was a big girl and had trouble fitting herself. Finally she abandoned the plum-colored wool and compromised on a dark tartan, size 12, $120 reduced to $99.90. She located a salesbook and pencil, blew the dust off, and carefully wrote: *I.O.U. $99.90. Linda Nielsen.*

She returned to the library and went through the main doors which had taken her a week to batter in with a sledgehammer. She ran across the great hall, filthied with five years of droppings from the pigeons roosting there. As she ran, she clapped her arms over her head to shield her hair from stray shots. She climbed the stairs to the third floor and entered the Print Room. As always, she signed the register: *Date—June 20, 1981. Name—Linda Nielsen. Address—Central Park Model Boat Pond. Business or Firm—Last Man on Earth.*

She had had a long debate with herself about *Business or Firm* the last time she broke into the library. Strictly speaking, she was the last woman on earth, but she had felt that if she wrote that it would seem chauvinistic; and "Last Person on Earth" sounded silly, like calling a drink a beverage.

She pulled portfolios out of racks and leafed through them. She knew exactly what she wanted; something warm with blue accents to fit a twenty by thirty frame for her bedroom. In a priceless collection of Hiroshige prints she found a lovely landscape. She filled out a slip, placed it carefully on the librarian's desk, and left with the print.

Downstairs, she stopped off in the main circulation room, went to the back shelves, and selected two Italian grammars and an Italian dictionary. Then she backtracked through the main hall, went out to the jeep, and placed the books and print on the front seat alongside her companion, an exquisite Dresden china doll. She picked up a list that read:

Jap. print
Italian
20 X 30 pict. fr.
Lobster bisque
Brass polish
Detergent
Furn. polish
Wet mop

She crossed off the first two items, replaced the list on the dashboard, got into the jeep, and bounced down the library steps. She drove up Fifth Avenue, threading her way through crumbling wreckage. As she was passing the ruins of St. Patrick's Cathedral at 50th Street, a man appeared from nowhere.

He stepped out of the rubble and, without looking left or right, started crossing the avenue just in front of her. She exclaimed, banged on the horn which remained mute, and braked so sharply that the jeep slewed and slammed into the remains of a No. 3 bus. The man let out a squawk, jumped ten feet, and then stood frozen, staring at her.

"You crazy jaywalker," she yelled. "Why don't you look where you're going? D'you think you own the whole city?"

He stared and stammered. He was a big man, with thick, grizzled hair, a red beard, and weathered skin. He was wearing army fatigues, heavy ski boots, and had a bursting knapsack and blanket roll on his back. He carried a battered shotgun, and his pockets were crammed with odds and ends. He looked like a prospector.

"My God," he whispered in a rusty voice. "Somebody at last. I knew it. I always knew I'd find someone." Then, as he noticed her long, fair hair, his face fell. "But a woman," he muttered. "Just my goddamn lousy luck."

"What are you, some kind of nut?" she demanded. "Don't you know better than to cross against the lights?"

He looked around in bewilderment. "What lights?"

"So all right, there aren't any lights, but couldn't you look where you were going?"

"I'm sorry, lady. To tell the truth, I wasn't expecting any traffic."

"Just plain common sense," she grumbled, backing the jeep off the bus.

"Hey lady, wait a minute."

"Yes?"

"Listen, you know anything about TV? Electronics, how they say . . ."

"Are you trying to be funny?"

"No, this is straight. Honest."

She snorted and tried to continue driving up Fifth Avenue, but he wouldn't get out of the way.

"Please, lady," he persisted. "I got a reason for asking. Do you know?"

"No."

"Damn! I never get a break. Lady, excuse me, no offense, got any guys in this town?"

"There's nobody but me. I'm the last man on earth."

"That's funny. I always thought I was."

"So all right, I'm the last woman on earth."

He shook his head. "There's got to be other people; there just has to. Stands to reason. South, maybe you think? I'm down from New Haven, and I figured if I headed where the climate was like warmer, there'd be some guys I could ask something."

"Ask what?"

"Aw, a woman wouldn't understand. No offense."

"Well, if you want to head south you're going the wrong way."

"That's south, ain't it?" he said, pointing down Fifth Avenue.

"Yes, but you'll just come to a dead end. Manhattan's an island. What you have to do is go uptown and cross the George Washington Bridge to Jersey."

"Uptown? Which way is that?"

"Go straight up Fifth to Cathedral Parkway, then over to the West Side and up Riverside. You can't miss it."

He looked at her helplessly.

"Stranger in town?"

He nodded.

"Oh, all right," she said. "Hop in. I'll give you a lift."

She transferred the books and the china doll to the back seat, and he squeezed in alongside her. As she started the jeep she looked down at his worn ski boots.

"Hiking?"

"Yeah."

"Why don't you drive? You can get a car working, and there's plenty of gas and oil."

"I don't know how to drive," he said despondently. "It's the story of my life."

He heaved a sigh, and that made his knapsack jolt massively against her shoulder. She examined him out of the corner of her eye. He had a powerful chest, a long, thick back, and strong legs. His hands were big and hard, and his neck was corded with muscles. She thought for a moment, then nodded to herself and stopped the jeep.

"What's the matter?" he asked. "Won't it go?"

"What's your name?"

"Mayo. Jim Mayo."

"I'm Linda Nielsen."

"Yeah. Nice meeting you. Why don't it go?"

"Jim, I've got a proposition for you."

"Oh?" He looked at her doubtfully. "I'll be glad to listen, lady—I mean Linda, but I ought to tell you, I got something on my mind that's going to keep me pretty busy for a long t . . ." His voice trailed off as he turned away from her intense gaze.

"Jim, if you'll do something for me, I'll do something for you."

"Like what, for instance?"

"Well, I get terribly lonesome, nights. It isn't so bad during the day—there's always a lot of chores to keep you busy—but at night it's just awful."

"Yeah, I know," he muttered.

"I've got to do something about it."

"But how do I come into this?" he asked nervously.

"Why don't you stay in New York for a while? If you do, I'll teach you how to drive, and find you a car so you don't have to hike south."

"Say, that's an idea. Is it hard, driving?"

"I could teach you in a couple of days."

"I don't learn things so quick."

"All right, a couple of weeks, but think of how much time you'll save in the long run."

"Gee," he said, "that sounds great." Then he turned away again. "But what do I have to do for you?"

Her face lit up with excitement. "Jim, I want you to help me move a piano."

"A piano? What piano?"

"A rosewood grand from Steinway's on Fifty-seventh Street. I'm dying to have it in my place. The living room is just crying for it."

"Oh, you mean you're furnishing, huh?"

"Yes, but I want to play after dinner, too. You can't listen to records all the time. I've got it all planned; books on how to play, and books on how to tune a piano. . . . I've been able to figure everything except how to move the piano in."

"Yeah, but . . . but there's apartments all over this town with pianos in them," he objected. "There must be hundreds, at least. Stands to reason. Why don't you live in one of them?"

"Never! I love my place. I've spent five years decorating it, and it's beautiful. Besides, there's the problem of water."

He nodded. "Water's always a headache. How do you handle it?"

"I'm living in the house in Central Park where they used to keep the model yachts. It faces the boat pond. It's a darling place, and I've got it all fixed up. We could get the piano in together, Jim. It wouldn't be hard."

"Well, I don't know, Lena . . ."

"Linda."

"Excuse me. Linda. I—"

"You look strong enough. What'd you do, before?"

"I used to be a pro rassler."

"There! I knew you were strong."

"Oh, I'm not a rassler anymore. I became a bartender and went into the restaurant business. I opened 'The Body Slam' up in New Haven. Maybe you heard of it?"

"I'm sorry."

"It was sort of famous with the sports crowd. What'd you do before?"

"I was a researcher for BBDO."

"What's that?"

"An advertising agency," she explained impatiently. "We can talk about that later, if you'll stick around. And I'll teach you how to drive, and we can move in the piano, and there're a few other things that I—but that can wait. Afterward you can drive south."

"Gee, Linda, I don't know . . ."

She took Mayo's hands. "Come on, Jim, be a sport. You can stay with me. I'm a wonderful cook, and I've got a lovely guest room . . ."

"What for? I mean, thinking you was the last man on earth."

"That's a silly question. A proper house has to have a guest room. You'll love my place. I turned the lawns into a farm and gardens, and you can swim in the pond, and we'll get you a new Jag . . . I know where there's a beauty up on blocks."

"I think I'd rather have a Caddy."

"You can have anything you like. So what do you say, Jim? Is it a deal?"

"All right, Linda," he muttered reluctantly. "You've a deal."

It was indeed a lovely house with its pagoda roof of copper weathered to verdigris green, fieldstone walls, and deep recessed windows. The oval pond before it glittered blue in the soft June sunlight, and mallard ducks paddled and quacked busily. The sloping lawns that formed a bowl around the pond were terraced and cultivated. The house faced west, and Central Park stretched out beyond like an unkempt estate.

Mayo looked at the pond wistfully. "It ought to have boats."

"The house was full of them when I moved in," Linda said.

"I always wanted a model boat when I was a kid. Once I even—" Mayo broke off. A penetrating pounding sounded somewhere; an irregular sequence of heavy knocks that sounded like the dint of stones under water. It stopped as suddenly as it had begun. "What was that?" Mayo asked.

Linda shrugged. "I don't know for sure. I think it's the city falling apart. You'll see buildings coming down every now and then. You get used to it." Her enthusiasm rekindled. "Now come inside. I want to show you everything."

She was bursting with pride and overflowing with decorating details that bewildered Mayo, but he was impressed by her Victorian living room. Empire bedroom, and country kitchen with a working kerosene cooking stove. The colonial guest room, with fourposter bed, hooked rug, and tole lamps, worried him.

"This is kind of girlie-girlie, huh?"

"Naturally, I'm a girl."

"Yeah. Sure. I mean . . ." Mayo looked around doubtfully. "Well, a guy is used to stuff that ain't so delicate. No offense."

"Don't worry, that bed's strong enough. Now remember, Jim, no feet on the spread, and remove it at night. If your shoes are dirty, take them off before you come in. I got that rug from the museum and I don't want it messed up. Have you got a change of clothes?"

"Only what I got on."

"We'll have to get you new things tomorrow. What you're wearing is so filthy it's not worth laundering."

"Listen," he said desperately, "I think maybe I better camp out in the park."

"Why on earth?"

"Well, I'm like more used to it than houses. But you don't have to worry, Linda. I'll be around in case you need me."

"Why should I need you?"

"All you have to do is holler."

"Nonsense," Linda said firmly. "You're my guest and you're staying here. Now get cleaned up; I'm going to start dinner. Oh damn! I forgot to pick up the lobster bisque."

She gave him a dinner cleverly contrived from canned goods and served on exquisite Fornisetti china with Danish silver flatware. It was a typical girl's meal, and Mayo was still hungry when it was finished, but too polite to mention it. He was too tired to fabricate an excuse to go out and forage for something substantial. He lurched off to bed, remembering to remove his shoes but forgetting all about the spread.

He was awakened next morning by a loud honking and clattering of wings. He rolled out of bed and went to the windows just in time to see the mallards dispossessed from the pond by what appeared to be a red balloon. When he got his eyes working properly, he saw that it was a bathing cap. He wandered out to the pond, stretching and groaning. Linda yelled cheerfully and swam toward him. She heaved herself up out of the pond onto the curbing. The bathing cap was all that she wore. Mayo backed away from the splash and spatter.

"Good morning," Linda said. "Sleep well?"

"Good morning," Mayo said. "I don't know. The bed put kinks in my back. Gee, that water must be cold. You're all gooseflesh."

"No, it's marvelous." She pulled off the cap and shook her hair down. "Where's that towel? Oh, here. Go on in, Jim. You'll feel wonderful."

"I don't like it when it's cold."

"Don't be a sissy."

A crack of thunder split the quiet morning. Mayo looked up at the clear sky in astonishment. "What the hell was that?" he exclaimed.

"Watch," Linda ordered.

"It sounded like a sonic boom."

"There!" she cried, pointing west. "See?"

One of the West Side skyscrapers crumbled majestically, sinking into itself like a collapsible cup and raining masses of cornice and brick. The flayed girders twisted and contorted. Moments later they could hear the roar of the collapse.

"Man, that's a sight," Mayo muttered in awe.

"The decline and fall of the Empire City. You get used to it. Now take a dip, Jim. I'll get you a towel."

She ran into the house. He dropped his shorts and took off his socks, but was still standing on the curb, unhappily dipping his toe into the water when she returned with a huge bath towel.

"It's awful cold, Linda," he complained.

"Didn't you take cold showers when you were a wrestler?"

"Not me. Boiling hot."

"Jim, if you just stand there, you'll never go in. Look at you, you're starting to shiver. Is that a tattoo around your waist?"

"What? Oh, yea. It's a python, in five colors. It goes all the way around. See?" He revolved proudly. "Got it when I was with the Army in Saigon back in '64. It's a Oriental-type python. Elegant, huh?"

"Did it hurt?"

"To tell the truth, no. Some guys try to make out like it's Chinese torture to get tattooed, but they're just showin' off. It itches more than anything else."

"You were a soldier in '64?"

"That's right."

"How old were you?"

"Twenty."

"You're thirty-seven now?"

"Thirty-six going on thirty-seven."

"Then you're prematurely grey?"

"I guess so."

She contemplated him thoughtfully. "I tell you what, if you do go in, don't get your head wet."

She ran back into the house. Mayo, ashamed of his vacillation, forced himself to jump feet first into the pond. He was standing, chest deep, splashing his face and shoulders with water when Linda returned. She carried a stool, a pair of scissors, and a comb.

"Doesn't it feel wonderful?" she called.

"No."

She laughed. "Well, come out. I'm going to give you a haircut."

He climbed out of the pond, dried himself, and obediently sat on the stool while she cut his hair. "The beard, too," Linda insisted. "I want to see what you really look like." She trimmed him close enough for shaving, inspected him, and nodded with satisfaction. "Very handsome."

"Aw, go on," he blushed.

"There's a bucket of hot water on the stove. Go and shave. Don't bother to dress. We're going to get you new clothes after breakfast, and then . . . the Piano."

"I couldn't walk around the streets naked," he said, shocked.

"Don't be silly. Who's to see? Now hurry."

They drove down to Abercrombie & Fitch on Madison and 45th Street, Mayo wrapped modestly in his towel. Linda told him she'd been a customer for years, and showed him the pile of sales slips she had accumulated. Mayo examined them curiously while she took his measurements and went off in search of clothes. He was almost indignant when she returned with her arms laden.

"Jim, I've got some lovely elk moccasins, and a safari suit, and wool socks, and shipboard shirts, and—"

"Listen," he interrupted, "do you know what your whole tab comes to? Nearly fourteen hundred dollars."

"Really? Put on the shorts first. They're drip-dry."

"You must have been out of your mind, Linda. What'd you want all that junk for?"

"Are the socks big enough? What junk? I needed everything."

"Yeah? Like . . ." He shuffled the signed sales slips. "Like one Underwater Viewer with Plexiglas Lens, nine ninety-five? What for?"

"So I could see to clean the bottom of the pond."

"What about this Stainless Steel Service for Four, thirty-nine fifty?"

"For when I'm lazy and don't feel like heating water. You can wash stainless steel in cold water." She admired him. "Oh, Jim, come look in the mirror. You're real romantic, like the big-game hunter in that Hemingway story."

He shook his head. "I don't see how you're ever going to get out of hock. You got to watch your spending, Linda. Maybe we better forget about that piano, huh?"

"Never," Linda said adamantly. "I don't care how much it costs. A piano is a lifetime investment, and it's worth it."

She was frantic with excitement as they drove uptown to the Steinway showroom, and helpful and underfoot by turns. After a long afternoon of muscle-cracking and critical engineering involving makeshift gantries and an agonizing dolly-haul up Fifth Avenue, they had the piano in place in Linda's living room. Mayo gave it one last shake to make sure it was firmly on its legs and then sank down, exhausted. "Je-zuz!" he groaned. "Hiking south would've been easier."

"Jim!" Linda ran to him and threw herself on him with a fervent hug. "Jim, you're an angel. Are you all right?"

"I'm okay." He grunted. "Get off me, Linda. I can't breathe."

"I just can't thank you enough. I've been dreaming about this for ages. I don't know what I can do to repay you. Anything you want, just name it."

"Aw," he said, "you already cut my hair."

"I'm serious."

"Ain't you teaching me how to drive?"

"Of course. As quickly as possible. That's the least I can do." Linda backed to a chair and sat down, her eyes fixed on the piano.

"Don't make such a fuss over nothing," he said, climbing to his feet. He sat down before the keyboard, shot an embarrassed grin at her over his shoulder, then reached out and began stumbling through *The Minuet in G.*

Linda gasped and sat bolt upright. "You play," she whispered.

"Naw. I took piano when I was a kid."

"Can you read music?"

"I used to."

"Could you teach me?"

"I guess so; it's kind of hard. Hey, here's another piece I had to take." He began mutilating *The Rustle of Spring.* What with the piano out of tune and his mistakes, it was ghastly.

"Beautiful," Linda breathed. "Just beautiful!" She stared at his back while an expression of decision and determination stole across her face. She arose, slowly crossed to Mayo, and put her hands on his shoulders.

He glanced up. "Something?" he asked.

"Nothing," she answered. "You practice the piano. I'll get dinner."

But she was so preoccupied for the rest of the evening that she made Mayo nervous. He stole off to bed early.

It wasn't until three o'clock the following afternoon that they finally got a car working, and it wasn't a Caddy, but a Chevy—a hardtop because Mayo didn't like the idea of being exposed to the weather in a convertible. They drove out of the Tenth Avenue garage and back to the East Side, where Linda felt more at home. She confessed that the boundaries of her world were from Fifth Avenue to Third, and from 42nd Street to 86th. She was uncomfortable outside this pale.

She turned the wheel over to Mayo and let him creep up and down Fifth and Madison, practicing starts and stops. He sideswiped five wrecks, stalled eleven times, and reversed through a storefront which, fortunately, was devoid of glass. He was trembling with nervousness.

"It's real hard," he complained.

"It's just a question of practice," she reassured him. "Don't worry. I promise you'll be an expert if it takes us a month."

"A whole month!"

"You said you were a slow learner, didn't you? Don't blame me. Stop here a minute."

He jolted the Chevy to a halt. Linda got out.

"Wait for me."

"What's up?"

"A surprise."

She ran into a shop and was gone for half an hour. When she reappeared she was wearing a pencil-thin black sheath, pearls, and high-heeled opera pumps. She had twisted her hair into a coronet. Mayo regarded her with amazement as she got into the car.

"What's all this?" he asked.

"Part of the surprise. Turn east on Fifty-second Street."

He labored, started the car, and drove east. "Why'd you get all dressed up in an evening gown?"

"It's a cocktail dress."

"What for?"

"So I'll be dressed for where we're going. Watch out, Jim!" Linda wrenched the wheel and sheared off the stern of a shattered sanitation truck. "I'm taking you to a famous restaurant."

"To eat?"

"No, silly, for drinks. You're my visiting fireman, and I have to entertain you. That's it on the left. See if you can park somewhere."

He parked abominably. As they got out of the car, Mayo stopped and began to sniff curiously.

"Smell that?" he asked.

"Smell what?"

"That sort of sweet smell."

"It's my perfume."

"No, it's something in the air, kind of sweet and choky. I know that smell from somewhere, but I can't remember."

"Never mind. Come inside." She led him into the restaurant. "You ought to be wearing a tie," she whispered, "but maybe we can get away with it."

Mayo was not impressed by the restaurant decor, but was fascinated by the portraits of celebrities hung in the bar. He spent rapt minutes burning his fingers with matches, gazing at Mel Allen, Red Barber, Casey Stengel, Frank Gifford, and Rocky Marciano. When Linda finally came back from the kitchen with a lighted candle, he turned to her eagerly.

"You ever see any of them TV stars in here?" he asked.

"I suppose so. How about a drink?"

"Sure. Sure. But I want to talk more about them TV stars."

He escorted her to a bar stool, blew the dust off, and helped her up most gallantly. Then he vaulted over the bar, whipped out his handkerchief, and polished the mahogany professionally. "This is my specialty," he grinned. He assumed the impersonally friendly attitude of the bartender. "Evening, ma'am. Nice night. What's your pleasure?"

"God, I had a rough day in the shop! Dry martini on the rocks. Better make it a double."

"Certainly, ma'am. Twist or olive?"

"Onion."

"Double-dry Gibson on the rocks. Right." Mayo searched behind the bar and finally produced whiskey, gin, and several bottles of soda, as yet only partially evaporated through their sealed caps. "Afraid we're fresh out of martinis, ma'am. What's your second pleasure?"

"Oh, I like that. Scotch, please."

"This soda'll be flat," he warned, "and there's no ice."

"Never mind."

He rinsed a glass with soda and poured her a drink.

"Thank you. Have one on me, bartender. What's your name?"

"They call me Jim, ma'am. No thanks. Never drink on duty."

"Then come off duty and join me."

"Never drink off duty, ma'am."

"You can call me Linda."

"Thank you, Miss Linda."

"Are you serious about never drinking, Jim?"

"Yeah."

"Well, happy days."

"And long nights."

"I like that, too. Is it your own?"

"Gee, I don't know. It's sort of the usual bartender's routine, a specially with guys. You know? Suggestive. No offense."

"None taken."

"Bees!" Mayo burst out.

Linda was startled. "Bees what?"

"That smell. Like inside beehives."

"Oh? I wouldn't know," she said indifferently. "I'll have another, please."

"Coming right up. Now listen, about them TV celebrities, you actually saw them here? In person?"

"Why of course. Happy days, Jim."

"May they all be Saturdays."

Linda pondered. "Why Saturdays?"

"Day off."

"Oh."

"Which TV stars did you see?"

"You name 'em, I saw 'em." She laughed. "You remind me of the kid next door. I always had to tell him the celebrities I'd seen. One day I told him I saw Jean Arthur in here, and he said, 'With his horse?'"

Mayo couldn't see the point, but was wounded nevertheless. Just as Linda was about to soothe his feelings, the bar began a gentle quivering, and at the same time a faint subterranean rumbling commenced. It came from a distance, seemed to approach slowly, and then faded away. The vibration stopped. Mayo stared at Linda.

"Je-zus! You think maybe this building's going to go?"

She shook her head. "No. When they go, it's always with that boom. You know what that sounded like? The Lexington Avenue subway."

"The subway?"

"Uh-huh. The local train."

"That's crazy. How could the subway be running?"

"I didn't say it *was*. I said it *sounded* like. I'll have another, please."

"We need more soda." Mayo explored and reappeared with bottles and a large menu. He was pale. "You better take it easy, Linda," he said. "You know what they're charging per drink? A dollar seventy-five. Look."

"To hell with the expense. Let's live a little. Make it a double, bartender. You know something, Jim? If you stayed in town, I could show you where all your heroes lived. Thank you. Happy days. I could take you up to BBDO and show you their tapes and films. How about that? Stars like . . . like Red . . . Who?"

"Barber."

"Red Barber, and Rocky Gifford, and Rocky Casey, and Rocky the Flying Squirrel."

"You're putting me on," Mayo said, offended again.

"Me, sir? Putting you on?" Linda said with dignity. "Why would I do a thing like that? Just trying to be pleasant. Just trying to give you a good time. My mother told me, 'Linda,' she told me, 'just remember this, about a man. Wear what he wants and say what he likes,' is what she told me. You want this dress?" she demanded.

"I like it, if that's what you mean."

"Know what I paid for it? Ninety-nine fifty."

"What? A hundred dollars for a skinny black thing like that?"

"It is not a skinny black thing like that. It is a basic black cocktail frock. And I paid twenty dollars for the pearls. Simulated," she explained. "And sixty for the opera pumps. And forty for the perfume. Two hundred and twenty dollars to give you a good time. You having a good time?"

"Sure."

"Want to smell me?"

"I already have."

"Bartender, give me another."

"Afraid I can't serve you, ma'am."

"Why not?"

"You've had enough already."

"I have not had enough already," Linda said indignantly. "Where's your manners?" She grabbed the whiskey bottle. "Come on, let's have a few drinks and talk up a storm about TV stars. Happy days. I could take you up to BBDO and show you their tapes and films. How about that?"

"You just asked me."

"You didn't answer. I could show you movies, too. You like movies? I hate 'em, but I can't knock 'em anymore. Movies saved my life when the big bang came."

"How was that?"

"This is a secret, understand? Just between you and me. If any other agency ever found out . . ." Linda looked around and then lowered her voice. "BBDO located this big cache of silent films. Lost films, see? Nobody knew the prints were around. Make a great TV series. So they sent me to this abandoned mine in Jersey to take inventory."

"In a mine?"

"That's right. Happy days."

"Why were they in a mine?"

"Old prints. Nitrate. Catch fire. Also rot. Have to be stored like wine. That's why. So took two of my assistants with me to spend weekend down there, checking."

"You stayed in the mine a whole weekend?"

"Uh-huh. Three girls. Friday to Monday. That was the plan. Thought it would be a fun deal. Happy days. So . . . Where was I? Oh. So, took lights, blankets, linen, plenty of picnic, the whole schmeer, and went to work. I remember exact moment when blast came. Was looking for third reel of a UFA film, *Gekronter Blumenorden an der Pegnitz*. Had reel one, two, four, five, six. No three. Bang! Happy days."

"Jesus. Then what?"

"My girls panicked. Couldn't keep 'em down there. Never saw them again. But I knew. I knew. Stretched that picnic forever. Then starved even longer. Finally came up, and for what? For who? Whom?" She began to weep. "For nobody. Nobody left. Nothing." She took Mayo's hands. "Why won't you stay?"

"Stay? Where?"

"Here."

"I am staying."

"I mean for a long time. Why not? Haven't I got lovely home? And there's all New York for supplies. And farm for flowers and vegetables. We could keep cows and chickens. Go fishing. Drive cars. Go to museums. Art galleries. Entertain . . ."

"You're doing all that right now. You don't need me."

"But I do. I do."

"For what?"

"For piano lessons."

After a long pause he said, "You're drunk."

"Not wounded, sire, but dead."

She lay her head on the bar, beamed up at him roguishly, and then closed her eyes. An instant later, Mayo knew she had passed out. He compressed his lips. Then he climbed out of the bar, computed the tab, and left fifteen dollars under the whiskey bottle.

He took Linda's shoulder and shook her gently. She collapsed into his arms, and her hair came tumbling down. He blew out the candle, picked Linda up, and carried her to the Chevy. Then, with anguished concentration, he drove through the dark to the boat pond. It took him forty minutes.

He carried Linda into her bedroom and sat her down on the bed, which was decorated with an elaborate arrangement of dolls. Immediately she rolled over and curled up with a doll in her arms, crooning to it. Mayo lit a lamp and tried to prop her upright. She went over again, giggling.

"Linda," he said, "you got to get that dress off."

"Mf."

"You can't sleep in it. It cost a hundred dollars."

"Nine'nine-fif'y."

"Now come on, honey."

"Fm."

He rolled his eyes in exasperation and then undressed her, carefully hanging up the basic black cocktail frock, and standing the sixty-dollar pumps in a corner. He could not manage the clasp of the pearls (simulated), so he put her to bed still wearing them. Lying on the pale blue sheets, nude except for the necklace, she looked like a Nordic odalisque.

"Did you muss my dolls?" she mumbled.

"No. They're all around you."

"Tha's right. Never sleep without 'em." She reached out and petted them lovingly. "Happy days. Long nights."

"Women!" Mayo snorted. He extinguished the lamp and tramped out, slamming the door behind him.

Next morning Mayo was again awakened by the clatter of dispossessed ducks. The red balloon was sailing on the surface of the pond, bright in the warm June sunshine. Mayo wished it was a model boat instead of the kind of girl who got drunk in bars. He stalked out and jumped into the water as far from Linda as possible. He was sluicing his chest when something seized his ankle and nipped him. He let out a yell, and was confronted by Linda's beaming face bursting out of the water before him.

"Good morning," she laughed.

"Very funny," he muttered.

"You look mad this morning."

He grunted.

"And I don't blame you. I did an awful thing last night. I didn't give you any dinner, and I want to apologize."

"I wasn't thinking about dinner," he said with baleful dignity.

"No? Then what on earth are you mad about?"

"I can't stand women who get drunk."

"Who was drunk?"

"You."

"I was not," she said indignantly.

"No? Who had to be undressed and put to bed like a kid?"

"Who was too dumb to take off my pearls?" she countered. "They broke and I slept on pebbles all night. I'm covered with black and blue marks. Look. Here and here and—"

"Linda," he interrupted sternly, "I'm just a plain guy from New Haven. I got no use for spoiled girls who run up charge accounts and all the time decorate theirselves and hang around society-type saloons getting loaded."

"If you don't like my company, why do you stay?"

"I'm going," he said. He climbed out and began drying himself. "I'm starting south this morning."

"Enjoy your hike."

"I'm driving."

"What? A kiddie-car?"

"The Chevy."

"Jim, you're not serious?" She climbed out of the pond, looking alarmed. "You really don't know how to drive yet."

"No? Didn't I drive you home falling-down drunk last night?"

"You'll get into awful trouble."

"Nothing I can't get out of. Anyway, I can't hang around here forever. You're a party girl; you just want to play. I got serious things on my mind. I got to go south and find guys who know about TV."

"Jim, you've got me wrong. I'm not like that at all. Why, look at the way I fixed up my house. Could I have done that if I'd been going to parties all the time?"

"You done a nice job," he admitted.

"Please don't leave today. You're not ready yet."

"Aw, you just want me to hang around and teach you music."

"Who said that?"

"You did. Last night."

She frowned, pulled off her cap, then picked up her towel and began drying herself. At last she said, "Jim, I'll be honest with you. Sure, I want you to stay a while. I won't deny it. But I wouldn't want you around permanently. After all, what have we got in common?"

"You're so damn uptown," he growled.

"No, no, it's nothing like that. It's simply that you're a guy and I'm a girl, and we've got nothing to offer each other. We're different. We've got different tastes and interests. Fact?"

"Absolutely."

"But you're not ready to leave yet. So I tell you what; we'll spend the whole morning practicing driving, and then we'll have some fun. What would you like to do? Go window-shopping? Buy more clothes? Visit the Modern Museum? Have a picnic?"

His face brightened. "Gee, you know something? I was never to a picnic in my whole life. Once I was bartender at a clambake, but that's not the same thing; not like when you're a kid."

She was delighted. "Then we'll have a real kid-type picnic."

And she brought her dolls. She carried them in her arms while Mayo toted the picnic basket to the Alice in Wonderland monument. The statue perplexed Mayo, who had never heard of Lewis Carroll. While Linda seated her pets and unpacked the picnic, she gave Mayo a summary of the story, and described how the bronze heads of Alice, the Mad Hatter, and the March Hare had been polished bright by the swarms of kids playing King of the Mountain.

"Funny, I never heard of that story," he said.

"I don't think you had much of a childhood, Jim."

"Why would you say a—" He stopped, cocked his head, and listened intently.

"What's the matter?" Linda asked.

"You hear that bluejay?"

"No."

"Listen. He's making a funny sound; like steel."

"Steel?"

"Yeah. Like . . . like swords in a duel."

"You're kidding."

"No. Honest."

"But birds sing; they don't make noises."

"Not always. Bluejays imitate noises a lot. Starlings, too. And parrots. Now why would he be imitating a sword fight? Where'd he hear it?"

"You're a real country boy, aren't you, Jim? Bees and bluejays and starlings and all that . . ."

"I guess so. I was going to ask; why would you say a thing like that, me not having any childhood?"

"Oh, things like not knowing Alice, and never going on a picnic, and always wanting a model yacht." Linda opened a dark bottle. "Like to try some wine?"

"You better go easy," he warned.

"Now stop it, Jim. I'm not a drunk."

"Did you or didn't you get smashed last night?"

She capitulated. "All right, I did; but only because it was my first drink in years."

He was pleased by her surrender. "Sure. Sure. That figures."

"So? Join me?"

"What the hell, why not?" He grinned. "Let's live a little. Say, this is one swingin' picnic, and I like the plates, too. Where'd you get them?"

"Abercrombie & Fitch," Linda said, deadpan. "Stainless Steel Service for Four, thirty-nine fifty. Skoal."

Mayo burst out laughing. "I sure goofed, didn't I, kicking up all that fuss? Here's looking at you."

"Here's looking right back."

They drank and continued eating in warm silence, smiling companionably at each other. Linda removed her madras silk shirt in order to tan in the blazing afternoon sun, and Mayo politely hung it up on a branch. Suddenly Linda asked, "Why didn't you have a childhood, Jim?"

"Gee, I don't know." He thought it over. "I guess because my mother died when I was a kid. And something else, too; I had to work a lot."

"Why?"

"My father was a schoolteacher. You know how they get paid."

"Oh, so that's why you're anti-egghead."

"I am?"

"Of course. No offense."

"Maybe I am," he conceded. "It sure was a letdown for my old man, me playing fullback in high school and him wanting like an Einstein in the house."

"Was football fun?"

"Not like playing games. Football's a business. Hey, remember when we were kids how we used to choose up sides? *Ibbety, bibbety, zibbety, zab?*"

"We used to say, *Eenie, meenie, miney, mo.*"

"Remember: *April Fool, go to school, tell your teacher you're a fool?*"

"*I love coffee, I love tea, I love the boys, and the boys love me.*"

"I bet they did at that," Mayo said solemnly.

"Not me."

"Why not?"

"I was always too big."

He was astonished. "But you're not big," he assured her. "You're just the right size. Perfect. And really built, I noticed when we moved the piano in. You got muscle, for a girl. A specially in the legs, and that's where it counts."

She blushed. "Stop it, Jim."

"No. Honest."

"More wine?"

"Thanks. You have some, too."

"All right."

A crack of thunder split the sky with its sonic boom, and was followed by the roar of collapsing masonry.

"There goes another skyscraper," Linda said. "What were we talking about?"

"Games," Mayo said promptly. "Excuse me for talking with my mouth full."

"Oh yes. Jim did you play *Drop the Handkerchief* up in New Haven?" Linda sang. *"A tisket, a tasket, a green and yellow basket. I sent a letter to my love, and on the way I dropped it . . ."*

"Gee," he said, much impressed. "You sing real good."

"Oh, go on!"

"Yes you do. You got a swell voice. Now don't argue with me. Keep quiet a minute. I got to figure something out." He thought intently for a long time, finishing his wine and absently accepting another glass. Finally he delivered himself of a decision. "You got to learn music."

"You know I'm dying to, Jim."

"So I'm going to stay awhile and teach you; as much as I know. Now hold it! Hold it!" he added hastily, cutting off her excitement. "I'm not going to stay in your house. I want a place of my own."

"Of course, Jim. Anything you say."

"And I'm still headed south."

"I'll teach you to drive, Jim. I'll keep my word."

"And no strings, Linda."

"Of course not. What kind of strings?"

"You know. Like the last minute you all of a sudden got a Looey Cans couch you want me to move in."

"Louis Quinze!" Linda's jaw dropped. "Wherever did you learn that?"

"Not in the army, that's for sure."

They laughed, clinked glasses, and finished their wine. Suddenly Mayo leaped up, pulled Linda's hair, and ran to the Wonderland monument. In an instant he had climbed to the top of Alice's head.

"I'm King of the Mountain," he shouted, looking around in imperial survey. "I'm King of the—" He cut himself off and stared down behind the statue.

"Jim, what's the matter?"

Without a word, Mayo climbed down and strode to a pile of debris half-hidden inside overgrown forsythia bushes. He knelt and began turning over the wreckage with gentle hands. Linda ran to him.

"Jim, what's wrong?"

"These used to be model boats," he muttered.

"That's right. My God, is that all? I thought you were sick or something."

"How come they're here?"

"Why, I dumped them, of course."

"You?"

"Yes. I told you. I had to clear out the boathouse when I moved in. That was ages ago."

"You did this?"

"Yes. I—"

"You're a murderer," he growled. He stood up and glared at her. "You're a killer. You're like all women, you got no heart and soul. To do a thing like this!"

He turned and stalked toward the boat pond. Linda followed him, completely bewildered.

"Jim, I don't understand. Why are you so mad?"

"You ought to be ashamed of yourself."

"But I had to have house room. You wouldn't expect me to live with a lot of model boats."

"Just forget everything I said. I'm going to pack and go south, I wouldn't stay with you if you was the last person on earth."

Linda gathered herself and suddenly darted ahead of Mayo. When he tramped into the boathouse, she was standing before the door of the guest room. She held up a heavy iron key.

"I found it," she panted. "Your door's locked."

"Gimme that key, Linda."

"No."

He stepped toward her, but she faced him defiantly and stood her ground.

"Go ahead," she challenged. "Hit me."

He stopped. "Aw, I wouldn't pick on anybody that wasn't my own size."

They continued to face each other, at a complete impasse.

"I don't need my gear," Mayo muttered at last. "I can get more stuff somewheres."

"Oh, go ahead and pack," Linda answered. She tossed him the key and stood aside. Then Mayo discovered there was no lock in the bedroom door. He opened the door, looked inside, closed it, and looked at Linda. She kept her face straight but began to sputter. He grinned. Then they both burst out laughing.

"Gee," Mayo said, "you sure made a monkey out of me. I'd hate to play poker against you."

"You're a pretty good bluffer yourself, Jim. I was scared to death you were going to knock me down."

"You ought to know I wouldn't hurt nobody."

"I guess I do. Now, let's sit down and talk this over sensibly."

"Aw, forget it, Linda. I kind of lost my head over them boats, and I—"

"I don't mean the boats; I mean going south. Every time you get mad you start south again. Why?"

"I told you, to find guys who know about TV."

"Why?"

"You wouldn't understand."

"I can try. Why don't you explain what you're after—specifically? Maybe I can help you."

"You can't do nothing for me; you're a girl."

"We have our uses. At least I can listen. You can trust me, Jim. Aren't we chums? Tell me about it."

Well, when the blast come (Mayo said) I was up in the Berkshires with Gil Watkins. Gil was my buddy, a real nice guy and a real bright guy. He took two years from M.I.T. before he quit college. He was like chief engineer or something at WNHA, the TV station in New Haven. Gil had a million hobbies. One of them was spee—speel—I can't remember. It meant exploring caves.

So anyway we were up in this flume in the Berkshires, spending the weekend inside, exploring and trying to map everything and figure out where the underground river comes from. We brought food and stuff along, and bedrolls. The compass we were using went crazy for like twenty minutes, and that should have give us a clue, but Gil talked about magnetic ores and stuff. Only when we come out Sunday night, I tell you it was pretty scary. Gil knew right off what happened.

"By Christ, Jim," he said, "they up and done it like everybody always knew they would. They've blew and gassed and poisoned and radiated themselves straight to hell, and we're going back to that goddamn cave until it all blows over."

So me and Gil went back and rationed the food and stayed as long as we could. Finally we come out again and drove back to New Haven. It was dead like all the rest. Gil put together some radio stuff and tried to pick up broadcasts. Nothing. Then we packed some canned goods and drove all around: Bridgeport, Waterbury, Hartford, Springfield, Providence, New London . . . a big circle. Nobody. Nothing. So we come back to New Haven and settled down, and it was a pretty good life.

Daytime, we'd get in supplies and stuff, and tinker with the house to keep it working right. Nights, after supper, Gil would go off to WNHA around seven o'clock and start the station. He was running it on the emergency generators. I'd go down to "The Body Slam," open it up, sweep it out, and then start the bar TV set. Gil fixed me a generator for it to run on.

It was a lot of fun watching the shows Gil was broadcasting. He'd start with the news and weather, which he always got wrong. All he had was some Farmer's Almanacs and a sort of antique barometer that looked like that clock you got there on the wall. I don't think it worked so good, or maybe Gil never took weather at M.I.T. Then he'd broadcast the evening show.

I had my shotgun in the bar in case of holdups. Anytime I saw something that bugged me, I just up with the gun and let loose at the set. Then I'd take it and throw it out the front door and put another one in its place. I must have had hundreds waiting in the back. I spent two days a week just collecting reserves.

Midnight, Gil would turn off WNHA, I'd lock up the restaurant, and we'd meet home for coffee. Gil would ask how many sets I shot, and laugh when I told him. He said I was the most accurate TV poll ever invented. I'd ask him about what shows were coming up next week and argue with him about . . . oh . . . about like what movies or football games WNHA was scheduling. I didn't like Westerns much, and I hated them high-minded panel discussions.

But the luck had to turn lousy; it's the story of my life. After a couple of years, I found out I was down to my last set, and then I was in trouble. This night Gil run one of them icky commercials where this smart-aleck woman saves a marriage with the right laundry soap. Naturally I reached for my gun, and only at the last minute remembered not to shoot. Then he run an awful movie about a misunderstood composer, and the same thing happened. When we met back at the house, I was all shook up.

"What's the matter?" Gil asked.

I told him.

"I thought you liked watching the shows," he said.

"Only when I could shoot 'em."

"You poor bastard," he laughed, "you're a captive audience now."

"Gil, could you maybe change the programs, seeing the spot I'm in?"

"Be reasonable, Jim. WNHA has to broadcast variety. We operate on the cafeteria basis; something for everybody. If you don't like a show, why don't you switch channels?"

"Now that's silly. You know damn well we only got one channel in New Haven."

"Then turn your set off."

"I can't turn the bar set off, it's part of the entertainment. I'd lose my whole clientele. Gil, do you *have* to show them awful movies, like that army musical last night, singing and dancing and kissing on top of Sherman tanks for Jezus sake!"

"The women love uniform pictures."

"And those commercials; women always sneering at somebody's girdle, and fairies smoking cigarettes, and—"

"Aw," Gil said, "write a letter to the station."

So I did, and a week later I got an answer. It said: *Dear Mr. Mayo: We are very glad to learn that you are a regular viewer of WNHA, and thank you for your interest in our programming. We hope you will continue to enjoy our broadcasts. Sincerely yours, Gilbert O. Watkins, Station Manager.* A couple of tickets for an interview show were enclosed. I showed the letter to Gil, and he just shrugged.

"You see what you're up against, Jim," he said. "They don't care about what you like or don't like. All they want to know is if you are watching."

I tell you, the next couple of months were hell for me. I couldn't keep the set turned off, and I couldn't watch it without reaching for my gun a dozen times a night. It took all my willpower to keep from pulling the trigger. I got so nervous and jumpy that I knew I had to do something about it before I went off my rocker. So one night I brought the gun home and shot Gil.

Next day I felt a lot better, and when I went down to "The Body Slam" at seven o'clock to clean up, I was whistling kind of cheerful. I swept out the restaurant, polished the bar, and then turned on the TV to get the news and weather. You wouldn't believe it, but the set was busted. I couldn't get a picture. I couldn't even get a sound. My last set, busted.

So you see, that's why I have to head south (Mayo explained)—I got to locate a TV repairman.

There was a long pause after Mayo finished his story. Linda examined him keenly, trying to conceal the gleam in her eye. At last she asked with studied carelessness, "Where did he get the barometer?"

"Who? What?"

"Your friend, Gil. His antique barometer. Where did he get it?"

"Gee, I don't know. Antiquing was another one of his hobbies."

"And it looked like that clock?"

"Just like it."

"French?"

"I couldn't say."

"Bronze?"

"I guess so. Like your clock. Is that bronze?"

"Yes. Shaped like a sunburst?"

"No, just like yours."

"That's a sunburst. The same size?"

"Exactly."

"Where was it?"

"Didn't I tell you? In our house."

"Where's the house?"

"On Grant Street."

"What number?"

"Three fifteen. Say, what is all this?"

"Nothing, Jim. Just curious. No offense. Now I think I'd better get our picnic things."

"You wouldn't mind if I took a walk by myself?"

She cocked an eye at him. "Don't try driving alone. Garage mechanics are scarcer than TV repairmen."

He grinned and disappeared; but after dinner the true purpose of his disappearance was revealed when he produced a sheaf of sheet music, placed it on the piano rack, and led Linda to the piano bench. She was delighted and touched.

"Jim, you angel! Wherever did you find it?"

"In the apartment house across the street. Fourth floor, rear. Name of Horowitz. They got a lot of records, too. Boy, I can tell you it was pretty spooky snooping around in the dark with only matches. You know something funny, the whole top of the house is full of glop."

"Glop?"

"Yeah. Sort of white jelly, only it's hard. Like clear concrete. Now look, see this note? It's C. Middle C. It stands for this white key here. We better sit together. Move over . . ."

The lesson continued for two hours of painful concentration and left them both so exhausted that they tottered to their rooms with only perfunctory good nights.

"Jim," Linda called.

"Yeah?" he yawned.

"Would you like one of my dolls for your bed?"

"Gee, no. Thanks a lot, Linda, but guys really ain't interested in dolls."

"I suppose not. Never mind. Tomorrow I'll have something for you that really interests guys."

Mayo was awakened next morning by a rap on his door. He heaved up in bed and tried to open his eyes.

"Yeah? Who is it?" he called.

"It's me. Linda. May I come in?"

He glanced around hastily. The room was neat. The hooked rug was clean. The precious candlewick bedspread was neatly folded on top of the dresser.

"Okay. Come on in."

Linda entered, wearing a crisp seersucker dress. She sat down on the edge of the fourposter and gave Mayo a friendly pat. "Good morning," she said. "Now listen. I'll have to leave you alone for a few hours. I've got things to do. There's breakfast on the table, but I'll be back in time for lunch. All right?"

"Sure."

"You won't be lonesome?"

"Where you going?"

"Tell you when I get back." She reached out and tousled his head. "Be a good boy and don't get into mischief. Oh, one other thing. Don't go into my bedroom."

"Why should I?"

"Just don't anyway."

She smiled and was gone. Moments later, Mayo heard the jeep start and drive off. He got up at once, went into Linda's bedroom, and looked around. The room was neat, as ever. The bed was made, and her pet dolls were lovingly arranged on the coverlet. Then he saw it.

"Gee," he breathed.

It was a model of a full-rigged clipper ship. The spars and rigging were intact, but the hull was peeling, and the sails were shredded. It stood before Linda's closet, and alongside it was her sewing basket. She had already cut out a fresh set of white linen sails. Mayo knelt down before the model and touched it tenderly.

"I'll paint her black with a gold line around her," he murmured, "and I'll name her the *Linda N.*"

He was so deeply moved that he hardly touched his breakfast. He bathed, dressed, took his shotgun and a handful of shells, and went out to wander through the park. He circled south, passed the playing fields, the decaying carousel, and the crumbling skating rink, and at last left the park and loafed down Seventh Avenue.

He turned east on 50th Street and spent a long time trying to decipher the tattered posters advertising the last performance at Radio City Music Hall. Then he turned south again. He was jolted to a halt by the sudden clash of steel. It sounded like giant sword blades in a titanic duel. A small herd of stunted horses burst out of a side street, terrified by the clangor. Their shoeless hooves thudded bluntly on the pavement. The sound of steel stopped.

"That's where that bluejay got it from," Mayo muttered. "But what the hell is it?"

He drifted eastward to investigate, but forgot the mystery when he came to the diamond center. He was dazzled by the blue-white stones glittering in the showcases. The door of one jewel mart had sagged open, and Mayo tipped in. When he emerged it was with a strand of genuine matched pearls which had cost him an I.O.U. worth a year's rent on "The Body Slam."

His tour took him to Madison Avenue where he found himself before Abercrombie & Fitch. He went in to explore and came at last to the gun racks. There he lost all sense of time, and when he recovered his senses, he was walking up Fifth Avenue toward the boat pond. An Italian Cosmi automatic rifle was cradled in his arms, guilt was in his heart, and a sales slip in the store read: *I.O.U. 1 Cosmi Rifle, $750.00. 6 Boxes Ammo. $18.00. James Mayo*.

It was past three o'clock when he got back to the boathouse. He eased in, trying to appear casual, hoping the extra gun he was carrying would go unnoticed. Linda was sitting on the piano bench with her back to him.

"Hi," Mayo said nervously. "Sorry I'm late. I . . . I brought you a present. They're real." He pulled the pearls from his pocket and held them out. Then he saw she was crying.

"Hey, what's the matter?"

She didn't answer.

"You wasn't scared I'd run out on you? I mean, well, all my gear is here. The car, too. You only had to look."

She turned. "I hate you!" she cried.

He dropped the pearls and recoiled, startled by her vehemence. "What's the matter?"

"You're a lousy rotten liar!"

"Who? Me?"

"I drove up to New Haven this morning." Her voice trembled with passion. "There's no house standing on Grant Street. It's all wiped out. There's no Station WNHA. The whole building's gone."

"No."

"Yes. And I went to your restaurant. There's no pile of TV sets out in the street. There's only one set, over the bar. It's rusted to pieces. The rest of the restaurant is a pigsty. You were living there all the time. Alone. There was only one bed in back. It was lies! All lies!"

"Why would I lie about a thing like that?"

"You never shot any Gil Watkins."

"I sure did. Both barrels. He had it coming."

"And you haven't got any TV set to repair."

"Yes I do."

"And even if it is repaired, there's no station to broadcast."

"Talk sense," he said angrily. "Why would I shoot Gil if there wasn't any broadcast."

"If he's dead, how can he broadcast?"

"See? And you just now said I didn't shoot him."

"Oh, you're mad! You're insane!" she sobbed. "You just described that barometer because you happened to be looking at my clock. And I believed your crazy lies. I had my heart set on a barometer to match my clock. I've been looking for years." She ran to the wall arrangement and hammered her fist alongside the clock. "It belongs right here. Here. But you lied, you lunatic. There never was a barometer."

"If there's a lunatic around here, it's you," he shouted. "You're so crazy to get this house decorated that nothing's real for you anymore."

She ran across the room, snatched up his old shotgun, and pointed it at him. "You get out of here. Right this minute. Get out or I'll kill you. I never want to see you again."

The shotgun kicked off in her hands, knocking her backward, and spraying shot over Mayo's head into a corner bracket. China shattered and clattered down. Linda's face went white.

"Jim! My God, are you all right? I didn't mean to . . . it just went off . . ."

He stepped forward, too furious to speak. Then, as he raised his hand to cuff her, the sound of distant reports came, BLAM-BLAM-BLAM. Mayo froze.

"Did you hear that?" he whispered.

Linda nodded.

"That wasn't any accident. It was a signal."

Mayo grabbed the shotgun, ran outside, and fired the second barrel into the air. There was a pause. Then again came the distant explosions in a stately triplet, BLAM-BLAM-BLAM. They had an odd, sucking sound, as though they were implosions rather than explosions. Far up the park, a canopy of frightened birds mounted into the sky.

"There's somebody," Mayo exulted. "By God, I told you I'd find somebody. Come on."

They ran north, Mayo digging into his pockets for more shells to reload and signal again.

"I got to thank you for taking that shot at me, Linda."

"I didn't shoot at you," she protested. "It was an accident."

"The luckiest accident in the world. They could be passing through and never know about us. But what the hell kind of guns are they using? I never heard no shots like that before, and I heard 'em all. Wait a minute."

On the little piazza before the Wonderland monument, Mayo halted and raised the shotgun to fire. Then he slowly lowered it. He took a deep breath. In a harsh voice he said, "Turn around. We're going back to the house." He pulled her around and faced her south.

Linda stared at him. In an instant he had become transformed from a gentle teddy bear into a panther.

"Jim, what's wrong?"

"I'm scared," he growled. "I'm goddam scared, and I don't want you to be, too." The triple salvo sounded again. "Don't pay any attention," he ordered. "We're going back to the house. Come on!"

She refused to move. "But why? Why?"

"We don't want any part of them. Take my word for it."

"How do you know? You've got to tell me."

"Christ! You won't let it alone until you find out, huh? All right. You want the explanation for that bee smell, and them buildings falling down, and all the rest?" He turned Linda around with a hand on her neck, and directed her gaze at the Wonderland monument. "Go ahead. Look."

A consummate craftsman had removed the heads of Alice, the Mad Hatter, and the March Hare, and replaced them with towering mantis heads, all saber mandibles, antennae, and faceted eyes. They were of a burnished steel and gleamed with unspeakable ferocity. Linda let out a sick whimper and sagged against Mayo. The triple report signaled once more.

Mayo caught Linda, heaved her over his shoulder, and loped back toward the pond. She recovered consciousness in a moment and began to moan. "Shut up," he growled. "Whining won't help." He set her on her feet before the boathouse. She was shaking but trying to control herself. "Did this place have shutters when you moved in? Where are they?"

"Stacked." She had to squeeze the words out. "Behind the trellis."

"I'll put 'em up. You fill buckets with water and stash 'em in the kitchen. Go!"

"Is it going to be a siege?"

"We'll talk later. Go!"

She filled buckets and then helped Mayo jam the last of the shutters into the window embrasures. "All right, inside," he ordered. They went into the house and shut and barred the door. Faint shafts of the late afternoon sun filtered through the louvers of the shutters. Mayo began unpacking the cartridges for the Cosmi rifle. "You got any kind of gun?"

"A .22 revolver somewhere."

"Ammo?"

"I think so."

"Get it ready."

"Is it going to be a siege?" she repeated.

"I don't know. I don't know who they are, or what they are, or where they come from. All I know is, we got to be prepared for the worst."

The distant implosions sounded. Mayo looked up alertly, listening. Linda could make him out in the dimness now. His face looked carved. His chest gleamed with sweat. He exuded the musky odor of caged lions. Linda had an overpowering impulse to touch him. Mayo loaded the rifle, stood it alongside the shotgun, and began padding from shutter to shutter, peering out vigilantly, waiting with massive patience.

"Will they find us?" Linda asked.

"Maybe."

"Could they be friendly?"

"Maybe."

"Those heads looked so horrible."

"Yeah."

"Jim, I'm scared. I've never been so scared in my life."

"I don't blame you."

"How long before we know?"

"An hour, if they're friendly; two or three, if they're not."

"W-Why longer?"

"If they're looking for trouble, they'll be more cautious."

"Jim, what do you really think?"

"About what?"

"Our chances."

"You really want to know?"

"Please."

"We're dead."

She began to sob. He shook her savagely. "Stop that. Go get your gun ready."

She lurched across the living room, noticed the pearls Mayo had dropped, and picked them up. She was so dazed that she put them on automatically. Then she went into her darkened bedroom and pulled Mayo's model yacht away from the closet door. She located the .22 in a hatbox on the closet floor and removed it along with a small carton of cartridges.

She realized that a dress was unsuited to this emergency. She got a turtleneck sweater, jodhpurs, and boots from the closet. Then she stripped naked to change. Just as she raised her arms to unclasp the pearls, Mayo entered, paced to the shuttered south window, and peered out. When he turned back from the window, he saw her.

He stopped short. She couldn't move. Their eyes locked, and she began to tremble, trying to conceal herself with her arms. He stepped forward, stumbled on the model yacht, and kicked it out of the way. The next instant he had taken possession of her body, and the pearls went flying, too. As she pulled him down on the bed, fiercely tearing the shirt from his back, her pet dolls also went into the discard heap along with the yacht, the pearls, and the rest of the world.

WILL YOU WAIT?

They keep writing those antiquated stories about bargains with the Devil. You know—sulfur, spells and pentagrams; tricks, snares and delusions. They don't know what they're talking about. Twentieth-century diabolism is slick and streamlined, like jukeboxes and automatic elevators and television and all the other modern efficiencies that leave you helpless and infuriated.

A year ago I got fired from an agency job for the third time in ten months. I had to face the fact that I was a failure. I was also dead broke. I decided to sell my soul to the Devil, but the problem was how to find him. I went down to the main reference room of the library and read everything on demonology and devillore. Like I said,

it was all just talk. Anyway, if I could have afforded the expensive in-
gredients which they claimed could raise the Devil, I wouldn't have
had to deal with him in the first place.

I was stumped, so I did the obvious thing; I called Celebrity Service. A delicate young man answered.

I asked, "Can you tell me where the Devil is?"

"Are you a subscriber to Celebrity Service?"

"No."

"Then I can give you no information."

"I can afford to pay a small fee for one item."

"You wish limited service?"

"Yes."

"Who is the celebrity, please?"

"The Devil."

"Who?"

"The Devil—Satan, Lucifer, Scratch, Old Nick—the Devil."

"One moment, please." In five minutes he was back, extremely
annoyed. "Veddy soddy. The Devil is no longer a celebrity."

He hung up. I did the sensible thing and looked through the
telephone directory. On a page decorated with ads for Sardi's
Restaurant I found Satan, Shaitan, Carnage & Bael, 477 Madison
Avenue, Judson 3-1900. I called them. A bright young woman
answered.

"SSC&B. Good morning."

"May I speak to Mr. Satan, please?"

"The lines are busy. Will you wait?"

I waited and lost my dime. I wrangled with the operator and lost
another dime but got the promise of a refund in postage stamps. I
called Satan, Shaitan, Carnage & Bael again.

"SSC&B. Good morning."

"May I speak to Mr. Satan? And please don't leave me hanging
on the phone. I'm calling from a—"

The switchboard cut me off and buzzed. I waited. The coin box
gave a warning click. At last a line opened.

"Miss Hogan's office."

"May I speak to Mr. Satan?"

"Who's calling?"

"He doesn't know me. It's a personal matter."

"I'm sorry. Mr. Satan is no longer with our organization."

"Can you tell me where I can find him?"

There was muffled discussion in broad Brooklyn and then Miss Hogan spoke in crisp Secretary: "Mr. Satan is now with Beelzebub, Belial, Devil & Orgy."

I looked them up in the phone directory. 383 Madison Avenue, Murray Hill 2-1900. I dialed. The phone rang once and then choked. A metallic voice spoke in sing-song: "The number you are dialing is not a working number. Kindly consult your directory for the correct number. This is a recorded message." I consulted my directory. It said Murray Hill 2-1900. I dialed again and got the same recorded message.

I finally broke through to a live operator, who was persuaded to give me the new number of Beelzebub, Belial, Devil & Orgy. I called them. A bright young woman answered.

"BBDO. Good morning."

"May I speak to Mr. Satan, please?"

"Who?"

"Mr. Satan."

"I'm sorry. There is no such person with our organization."

"Then give me Beelzebub or the Devil."

"One moment, please."

I waited. Every half minute she opened my wire long enough to gasp, "Still ringing the Dev—" and then cut off before I had a chance to answer. At last a bright young woman spoke. "Mr. Devil's office."

"May I speak to him?"

"Who's calling?"

I gave her my name.

"He's on another line. Will you wait?"

I waited. I was fortified with a dwindling reserve of nickels and dimes. After twenty minutes, the bright young woman spoke again: "He's just gone into an emergency meeting. Can he call you back?"

"No. I'll try again."

Nine days later I finally got him.

"Yes, sir? What can I do for you?"

I took a breath. "I want to sell you my soul."

"Have you got anything on paper?"

"What do you mean, anything on paper?"

"The Property, my boy. The Sell. You can't expect BBDO to buy a pig in a poke. We may drink out of Dixie cups up here, but the sauce has got to be a hundred proof. Bring in your Presentation. My girl'll set up an appointment."

I prepared a Presentation of my soul with plenty of Sell. Then I called his girl.

"I'm sorry, he's on the Coast. Call back in two weeks."

Five weeks later she gave me an appointment. I went up and sat in the photomontage reception room of BBDO for two hours, balancing my Sell on my knees. Finally I was ushered into a corner office decorated with Texas brands in glowing neon. The Devil was lounging on his contour chair, dictating to an Iron Maiden. He was a tall man with the phony voice of a sales manager; the kind that talks loud in elevators. He gave me a Sincere handshake and immediately looked through my Presentation.

"Not bad," he said. "Not bad at all. I think we can do business. Now, what did you have in mind? The usual?"

"Money, success, happiness."

He nodded. "The usual. Now, we're square-shooters in this shop. BBDO doesn't dry-gulch. We'll guarantee money, success, and happiness."

"For how long?"

"Normal life span. No tricks, my boy. We take our estimates from the actuary tables. Offhand I'd say you're good for another forty, forty-five years. We can pinpoint that in the contract later."

"No tricks?"

He gestured impatiently. "That's all bad public relations, what you're thinking. I promise you, no tricks."

"Guaranteed?"

"Not only do we guarantee service; we *insist* on giving service. BBDO doesn't want any beefs going up to the Fair Practice Committee. You'll have to call on us for service at least twice a year or the contract will be terminated."

"What kind of service?"

He shrugged. "Any kind. Shine your shoes; empty ashtrays; bring you dancing girls. That can be pinpointed later. We just insist that you use us at least twice a year. We've got to give you a *quid* for your *quo. Quid pro quo.* Check?"

"But no tricks?"

"No tricks. I'll have our legal department draw up the contract. Who's representing you?"

"You mean an agent? I haven't got one."

He was startled. "Haven't got an agent? My boy, you're living dangerously. Why, we could skin you alive. Get yourself an agent and tell him to call me."

"Yes, sir. M-may I . . . Could I ask a question?"

"Shoot. Everything is open and aboveboard at BBDO."

"What will it be like for me—wh-when the contract terminates?"

"You really want to know?"

"Yes."

"I don't advise it."

"I want to know."

He showed me. It was like a hideous session with a psychoanalyst, in perpetuity—an eternal, agonizing self-indictment. It was hell. I was shaken.

"I'd rather have inhuman fiends torturing me," I said.

He laughed. "They can't compare to man's inhumanity to himself. Well . . . changed your mind, or is it a deal?"

"It's a deal."

We shook hands and he ushered me out. "Don't forget," he warned. "Protect yourself. Get an agent. Get the best."

I signed with Sibyl & Sphinx. That was on March third. I called S&S on March fifteenth. Mrs. Sphinx said, "Oh, yes, there's been a hitch. Miss Sibyl was negotiating with BBDO for you, but she had to fly to Sheol. I've taken over for her."

I called April first. Miss Sibyl said, "Oh, yes, there's been a slight delay. Mrs. Sphinx had to go to Salem for a tryout. A witch-burning. She'll be back next week."

I called April fifteenth. Miss Sibyl's bright young secretary told me that there was some delay getting the contracts typed. It seemed that BBDO was reorganizing its legal department. On May first Sibyl & Sphinx told me that the contracts had arrived and that *their* legal department was looking them over.

I had to take a menial job in June to keep body and soul together. I worked in the stencil department of a network. At least once a week a script would come in about a bargain with the Devil that was signed, sealed and delivered before the opening commercial.

I used to laugh at them. After four months of negotiation I was still threadbare.

I saw the Devil once, bustling down Park Avenue. He was running for Congress and was very busy being jolly and hearty with the electorate. He addressed every cop and doorman by his first name. When I spoke to him he got a little frightened, thinking I was a Communist or worse. He didn't remember me at all.

In July, all negotiations stopped; everybody was away on vacation. In August everybody was overseas for some Black Mass Festival. In September Sibyl & Sphinx called me to their office to sign the contract. It was thirty-seven pages long, and fluttered with pasted-in corrections and additions. There were half a dozen tiny boxes stamped on the margin of every page.

"If you only knew the work that went into this contract," Sibyl & Sphinx told me with satisfaction.

"It's kind of long, isn't it?"

"It's the short contracts that make all the trouble. Initial every box, and sign on the last page. All six copies."

I initialed and signed. When I was finished, I didn't feel any different. I'd expected to start tingling with money, success, and happiness.

"Is it a deal now?" I asked.

"Not until *he's* signed it."

"I can't hold out much longer."

"We'll send it over by messenger."

I waited a week and then called.

"You forgot to initial one of the boxes," they told me.

I went to the office and initialed. After another week I called.

"*He* forgot to initial one of the boxes," they told me that time.

On October first I received a special-delivery parcel. I also received a registered letter. The parcel contained the signed, sealed and delivered contract between me and the Devil. I could at last be rich, successful, and happy. The registered letter was from BBDO and informed me that in view of my failure to comply with Clause 27-A of the contract, it was considered terminated, and I was due for collection at their convenience. I rushed down to Sibyl & Sphinx.

"What's Clause 27-A?" they asked.

We looked it up. It was the clause that required me to use the services of the Devil at least once every six months.

"What's the date of the contract?" Sibyl & Sphinx asked.

We looked it up. The contract was dated March first, the day I'd had my first talk with the Devil in his office.

"March, April, May . . ." Miss Sibyl counted on her fingers. "That's right. Seven months have elapsed. Are you sure you didn't ask for *any* service?"

"How could I? I didn't have a contract."

"We'll see about this," Mrs. Sphinx said grimly. She called BBDO and had a spirited argument with the Devil and his legal department. Then she hung up. "He says you shook hands on the deal March first," she reported. "He was prepared in good faith to go ahead with his side of the bargain."

"How could I know? I didn't have a contract."

"Didn't you ask for anything?"

"No. I was waiting for the contract."

Sibyl & Sphinx called in their legal department and presented the case.

"You'll have to arbitrate," the legal department said, and explained that agents are forbidden to act as their client's attorney.

I hired the legal firm of Wizard, Warlock, Vodoo, Dowser & Hag (99 Wall Street, Exchange 3-1900) to represent me before the Arbitration Board (479 Madison Avenue, Lexington 5-1900). They asked for a two-hundred-dollar retainer plus 20 percent of the contract's benefits. I'd managed to save thirty-four dollars during the four months I was working in the stencil department. They waived the retainer and went ahead with the Arbitration preliminaries.

On November fifteenth the network demoted me to the mail room, and I seriously contemplated suicide. Only the fact that my soul was in jeopardy in an arbitration stopped me.

The case came up December twelfth. It was tried before a panel of three impartial Arbitrators and took all day. I was told they'd mail me their decision. I waited a week and called Wizard, Warlock, Voodoo, Dowser & Hag.

"They've recessed for the Christmas holidays," they told me.

I called January second.

"One of them's out of town."

I called January tenth.

"He's back, but the other two are out of town."

"When will I get a decision?"

"It could take months."

"How do you think my chances look?"

"Well, we've never lost an arbitration."

"That sounds pretty good."

"But there can always be a first time."

That sounded pretty bad. I got scared and figured I'd better copper my bets. I did the sensible thing and hunted through the telephone directory until I found Seraphim, Cherubim and Angel, 666 Fifth Avenue, Templeton 4-1900. I called them. A bright young woman answered.

"Seraphim, Cherubim and Angel. Good morning."

"May I speak to Mr. Angel, please?"

"He's on another line. Will you wait?"

I'm still waiting.

THE FLOWERED
THUNDERMUG

We will conclude this first semester of Antiquities 107," Professor Paul Muni said, "with a reconstruction of an average day in the life of a mid-twentieth-century inhabitant of the United States of America, as Great L.A. was known five hundred years ago.

"Let us refer to him as Jukes, one of the proudest names of the times, immortalized in the Kallikak-Jukes-feud sagas. It is now generally agreed that the mysterious code letters JU, found in the directories of Hollywood East, or New York City as it was called then—viz., JU 6-0600 or JU 2-1914—indicate in some manner a genealogical relationship to the powerful Jukes dynasty.

"The year is 1950. Mr. Jukes, a typical 'loner'—i.e., 'bachelor'—lives on a small ranch outside New York. He rises at dawn, dresses in spurred boots, Daks slacks, rawhide shirt, gray flannel waistcoat and black knit tie. He arms himself with a Police Positive revolver or a Frontier Six Shooter and goes out to the Bar-B-Q to prepare his breakfast of curried plankton or converted algae. He may or may not surprise juvenile delinquents or red Indians on his ranch in the act of lynching a victim or rustling his automobiles, of which he has a herd of perhaps one hundred and fifty.

"These hooligans he disperses after single combat with his fists. Like all twentieth-century Americans, Jukes is a brute of fantastic strength, giving and receiving sledgehammer blows, or being battered by articles of furniture with inexhaustible resilience. He rarely uses his gun on such occasions; it is usually reserved for ceremonial rituals.

"Mr. Jukes journeys to his job in New York City on horseback, in a sports car (a kind of open automobile), or on an electric trolley car. He reads his morning newspaper, which will feature such stories as: 'The Discovery of the North Pole,' 'The Sinking of the Luxury Liner *Titanic*,' 'The Successful Orbiting of Mars by Manned Space Capsule,' or 'The Strange Death of President Harding.'

"Jukes works in an advertising agency situated on Madison Avenue (now Sunset Boulevard East), which, in those days, was a rough muddy highway, traversed by stagecoaches, lined with gin mills and populated by bullies, corpses, and beautiful night-club performers in abbreviated dresses. Jukes is an agency man, dedicated to the guidance of taste, the improvement of culture, the election of public officers, and the selection of national heroes.

"His office on the twentieth floor of a towering skyscraper is decorated in the characteristic style of the mid-twentieth century. He has a rolltop desk, a Null-G, or Free Fall chair and a brass spittoon. Illumination is by Optical Maser light pumps. Large fans suspended from the ceiling cool him in the summer, and an infrared Franklin stove warms him in the winter.

"The walls are decorated with rare pictures executed by such famous painters as Michelangelo, Renoir, and Sunday. Alongside the desk is a tape recorder, which he uses for dictation. His words are later written down by a secretary using a pen and carbon ink. (It has, by now, been clearly demonstrated that the typewriting machine was not developed until the onset of the Computer Age at the end of the twentieth century.)

"Mr. Jukes's work involves the creation of the spiritual slogans that uplift the consumer half of the nation. A few of these have come down to us in more or less fragmentary condition, and those of you who have taken Professor Rex Harrison's course, Linguistics 916, know the extraordinary difficulties we are encountering in our attempts to interpret: 'Good to the Last Drop' (for 'good' read 'God'?); 'Does She or Doesn't She?' (what?); and 'I Dreamed I Went to the Circus in My Maidenform Bra' (incomprehensible).

"At midday, Mr. Jukes takes a second meal, usually a community affair with thousands of others in a giant stadium. He returns to his office and resumes work, but you must understand that conditions were not ideal for concentration, which is why he was forced to labor as much as four and six hours a day. In those deplorable times there was a constant uproar of highway robberies, hijackings, gang wars and other brutalities. The air was filled with falling bodies as despairing brokers leaped from their office windows.

"Consequently it is only natural for Mr. Jukes to seek spiritual peace at the end of the day. This he finds at a ritual called a 'cocktail party.' He and many other believers stand close-packed in a small room, praying aloud, and filling the air with the sacred residues of marijuana and mescaline. The women worshippers often wear vestments called 'cocktail dresses,' otherwise known as 'basic black.'

"Afterward, Mr. Jukes may take his last meal of the day in a night club, an underground place of entertainment where raree shows are presented. He is often accompanied by his 'expense account,' a phrase difficult to interpret. Dr. David Niven argues most cogently that it was cant for 'a woman of easy virtue,' but Professor Nelson Eddy points out that this merely compounds the difficulty, since no one today knows what 'a woman of easy virtue' was.

"Finally, Mr. Jukes returns to his ranch on a 'commuters' special,' a species of steam car, on which he plays games of chance with the professional gamblers who infested all the transportation systems of the times. At home, he builds a small outdoor fire, calculates the day's expenses on his abacus, plays sad music on his guitar, makes love to one of the thousands of strange women who made it a practice of intruding on campfires at odd hours, rolls up in a blanket and goes to sleep.

"Such was the barbarism of that age—an age so hysteric that few men lived beyond one hundred years. And yet romantics today yearn for that monstrous era of turmoil and terror. Twentieth-century Americana is all the vogue. Only recently, a single copy of *Life*, a sort of mail-order catalogue, was bought at auction by the noted collector Clifton Webb for $150,000. I might mention, in passing, that in my analysis of that curio in the current *Phil. Trans.* I cast grave doubts on its authenticity. Certain anachronisms in the text indicate a possible forgery.

"And now a final word about your term examinations. There has been some talk about bias on the part of the computer. It has been suggested that when this department took over the Multi-III from Biochemistry various circuits were overlooked and left operative, prejudicing the computer in favor of the mathematical approach. This is utter nonsense. Our computer psychiatrist assures me that the Multi-III was completely brainwashed and reindoctrinated. Exhaustive checks have shown that all errors were the result of student carelessness.

"I urge you to observe the standard sterilization procedures before taking your examination. Do not scamp your wash-up. Make sure your surgical caps, gowns, masks, and gloves are properly adjusted. Be certain that your punching tools are in register and sterile. Remember that one speck of contamination on your answer card can wreck your results. The Multi-III is not a machine, it is a brain, and requires the same care and consideration you give your own bodies. Thank you, good luck, and I hope to see you all again next semester."

Coming out of the lecture hall, Professor Muni was met in the crowded corridor by his secretary, Ann Sothern. She was wearing a polka dot bikini, carried a tray of drinks and had a pair of the professor's swim trunks draped over her arm. Muni nodded in appreciation, swallowed a quick one and frowned at the traditional musical production number with which the students moved from class to class. He began reassembling his lecture notes as they hurried from the building.

"No time for a dip, Miss Sothern," he said. "I'm scheduled to sneer at a revolutionary discovery in the Medical Arts Building this afternoon."

"It's not on your calendar, Dr. Muni."

"I know. I know. But Raymond Massey is sick, and I'm standing in for him. Ray says he'll substitute for me the next time I'm due to advise a young genius to give up poetry."

They left the Sociology Building, passed the teardrop swimming pool, the book-shaped library, the heart-shaped Heart Clinic, and came to the faculty-shaped Faculty Building. It was in a grove of royal palms through which a miniature golf course meandered, its air conditioners emitting a sibilant sound. Inside the Faculty Building, concealed loudspeakers were broadcasting the latest noise-hit.

"What is it—Caruso's 'Niagara'?" Professor Muni asked absently.

"No, Callas's 'Johnstown Flood,'" Miss Sothern answered, opening the door of Muni's office. "Why, that's odd. I could have sworn I left the lights on." She felt for the light switch.

"Stop," Professor Muni snapped. "There's more here than meets the eye, Miss Sothern."

"You mean . . . ?"

"Who does one traditionally encounter on a surprise visit in a darkened room? I mean, *whom*."

"Th-the Bad Guys?"

"Precisely."

A nasal voice spoke. "You are so right, my dear professor, but I assure you this is purely a private business matter."

"Dr. Muni," Miss Sothern gasped. "There's someone in your office."

"Do come in, professor," the nasal voice said. "That is, if you will permit me to invite you into your own office. There is no use trying to turn on the lights, Miss Sothern. They have been—attended to."

"What is the meaning of this intrusion?" Professor Muni demanded.

"Come in. Come in. Boris, guide the professor to a chair. The goon who is taking your arm, Professor Muni, is my ruthless bodyguard, Boris Karloff. I am Peter Lorre."

"I demand an explanation," Muni shouted. "Why have you invaded my office? Why are the lights out? By what right do you—"

"The lights are out because it is best that people do not see Boris. He is a most useful man, but not, shall we say, an aesthetic delight. Why I have invaded your office will be made known to you after you have answered one or two trifling questions."

"I will do nothing of the sort. Miss Sothern, get the dean."

"You will remain where you are, Miss Sothern."

"Do as you're told, Miss Sothern. I will not permit this—"

"Boris, light something."

Something was lit. Miss Sothern screamed. Professor Muni was dumb-struck.

"All right, Boris, put it out. Now, my dear professor, to business. First, let me inform you that it will be worth your while to answer my questions honestly. Be good enough to put out your hand." Professor Muni extended his hand. A sheaf of bills was placed in it. "Here is one thousand dollars, your consultation fee. Would you care to count it? Shall I have Boris light something?"

"I believe you," Muni muttered.

"Very good. Professor Muni, where and how long did you study American history?"

"That's an odd question, Mr. Lorre."

"You have been paid, Professor Muni."

"Very true. Well . . . I studied at Hollywood High, Harvard High, Yale High, and the College of the Pacific."

"What is 'college'?"

"The old name for a high. They're traditionalists at Pacific— hidebound reactionaries."

"And how long did you study?"

"Some twenty years."

"How long have you been teaching here at Columbia High?"

"Fifteen years."

"Then that adds up to thirty-five years of experience. Would you say that you had an extensive knowledge of the merits and qualifications of the various living historians?"

"Fairly extensive. Yes."

"Then who, in your opinion, is the leading authority on twentieth-century Americana?"

"Ah. So. Very interesting. Harrison, of course, on advertising copy, newspaper headlines, and photo captions. Taylor on domestic science—that's Dr. Elizabeth Taylor. Gable is probably your best bet for transportation. Clark's at Cambridge High now, but he—"

"Excuse me, Professor Muni. I put the question badly. I should have asked: Who is the leading authority on twentieth-century objects of virtu? Antiques, paintings, furniture, curios, *objets d'art*, and so forth . . ."

"Ah! I have no hesitation in answering that, Mr. Lorre. Myself."

"Very good. Very good. Now listen carefully, Professor Muni. I have been delegated by a little group of powerful men to hire your professional services. You will be paid ten thousand dollars in advance. You will give your word that the transaction will be kept secret. And it must be understood that if your mission fails, we will do nothing to help you."

"That's a lot of money," Professor Muni said slowly. "How can I be sure that this offer is from the Good Guys?"

"You have my assurance that it is for freedom and justice, the man on the street, the underdogs, and the L.A. Way of Life. Of course, you can refuse this dangerous assignment, and it will not be held against you, but you are the one man in all Great L.A. who can carry it out."

"Well," Professor Muni said, "seeing that I have nothing better to do than mistakenly sneer at a cancer cure today, I might as well accept."

"I knew we could depend on you. You are the sort of little man that makes L.A. great. Boris, sing the national anthem."

"Thank you, but I need no praise. I'm just doing what any loyal, red-blooded, one-hundred-percent Angeleno would do."

"Very good. I will pick you up at midnight. You will be wearing rough tweeds, a felt hat pulled down over your face, and stout shoes. You will carry one hundred feet of mountaineering rope, prism binoculars, and an ugly snub-nosed fission gun. Your code identity will be .369."

"This," Peter Lorre said, "is .369. .369, may I have the pleasure of introducing you to X, Y, and Z?"

"Good evening, Professor Muni," the Italian-looking gentleman said. "I am Vittorio De Sica. This is Miss Garbo. That is Edward Everett Horton. Thank you, Peter. You may go."

Mr. Lorre exited. Muni stared around. He was in a sumptuous penthouse apartment decorated entirely in white. Even the fire burning in the grate was, by some miracle of chemistry, composed entirely of milk-white flames. Mr. Horton was pacing nervously before the fire. Miss Garbo reclined languidly on a polar-bear skin, an ivory cigarette holder drooping from her hand.

"Let me relieve you of that rope, professor," De Sica said. "And the customary binoculars and snub-nosed pistol, I presume? I'll take them too. Do make yourself comfortable. You must forgive our being in faultless evening dress; our cover identities, you understand. We operate the gambling hell downstairs. Actually we are—"

"No!" Mr. Horton cried in alarm.

"Unless we have full faith in Professor Muni and are perfectly candid, we will get nowhere, my dear Horton. You agree, Greta?"

Miss Garbo nodded.

"Actually," De Sica continued, "we are a little group of powerful art dealers."

Muni stammered. "Th-then . . . Then you're *the* De Sica, and *the* Garbo, and *the* Horton?"

"We are."

"B-but . . . But everyone says you don't exist. Everyone believes that the organization known as the Little Group of Powerful Art Dealers is really owned by 'The Thirty-nine Steps,' with the controlling interest vested in *Cosa Vostro*. It is said that—"

"Yes, yes," De Sica interrupted. "That is what we desire to have believed; hence our cover identity as the sinister trio operating this gambling syndicate. But it is we three who control the art of the world, and that is why you are here."

"I don't understand."

"Show him the list," Miss Garbo growled.

De Sica produced a sheet of paper and handed it to Muni. "Be good enough to read this list of articles, Professor. Study it carefully. A great deal will depend on the conclusions you draw."

Automatic grill-waffler
Steam-spray iron
12-speed electric mixer
Automatic 6-cup percolator
Electric aluminum fry pan
4-burner gas heater-range w. griddle
11-cubic-foot refrigerator plus 170-lb. freezer
Power sweeper, canister-type, w. vinyl bumper

Sewing machine w. bobbins and needles
Maple-finished-pine wagon-wheel chandelier
Opal-glass ceiling-fixture lamp
Hobnail-glass Provincial-style lamp
Pull-down brass lamp w. beaded glass diffuser
Double-bell black-faced alarm clock
50-piece service for 8, mirror-lite flatware
16-piece service for 4, Du Barry–pattern dinnerware
All-nylon pile rug, 9x12, spice beige
Colonial rug, oval, 9x12, fern green
Hemp outdoor "Welcome" mat, 18x30
Sofa-bed and chair, sage green
Round foam-rubber hassock
Serofoam recliner chair w. 3-way mechanism
Drop-leaf extension table, seats 8
4 captain's chairs w. scoop seats
Colonial oak bachelor's chest, 3 drawers
Colonial oak double dresser, 6 drawers
French Provincial canopy bed, 54 in. wide

After studying the list for ten minutes, Professor Muni put the paper down and heaved a deep sigh. "It reads like the most fabulous buried treasure in history," he said.

"Oh, it is not buried, Professor."

Muni sat bolt upright. "You mean these objects actually exist?" he exclaimed.

"Most certainly they do. More of that later. First, have you absorbed the items?"

"Yes."

"You have them in your mind's eye?"

"I do."

"Then can you answer this question: Are these treasures all of a kind, of a style, of a taste?"

"You are obscure, Vittorio," Miss Garbo growled.

"What we want to know," Edward Everett Horton burst out, "is whether one man could—"

"Gently, my dear Horton. Each question in its proper sequence. Professor, perhaps I have been obscure. What I am asking is this: Do these treasures represent one man's taste? That is to say, could the man who—let us say—collected the twelve-speed electric mixer also be the man who collected the hemp outdoor 'Welcome' mat?"

"If he could afford both," Muni chuckled.

"We will, for the sake of argument, say that he can afford all the items on that list."

"A national government couldn't afford all of them," Muni replied. "However, let me think. . . ." He leaned back in his chair and squinted at the ceiling, hardly aware that the Little Group of Powerful Art Dealers was watching him intently. After much face-contorting concentration, Muni opened his eyes and looked around.

"Well? Well?" Horton demanded anxiously.

"I've been visualizing those treasures in one room," Muni said. "They go remarkably well together. In fact, they would make one of the most impressive and beautiful rooms in the world. If one were to walk into such a room, one would immediately want to know who the genius was who decorated it?"

"Then . . . ?"

"Yes. I would say this was the taste of one man."

"Aha! Then your guess was right, Greta. We are dealing with a lone shark."

"No, no, no. It's impossible." Horton hurled his B&B glass into the fire, and then flinched at the crash. "It can't be a lone shark. It must be many men, all kinds, operating independently. I tell you—"

"My dear Horton, pour yourself another drink and calm yourself. You are only confusing the good doctor. Professor Muni, I told you that the items on that list exist. They do. But I did not tell you that we don't know where they are at present. We do not for a very good reason; they have all been stolen."

"No! I can't believe it."

"But yes, plus perhaps a dozen more rarities, which we have not bothered to itemize because they are rather minor."

"Surely this was not a single, comprehensive collection of Americana. I would have been aware of its existence."

"No. Such a single collection never was and never will be."

"Ve vould not permit it," Miss Garbo said.

"Then how were they stolen? Where?"

"By crooks," Horton exclaimed, waving the Brandy & Banana

decanter. "By dozens of different thieves. It can't be one man's work."

"The professor has said it is one man's taste."

"It's impossible. Forty daring robberies in fifteen months? I won't believe it."

"The rare objects on that list," De Sica continued to Muni, "were stolen over a period of fifteen months from collectors, museums, dealers, and importers, all in the Hollywood East area. If, as you say, the objects represent one man's taste—"

"I do."

"Then it is obvious we have on our hands a *rara avis*, a clever criminal who is also a connoisseur, or, what is perhaps even more dangerous, a connoisseur who has turned criminal."

"But why particularize?" Muni asked. "Why must he be a connoisseur? Any average art dealer could tell a crook the value of antique *objets d'art*. The information could even be obtained from a library."

"I say connoisseur," De Sica answered, "because none of the stolen objects has ever been seen again. None has been offered for sale anywhere in the four orbits of the world, despite the fact that any one of them would be worth a king's ransom. Ergo, we are dealing with a man who steals to add to his own collection."

"Enough, Vittorio," Miss Garbo growled. "Ask him the next qvestion."

"Professor, we now assume we are dealing with a man of taste. You have seen the list of what he has stolen thus far. I ask you, as a historian: can you suggest any object of virtu that obviously belongs in his collection? If a rare item were to come to his attention, something that would fit in beautifully with that hypothetical room you visualized—what might it be? What would tempt the connoisseur in the criminal?"

"Or the criminal in the connoisseur," Muni added. Again he squinted at the ceiling while the others watched breathlessly. At last he muttered, "Yes . . . Yes . . . That's it. It must be. It would be the focal point of the entire collection."

"What?" Horton cried. "What are you talking about?"

"The Flowered Thundermug," Muni answered solemnly.

The three art dealers looked so perplexed that Muni was forced to elaborate. "It is a blue porcelain jardiniere of uncertain function, decorated with a border of white and gold marguerites. It was discovered over a century ago by a French interpreter in Nigeria. He brought it to Greece, where he offered it for sale, but he was murdered, and the mug disappeared. It next turned up in possession of an Uzbek prostitute traveling under a Formosan passport who surrendered it to a quack in Civitavecchia in return for an alleged aphrodisiac.

"The quack hired a Swiss, a deserter from the Vatican Guards, to safeguard him to Quebec, where he hoped to sell the mug to a Canadian uranium tycoon, but he disappeared en route. Ten years later a French acrobat with a Korean passport and a Swiss accent sold the mug in Paris. It was bought by the ninth Duke of Stratford for one million gold francs, and has remained in the Olivier family ever since."

"And this," De Sica asked keenly, "could be the focal point of our connoisseur's entire collection?"

"Most definitely. I stake my reputation on it."

"Bravo! Then our plan is simplicity itself. We much publicize a pretended sale of the Flowered Thundermug to a prominent Hollywood East collector. Perhaps Mr. Clifton Webb is best suited to the role. We much publicize the shipment of the rare treasure to Mr. Webb. We bait a trap in the home of Mr. Webb for our criminal, and—*Mah!* We have him."

"Will the Duke and Mr. Webb cooperate?" Muni asked.

"They will. They must."

"They must? Why?"

"Because we have sold art treasures to both of them, Professor Muni."

"I don't follow."

"My good doctor, sales today are entirely on the residual basis. From five to fifty percent of ownership, control and resale value of all works of art remain in our possession. We own residual rights in all those stolen objects too, which is why they must be recovered. Do you understand now?"

"I do, and I see that I'm in the wrong business."

"So. Peter has paid you already?"

"Yes."

"And pledged you to secrecy?"

"I gave my word."

"*Grazie.* Then if you will excuse us, we have much work to do."

As De Sica handed Muni the coil of rope, binoculars, and snub-nosed gun, Miss Garbo said, "No."

De Sica gave her an inquiring glance. "Is there something else, *cara mia?*"

"You and Horton go and do your vork somevhere else," she growled. "Peter may have paid him, but I have not. Ve vant to be alone." And she beckoned Professor Muni to the bearskin.

In the ornate library of the Clifton Webb mansion on Skouras Drive, Detective Inspector Edward G. Robinson introduced his assistants to the Little Group of Powerful Art Dealers. His staff was lined up before the exquisitely simulated trompe-l'oeil bookshelves, and were rather trompe-l'oeil themselves in their uniforms of household servants.

"Sergeant Eddie Brophy, footman," Inspector Robinson announced. "Sergeant Eddie Albert, second footman. Sergeant Ed Begley, chef. Sergeant Eddie Mayhoff, second chef. Detectives Edgar Kennedy, chauffeur, and Edna May Oliver, maid."

Inspector Robinson himself was in the uniform of a butler. "Now, ladies and gents, the trap is baited and set, with the invaluable aid of the Police Costume, Prop and Makeup Department, Deputy Commissioner Eddie Fisher in charge, than which there is none better."

"We congratulate you," De Sica said.

"As you very well know," Robinson continued, "everybody believes that Mr. Clifton Webb has bought the Thundermug from Duke Stratford for two million dollars. They are well aware that it was secretly shipped to Hollywood East under armed guard and that at this very moment the art treasure reposes in a concealed safe in Mr. Webb's library." The inspector pointed to a wall, where the combination dial of a safe was artfully set in the navel of a nude by Amedeo Modigliani (2381–2431), and highlighted by a concealed pin spot.

"Vhere is Mr. Vebb now?" Miss Garbo asked.

"Having turned over his palatial mansion to us at your request," Robinson answered, "he is presently on a pleasure cruise of the Carib with his family and servants. As you very well know, this is a closely guarded secret."

"And the Thundermug?" Horton asked nervously. "Where is it?"

"Why, sir, in that safe."

"You mean—you mean you actually brought it over from Stratford? It's here? Oh, my God! Why? Why?"

"We had to have the art treasure transported, Mr. Horton. How else could we have leaked the closely guarded secret to Associated Press, United Television, Reuters News, and the Satellite Syndicate, thus enabling them to take sneak photographs?"

"B-but . . . But if it's actually stolen. . . . Oh, my God! This is awful."

"Ladies and gents," Robinson said. "Me and my associates, the best cops on the Hollywood East force, the Honorable Edmund Kean, Commissioner, will be here, nominally going through the duties of the household staff, actually keeping our eyes peeled, leaving no stone unturned, up to every trick and dodge known in the annals of crime. If anything's taken, it will not be the Flowered Thundermug; it will be the Artsy-Craftsy Kid."

"The who?" De Sica asked.

"Your crooked connoisseur, sir. That's our nickname for him on the Bunco Squad. And now, if you will be good enough to slip out under cover of darkness, using a little-known door in the back garden, me and my associates will begin our simulated domestic duties. We have a hot tip from the underworld that the Artsy-Craftsy Kid will strike—tonight."

The Little Group of Powerful Art Dealers departed under cover of darkness; the Bunco Squad began the evening household routine to reassure any suspicious observer that life was proceeding normally in the Webb pleasance. Inspector Robinson was to be seen, gravely pacing back and forth before the living room windows, carrying a silver salver on which was glued a wineglass, its interior ingeniously painted red to simulate claret.

Sergeants Brophy and Albert, the footmen, alternately opened the front door for each other with much elaborate formality as they took turns going out to mail letters. Detective Kennedy painted the garage. Detective Edna May Oliver hung the bedding out the upstairs windows to air. And at frequent intervals Sergeant Begley (chef) chased Sergeant Mayhoff (second chef) through the house with a meat cleaver.

At 2300 hours, Inspector Robinson put the salver down and yawned prodigiously. The cue was picked up by his staff, and the entire mansion echoed with yawns. In the living room, Inspector Robinson undressed, put on a nightgown and nightcap, lit a candle and extinguished the lights. He put out the library lights, leaving only the pin spot focused on the safe dial. Then he trudged upstairs. In other parts of the house his staff also changed to nightgowns, and then joined him. The Webb home was dark and silent.

An hour passed; a clock chimed twenty-four. A loud clank sounded from the direction of Skouras Drive.

"The front gate," Ed whispered.

"Someone's coming in," Ed said.

"It's the Artsy-Craftsy Kid," Ed added.

"Keep your voices down!"

"Right, Chief."

There was a crunch-crunch-crunch of gravel.

"Coming up the front drive," Ed muttered.

"Oh, he's a deep one," Ed said.

The gravel noises changed to mushy sounds.

"Crossing the flower border," Ed said.

"You got to hand it to him," Ed said.

There was a dull thud, a stumble and an imprecation.

"Stepped into a flowerpot," Ed said.

There came a series of thuddy noises at irregular intervals.

"Can't get it off," Ed said.

A crack and a clatter.

"Got it off now," Ed said.

"Oh, he's slick all right," Ed said.

There came exploratory taps on glass.

"At the library window," Ed said.

"Did you unlock it?"

"I thought Ed was going to do that, Chief."

"Did you, Ed?"

"No, Chief. I thought Ed was supposed to."

"He'll never get in. Ed, see if you can unlock it without him seeing—"

A crash of glass.

"Never mind, he's got it open. You can always trust a pro."

The window creaked up; there were scrapes and grunts as the midnight intruder climbed through. When he finally stood upright in the library, his silhouette against the beam of the pin spot was

apelike. He looked around uncertainly for some time, and at last began searching aimlessly through drawers and cupboards.

"He'll never find it," Ed whispered. "I told you we should of put
a sign under the dial, Chief."

"No, trust an old pro. See? What'd I tell you? He's spotted it. All
set now?"

"Don't you want to wait for him to crack it, Chief?"

"Why?"

"Catch him red-handed."

"For God's sake, that safe's burglar proof. Come on now. Ready?
Go!"

The library was flooded with light. The thief started back from the
concealed safe in consternation, to find himself surrounded by seven
grim detectives, all leveling guns at his head. The fact that they were
wearing night-shirts did not make them look any less resolute. For
their part, the detectives saw a broad-shouldered, bull-necked burglar
with a lantern jaw. The fact that he had not altogether shaken off the
contents of the flowerpot, and wore a Parma violet (*Viola pallida
plena*) on his right shoe, did not make him look any less vicious.

"And now, Kid, *if* you please," Inspector Robinson said with the
exaggerated courtesy that made his admirers call him the Beau
Brummel of the Bunco Squad.

They bore the malefactor off to headquarters in triumph.

Five minutes after the detectives departed with their captive, a
gentleman in full evening cloak sauntered up to the front door of the
Webb mansion. He rang the doorbell. From within came the music of
the first eight bars of Ravel's *Bolero* played on full carillon orchestra
in waltz tempo. While the gentleman appeared to wait carelessly, his
right hand slid through a slit in his cloak and rapidly tried a series of
keys in the lock. The gentleman rang the bell again. Midway through
the second rendition of the *Bolero,* he found a key that fitted.

He turned the lock, thrust the door open a few inches with a
twist of his toe, and spoke pleasantly, as to an invisible servant inside.

"Good evening. I'm afraid I'm rather late. Is everybody asleep, or
am I still expected? Oh, good. Thank you." The gentleman entered
the house, shut the door behind him softly, looked around at the
dark, empty foyer, and grinned. "Like taking candy from kids," he
murmured. "I ought to be ashamed of myself."

He located the library, entered and turned on all the lights. He removed his cloak, lit a cigarette, noticed the bar and then poured himself a drink from one of the more appealing decanters. He tried it and gagged. "Ack! A new horror, and I thought I knew them all. What the hell is it?" He dipped his tongue into the glass. "Scotch, yes; but Scotch and what?" He sampled again. "My God, it's broccoli juice."

He glanced around, found the safe, crossed to it and inspected it. "Great heavens!" he exclaimed. "A whole three-number dial—all of twenty-seven possible combinations. Absolutely burglar-proof. I really am impressed."

He reached for the dial, looked up, met the nude's melting glance, and smiled apologetically. "I beg your pardon," he said, and began twisting the dial: 1-1-1, 1-1-2, 1-1-3, 1-2-1, 1-2-2, 1-2-3, and so on, each time trying the handle of the safe, which had been cleverly disguised as the nude's forefinger. At 3-2-1, the handle came down with a smart click. The safe door opened, eviscerating, as it were, the lovely belly. The cracksman reached in and brought out the Flowered Thundermug. He contemplated it for a full minute.

A low voice spoke. "Remarkable, isn't it?"

The cracksman looked up quickly. A girl was standing in the library door, examining him casually. She was tall and slender, with chestnut hair and very dark blue eyes. She was wearing a revealing white sheath, and her clear skin gleamed under the lights.

"Good evening, Miss Webb—Mrs.—?"

"Miss." She flicked the third finger of her left hand at him.

"I'm afraid I didn't hear you come in."

"Nor I you." She strolled into the library. "You do think it's remarkable, don't you? I mean, I hope you're not disappointed."

"No, I'm not. It's unique."

"Who do you suppose designed it?"

"We'll never know."

"Do you think he didn't make many? Is that why it's so rare?"

"It would be pointless to speculate, Miss Webb. That's rather like asking how many colors an artist used in a painting, or how many notes a composer used in an opera."

She flowed onto a lounge. "Cigarette, please? Are you by any chance being condescending?"

"Not at all. Light?"

"Thank you."

"When we contemplate beauty we should see only the *Ding an sich*, the thing in itself. Surely you're aware of that, Miss Webb."

"I suspect you're rather detached."

"Me? Detached? Not at all. When I contemplate you, I also see only the beauty in itself. And while you're a work of art, you're hardly a museum piece."

"So you're also an expert in flattery."

"You could make any man an expert, Miss Webb."

"And now that you've broken into my father's safe, what next?"

"I intend to spend many hours admiring this work of art."

"Make yourself at home."

"I couldn't think of intruding. I'll take it along with me."

"So you're going to steal it."

"I beg you to forgive me."

"You're doing a very cruel thing, you know."

"I'm ashamed of myself."

"Do you know what the mug means to my father?"

"Certainly. A two-million-dollar investment."

"You think he trades in beauty, like brokers on the stock exchange?"

"Of course. All wealthy collectors do. They buy to own to sell at a profit."

"My father isn't wealthy."

"Oh come now, Miss Webb. Two million dollars?"

"He borrowed the money."

"Nonsense."

"He did." She spoke with great intensity, and her dark-blue eyes narrowed. "He has no money, not really. He has nothing but credit. You must know how Hollywood financiers manage that. He borrowed the money, and that mug is the security." She surged up from the lounge. "If it's stolen it will be a disaster for him—and for me."

"Miss Webb, I—"

"I beg you, don't take it. Can I persuade you?"

"Please don't come any closer."

"Oh, I'm not armed."

"You're endowed with deadly weapons that you're using ruthlessly."

"If you love this work of art for its beauty alone, why not share it with us? Or are you the kind of man you hate, the kind that must own?"

"I'm getting the worst of this."

"Why can't you leave it here? If you give it up now, you'll have won a half interest in it forever. You'll be free to come and go as you please. You'll have won a half interest in our family—my father, me, all of us. . . ."

"My God! I'm completely outclassed. All right, keep your confounded—" He broke off.

"What's the matter?"

He was staring at her left arm. "What's that on your arm?" he asked slowly.

"Nothing."

"What is it?" he persisted.

"It's a scar. I fell when I was a child and—"

"That's no scar. It's a vaccination mark."

She was silent.

"It's a vaccination mark," he repeated in awe. "They haven't vaccinated in four hundred years—not like that, they haven't."

She stared at him. "How do you know?"

In answer he rolled up his left sleeve and showed her his vaccination mark.

Her eyes widened. "You too?"

He nodded.

"Then we're both from . . ."

"From then? Yes."

They gazed at each other in amazement. Then they began to laugh with incredulous delight. They embraced and thumped each other, very much like tourists from the same home town meeting unexpectedly on top of the Eiffel Tower. At last they separated.

"It's the most fantastic coincidence in history," he said.

"Isn't it?" She shook her head in bewilderment. "I still can't quite believe it. When were you born?"

"Nineteen fifty. You?"

"You're not supposed to ask a lady."

"Come on! Come on!"

"Nineteen fifty-four."

"Fifty-four?" He grinned. "You're five hundred and ten years old."

"See? Never trust a man."

"So you're not the Webb girl. What's your real name?"

"Dugan. Violet Dugan."

"What a nice, plain, wholesome sound that has."

"What's yours?"

"Sam Bauer."

"That's even plainer and nicer. Well!"

"Shake, Violet."

"Pleased to meet you, Sam."

"It's a pleasure."

"Likewise, I'm sure."

"I was a computer man at the Denver Project in seventy-five,"
Bauer said, sipping his gin and gingersnap, the least horrific combination from the Webb bar.

"Seventy-five?" Violet exclaimed. "That was the year it blew up."

"Don't I know it. They'd bought one of the new IBM 1709s, and
IBM sent me along as installation engineer to train the Army personnel. I remember the night of the blast—at least I figure it was the
blast. All I know is, I was showing them how to program some new
algorisms for the computer when—"

"When what?"

"Somebody put out the lights. When I woke up, I was in a hospital in Philadelphia—Santa Monica East, they call it—and I learned
that I'd been kicked five centuries into the future. I'd been picked up,
naked, half dead, no identification."

"Did you tell them who you really were?"

"No. Who'd believe me? So they patched me up and discharged
me, and I hustled around until I found a job."

"As a computer engineer?"

"Oh, no; not for what they pay. I calculate odds for one of the
biggest bookies in the East. Now, what about you?"

"Practically the same story. I was on assignment at Cape
Kennedy, doing illustrations for a magazine piece on the first Mars
shoot. I'm an artist by trade—"

"The Mars shoot? That was scheduled for seventy-six, wasn't it?
Don't tell me they loused it."

"They must have, but I can't find out much in the history books."

"They're pretty vague about our time. I think that war must
have wiped most of it out."

"Anyway, I was in the control center doing sketches and making color notes during the countdown, when—well, the way you said, somebody put out the lights."

"My God! The first atomic shoot, and they blew it."

"I woke up in a hospital in Boston—Burbank North—exactly like you. After I got out, I got a job."

"As an artist?"

"Sort of. I'm an antique-faker. I work for one of the biggest art dealers in the country."

"So here we are, Violet."

"Here we are. How do you think it happened, Sam?"

"I have no idea, but I'm not surprised. When you fool around with atomic energy on such a massive scale, anything can happen. Do you think there are any more of us?"

"Shot forward?"

"Uh huh."

"I couldn't say. You're the first I ever met."

"If I thought there were, I'd look for them. My God, Violet, I'm so homesick for the twentieth century."

"Me too."

"It's grotesque here; it's all B picture," Bauer said. "Pure Hollywood cliché. The names. The homes. The way they talk. The way they carry on. All like it's straight out of the world's worst double feature."

"It is. Didn't you know?"

"Know? Know what? Tell me."

"I got it from their history books. It seems after that war nearly everything was wiped out. When they started building a new civilization, all they had for a pattern was the remains of Hollywood. It was comparatively untouched in the war."

"Why?"

"I guess nobody thought it was worth bombing."

"Who were the two sides, us and Russia?"

"I don't know. Their history books just call them the Good Guys and the Bad Guys."

"Typical. Christ, Violet, they're like idiot children. No, they're like extras in a bad movie. And what kills me is that they're happy. They're all living this grade Z synthetic life out of a Cecil B. DeMille spectacle, and the idiots love it. Did you see President

Spencer Tracy's funeral? They carried the coffin in a full-sized Sphinx."

"That's nothing. Did you see Princess Joan's wedding?"

"Fontaine?"

"Crawford. She was married under anesthesia."

"You're kidding."

"I am not. She and her husband were joined in holy matrimony by a plastic surgeon."

Bauer shuddered. "Good old Great L.A. Have you been to a football game?"

"No."

"They don't play football; they just give two hours of half-time entertainment."

"Like the marching bands; no musicians, nothing but drum majorettes with batons."

"They've got everything air-conditioned, even outdoors."

"With Muzak in every tree."

"Swimming pools on every street corner."

"Klieg lights on every roof."

"Commissaries for restaurants."

"Vending machines for autographs."

"And for medical diagnosis. They call them Medicmatons."

"Cheesecake impressions in the sidewalks."

"And here we are, trapped in hell," Bauer grunted. "Which reminds me, shouldn't we get out of this house? Where's the Webb family?"

"On a cruise. They won't be back for days. Where's the cops?"

"I got rid of them with a decoy. They won't be back for hours. Another drink?"

"All right. Thanks." Violet looked at Bauer curiously. "Is that why you're stealing, Sam, because you hate it here? Is it revenge?"

"No, nothing like that. It's because I'm homesick. . . . Try this; I think it's Rum and Rhubarb. . . . I've got a place out on Long Island—Catalina East, I ought to say—and I'm trying to turn it into a twentieth-century home. Naturally I have to steal the stuff. I spend weekends there, and it's bliss, Violet. It's my only escape."

"I see."

"Which again reminds me. What the devil were you doing here, masquerading as the Webb girl?"

"I was after the Flowered Thundermug too."

"You were going to steal it?"

"Of course. Who was as surprised as I when I discovered someone was ahead of me?"

"And that poor-little-rich-girl routine—you were trying to swindle it out of me?"

"I was. As a matter of fact, I did."

"You did indeed. Why?"

"Not the same reason as you. I want to go into business for myself."

"As an antique-faker?"

"Faker and dealer both. I'm building up my stock, but I haven't been nearly as successful as you."

"Then was it you who got away with that three-panel vanity mirror framed in simulated gold?"

"Yes."

"And that brass bedside reading lamp with adjustable extension?"

"That was me."

"Too bad; I really wanted that. How about the tufted chaise longue covered in crewel?"

She nodded. "Me again. It nearly broke my back."

"Couldn't you get help?"

"How could I trust anyone? Don't you work alone?"

"Yes," Bauer said thoughtfully. "Up to now, yes; but I don't see any reason for going on that way. Violet, we've been working against each other without knowing it. Now that we've met, why don't we set up housekeeping together?"

"What housekeeping?"

"We'll work together, furnish my house together and make a wonderful sanctuary. And at the same time you can be building up your stock, I mean, if you want to sell a chair out from under me, that'll be all right. We can always pinch another one."

"You mean share your house together?"

"Sure."

"Couldn't we take turns?"

"Take turns how?"

"Sort of like alternate weekends?"

"Why?"

"You know."

"I don't know. Tell me."

"Oh, forget it."

"No, tell me why."

She flushed. "How can you be so stupid? You know perfectly well why. Do you think I'm the kind of girl who spends weekends with men?"

Bauer was taken aback. "But I had no such proposition in mind, I assure you. The house has two bedrooms. You'll be perfectly safe. The first thing we'll do is steal a Yale lock for your door."

"It's out of the question," she said. "I know men."

"I give you my word, this will be entirely on a friendly basis. Every decorum will be observed."

"I know men," she repeated firmly.

"Aren't you being a little unrealistic?" he asked. "Here we are, refugees in this Hollywood nightmare; we ought to be helping and comforting each other; and you let a silly moral issue stand between us."

"Can you look me in the eye and tell me that sooner or later the comfort won't wind up in bed?" she countered. "Can you?"

"No, I can't," he answered honestly. "That would be denying the fact that you're a damned attractive girl. But I—"

"Then it's out of the question, unless you want to legalize it; and I'm not promising that I'll accept."

"No," Bauer said sharply. "There I draw the line, Violet. That would be doing it the L.A. way. Every time a couple want a one-night stand they go to a Wedmaton, put in a quarter and get hitched. The next morning they go to a Renomaton and get unhitched, and their conscience is clear. It's hypocrisy! When I think of the girls who've put me through that humiliation: Jane Russell, Jane Powell, Jayne Mansfield, Jane Withers, Jane Fonda, Jane Tarzan—Iyeuch!"

"Oh! You!" Violet Dugan leaped to her feet in a fury. "So, after all that talk about loathing it here, you've gone Hollywood too."

"Go argue with a woman." Bauer was exasperated. "I just said I didn't want to do it the L.A. way, and she accuses me of going Hollywood. Female logic!"

"Don't you pull your male supremacy on me," she flared. "When I listen to you, it takes me back to the old days, and it makes me sick."

"Violet . . . Violet . . . Don't let's fight. We have to stick together. Look, I'll go along with it your way. What the hell, it's only a quarter. But we'll put that lock on your door anyway. All right?"

"Oh! You! Only a quarter! You're disgusting." She picked up the Flowered Thundermug and turned.

"Just a minute," Bauer said. "Where do you think you're going?"

"I'm going home."

"Then we don't team up?"

"No."

"We don't get together on any terms?"

"No. Go and comfort yourself with those tramps named Jane. Good night."

"You're not leaving, Violet."

"I'm on my way, Mr. Bauer."

"Not with that Thundermug."

"It's mine."

"I did the stealing."

"And I did the swindling."

"Put it down, Violet."

"You gave it to me. Remember?"

"I'm telling you, put it down."

"I will not. Don't you come near me!"

"You know men. Remember? But not all about them. Now put that mug down like a good girl or you're going to learn something else about male supremacy. I'm warning you, Violet. . . . All right, love, here it comes."

Pale dawn shone into the office of Inspector Edward G. Robinson, casting blue beams through the dense cigarette smoke. The Bunco Squad made an ominous circle around the apelike figure slumped in a chair. Inspector Robinson spoke wearily.

"All right, let's hear your story again."

The man in the chair stirred and attempted to raise his head. "My name is William Bendix," he mumbled. "I am forty years of age. I am a pinnacle expediter in the employ of Groucho, Chico, Harpo and Marx, construction engineers, at 12203 Goldwyn Terrace."

"What is a pinnacle expediter?"

"A pinnacle expediter is a specialist whereby when the firm builds like a shoe-shaped building for a shoe store, he ties the laces on top; also he puts the straws on top of an ice cream parlor; also he—"

"What was your last job?"

"The Memory Institute at 30449 Louis B. Mayer Boulevard."

"What did you do?"

"I put the veins in the brain."

"Have you got a police record?"

"No, *sir.*"

"What were you perpetrating in the luxurious residence of Clifton Webb on or about midnight last night?"

"Like I said, I was having a vodka-and-spinach in Ye Olde Moderne Beer Taverne—I put the foam on top when we built it—and this guy come up to me and got to talking. He told me all about this art treasury just imported by a rich guy. He told me he was a collector hisself, but couldn't afford to buy this treasury, and the rich guy was so jealous of him he wouldn't even let him see it. He told me he would give me a hundred dollars just to get a look at it."

"You mean steal it."

"No, *sir,* look at it. He said if I would just bring it to the window so he could look at it, he would pay me a hundred dollars."

"And how much if you handed it to him?"

"No, *sir,* just look at it. Then I was supposed to put it back from whence it come from, and that was the whole deal."

"Describe the man."

"He was maybe thirty years old. Dressed good. Talked a little funny, like a foreigner, and laughed a lot, like he had a joke he wanted to tell. He was maybe medium height, maybe taller. His eyes was dark. His hair was dark and thick and wavy; it would of looked good on top of a barbershop."

There was an urgent rap on the office door. Detective Edna May Oliver burst in, looking distressed.

"Well?" Inspector Robinson snapped.

"His story stands up, Chief," Detective Oliver reported. "He was seen in Ye Olde Moderne Banana Split last night—"

"No, no, no. It was Ye Olde Moderne Beer Taverne."

"Same place, Chief. They just renovated for another grand opening tonight."

"Who put the cherries on top?" Bendix wanted to know. He was ignored.

"This perpetrator was seen talking to the mystery man he described," Detective Oliver continued. "They left together."

"It was the Artsy-Craftsy Kid."

"Yes, Chief."

"Could anyone identify him?"

"No, Chief."

"Damn! Damn! Damn!" Inspector Robinson smote the desk in exasperation. "I have a hunch that we've been tricked."

"How, Chief?"

"Don't you see, Ed? There's a chance the Kid might have found out about our secret trap."

"I don't get it, Chief."

"Think, Ed. Think! Maybe *he* was the underworld informer who sent us the anonymous tip that the Kid would strike last night."

"You mean squeal on himself?"

"Exactly."

"But why, Chief?"

"To trick us into arresting the wrong man. I tell you, he's diabolical."

"But what did that get him, Chief? You already seen through the trick."

"You're right, Ed. The Kid's plan must go deeper than that. But how? How?" Inspector Robinson arose and began pacing, his powerful mind grappling with the tortuous complications of the Artsy-Craftsy Kid's caper.

"So how about me?" Bendix asked.

"Oh, you can go," Robinson said wearily. "You're just a pawn in a far bigger game, my man."

"No, I mean, can I go through with that deal now? He's prolly still waiting outside the house for a look."

"What's that you say? Waiting?" Robinson exclaimed. "You mean he was there when we arrested you?"

"He must of been."

"I've got it! I've got it!" Robinson cried. "Now I see it all."

"See what, Chief?"

"Don't you get the picture, Ed? The Kid watched us leave with this dupe. Then, after we left, *the Kid entered the house.*"

"You mean . . . ?"

"He's probably there right now, cracking that safe."

"Great Scot!"

"Ed, alert the Flying Squad and the Riot Squad."

"Right, Chief."

"Ed, I want roadblocks all around the house."

"Check, Chief."

"Ed, you and Ed come with me."

"Where to, Chief?"

"The Webb mansion."

"You can't, Chief. It's madness."

"I must. This town isn't big enough for both of us. This time it's the Artsy-Craftsy Kid—or me."

It made headlines: how the Bunco Squad had seen through the diabolical plan of the Artsy-Craftsy Kid and arrived at the fabled Webb mansion only moments after he had made off with the Flowered Thundermug; how they had found his unconscious victim, the plucky Audrey Hepburn, devoted assistant to the mysterious gambling overlord Greta "Snake Eyes" Garbo; how Audrey, intuitively suspecting that something was amiss, had taken it upon herself to investigate; how the canny cracksman had played a sinister cat-and-mouse game with her until the opportunity came to fell her with a brutal blow.

Interviewed by the news syndicates, Miss Hepburn said, "It was just a woman's intuition. I suspected something was amiss and took it upon myself to investigate. The canny cracksman played a sinister cat-and-mouse game with me until the opportunity came to fell me with a brutal blow."

She received seventeen proposals of marriage by Wedmaton, three offers of screen tests, twenty-five dollars from the Hollywood East Community Chest, the Darryl F. Zanuck Award for Human Interest and a reprimand from her boss.

"You should also have said you vere ravished, Audrey," Miss Garbo told her. "It vould have improved the story."

"I'm sorry, Miss Garbo. I'll try to remember next time. He did make an indecent proposal."

This was in Miss Garbo's secret atelier, where Violet Dugan (Audrey Hepburn) was busily engaged in faking a calendar of the Corn Exchange Bank for the year 1943, while the members of the Little Group of Powerful Art Dealers consulted.

"*Cara mia,*" De Sica asked Violet, "can you not give us a fuller description of the scoundrel?"

"I've told you everything I can remember, Mr. De Sica. The one detail that seems to help is the fact that he computes odds for one of the biggest bookies in the East."

"*Mah!* There are hundreds of that species. It is no help at all. You did not get a clue to his name?"

"No, sir; at least, not the name he uses now."

"The name he uses now? How do you mean that?"

"I—I meant—the name he uses when he isn't the Artsy-Craftsy Kid."

"I see. And his home?"

"He said somewhere in Catalina East."

"There are a hundred and forty miles of homes in Catalina East," Horton said irritably.

"I can't help that, Mr. Horton."

"Audrey," Miss Garbo commanded, "put down that calendar and look at me."

"Yes, Miss Garbo."

"You have fallen in love vith this man. To you he is a romantic figure, and you do not vant him brought to justice. Is that not so?"

"No, Miss Garbo," Violet answered vehemently. "If there's anything in the world I want, it's to have him arrested." She fingered her jaw. "In love with him? I hate him!"

"So." De Sica sighed. "It is a disaster. Plainly, we are obliged to pay his grace two million dollars if the Thundermug is not recovered."

"In my opinion," Horton burst out, "the police will never find it. They're dolts! Almost as big a pack of fools as we were to get mixed up in this thing in the first place."

"Then it must be a case for a private eye. With our unsavory underworld connections, we should have no difficulty contacting the right man. Are there any suggestions?"

"Nero Volfe," Miss Garbo said.

"Excellent, *cara mia.* A gentleman of culture and erudition."

"Mike Hammer," Horton said.

"The nomination is noted. What would you say to Perry Mason?"

"That shyster is too honest," Horton snapped.

"The shyster is scratched. Any further suggestions?"

"Mrs. North," Violet said.

"Who, my dear? Oh, yes, Pamela North, the lady detective. No—no, I think not. This is hardly a case for a woman."

"Why not, Mr. De Sica?"

"There are prospects of violence that make it unsuited to the tender sex, my dear Audrey."

"I don't see that," Violet said. "We women can take care of ourselves."

"She is right," Miss Garbo growled.

"I think not, Greta; and her experience last night proves it."

"He felled me with a brutal blow when I wasn't looking," Violet protested.

"Perhaps. Shall we vote? I say Nero Wolfe."

"Why not Mike Hammer?" Horton demanded. "He gets results, and he doesn't care how."

"But that carelessness may recover the Thundermug in pieces."

"My God! I never thought of that. All right, I'll go along with Wolfe."

"Mrs. North," Miss Garbo said.

"You are outvoted, *cara mia*. So, it is to be Wolfe, then. *Bene*. I think we had best approach him without Greta, Horton. He is notoriously *antipatico* to women. Dear ladies, *arrivederci*."

After two of the three Powerful Art Dealers had left, Violet glared at Miss Garbo. "Male chauvinists!" she grumbled. "Are we going to stand for it?"

"Vhat can ve do about it, Audrey?"

"Miss Garbo, I want permission to track that man down myself."

"You do not mean this?"

"I'm serious."

"But vhat could you do?"

"There has to be a woman in his life somewhere."

"Naturally."

"*Cherchez la femme*."

"But that is brilliant!"

"He mentioned a few likely names, so if I find her, I find him. May I have a leave of absence, Miss Garbo?"

"Go, Audrey. Bring him back alive."

The old lady wearing the Welsh hat, white apron, hexagonal spectacles, and carrying a mass of knitting bristling with needles, stumbled on the reproduction of the Spanish Stairs, which led to the King's Arms Residenza. The King's Arms was shaped like an imperial crown, with a fifty-foot replica of the Hope diamond sparkling on top.

"Damn!" Violet Dugan muttered. "I shouldn't have been so authentic with the shoes. Sandals are hell."

She entered the Residenza and mounted to the tenth floor, where she rang a hanging bell alongside a door flanked by a lion and a unicorn, which roared and brayed alternately. The door turned misty and then cleared, revealing an Alice in Wonderland with great innocent eyes.

"Lou?" she said eagerly. Then her face fell.

"Good morning, Miss Powell," Violet said, her eyes peering past the lady and examining the apartment. "I represent Slander Service, Inc. Does gossip give you the go-by? Are you missing out on the juiciest scandals? Our staff of trained mongers guarantees the latest news within five minutes after the event; news defamatory, news derogatory, news libelous, scurrilous, disparaging and vituperative—"

"Flam," Miss Powell said. The door turned opaque.

The Marquise de Pompadour, in full brocade skirt and lace bodice, her powdered wig standing no less than two feet high, entered the grilled portico of Birdies' Rest, a private home shaped like a birdcage. A cacophony of bird calls assailed the ears from the gilt dome. Madame Pompadour blew the bird whistle set in the door, which was shaped like a cuckoo clock. The little hatch above the clock face flew open, and a TV eye popped out with a cheerful "Cuckoo!" and inspected her.

Violet sank into a deep curtsy. "May I see the lady of the house, please?"

The door opened. Peter Pan stood there, dressed in Lincoln-green transparencies, which revealed her sex.

"Good afternoon, Miss Withers. This is Avon calling. Ignatz Avon, the Topper Tailor, designs wigs, transformations, chignons, merkins, toupees and hairpieces for fun, fashion and—"

"Fawf," Miss Withers said. The door slammed. The Marquise de Pompadour fawfed.

The Left Bank artiste in beret and velvet smock carried her palette and easel to the fifteenth floor of La Pyramide. Just under the apex there were six Egyptian columns fronting a massive basalt door.

When the artiste tossed baksheesh onto a stone beggar's plate, the door swung open on pivots, revealing a gloomy tomb in which stood a Cleopatra type dressed like a Cretan serpent goddess, with serpents to match.

"Good morning, Miss Russell. Tiffany's proudly presents a new coup in organic jewelry, the Tifftoo skin gems. Tattooed in high relief, Tifftoo skin gems incorporate a source of gamma radiation, warranted harmless for thirty days, which outscintillates diamonds of the finest water."

"Shlock!" Miss Russell said. The door closed on its pivots, accompanied by the closing bars of *Aïda*, softly moaned by a harmonica choir.

The schoolmarm in crisp *tailleur*, her hair skinned back into a tight bun, her eyes magnified by thick glasses, carried her schoolbooks across the drawbridge of The Manor House. She was lifted by a crenelated elevator to the twelfth floor, where she was forced to leap across a small moat before she could wield the door knocker, which was shaped like a mailed fist. The door rumbled upward, a miniature portcullis, and there stood Goldilocks.

"Louis?" she laughed. Then her face fell.

"Good evening, Miss Mansfield. Read-Eze offers a spectacular new personalized service. Why submit to the monotony of mechanical readers when Read-Eze experts with cultivated voices, capable of coloring each individual word, will, in person, read you comic books, true-confession and movie magazines at five dollars an hour; mysteries, westerns and society columns at—"

The portcullis rumbled down.

"First Lou, then Louis," Violet muttered. "I wonder."

The little pagoda was set in an exact reproduction of the landscape on a Willow Pattern plate, including the figures of three coolies posed on the bridge. The movie starlet wearing black sunglasses and a white sweater stretched over her forty-four-inch *poitrine*, patted their heads as she passed.

"That tickles, doll," the last one said.

"Oh, excuse me! I thought you were dummies."

"At fifty cents an hour we are, but that's show business."

Madame Butterfly came to the archway of the pagoda, hissing and bowing like a geisha, but rather oddly decorated with a black patch over her left eye.

"Good morning, Miss Fonda. Sky's The Limit is making an introductory offer of a revolutionary concept in bosom uplift. One application of Breast-G, our flesh-tinted antigravity powder, under the bust works miracles. Comes in three tints: blond, titian and brunette; and three uplifts: grapefruit, Persian melon and—"

"I don't need no balloon ascension," Miss Fonda said drearily. "Fawf."

"Sorry to have bothered you." Violet hesitated. "Forgive me, Miss Fonda, but isn't that eye patch out of character?"

"It ain't no prop, dearie; it's for Real City. That Jourdan's a bastard."

"Jourdan," Violet said to herself, retracing her steps across the bridge. "Louis Jourdan. Could it be?"

The frogman in black rubber, complete with full scuba equipment including face mask, oxygen tank, and harpoon, trudged through the jungle path to Strawberry Hill Place, frightening the chimpanzees. In the distance an elephant trumpeted. The frogman banged on a brazen gong suspended from a coconut palm, and African drums answered. A seven-foot Watusi appeared and conducted the visitor to the rear of the house, where a Pocahontas type was dangling her legs in a hundred-foot replica of the Congo.

"Is it Louis Bwana?" she called. Then her face fell.

"Good afternoon, Miss Tarzan," Violet said. "Up-Chuck, with a fifty-year record of bonded performance, guarantees sterile swimming pleasure whether it's an Olympic pool or just a plain, old-fashioned swimming hole. With its patented mercury-pump vacuum-cleaning system, Up-Chuck chucks up mud, sand, silt, drunks, dregs, debris—"

The brazen gong sounded, and was again answered by drums.

"Oh! That must be Louis now," Miss Tarzan cried. "I knew he'd keep his promise."

Miss Tarzan ran around to the front of the house. Miss Dugan pulled the mask down over her face and plunged into the Congo. On the far side she came to the surface behind a frond of bamboo, alongside a most realistic alligator. She poked its head once to make sure it was stuffed. Then she turned just in time to see Sam Bauer come strolling into the jungle garden, arm in arm with Jane Tarzan.

Concealed in the telephone-shaped booth across the street from Strawberry Hill Place, Violet Dugan and Miss Garbo argued heatedly.

"It vas a mistake to call the police, Audrey."

"No, Miss Garbo."

"Inspector Robinson has been in that house ten minutes already. He vill blunder again."

"That's what I'm counting on, Miss Garbo."

"Then I vas right. You do not vant this—this Louis Jourdan to be caught."

"I do, Miss Garbo. I do! If you'll just let me explain!"

"He captured your fancy vith his indecent proposal."

"Please listen, Miss Garbo. The important thing isn't so much to catch him as it is to recover the stolen loot. Isn't that right?"

"Excuses! Excuses!"

"If he's arrested now, he may never tell us where the Thunder-mug is."

"So?"

"So we've got to make him show us where it is."

"But how?"

"I've taken a leaf from his book. Remember how he duped a decoy into fooling the police?"

"That stupid creature Bendix."

"Well, Inspector Robinson is our decoy. Oh, look! Something's happening."

Pandemonium was breaking loose in Strawberry Hill Place. The chimpanzees were screaming and flitting from branch to branch. The Watusi appeared, running hard, pursued by Inspector Robinson. The elephant began trumpeting. A giant alligator crawled hastily through the heavy grass. Jane Tarzan appeared, running hard, pursued by Inspector Robinson. The African drums pounded.

"I could have sworn that alligator was stuffed," Violet muttered.

"Vhat vas that, Audrey?"

"That alligator . . . Yes, I was right! Excuse me, Miss Garbo. I've got to be going."

The alligator had risen to its hind legs and was now strolling down Strawberry Lane. Violet left the telephone booth and began following it at a leisurely pace. The spectacle of a strolling alligator followed, at a discreet distance, by a strolling frogman evoked no particular interest in the passers-by of Hollywood East.

The alligator glanced back over his shoulder once or twice and at last noticed the frogman. He quickened his pace. The frogman stayed with him. He began to run. The frogman ran, was outdistanced, turned on her oxygen tank and began to close the gap. The alligator leaped for a handle on the crosstown straphanger and was borne east, dangling from the cable. The frogman hailed a passing rickshaw. "Follow that alligator!" she cried into the hearing aid of the robot.

At the zoo, the alligator dropped off the straphanger and disappeared into the crowd. The frogman leaped out of the rickshaw and hunted frantically through the Berlin House, the Moscow House and the London House. In the Rome House, where sightseers were tossing pizzas to the specimens behind the bars, she saw one of the Romans lying naked and unconscious in a small corner cage. Alongside him was an empty alligator skin. Violet looked around hastily and saw Bauer slinking out, dressed in a striped suit and a Brosalino hat.

She ran after him. Bauer pulled a small boy off an electric carrousel pony, leaped on its back and began galloping west. Violet leaped onto the back of a passing Lama. "Follow that carrousel," she cried. The Lama began running. *"Ch-iao hsi-fu nan tso mei mi chou,"* he complained. "But that's always been my problem."

At Hudson Terminal, Bauer abandoned the pony, was corked in a bottle and jetted across the river. Violet leaped into the coxswain's seat of an eight-oared shell. "Follow that bottle," she cried. On the Jersey side (Nevada East) Violet pursued Bauer onto the Freeway and thence, by Dodge-Em Kar, to Old Newark, where Bauer leaped onto a trampoline and was catapulted up to the forward cylinder of the Block Island & Nantucket Monorail. Violet shrewdly waited until the monorail left the terminal, and then just made the rear cylinder.

Inside, at point of harpoon, she held up a teenage madam and forced her to exchange clothes. Dressed in opera pumps, black net stockings, checked skirt, silk blouse and hair rollers, she threw the cursing madam off the monorail at the East Vine Street station and began watching the forward cylinder more openly. At Montauk, the easternmost point on Catalina East, Bauer slipped off.

Again she waited until the monorail was leaving the station before she followed. On the platform below, Bauer slid into a Commuters' Cannon and was shot into space. Violet ran to the same cannon, carefully left the coordinate dials exactly as Bauer had set them, and slipped into the muzzle. She was shot off less than thirty seconds after Bauer, and bounced into the landing net just as he was climbing down the rope ladder.

"You!" he exclaimed.

"Me."

"Was that you in the frog suit?"

"Yes."

"I thought I ditched you in Newark."

"No, you didn't," she said grimly. "I've got you dead to rights, Kid."

Then she saw the house.

It was shaped like the house that children used to draw back in the twentieth century: two stories; peaked roof, covered with torn tar paper; dirty brown shingles, half of them hanging; plain windows with four panes in each sash; brick chimney overgrown with poison ivy; sagging front porch; the rotted remains of a two-car garage on the right; a clump of sickly sumac on the left. In the gloom of evening it looked like a haunted house.

"Oh, Sam," she breathed. "It's beautiful!"

"It's a home," he said simply.

"What's it like inside?"

"Come and see."

Inside it was unadulterated mail-order house; it was dime store, bargain basement, second hand, castoff, thrift shop, flea market.

"It's sheer heaven," Violet said. She lingered lovingly over the power sweeper, canister-type, w. vinyl bumper. "It's so—so soothing. I haven't been this happy in years."

"Wait, wait!" Bauer said, bursting with pride. He knelt before the fireplace and lit a birch-log fire. The flames crackled yellow and orange. "Look," he said. "Real wood, and real flames. And I know a museum where they've got a pair of matching andirons."

"No! Really?"

He nodded. "The Peabody, at Yale High."

Violet made up her mind. "Sam, I'll help you."

He stared at her.

"I'll help you steal them," she said. "I—I'll help you steal anything you want."

"You mean that, Violet?"

"I was a fool. I never realized. . . . I—You were right. I should never have let such a silly thing come between us."

"You're not just saying that to trick me, Violet?"

"I'm not, Sam. Honest."

"Or because you love my house?"

"Of course I love it, but that's not the whole reason."

"Then we're partners?"

"Yes."

"Shake."

Instead she flung her arms around his neck and pressed herself against him. Minutes later, on the Serofoam recliner chair w. three-way mechanism, she murmured in his ear, "It's us against everybody, Sam."

"Let 'em watch out, is all I have to say."

"And 'everybody' includes those women named Jane."

"Violet, I swear it was never serious with them. If you could see them—"

"I have."

"You have? Where? How?"

"I'll tell you some other time."

"But—"

"Oh, hush!"

Much later he said, "If we don't put a lock on that bedroom door, we're in for trouble."

"To hell with the lock," Violet said.

"ATTENTION LOUIS JOURDAN," a voice blared.

Sam and Violet scrambled out of the chair in astonishment. Blue-white light blazed through the windows of the house. There came the excited clamor of a lynch mob, the galloping crescendo of the *William Tell Overture,* and sound effects of the Kentucky Derby, a 4-6-4 locomotive, destroyers at battle stations, and the Saskatchewan Rapids.

"ATTENTION LOUIS JOURDAN," the voice brayed again.

They ran to a window and peered out. The house was surrounded by blinding Klieg lights. Dimly they could see a horde of *Jacqueries* with a guillotine, television and news cameras, a ninety-piece orchestra, a battery of sound tables manned by technicians wearing earphones, a director in jodhpurs carrying a megaphone, Inspector Robinson at a microphone, and a ring of canvas deck chairs in which were seated a dozen men and women wearing theatrical makeup.

"ATTENTION LOUIS JOURDAN. THIS IS INSPECTOR EDWARD G. ROBINSON SPEAKING. YOU ARE SURROUNDED. WE—WHAT? OH, TIME FOR A COMMERCIAL? ALL RIGHT. GO AHEAD."

Bauer glared at Violet. "So it was a trick."

"No, Sam, I swear it."

"Then what are they doing here?"

"I don't know."

"You brought them."

"No, Sam, no! I—Maybe I wasn't as smart as I thought I was. Maybe they trailed me when I was chasing you; but I swear I never saw them."

"You're lying."

"No, Sam." She began to cry.

"You sold me out."

"ATTENTION LOUIS JOURDAN. ATTENTION LOUIS JOURDAN. YOU WILL RELEASE AUDREY HEPBURN AT ONCE."

"Who?" Bauer was confused.

"Th-that's me," Violet sobbed. "It's the name I took, just like you. Audrey Hepburn and Violet Dugan are one and the s-same person. They think you captured me; but I didn't sell you out, S-Sam. I'm no fink."

"You're leveling with me?"

"Honest."

"ATTENTION LOUIS JOURDAN. WE KNOW YOU ARE THE ARTSY-CRAFTSY KID. COME OUT WITH YOUR HANDS UP. RELEASE AUDREY HEPBURN AND COME OUT WITH YOUR HANDS UP."

Bauer flung the window open. "Come and get me, copper," he yelled.

"WAIT UNTIL AFTER THE NETWORK I.D., WISE GUY."

There was a ten-second pause for network identification. Then a fusillade of shots rang out. Minuscule mushroom clouds arose where the fission slugs struck. Violet screamed. Bauer slammed the window down.

"Got their ammunition damped to the lowest exponent," he said. "Afraid of hurting the goodies in here. Maybe there's a chance, Violet."

"No! Please, darling, don't try to fight them."

"I can't. I haven't got anything to fight with."

The shots came continuously now. A picture fell off the wall.

"Sam, listen to me," she pleaded. "Give yourself up. I know it's ninety days for burglary, but I'll be waiting for you when you come out."

A window shattered.

"You'll wait for me, Violet?"

"I swear it."

A curtain caught fire.

"But ninety days! Three whole months!"

"We'll make a new life together."

Outside, Inspector Robinson suddenly groaned and clutched his shoulder.

"All right," Bauer said, "I'll quit. But look at them, turning it into a damned Spectacular—'Gang Busters' and 'The Untouchables' and 'The Roaring Twenties.' I'm damned if I let them get anything I've pinched. Wait a minute. . . ."

"What are you going to do?"

Outside, the Bunco Squad began coughing, as if from tear gas.

"Blow it all up," Bauer said, rooting around in a sugar canister.

"Blow it up? How?"

"I've got some dynamite I lifted from Groucho, Chico, Harpo and Marx when I was after their pickax collection. Didn't get a pickax, but I got this." He displayed a small red stick with a clockwork top. On the side of the stick was stenciled: TNT.

Outside, Ed (Begley) clutched his heart, smiled bravely and collapsed.

"I don't know how much time the fuse will give us," Bauer said. "So when I start it, go like hell. All set?"

"Y-yes," she quavered.

He snapped the fuse, which began an ominous ticking, and tossed the TNT onto the sage-green sofabed.

"Run!"

They charged out through the front door into the blinding light with their hands up.

The TNT stood for thermonuclear toluene.

"Dr. Culpepper," Mr. Pepys said, "this is Mr. Christopher Wren. That is Mr. Robert Hooke. Pray, be seated, sir. We have begged you to wait upon the Royal Society and advantage us with your advice as the foremost physician-astrologer in London. However, we must pledge you to secrecy."

Dr. Culpepper nodded gravely and stole a glance at the mysterious basket resting on the table before the three gentlemen. It was covered with green felt.

"*Imprimis,*" Mr. Hooke said, "the articles we shall show you were sent to the Royal Society from Oxford, where they were required of various artificers, the designs for same being supplied by the purchaser. We obtained these specimens from the said craftsmen by stealth. *Secundo,* the fabrication of the objects was commissioned in secret by certain persons who have attained great power and wealth at the colleges through sundry soothsayings, predictions, auguries and premonstrations. Mr. Wren?"

Mr. Wren delicately lifted the felt cloth as though he feared infection. Displayed in the basket were: a neat pile of soft paper napkins; twelve wooden splinters, their heads curiously dipped in sulphur; a pair of tortoise shell spectacles with lenses of a dark, smoky color; an extraordinary pin, doubled upon itself so that the point locked in a cap; and two large fluffy flannel cloths, one embroidered HIS, and the other, HERS.

"Dr. Culpepper," Mr. Pepys asked in sepulchral tones, "are these the amulets of witchcraft?"

ADAM AND NO EVE

Krane knew this must be the seacoast. Instinct told him; but more than instinct, the few shreds of knowledge that clung to his torn brain told him; the stars that had shown at night through the rare breaks in the clouds, and his compass that still pointed a trembling finger north. That was strangest of all, Krane thought. The rubbled Earth still retained its polarity.

It was no longer a coast; there was no longer any sea. Only the faint line of what had been a cliff stretched north and south for endless miles. It was a line of gray ash; the same gray ash and cinders that lay behind him and stretched before him. . . . Fine silt, knee-deep, that swirled up at every motion and choked him; cinders that

scudded in dense night clouds when the mad winds blew; black dust
that was churned to mud when the frequent rains fell.

The sky was jet overhead. The heavy clouds rode high and were
pierced with shafts of sunlight that marched swiftly over the Earth.
Where the light struck a cinder storm, it was filled with gusts of
dancing, gleaming particles. Where it played through rain it brought
the arches of rainbows into being. Rain fell; cinder-storms blew; light
thrust down—together, alternately and continually in jigsaw of black
and white violence. So it had been for months. So it was over every
mile of the broad Earth.

Krane passed the edge of the ashen cliffs and began crawling
down the even slope that had once been the ocean bed. He had been
traveling so long that pain had become part of him. He braced elbows
and dragged his body forward. Then he brought his right knee under
him and reached forward with elbows again. Elbows, knee, elbows,
knee—He had forgotten what it was to walk.

Life, he thought dazedly, is miraculous. It adapts itself to anything. If it must crawl, it crawls. Callus forms on the elbows and
knees. The neck and shoulders toughen. The nostrils learn to snort
away the ashes before they breathe. The bad leg swells and festers. It
numbs, and presently it will rot and fall off.

"I beg pardon?" Krane said, "I didn't quite get that—"

He peered up at the tall figure before him and tried to understand the words. It was Hallmyer. He wore his stained lab coat and
his gray hair was awry. Hallmyer stood delicately on top of the ashes
and Krane wondered why he could see the scudding cinder clouds
through his body.

"How do you like your world, Steven?" Hallmyer asked.

Krane shook his head miserably.

"Not very pretty, eh?" said Hallmyer. "Look around you. Dust,
that's all; dust and ashes. Crawl, Steven, crawl. You'll find nothing
but dust and ashes—"

Hallmyer produced a goblet of water from nowhere. It was clear
and cold. Krane could see the fine mist of dew on its surface and his
mouth was suddenly coated with grit.

"Hallmyer!" he cried. He tried to get to his feet and reach for
the water, but the jolt of pain in his right leg warned him. He
crouched back. Hallmyer sipped and then spat in his face. The water
felt warm.

"Keep crawling," said Hallmyer bitterly. "Crawl round and round the face of the Earth. You'll find nothing but dust and ashes—" He emptied the goblet on the ground before Krane. "Keep crawling. How many miles? Figure it out for yourself. Pi-times D. The diameter is eight thousand or so—"

He was gone, coat and goblet. Krane realized that rain was falling again. He pressed his face into the warm cinder mud, opened his mouth and tried to suck the moisture. Presently he began crawling again.

There was an instinct that drove him on. He had to get somewhere. It was associated, he knew, with the sea—with the edge of the sea. At the shore of the sea something waited for him. Something that would help him understand all this. He had to get to the sea—that is, if there was a sea any more.

The thundering rain beat his back like heavy planks. Krane paused and yanked the knapsack around to his side where he probed in it with one hand. It contained exactly three things. A gun, a bar of chocolate and a can of peaches. All that was left of two months' supplies. The chocolate was pulpy and spoiled. Krane knew he had best eat it before all the value rotted away. But in another day he would lack the strength to open the can. He pulled it out and attacked it with the opener. By the time he had pierced and pried away a flap of tin, the rain had passed.

As he munched the fruit and sipped the juice, he watched the wall of rain marching before him down the slope of the ocean bed. Torrents of water were gushing through the mud. Small channels had already been cut—channels that would be new rivers some day; a day he would never see; a day that no living thing would ever see. As he flipped the empty can aside, Krane thought: The last living thing on Earth eats its last meal. Metabolism begins the last act.

Wind would follow the rain. In the endless weeks that he had been crawling, he had learned that. Wind would come in a few minutes and flog him with its clouds of cinders and ashes. He crawled forward, bleary eyes searching the flat gray miles for cover.

Evelyn tapped his shoulder.

Krane knew it was she before he turned his head. She stood

alongside, fresh and gay in her bright dress, but her lovely face was puckered with alarm.

"Steven," she said, "you've got to hurry!"

He could only admire the way her smooth hair waved to her shoulders.

"Oh, darling!" she said, "you've been hurt!" Her quick gentle hands touched his legs and back. Krane nodded.

"Got it landing," he said. "I wasn't used to a parachute. I always thought you came down gently—like plumping onto a bed. But the earth came up at me like a fist—And Umber was fighting around in my arms. I couldn't let him drop, could I?"

"Of course not, dear," Evelyn said.

"So I just held on to him and tried to get my legs under me," Krane said. "And then something smashed my legs and side—"

He hesitated, wondering how much she knew of what really had happened. He didn't want to frighten her.

"Evelyn, darling—" he said, trying to reach up his arms.

"No dear," she said. She looked back in fright. "You've got to hurry. You've got to watch out behind!"

"The cinder storms?" He grimaced. "I've been through them before."

"Not the storms!" Evelyn cried. "Something else. Oh, Steven—"

Then she was gone, but Krane knew she had spoken the truth. There was something behind—something that had been following him. In the back of his mind he had sensed the menace. It was closing in on him like a shroud. He shook his head. Somehow that was impossible. He was the last living thing on Earth. How could there be a menace?

The wind roared behind him, and an instant later came the heavy clouds of cinders and ashes. They lashed over him, biting his skin. With dimming eyes, he saw the way they coated the mud and covered it with a fine dry carpet. Krane drew his knees under him and covered his head with his arms. With the knapsack as a pillow, he prepared to wait out the storm. It would pass as quickly as the rain.

The storm whipped up a great bewilderment in his sick head. Like a child he pushed at the pieces of his memory, trying to fit them together. Why was Hallmyer so bitter toward him? It couldn't have been that argument, could it?

What argument?

Why, that one before all this happened.

Oh, that!

Abruptly, the pieces locked together.

Krane stood alongside the sleek lines of his ship and admired it tremendously. The roof of the shed had been removed and the nose of the ship hoisted so that it rested on a cradle pointed toward the sky. A workman was carefully burnishing the inner surfaces of the rocket jets.

The muffled sounds of swearing came from within the ship and then a heavy clanking. Krane ran up the short iron ladder to the port and thrust his head inside. A few feet beneath him, two men were clamping the long tanks of ferrous solution into place.

"Easy there," Krane called. "Want to knock the ship apart?"

One looked up and grinned. Krane knew what he was thinking. That the ship would tear itself apart. Everyone said that. Everyone except Evelyn. She had faith in him. Hallmyer never said it either, but Hallmyer thought he was crazy in another way. As he descended the ladder, Krane saw Hallmyer come into the shed, lab coat flying.

"Speak of the devil!" Krane muttered.

Hallmyer began shouting as soon as he saw Krane. "Now listen—"

"Not all over again," Krane said.

Hallmyer dug a sheaf of papers out of his pocket and waved it under Krane's nose.

"I've been up half the night," he said, "working it through again. I tell you I'm right. I'm absolutely right—"

Krane looked at the tight-written equations and then at Hallmyer's bloodshot eyes. The man was half mad with fear.

"For the last time," Hallmyer went on. "You're using your new catalyst on iron solution. All right. I grant that it's a miraculous discovery. I give you credit for that."

Miraculous was hardly the word for it. Krane knew that without conceit, for he realized he'd only stumbled on it. You had to stumble on a catalyst that would induce atomic disintegration of iron and give 10×10^{10} foot-pounds of energy for every gram of fuel. No man was smart enough to think all that up by himself.

"You don't think I'll make it?" Krane asked.

"To the Moon? Around the Moon? Maybe. You've got a fifty-fifty chance." Hallmyer ran fingers through his lank hair. "But for God's sake, Steven, I'm not worried about you. If you want to kill yourself, that's your own affair. It's the Earth I'm worried about—"

"Nonsense. Go home and sleep it off."

"Look—" Hallmyer pointed to the sheets of paper with a shaky hand—"No matter how you work the feed and mixing system you can't get 100 per cent efficiency in the mixing and discharge."

"That's what makes it a fifty-fifty chance," Krane said. "So what's bothering you?"

"The catalyst that will escape through the rocket tubes. Do you realize what it'll do if a drop hits the Earth? It'll start a chain of disintegration that'll envelop the globe. It'll reach out to every iron atom—and there's iron everywhere. There won't be any Earth left for you to return to—"

"Listen," Krane said wearily, "we've been through all this before."

He took Hallmyer to the base of the rocket cradle. Beneath the iron framework was a two-hundred-foot pit, fifty feet wide and lined with firebrick.

"That's for the initial discharge flames. If any of the catalyst goes through, it'll be trapped in this pit and taken care of by the secondary reactions. Satisfied now?"

"But while you're in flight," Hallmyer persisted, "you'll be endangering the Earth until you're beyond Roche's limit. Every drop of non-activated catalyst will eventually sink back to the ground and—"

"For the very last time," Krane said grimly, "the flame of the rocket discharge takes care of that. It will envelop any escaped particles and destroy them. Now get out. I've got work to do."

As Krane pushed him to the door, Hallmyer screamed and waved his arms. "I won't let you do it!" he repeated over and over. "I won't let you risk it—"

Work? No, it was sheer intoxication to labor over the ship. It had the fine beauty of a well-made thing. The beauty of polished armor, of a balanced swept-hilt rapier, of a pair of matched guns. There was no thought of danger and death in Krane's mind as he wiped his hands with waste after the last touches were finished.

She lay in the cradle ready to pierce the skies. Fifty feet of slender steel, the rivet heads gleaming like jewels. Thirty feet were given over to fuel and catalyst. Most of the forward compartment contained the spring hammock Krane had devised to absorb the acceleration strain. The ship's nose was a porthole of natural crystal that stared upward like a cylopian eye.

Krane thought: She'll die after this trip. She'll return to the Earth and smash in a blaze of fire and thunder, for there's no way yet of devising a safe landing for a rocket ship. But it's worth it. She'll have had her one great flight, and that's all any of us should want. One great beautiful flight into the unknown—

As he locked the workshop door, Krane heard Hallmyer shouting from the cottage across the fields. Through the evening gloom he could see him waving urgently. He trotted through the crisp stubble, breathing the sharp air deeply, grateful to be alive.

"It's Evelyn on the phone," Hallmyer said.

Krane stared at him. Hallmyer refused to meet his eyes.

"What's the idea?" Krane asked. "I thought we agreed that she wasn't to call—wasn't to get in touch with me until I was ready to start? You been putting ideas into her head? Is this the way you're going to stop me?"

Hallmyer said: "No—" and studiously examined the darkening horizon

Krane went into his study and picked up the phone.

"Now listen, darling," he said without preamble, "there's no sense getting alarmed now. I explained everything very carefully. Just before the ship crashes, I take to a parachute. I love you very much and I'll see you Wednesday when I start. So long—"

"Good-bye, sweetheart," Evelyn's clear voice said, "and is that what you called me for?"

"Called you!"

A brown hulk disengaged itself from the hearth rug and lifted itself to strong legs. Umber, Krane's mastiff, sniffed and cocked an ear. Then he whined.

"Did you say I called you?" Krane repeated.

Umber's throat suddenly poured forth a bellow. He reached Krane in a single bound, looked up into his face and whined and roared all at once.

"Shut up, you monster!" Krane said. He pushed Umber away with his foot.

"Give Umber a kick for me," Evelyn laughed. "Yes, dear. Some-one called and said you wanted to speak to me."

"They did, eh? Look, honey, I'll call you back—"

Krane hung up. He arose doubtfully and watched Umber's un-easy actions. Through the windows, the late evening glow sent flick-ering shadows of orange light. Umber gazed at the light, sniffed and bellowed again. Suddenly struck, Krane leaped to the window.

Across the fields a mass of flame thrust high into the air, and within it was the crumbling walls of the workshop. Silhouetted against the blaze, the figures of half a dozen men darted and ran.

Krane shot out of the cottage and with Umber hard at his heels, sprinted toward the shed. As he ran he could see the graceful nose of the spaceship within the fire, still looking cool and untouched. If only he could reach it before the flames softened its metal and started the rivets.

The workmen trotted up to him, grimy and panting. Krane gaped at them in a mixture of fury and bewilderment.

"Hallmyer!" he shouted. "Hallmyer!"

Hallmyer pushed through the crowd. His eyes gleamed with tri-umph.

"Too bad," he said. "I'm sorry, Steven—"

"You bastard!" Krane shouted. He grasped Hallmyer by the lapels and shook him once. Then he dropped him and started into the shed.

Hallmyer snapped orders to the workmen and an instant later a body hurtled against Krane's calves and spilled him to the ground. He lurched to his feet, fists swinging. Umber was alongside, growling over the roar of the flames. Krane battered a man in the face, and saw him stagger back against a second. He lifted a knee in a vicious drive that sent the last workman crumpling to the ground. Then he ducked his head and plunged into the shop.

The scorch felt cool at first, but when he reached the ladder and began mounting to the port, he screamed with the agony of his burns. Umber was howling at the foot of the ladder, and Krane real-ized that the dog could never escape from the rocket blasts. He reached down and hauled Umber into the ship.

Krane was reeling as he closed and locked the port. He retained consciousness barely long enough to settle himself in the spring hammock. Then instinct alone prompted his hands to reach out toward the control board; instinct and the frenzied refusal to let his beautiful ship waste itself in the flames. He would fail—yes. But he would fail trying.

His fingers tripped the switches. The ship shuddered and roared. And blackness descended over him.

How long was he unconscious? There was no telling. Krane awoke with cold pressing against his face and body, and the sound of frightened yelps in his ears. Krane looked up and saw Umber tangled in the springs and straps of the hammock. His first impulse was to laugh, then suddenly he realized; he had looked *up!* He had looked up at the hammock.

He was lying curled in the cup of the crystal nose. The ship had risen high—perhaps almost to Roche's zone, to the limit of the Earth's gravitational attraction, but then without guiding hands at the controls to continue its flight, had turned and was dropping back toward Earth. Krane peered through the crystal and gasped.

Below him was the ball of the Earth. It looked three times the size of the Moon. And it was no longer his Earth. It was a globe of fire mottled with black clouds. At the northernmost pole there was a tiny patch of white, and even as Krane watched, it was suddenly blotted over with hazy tones of red, scarlet, and crimson. Hallmyer had been right.

Krane lay frozen in the cup of the nose as the ship descended, watching the flames gradually fade away to leave nothing but the dense blanket of black around the Earth. He lay numb with horror, unable to understand—unable to reckon up a people snuffed out, a green fair planet reduced to ashes and cinders. Everything that was once dear and close to him—gone. He could not think of Evelyn.

Air, whistling outside, awoke some instinct in him. The few shreds of reason left told him to go down with his ship and forget everything in the thunder and destruction, but the instinct of life forced him to action. He climbed up to the store chest and prepared for the landing. Parachute, a small oxygen tank—a knapsack of supplies. Only half aware of what he was doing he dressed for the descent, buckled on the 'chute and opened the port. Umber whined pathetically, and he took the heavy dog in his arms and stepped out into space.

But space hadn't been so clogged, the way it was now. Then it had been difficult to breathe. But that was because the air had been rare—not filled with clogging grit like now.

Every breath was a lungful of ground glass—or ashes—or cinders—he had returned to a suffocating black present that hugged him with soft weight and made him fight for breath. Krane struggled in panic, and then relaxed.

It had happened before. A long time past he'd been buried deep under ashes when he'd stopped to remember. Weeks ago—or days—or months. Krane clawed with his hands, inching out of the mound of cinders that the wind had thrown over him. Presently he emerged into the light again. The wind had died away. It was time to begin his crawl to the sea once more.

The vivid pictures of his memory scattered again before the grim vista that stretched out ahead. Krane scowled. He remembered too much, and too often. He had the vague hope that if he remembered hard enough, he might change one of the things he had done—just a very little thing—and then all this would become untrue. He thought: It might help if everyone remembered and wished at the same time—but there isn't any everyone. I'm the only one. I'm the last memory on Earth. I'm the last life.

He crawled. Elbows, knee, elbows, knee—And then Hallmyer was crawling alongside and making a great game of it. He chortled and plunged in the cinders like a happy sea lion.

Krane said: "But why do we have to get to the sea?"

Hallmyer blew a spume of ashes.

"Ask her," he said, pointing to Krane's other side.

Evelyn was there, crawling seriously, intently, mimicking Krane's smallest action.

"It's because of our house," she said. "You remember our house, darling? High on the cliff. We were going to live there forever and ever. I was there when you left. Now you're coming back to the house at the edge of the sea. Your beautiful flight is over, dear, and you're coming back to me. We'll live together, just we two, like Adam and Eve—"

Krane said: "That's nice."

Then Evelyn turned her head and screamed: "Oh, Steven! Watch out!" and Krane felt the menace closing in on him again. Still crawling, he stared back at the vast gray plains of ash, and saw nothing. When he looked at Evelyn again he saw only his shadow, sharp and black. Presently, it, too, faded away as the marching shaft of sunlight passed.

But the dread remained. Evelyn had warned him twice, and she was always right. Krane stopped and turned, and settled himself to watch. If he was really being followed, he would see whatever it was, coming along his tracks.

There was a painful moment of lucidity. It cleaved through his fever and bewilderment, bringing with it the sharpness and strength of a knife.

I'm mad, he thought. The corruption in my leg has spread to my brain. There is no Evelyn, no Hallmyer, no menace. In all this land there is no life but mine—and even ghosts and spirits of the underworld must have perished in the inferno that girdled the planet. No—there is nothing but me and my sickness. I'm dying—and when I perish, everything will perish. Only a mass of lifeless cinders will go on.

But there was a movement.

Instinct again—Krane dropped his head and lay still. Through slitted eyes he watched the ashen plains, wondering if death was playing tricks with his eyes. Another façade of rain was beating down toward him, and he hoped he could make sure before all vision was obliterated.

Yes. There.

A quarter mile back, a gray-brown shape was flitting along the gray surface. Despite the drone of the distant rain, Krane could hear the whisper of trodden cinders and see the little clouds kicking up. Stealthily he groped for the revolver in the knapsack as his mind reached feebly for explanations and recoiled from fear.

The thing approached, and suddenly Krane squinted and understood. He recalled Umber kicking with fear and springing away from him when the 'chute landed them on the ashen face of the Earth.

"Why, it's Umber," he murmured. He raised himself. The dog halted. "Here, boy!" Krane croaked gaily. "Here, boy!"

He was overcome with joy. He realized that loneliness had hung over him, a horrible sensation of oneness in emptiness. Now his was not the only life. There was another. A friendly life that could offer love and companionship. Hope kindled again.

"Here, boy!" he repeated. "Come on, boy—"

After a while he stopped trying to snap his fingers. The Mastiff hung back, showing fangs and a lolling tongue. The dog was emaciated and its eyes gleamed red in the dusk. As Krane called once more, the dog snarled. Puffs of ash leaped beneath its nostrils.

He's hungry, Krane thought, that's all. He reached into the knapsack and at the gesture the dog snarled again. Krane withdrew the chocolate bar and laboriously peeled off the paper and silver foil. Weakly he tossed it toward Umber. It fell far short. After a minute of savage uncertainty, the dog advanced slowly and snapped up the food. Ashes powered its muzzle. It licked its chops ceaselessly and continued to advance on Krane.

Panic jerked within him. A voice persisted: This is no friend. He has no love or companionship for you. Love and companionship have vanished from the land along with life. Now there is nothing left but hunger.

"No—" Krane whispered. "That isn't right that we should tear at each other and seek to devour—"

But Umber was advancing with a slinking sidle, and his teeth showed sharp and white. And even as Krane stared at him, the dog snarled and lunged.

Krane thrust up an arm under the dog's muzzle, but the weight of the charge carried him backward. He cried out in agony as his broken, swollen leg was struck by the weight of the dog. With his free hand he struck weakly, again and again, scarcely feeling the grind of teeth on his left arm. Then something metallic was pressed under him and he realized he was lying on the revolver he had let fall.

He groped for it and prayed the cinders had not clogged it. As Umber let go his arm and tore at his throat, Krane brought the gun up and jabbed the muzzle blindly against the dog's body. He pulled and pulled the trigger until the roars died away and only empty clicks sounded. Umber shuddered in the ashes before him, his body nearly shot in two. Thick scarlet stained the gray.

Evelyn and Hallmyer looked down sadly at the broken animal. Evelyn was crying, and Hallmyer reached nervous fingers through his hair in the same old gesture.

"This is the finish, Steven," he said. "You've killed part of yourself. Oh—you'll go on living, but not all of you. You'd best bury that body, Steven. It's the corpse of your soul."

"I can't," Krane said. "The wind will blow the cinders away."

"Then burn it," Hallmyer ordered with dream-logic.

It seemed that they helped him thrust the dead dog into his knapsack. They helped him take off his clothes and packed them underneath. They cupped their hands around the matches until the cloth caught fire, and blew on the weak flame until it sputtered and burned limply. Krane crouched by the fire and nursed it. Then he turned and once again began crawling down the ocean bed. He was naked now. There was nothing left of what-had-been but his flickering little life.

He was too heavy with sorrow to notice the furious rain that slammed and buffeted him, or the searing pains that were searing through his blackened leg and up his hip. He crawled. Elbows, knee, elbows, knee— Woodenly, mechanically, apathetic to everything . . . to the latticed skies, the dreary ashen plains and even the dull glint of water that lay far ahead.

He knew it was the sea—what was left of the old, or a new one in the making. But it would be an empty, lifeless sea that some day would lap against a dry, lifeless shore. This would be a planet of stone and dust, of metal and snow and ice and water, but that would be all. No more life. He, alone, was useless. He was Adam, but there was no Eve.

Evelyn waved gaily to him from the shore. She was standing alongside the white cottage with the wind snapping her dress to show the slender lines of her figure. And when he came a little closer, she ran out to him and helped him. She said nothing—only placed her hands under his shoulders and helped him lift the weight of his heavy pain-ridden body. And so at last he reached the sea.

It was real. He understood that. For even after Evelyn and the cottage had vanished, he felt the cool waters bathe his face.

Here's the sea, Krane thought, and here am I. Adam and no Eve. It's hopeless.

He rolled a little farther into the waters. They laved his torn body. He lay with his face to the sky, peering at the high menacing heavens, and the bitterness within him welled up.

"It's not right!" he cried. "It's not right that all this should pass away. Life is too beautiful to perish at the mad act of one mad creature—"

Quietly the waters laved him. Quietly . . . Calmly . . .

The sea rocked him gently, and even the death that was reaching up toward his heart was no more than a gloved hand. Suddenly the skies split apart—for the first time in all those months—and Krane stared up at the stars.

Then he knew. This was not the end of life. There could never be an end of life. Within his body, within the rotting tissues rocking gently in the sea was the source of ten million-million lives. Cells—tissues—bacteria—amoeba— Countless infinities of life that would take new root in the waters and live long after he was gone.

They would live on his rotting remains. They would feed on each other. They would adapt themselves to the new environment and feed on the minerals and sediments washed into this new sea. They would grow, burgeon, evolve. Life would reach out to the lands once more. It would begin again the same old repeated cycle that had begun perhaps with the rotting corpse of some last survivor of interstellar travel. It would happen over and over in the future ages.

And then he knew what had brought him back to the sea. There need be no Adam—no Eve. Only the sea, the great mother of life was needed. The sea had called him back to her depths that presently life might emerge once more, and he was content.

Quietly the waters comforted him. Quietly . . . Calmly . . . The mother of life rocked the last-born of the old cycle who would become the first-born of the new. And with glazing eyes Steven Krane smiled up at the stars, stars that were sprinkled evenly across the sky. Stars that had not yet formed into the familiar constellations, and would not for another hundred million centuries.

AND 3½ TO GO

Editor's note: This is a fragment of a story that Bester did not complete before his death. However, because it contains Bester's unique style and trademark radical ideas, we felt it should be included in this definitive collection.

Sociologists have never agreed on whether societies through the ages have demanded conformity because they think that the status quo is perfection, or believe that the majority, ipso facto, must be the yardstick—in which case we should make way for the insects—or because they resent extraordinary talents which produce extraordinary results and sometimes strange behavior.

There have been so many of these singular sports, perhaps multitudes of mutations through the millennia, who were forced to conceal their unique powers from mob hostility or else run for cover like hunted animals. This is the story of a batch who took off singing:

> One for the money,
> Two for the show.
> $F^\sharp - E^\flat - A - 2^\sharp - D$,
> And $3\frac{1}{2}$ to go!

Patience. All will be made clear very shortly.

These marvels or misfits, depending on your point of view, banded together and roamed the known universe, peddling their talents. They knew they could never settle down anywhere unless they concealed their faculties and conformed, something none was willing to, or even could, do. They were sometimes called "The Wandering Blues" and other times "The Blue Devils," again depending on the point of view. Word about them got around.

There's no doubt that they were often a curious blue when they emerged from their ship to sell their genius on some boondock planet or satellite. Long hauls through space forced them to conserve oxygen at the minimal survival level, turning them cyanotic. They recovered normal color if the new environment was hospitable, which, occasionally, it was most emphatically not. The same was true of their social reception now and then, forcing them to cut and run. They were, well, unusual.

Van Ryn, for instance, was a magnificent artist. (He was born Sam Katz but that's a hell of a name for a fashionable painter.) Rynny was astigmatic. There was a distortion in the lenses of his eyes that caused rays of light from an external point to converge unequally and form warped images. This is the common-or-garden-variety of astigmatism that afflicted El Greco and caused him to paint elongated faces and figures. The sixteenth century hadn't yet got around to prescription glasses.

What was strange about Rynny's astigmatism was the fact that some of the external point sources of light were far in the future of whatever or whoever he was painting, and he got mixed up. He didn't know what to believe so he settled for painting anything he saw, sometimes the present, more often the future. The twenty-fifth century hadn't yet got around to prescribing for anything as bizarre as that.

Clients got sore as hell at being depicted as decrepit ancients or embalmed corpses in the coffin (one was portrayed as a suicide hanging by the neck from a flagpole) and naturally refused to pay. But when Rynny was commissioned to paint the chateau of a royal mistress and produced a bijou of her in the garden of same, flagrante with another lover, that was the end. He had to leave, quickly.

Hertzing Matilda was a composer. He came from New South Wales, hence the odd play on the famous Aussie tune, "Waltzing Matilda," which gave him the girl part of his nickname. He was a brilliant musician, a genius in fact, but born with a deformity in his ears which gave him the front part of his name.

You see, all of us hear the audio-frequency band from around 30 Hz to 15,000 Hz. "Hz" is the abbreviation for "hertz," the symbol for cycles-per-second, and honoring the great physicist, Heinrich Rudolph Hertz (1857–1894). The infrasonic lies below 30 Hz, the ultrasonic is above 15,000 Hz, and only a few rare creatures can sense them, humans not among them.

Well, as Hertzing Matilda grew older, he and the rest of the world thought he was going deaf. By the time he was thirty he seemed to be stone deaf, a tragedy for a composer, and it showed in his music, for, like Beethoven, he went on composing. But his work got crazier and crazier until it was so far out that he was run out of the business. Nobody could read his scores, which looked like paradigms in symbolic logic, as in the third line of the "One for the money" jingle, which he arranged.

It was a skilled audiologist who discovered what had really happened to Hertz. He hadn't gone deaf. His hearing had shifted from the normal audio-frequency band up into the ultrasonic, higher and higher. He was sensing 30,000, 40,000, and 50,000 hertz and trying to translate the *outré* hyperworld he heard into conventional music, which was like trying to divide apples by pears. The audiologist's paper on the discovery created a sensation in the medical journals, but all it earned for Hertz was his nickname.

Fay Damien had been an actress. She was most attractive without being pretty, sweet, warm, appealing to the public, cooperative, and hardworking with her colleagues. She had everything going for her except the one kink that ruined all chances for success; she was a jinx.

Wherever she went, bad luck was sure to follow; props failed, sets collapsed, lights exploded and fell on heads, cameras jammed. Everybody was afraid to work with this hoodoo and stars flatly refused. The end came when a producer took her along to dine with a new potential backer and help coax him into putting up front money for a new series. The backer's wife suddenly appeared at the table and shot him dead. Out of the blue it had occurred to her that he and Fay were having an affair.

All this was a mystery to Ms. Damien until she happened to meet Hertzing Matilda at an audition where they were both desperately trying to get work. They'd heard of each other but never met. They chatted and exchanged sympathy for their perplexing problems—Hertz had trained himself to read lips and body language—when suddenly he cocked an ear, then winked and said in the strange singsong tones imposed by his ultrasonic handicap, "It's all right. He says to tell you not to worry. He likes me."

"What? He? Who?"

"Your brother." Hertz grinned. "He says we're a pair of fruitcakes and ought to stick together."

Fay was bewildered. "What brother? I haven't got a brother."

"Sure you do. Inside."

"Inside? Inside where?"

"Inside you."

"Are you saying I've got a brother inside me and you're talking to him?"

"Uh-huh. Ultrasonics."

Fay burst out laughing. "This is a brand-new come-on and I'd love to fall for it. God knows, most men on the make are so damn unoriginal."

"I'm not on the make; this is straight. You've got your brother Morgan inside you. Didn't you know?"

She didn't, and for an interesting reason. When mama Damien discovered she was expecting she resolved that, boy or girl, she'd name the baby Morgan. If a boy, after Sir Henry Morgan, the bold buccaneer, because she wanted him to be piratical, devil-may-care, and successful in a cutthroat world. If a girl, after Morgan le Fay, the fairy sister of King Arthur, because she wanted her to enchant and captivate the whole world. Mama was devoted to romantic literature.

Well, fraternal twins developed, brother and sister, which is not unique; it's simply a case of two fertilized ova. Only in this gestation the sister embryo overgrew the brother embryo, quite by accident, engulfed him and incorporated him in herself as a fraternal cyst. This is most unusual but, again, not unique.

What *was* unique was the fact that Morgan, the enclosed brother, was alive. And Morgan was not only piratical, he was also a witch, a living, fraternal devil-cyst with a will and ideas of his own. *He* was Fay's jinx because he had a hot temper and the most trivial things could sting him into casting malevolent spells. The backer's table conversation had annoyed him, hence the murdering wife. Morgan was the invisible, unpredictable "half" in the jingle and his motto was, *Incipere multost quam impetrare facilius.*

IT'S MUCH EASIER TO BEGIN A THING THAN TO FINISH IT

GALATEA GALANTE

He was wearing a prefaded jump suit, beautifully tailored, the *dernier cri* in the nostalgic 2100s, but really too youthful for his thirty-odd years. Set square on his head was a vintage (circa 1950) English motoring cap with the peak leveled on a line with his brows, masking the light of lunacy in his eyes.

Dead on a slab, he might be called distinguished, even handsome, but alive and active? That would depend on how much demented dedication one could stomach. He was shouldering his way through the crowded aisles of

GALATEA GALANTE

THE SATURN CIRCUS
50 PHANTASTIK PHREAKS 50
!!!ALL ALIENS!!!

He was carrying a mini sound-camera that looked like a chrome-and-ebony pepper mill, and he was filming the living, crawling, spasming, gibbering monstrosities exhibited in the large showcases and small vitrines, with a murmured running commentary. His voice was pleasant; his remarks were not.

"Ah, yes, the *Bellatrix basilisk,* so the sign assures us. Black-and-yellow bod of a serpent. Looks like a Gila-monster head attached. Work of that Tejas tailor who's so nitzy with surgical needle and thread. Peacock coronet on head. Good theater to blindfold its eyes. Conveys the conviction that its glance will kill. Hmmm. Ought to gag the mouth, too. According to myth the basilisk's breath also kills. . . .

"And the *Hyades hydra.* Like wow. Nine heads, as per revered tradition. Looks like a converted iguana. The Mexican again. That seamstress has access to every damn snake and lizard in Central America. She's done a nice join of necks to trunk—got to admit that—but her stitching shows to *my* eye. . . .

"*Canopus cerberus.* Three dog heads. Look like oversized Chihuahuas. Mastiff bod. Rattlesnake tail. Ring of rattlers around the waist. Authentic but clumsy. That Tejas woman ought to know you can't graft snake scales onto hound hide. They look like crud; but at least all three heads are barking. . . .

"Well, well, well, here's the maladroit who claims he's my rival; the Berlin butcher with his zoo castoffs. His latest spectacular, the *Rigel griffin.* Ta-daaa! Do him justice, it's classic. Eagle head and wings, but it's molting. Lion bod implanted with feathers. And he's used ostrich claws for the feet. *I* would have generated authentic dragon's feet. . . .

"Now *Martian monoceros;* horse bod, elephant legs, stag's tail. Yes, convincing, but why isn't it howling as it should, according to legend? *Mizar manticora.* Kosher. Kosher. Three rows of teeth. Look like implanted shark's. Lion bod. Scorpion tail. Wonder how they produced that red-eyed effect. The *Ares assida.* Dull. Dull. Dullsville. Just an ostrich with camel feet, and stumbling all over them, too. No creative imagination!

"Ah, but I call that poster over the *Sirius sphinx* brilliant theater.

My compliments to the management. It's got to be recorded for posterity: THE PUBLIC IS RESPECTFULLY REQUESTED NOT TO GIVE THE CORRECT ANSWER TO THE ENIGMA POSED BY THE SPHINX.

"Because if you do give the correct answer, as Oedipus found out, she'll destroy herself out of chagrin. A sore loser. I ought to answer the riddle, just to see how they stage it, but no. Theater isn't my shtick; my business is strictly creative genesis. . . .

"The Berlin butcher again, *Castor chimera.* Lion head. Goat's bod. Looks like an anaconda tail. How the hell did he surgify to get it to vomit those flames? Some sort of catalytic gimmick in the throat, I suppose. It's only a cold corposant fire, quite harmless but very dramatic—and those fire extinguishers around the showcase are a lovely touch. Damn good theater. Again, my compliments to the management. . . .

"Aha! Beefcake on the hoof. *Zosma centaur.* Good-looking Greek joined to that Shetland pony. Blood must have been a problem. They probably drained both and substituted a neutral surrogate. The Greek looks happy enough; in fact, damn smug. Anyone wondering why has only to see how the pony's hung. . . .

"What have we here? *Antares unicorn,* complete with grafted narwhal tusk but not with the virgin who captured it, virgin girls being the only types that can subdue unicorns, legend saith. I thought narwhals were extinct. They may have bought the tusk from a walking-stick maker. I know virgins are not extinct. *I* make 'em every month; purity guaranteed or your money back. . . .

"And a *Spica siren.* Lovely girl. Beautiful. She— But damn my eyes, she's no manufactured freak! That's Sandra, *my* Siren! I can recognize my genesis anywhere. What the hell is Sandy doing in this damn disgusting circus? Naked in a showcase! This is an outrage!"

He charged the showcase in his rage. He was given to flashes of fury that punctuated his habitual exasperated calm. (His deep conviction was that it was a damned intransigent world because it wasn't run *his* way, which was the *right* way.)

He beat and clawed at the supple walls, which gave but did not break. He cast around wildly for anything destructive, then darted to the *chimera* exhibit, grabbed a fire extinguisher, and dashed back to the Siren. Three demoniac blows cracked the plastic, and three more shattered an escape hatch. His fury outdrew the freaks, and a fascinated crowd gathered.

He reached in and seized the smiling Siren. "Sandy, get the hell out. What were you doing there in the first place?"

"Where's your husband?"

"For God's sake!" He pulled off his cap, revealing pale, streaky hair. "Here, cover yourself with this. No, no, girl, downstairs. Use an arm for upstairs, and hide your rear elevation against my back."

"No, I am *not* prudish. I simply will not have my beautiful creation on public display. D'you think I—" He turned fiercely on three security guards closing in on him and brandished the heavy brass cylinder. "One more step, and I let you have it with this. In the eyes. Ever had frozen eyeballs?"

They halted. "Now look, mister, you got no—"

"I am *not* called 'mister.' My degree is Dominie, which means master professor. I am addressed as Dominie, Dominie Manwright, and I want to see the owner at once. Immediately. Here and now. *Sofort! Immediatamente!* Mr. Saturn or Mr. Phreak or whatever!

"Tell him that Dominie Regis Manwright wants him here now. He'll know my name, or he'd better, by God! Now be off with you. Split. Cut." Manwright glared around at the enthralled spectators. "You turkeys get lost, too. All of you. Go eyeball the other sights. The Siren show is *kaput.*"

As the crowd shuffled back from Manwright's fury, an amused gentleman in highly unlikely twentieth-century evening dress stepped forward. "I see you understand Siren, sir. Most impressive." He slung the opera cape off his shoulders and offered it to Sandra. "You must be cold, madame. May I?"

"Thank you," Manwright growled. "Put it on, Sandy. Cover yourself. And thank the man."

"I don't give a damn whether you're cold or not. Cover yourself. I won't have you parading that beautiful body I created. And give me back my cap."

"Women!" Manwright grumbled. "This is the last time I ever generate one. You slave over them. You use all your expertise to create beauty and implant sense and sensibility, and they all turn out the same. Irrational! Women! A race apart! And where the hell's 50 Phantastik Phreaks 50?"

"At your service, Dominie," the gentleman smiled.

"What? You? The management?"

"Indeed yes."

"In that ridiculous white tie and tails?"

"So sorry, Dominie. The costume is traditional for the role. And by day I'm required to wear hunting dress. It *is* grotesque, but the public expects it of the ringmaster."

"Hmph! What's your name? I'd like to know the name of the man I skin alive."

"Corque."

"Cork? As in Ireland?"

"But with a *Q U E.*"

"Corque? Cor-kew-ee?" Manwright's eyes kindled. "Would you by any chance be related to Charles Russell Corque, Syrtus professor of ETM biology? I'll hold that in your favor."

"Thank you, Dominie. I *am* Charles Russell Corque, professor of extraterrestrial and mutation biology at Syrtus University."

"What!"

"Yes."

"In that preposterous costume?"

"Alas, yes."

"Here? On Terra?"

"In person."

"What a crazy coincidence. D'you know I was going to make that damned tedious trip to Mars just to rap with you."

"And I brought my circus to Terra hoping to meet and consult with you."

"How long have you been here?"

"Two days."

"Then why haven't you called?"

"Setting up a circus show takes time, Dominie. I haven't had a moment to spare."

"This monstrous fakery is really yours?"

"It is."

"You? The celebrated Corque? The greatest researcher into alien life forms that science has ever known? Revered by all your colleagues, including myself, and swindling the turkeys with a phony freak show? Incredible, Corque! Unbelievable!"

"But understandable, Manwright. Have you any idea of the cost of ETM research? And the reluctance of the grants committees to allocate an adequate amount of funds? No, I suppose not. You're in private practice and can charge gigantic fees to support your research, but I'm forced to moonlight and operate this circus to raise the money I need."

"Nonsense, Corque. You could have patented one of your brilliant discoveries—that fantastic Jupiter III methophyte, for instance. Gourmets call it 'The Ganymede Truffle.' D'you know what an ounce sells for?"

"I know, and there *are* discovery rights and royalties. Enormous. But you don't know university contracts, my dear Dominie. By contract, the royalties go to Syrtus, where"—Professor Corque's smile soured—"where they are spent on such studies as Remedial Table Tennis, Demonia Orientation, and The Light Verse of Leopold von Sacher-Masoch."

Manwright shook his head in exasperation. "Those damned faculty clowns! I've turned down a dozen university offers, and no wonder. It's an outrage that you should be forced to humiliate yourself and—Listen, Corque, I've been dying to get the details on how you discovered that Ganymede methophyte. When will you have some time? I thought— Where are you staying on Terra?"

"The Borealis."

"What? That fleabag?"

"I have to economize for my research."

"Well, you can economize by moving in with me. It won't cost you a cent. I've got plenty of room, and I'll put you up for the duration, with pleasure. I've generated a housekeeper who'll take good care of you—and rather startle you, I think. Now do say yes, Corque.

We've got a hell of a lot of discussing to do and I've got a lot to learn from you."

"I think it will be the other way around, my dear Dominie."

"Don't argue! Just pack up, get the hell out of the Borealis, and—"

"What, Sandy?"

"Where?"

"Oh, yes. I see the rat-fink."

"What now, Manwright?"

"Her husband. I'll trouble you to use restraint on me, or he'll become her *late* husband."

An epicene hove into view—tall, slender, elegant, in flesh-colored SkinAll—with chest, arms, and legs artfully padded to macho dimensions, as was the ornamented codpiece. Manwright juggled the extinguisher angrily, as though groping for the firing pin of a grenade. He was so intent on the encounter that Corque was able to slip the cylinder out of his hands as the epicene approached, surveyed them, and at last spoke.

"Ah, Manwright."

"Jessamy!" Manwright turned the name into a denunciation.

"Sandra."

"And our impresario."

"Good evening, Mr. Jessamy."

"Manwright, I have a bone to pick with you."

"You? Pick? A bone? With me? Why, you damned pimp, putting your own wife, my magnificent creation, into a damned freak show!" He turned angrily on Professor Corque. "And you bought her, eh?"

"Not guilty, Dominie. I can't supervise everything. The Freak Foreman made the purchase."

"He did, did he?" Manwright returned to Jessamy. "And how much did you get for her?"

"That is not germane."

"That little? Why, you padded procurer? Why? God knows, you don't need the money."

"Dr. Manwright—"

"Don't you 'Doctor' me. It's Dominie."

"Dominie—"

"Speak."

"You sold me a lemon."

"What!"

"You heard me. You sold me a lemon."

"How dare you!"

"I admit I'm a jillionaire."

"Admit it? You broadcast it."

"But nevertheless I resent a rip-off."

"Rip! I'll kill the man. Don't restrain me. I'll kill! Look, you damned minty macho, you came to me and contracted for the perfect wife. A Siren, you said. The kind that a man would have to lash himself to the mast to resist, à la Ulysses. Well? Didn't you?"

"Yes, I did."

"Yes, you did. And did I or did I not generate a biodroid miracle of beauty, enchantment, and mythological authenticity, guaranteed or your money back?"

"Yes, you did."

"And one week after delivery I discover my Pearl of Perfection sold to the distinguished Charles Russell Corque's obscene freak show and displayed naked in a bizarre showcase. My beautiful face and neck! My beautiful back and buttocks! My beautiful breasts! My beautiful mons veneris! My—"

"That's what she wanted."

"Did you, Sandy?"

"Shame on you, girl. I know you're vain—that was a glitch in my programming—but you don't have to flaunt it. You're a damned exhibitionist." Back to Jessamy: "But that doesn't excuse your selling her. Why did you do it, dammit? Why?"

"She was tearing my sheets."

"What?"

"Your beautiful, enchanting Pearl of Perfection was tearing my monogrammed silk sheets, woven at incredible cost by brain-damaged nuns. She was tearing them with her mythologically authentic feet. Look at them."

There was no need to look. It was undeniable that the beautiful, enchanting Siren was feathered from the knees down and had delicate pheasant feet.

"So?" Manwright demanded impatiently.

"She was also scratching my ankles."

"Damn you!" Manwright burst out. "You asked for a Siren. You paid for a Siren. You received a Siren."

"With bird feet?"

"Of course with bird feet. Sirens are part bird. Haven't you read your Bulfinch? Aristotle? Sir Thomas Browne? Matter of fact, you're lucky Sandy didn't turn out bird from the waist down. Ha!"

"Very funny," Jessamy muttered.

"But it wasn't luck," Manwright went on. "No, it was genius. My biodroid genius for creative genesis, and my deep understanding of the sexual appetites."

"Don't be impudent, girl. I have sexual appetites, too, but when I guarantee a virgin, I— No matter. Take her home, Jessamy. Don't argue, or I'll kill you, if I can find that damned brass thing I thought I had. Take Sandra home. I'll refund Professor Corque in full. Got to support his brilliant research. Sandy, trim your talons, for God's sake! Sense and sensibility, girl! Corque, go pack up and move in with me. Here's my card with the address. What the devil are you doing with that silly-looking fire extinguisher?"

"And that's the full shmeer, Charles. I'm sorry I haven't any work in progress to show you, but you can see I'm no tailor or seamstress, cutting up mature animals, human or otherwise, and piecing parts together like you see with those show-biz monsters in your circus. No, I macrogenerate 'em, pure and whole, out of the basic DNA broth. Mine are all test-tube babies. Florence-flask babies, as a matter of fact, which is where I start 'em. Biodroids need womb space like any other animal."

"Fascinating, my dear Reg, and quite overwhelming. But what I can't fathom is your RNA process."

"Ah! The RNA messenger service, eh?"

"Exactly. Now we all know that DNA is the life reservoir—"

"All? We all know? Ha! Not bloody likely. Some time I'll show you the abuse I get from the Scripture freaks."

"And we know that RNA is the messenger service delivering commands to the developing tissues."

"Right on, Charles. That's where the control lies."

"But how do you control the controls? How do you direct the RNA to deliver specific commands from DNA to embryo? And how do you select the commands?"

"Penthouse."

"Wh-what?"

"Come up to the penthouse. I'll show you."

Manwright led Corque out of the enormous crimson-lit cellar laboratory which was softly glowing with ruby-colored glassware and liquids ("My babies *must* be insulated from light and noise") and up to the main floor of the house. It was decorated in the Dominie's demented style: a hodgepodge of Regency, classic Greek, African, and Renaissance. There was even a marble pool inhabited by iridescent manic fish, which gazed up at the two men eagerly.

"Hoping we'll fall in," Manwright laughed. "A cross between piranha and golden carp. One of my follies."

Thence to the second floor, twenty-five by a hundred, Manwright's library and study: four walls shelved and crammed with tapes, publications, and software; a rolling ladder leaning against each wall; a gigantic carpenter's workbench center, used as a desk and piled with clutter.

Third floor divided between dining room (front), kitchen and pantry (center), and servants' quarters (rear, overlooking garden).

Fourth floor, enjoying maximum sky and air, bedrooms. There were four, each with its own dressing room and bath, all rather severe and monastic. Manwright regarded sleep as a damned necessity which had to be endured but which should never be turned into a luxury.

"We all get enough sleep during our nine months in the womb," he had growled to Corque, "and we'll get more than we'll ever need after we die. But I'm working regenerative immortality, off and on. Trouble is, tissues just don't want to play ball." He led the professor up a narrow stair to the penthouse.

It was a clear plastic dome, firmly anchored against wind and weather. In the center stood a glimmering Rube Goldberg, Heath-Robinson, Da Vinci mechanical construct. If it resembled anything it would be a giant collapsing robot waiting for a handyman to put it together again. Corque stared at the gallimaufry and then at Manwright.

"Neutrinoscope," the Dominie explained. "My extrapolation of the electron microscope."

"What? Neutrinos? The beta-decay process?"

Manwright nodded. "Combined with a cyclotron. I get particular particle selection that way and acceleration up to ten Mev. Selection's the crux, Charles. Each genetic molecule in the RNA coil has a specific response to a specific particle bombardment. That way I've been able to identify and isolate somewhere in the neighborhood of ten thousand messenger commands."

"But-but—My dear Reg, this is positively fantastic!"

Manwright nodded again. "Uh-huh. Took me ten years."

"But I had no idea that— Why haven't you published?"

"What?" Manwright snorted in disgust. "Publish? And have every damned quack and campus cretin clowning around with the most sacred and miraculous phenomenon ever generated on our universe? Pah! No way!"

"*You're* into it, Reg."

Manwright drew himself up with hauteur. "*I*, sir, do not clown."

"But Reg—"

"But me no buts, professor. By heaven, if Christ, in whom I've never believed, ever returned to Terra and this house, I'd keep it a secret. You know damn well the hell that would break loose if I published. It'd be Golgotha all over again."

While Corque was wondering whether Manwright meant his biodroid techniques, Christ's epiphany, or both, there was a sound of a large object slowly falling upstairs. Manwright's scowl was transformed into a grin. "My housekeeper," he chuckled. "You didn't get the chance to see him when you moved in last night. A treasure."

An imbecile face, attached to a pinhead, poked through the penthouse door. It was followed by a skewed hunchback body with gigantic hands and feet. The mouth, which seemed to wander at will around the face, opened and spoke in a hoarse voice.

"Mahth-ter . . ."

"Yes, Igor?"

"Should I thteal you a brain today, mahth-ter?"

"Thank you, Igor. Not today."

"Then breakfahtht ith therved, mahth-ter."

"Thank you, Igor. This is our distinguished guest, the celebrated Professor Charles Corque. You will make him comfortable and obey him in everything."

"Yeth, mahth-ter. At your thervithe, thelebrated Profethor Charlth Corque. Should I thteal you a brain today?"

"Not today, thank you."

Igor bobbed his head, turned, disappeared, and there was a sound of a large object rapidly falling downstairs. Corque's face was convulsed with suppressed laughter. "What in the world—?"

"A reject," Manwright grinned. "Only one in my career. No, the first of two, if we count Sandy, but I do think Jessamy will keep his Siren. Anyway," he continued, leading Corque downstairs, "this client was absolutely hypnotized by the Frankenstein legend. Came to me and contracted for a faithful servitor, like the Baron's accomplice. Returned five months later, paid like a gent, but said he'd changed his mind. He was now on a Robinson Crusoe kick and wanted a Friday. I made him his Friday, but I was stuck with Igor."

"Couldn't you have dissolved him back into the DNA broth?"

"Good God, Charles! No way. Never. I generate life; I don't destroy it. Anyway, Igor's an ideal housekeeper. He does have this brain-stealing hang-up—that was part of the original model—and I have to lock him in a closet when there's thunder and lightning, but he cooks like an absolute genius."

"I hadn't known that Baron Frankenstein's henchman was a chef."

"To be quite honest, Charles, he wasn't. That was an error in programming—I *do* glitch now and then—with a happy ending. When Igor's cooking, he thinks he's making monsters."

The·card came in on the same tray with the Tomato-Onion Tart (ripe tomatoes, sliced onions, parsley, basil, Gruyère, bake in pastry shell forty minutes at 375°F), and Manwright snatched the embossed foil off the salver.

"What's this, Igor? 'Anthony Valera, Chairman, Vortex Syndicate, 69 Old Slip, CB: 0210-0012-036-216291'?"

"In the waiting room, maththt-ter."

"By God, Charles, a potential client. Now you may have your chance to watch my genesis from start to finish. Come on!"

"Oh, have a heart, Reg. Let the chairman wait. Igor's monster looks delicious."

"Thank you, thelebrated Profethor Charlth Corque."

"No, no, Igor. The thanks go from me to you."

"Pigs, both of you," Manwright snorted and dashed for the stairs. Corque rolled his eyes to heaven, grabbed a slice of tart, winked at Igor, and followed, chewing ecstatically.

One would expect the chairman of a syndicate with a seventeen-figure CB telephone number to look like Attila the Hun. Anthony Valera looked and dressed like a suave Spanish grandee; he was black and silver, including ribboned peruke. He was very much au courant, for as Corque entered he smiled, bowed, and murmured, "What a happy surprise, Professor Corque. Delighted. I had the pleasure of hearing you speak at the Trivium Charontis convention." And Mr. Valera considerately offered his left palm, Corque's right hand being busy with the tart.

"He wants an ideal executive secretary," Manwright refused to waste time on courtesies. "And I told him that my biodroid talents are damned expensive."

"To which I was about to respond when you most happily entered, Professor Corque, that Vortex is criminally solvent."

"Then it's to be a company contract?"

"No, Dominie, personal." Mr. Valera smiled. "I, also, am criminally solvent."

"Good. I hate doing business with committees. You must know

the old saw about camels. Let's discuss the specs and see whether we understand each other. Sex?"

"Female, of course."

"Of course. Physical appearance?"

"You don't take notes?"

"Total recall."

"You *are* lucky. Well, then. Fair. Medium tall. Endowed with soft grace. Soft voice. Blue eyes. Clear skin. Slender hands. Slender neck. Auburn hair."

"Mmm. Got any particular example of the type in mind?"

"Yes. Botticelli's *Birth of Venus.*"

"Ha! Venus on the Half-shell. Lovely model. Character?"

"What one would expect of a secretary: sterling, faithful, devoted . . . to my work, of course."

"To your work, of course."

"And clever."

"D'you mean clever or intelligent?"

"Aren't they the same?"

"No. Cleverness requires humor. Intelligence does not."

"Then clever. I'll provide the intelligence. She must be able to learn quickly and remember. She must be able to acquire any skill necessary for my work. She must be perceptive and understand the stresses and conflicts that make a chairman's life one constant battle."

"So far you could hire such a girl," Manwright objected. "Why come to me?"

"I haven't finished, Dominie. She must have no private life and be willing to drop everything and be instantly available at all times."

"Available for what?"

"Business luncheons, dinners, last-minute parties, client entertainment, and so forth. She must be chic and fashionable and able to dazzle men. You would not believe how many tough tycoons have been charmed into dubious deals by a seductive secretary."

"You've left out an important point. On what salary will she be seducing?"

"Oh, I'll provide the money for the wardrobe, the maquillage, and so forth. She must provide the taste, the charm, the wit, the entertaining conversation."

"Then you want a talker?"

"But only when I want her to talk. Otherwise, mum."

Corque whistled softly. "But you're describing a paragon, my dear sir."

"I would say a miracle, Professor Corque, but Dominie Manwright is celebrated for his miraculous creations."

"You married?" Manwright shot.

"Five times."

"Then you're a chaser."

"Dominie!"

"And easily landed."

"Really, you're extraordinarily blunt. A chaser? Well . . . let's say that I'm attracted occasionally."

"Would you want your executive secretary to be responsive—occasionally? Is that to be programmed?"

"Only unilaterally. If I should happen to desire, I would want a beautiful response. But she is not to make demands. Nevertheless she will, of course, be faithful to me."

"These parameters are preposterous," Corque exclaimed indignantly.

"Not at all, Charles, not at all," Manwright soothed. "Mr. Valera is merely describing what all men desire in a woman: an Aspasia, the beautiful *femme galante* who was the adoring mistress and advisor to Pericles of ancient Greece. It's wishful fantasy, but my business is turning fantasy into reality, and I welcome the challenge. This girl may be my magnum opus." Again he fired a shot at Valera. "And you'll become very bored."

"What?"

"Within six months this adoring, talented, dedicated slave will bore you to tears."

"But how? Why?"

"Because you've left out the crux of a kept woman's hold over a man. Don't protest, Valera. We know damn well you're ordering a mistress, and I make no moral judgment, but you've forgotten the drop of acid."

"Dominie. I do protest. I—"

"Just listen. You're contracting for an enchanting mistress, and it's my job to make sure that she remains enchanting, always. Now there are many sweet confections that require a drop of acid to bring out the full flavor and keep them enjoyable. Your Aspasia will need a drop of acid for the same reason. Otherwise, her perpetual perfection will cloy you in a matter of months."

"You know," Valera said slowly, "that's rather astute. Dominie. What would you advise? I'm all anticipation!"

"The acid in any woman who can hold a man: the unexpected, the quality that makes it impossible to live with them or without them."

"And what would that be in my . . . my secretary?"

"How the devil can I tell you?" Manwright shouted. "If you knew in advance, it wouldn't be unexpected; and anyway *I* won't know. I can't guarantee surprise and adventure with a woman. All I can do is program a deliberate error into the genesis of your perfect Aspasia, and the discovery of that kink will be the charming drop of acid. Understood?"

"You make it sound like a gamble."

"The irrational is always a gamble."

After a pause Valera said. "Then you're challenging me, Dominie?"

"We're both being challenged. You want the ideal mistress created to your specs; I've got to meet them to your complete satisfaction."

"And your own, Reg?" Corque murmured.

"Certainly my own. I'm a professional. The job is the boss. Well, Valera? Agreed?"

After another thoughtful pause, Valera nodded. "Agreed, Dominie."

"Splendid. I'll need your Persona Profile from the syndicate."

"Out of the question, Dominie! Persona Profiles are Inviolable Secret. How can I ask Vortex to make an exception?"

"Damn it, can't you understand?" Manwright was infuriated by this intransigence but controlled himself and tried to speak reasonably. "My dear chairman, I'm shaping and conditioning this Aspasia for your exclusive use. She will be the cynosure of all men, so I must make sure that she'll be implanted with an attraction for your qualities and drawn to you alone."

"Surely not all, Dominie. I have no delusions of perfection."

"Then perhaps to your defects, and that will be *your* charming drop of acid. Come back in twenty-one weeks."

"Why twenty-one specifically?"

"She'll be of age. My biodroids average out at a week of genesis for every physical year of the creation's maturity. One week for a dog; twenty-one weeks for an Aspasia. Good day, Mr. Valera."

After the chairman had left, Manwright cocked an eye at Corque and grinned. "This is going to be a magnificent experiment, Charles. I've never generated a truly contemporary biodroid before. You'll pitch in and help, I hope?"

"I'll be honored, Reg." Suddenly, Corque returned the grin. "But there's one abstruse reference I can't understand."

"Fear not, you'll learn to decipher me as we go along. What don't you understand?"

"The old saw about the camel."

Manwright burst out laughing. "What? Never heard it? Penalty of spending too much time on the outer planets. Question: What is a camel? Answer: A camel is a horse made by a committee." He sobered. "But by God, our gallant girl won't be any camel. She'll be devastating."

"Forgive the question, Reg. Too devastating for you to resist?"

"What? That? No way! Never! I've guaranteed and delivered too many virgin myths, deities, naiads, dryads, *und so weiter.* I'm seasoned, Charles; tough and hard and impervious to all their lures. But the breasts are going to be a problem," he added absently.

"My dear Reg! Please decipher."

"Her breasts, Charles. Botticelli made 'em too small in his Venus. I think I should program 'em fuller, but what size and shape? Like pears? Pomegranates? Melons? It's an aesthetic perplexity."

"Perhaps your deliberate error will solve it."

"Perhaps, but only the Good Lord, in whom I've never believed, can know what her mystery kink will turn out to be. *Selah!* Let's get to work on our perfect mistress, Charles, or, to use an antique expression that's just become a new vogue word, our perfect Popsy."

The Dominie's program for a devastating Popsy who was to be enchanting, trustworthy, loyal, helpful, friendly, courteous, kind, obedient, cheerful, clever, chic, soft-spoken, beautiful, busty, eloquent on demand, and always available to entertain, began as follows:

A	12-1	0	0	(scald)
B	12-2	1	1	

C	12-3	2	2	(V.S.O.P.)
D	12-4	3	3	
E	12-5	4	4	
F	12-6	5	5	(¼ dram)
G	12-7	6	6	
H	12-8	7	7	(crimped)
I	12-9	8	8	
J	11-1	9	9	(½ scruple)
K	11-2	(garni)		
L	⌐11-3	#	8-3	
M	11-4	!	11-8-2	
N	11-5	@	8-4	(eau)
O	11-6	$	11-8-3	
P	11-7	%	0-8-4	(MSG)
Q	11-8	¢	12-8-2	
R	11-9	&	12	
S	0-2	•	11-8-4	(only a dash)
T	0-3	+	0-8-3	
U	0-4	:	12-8-3	

Und so weiter for 147 pages. *Und* good luck to the computer software for creative biogenesis, which couldn't possibly interest anyone.

"Anyway, there's no point in reading the program, Charles. Numbers can't paint the picture. I'll just describe the sources I've used for the generation of our Popsy. You may not recognize some of the names, but I assure you that most of them were very real and famous celebrities in their time."

"What was your lecture to Igor the other day, Reg? 'A chef is no better than his materials.'"

"Right on. And I'm using the best. Beauty—Botticelli's Venus of course, but with Egyptian breasts. I thought of using Pauline Borghese, but there's a queen in a limestone relief from the Ptolemaic period who's the ideal model. Callipygian rear elevation. Maidenhair frontispiece, delicate and fritillary. Did you say something, Charles?"

"Not I, Reg."

"I've decided not to use Aspasia for the virtues."

"But you said that was what Valera wanted."

"So I did, but I was wrong. The real Aspasia was a damned premature Women's Rights activist. Too strong for the chairman's taste."

"And yours?"

"Any man's. So I'm using Egeria instead."

"Egeria? I haven't had an education in the classics, Reg."

"Egeria, the legendary fountain nymph who was the devoted adviser to King Numa of ancient Rome. She also possessed the gift of prophecy, which might come in handy for Valera. Let's see. Fashion and chic—a famous couturière named Coco Chanel. Subtle perceptions—the one and only Jane Austen. Voice and theater sense—Sarah Bernhardt. And she'll add a soupçon of lovely Jew."

"What on earth for?"

"It's obvious you haven't met many on the outer planets or you wouldn't ask. Remarkable race, Jews: freethinking, original, creative, obstinate, impossible to live with or without."

"That's how you described the ideal mistress, wasn't it?"

"I did."

"But if your Popsy is obstinate, how can she respond to Valera's desires?"

"Oh, I'm using Lola Montez for that. Apparently, she was a tigress in the sex department. Hmmm. Next? Victoria Woodhull for business acumen. La Pasionaria for courage. Hester Baterman—she was the first woman silversmith—for skills. Dorothy Parker for wit. Florence Nightingale for sacrifice. Mata Hari for mystery. What else?"

"Conversation."

"Quite right. Oscar Wilde."

"Oscar Wilde!"

"Why not? He was a brilliant talker; held dinner parties spellbound. I'm giving her dancer's hands, neck, and legs. Dolley Madison hostessing, and—I've omitted something. . . ."

"Your deliberate mistake."

"Of course. The mystery kink which will catch us all by surprise." Manwright flipped through the software. "It's programmed somewhere around here. No, that's Valera's Persona Profile. Charles, you won't believe the damned intransigent, stubborn, know-it-all, conceited egomania concealed beneath that polished veneer. It's going to be hell imprinting our girl with an attraction engram for such an impossible man. Oh, here's the unexpected in black and white."

Manwright pointed to:

$$R = L \times \sqrt{N}$$

"Wait a minute," Corque said slowly. "That equation looks familiar."

"Aha."

"I think I remember it from one of my boyhood texts."

"Oh-ho."

"The . . . the most probable distance . . ." Corque was dredging up the words ". . . from the lamppost after a certain number of . . . of irregular turns is equal to the average length of each track that is—"

"Straight track, Charles."

"Right. Each straight track that is walked, times the square root of their number." Corque looked at Manwright with a mixture of wonder and amusement. "Confound you, Reg! That's the solution to the famous 'Drunkard's Walk' problem from *The Law of Disorder.* And this is the deliberate uncertainty that you're programming? You're either a madman or a genius."

"A little of both, Charles. A little of both. Our Popsy will walk straight lines within my parameters, but we'll never know when or how she'll hang a right or a left."

"Surely she'll be aiming for Valera?"

"Of course. He's the lamppost. But she'll do some unexpected staggering on the way." Manwright chuckled and sang in an odd, husky voice. "There's a lamp on a post, There's a lamp on a post, And it sets the night aglowin'. Boy girl boy girl, Boy boy girl girl, But best when flakes is snowin'."

Regis Manwright's laboratory notes provide a less-than-dramatic description (to put it politely) of the genesis and embryological development of Galatea Galante, the Perfect Popsy.

GERMINAL

Day 1: One hundred milliliter Florence flask.
Day 2: Five hundred milliliter Florence flask.
Day 3: One thousand milliliter Florence flask.
Day 4: Five thousand milliliter Florence flask.
Day 5: Decanted.

(E & A charging *too damn much* for flasks!!!)

(Baby nominal. Charles enchanted with her. Too red for my taste. Poured out of the amnion blowing bubbles and talking. Couldn't shut her up. Just another fresh kid with a damn big mouth.)

"Reg. Gally must have a nurse."

"For heaven's sake, Charles! She'll be a year old next week."

"She must have someone to look after her."

"All right. All right. Igor. She can sleep in his room."

"No, no, no. He's a dear creature, but hardly my idea of a nurse-maid."

"I can convince him he made her. He'll be devoted."

"No good, Reg; he isn't child oriented."

"You want someone child oriented? Hmmm. Ah, yes. Got just the right number for you. I generated The Old Woman Who Lived in a Shoe for the Positively Peerless Imitation Plastic company to use in their genuine plastics sales promotion."

"'She had so many children she didn't know what to do'?"

"The same." Manwright punched the CB keyboard. "Sean-bhean? This is Regis."

The screen sparkled and cleared. A gypsy crone appeared with begging hand outstretched for alms.

"How's everything going, Seanbhean?"

"*Scanruil aduafar,* Regis."

"Why?"

"*Briseadh ina ghno e.*"

"What! PPIP gone bankrupt? That's shocking. So you're out of a job?"

"*Deanfaidh sin!*"

"Well perhaps I have something for you, Seanbhean. I've just generated—"

"Cut off, Reg," Corque broke in sharply.

Manwright was so startled by Corque's tone that he obeyed and looked up perplexedly. "Don't think she'll do, Charles?"

"That old hag? Out of the question."

"She isn't old," Manwright protested. "She's under thirty. I made her look like that according to specs: Seventy-year-old Irish gypsy. They call 'em 'tinkers' in Ireland. Speaks Irish and can handle kid actors who are a pain in the ass. And I delivered, by God."

"As you always do, but still out of the question. Please try someone else."

"Charles, has that damn infant got you enthralled?"

"No."

"Her first conquest, and she's just out of the flask! Can you imagine what she'll do to men in another twenty weeks? Be at each other's throats. Fighting duels. Ha! I *am* a genius, and I don't deny it."

"We need a nurse for Gally, Reg."

"Nag, nag, nag."

"Someone warm and comforting after the child has endured a session with you."

"I can't think what the man is implying. All right, cradle-snatcher, all right. I'll call Claudia." Manwright punched the CB. "She's warm and maternal and protective. Wish she'd been *my* nanny. Hello? Claudia? It's Regis. Switch on, darling." The screen sparkled and cleared. The magnificent head and face of a black mountain gorilla appeared.

"!!" she grunted.

"I'm sorry, love. Been too busy to call. You're looking well. How's that no-good husband of yours?"

"!"

"And the kids?"

"!!!"

"Splendid. Now don't forget. You promised to send them to me so I can surgify them into understanding our kind of speech. Same like you, love, and no charge. And speaking of kids, I've got a new one, a girl, that I'd like you to—"

At this point the stunned Corque collected himself enough to press the cutoff stud. Claudia faded.

"Are you mad?" he demanded.

Manwright was bewildered. "What's wrong, Charles?"

"You suggest that terrifying beast for the child's nurse?"

"Beast! She's an angel of mother love. She'll have the kid climbing all over her, hugging and kissing her. It's interesting," he reflected, "I can manipulate the cognition centers, but I can't overcome muscular limitations. I gave Claudia college-level comprehension of spoken and written communications, but I couldn't give her human speech. She's still forced to use Mountain, which is hardly a language of ideas. Damn frustrating. For both of us."

"And you actually want her to mother Gally?"

"Of course. Why not?"

"Your Claudia will frighten the daylights out of the infant."

"Ridiculous."

"She's hideous."

"Are *you* mad? She's beautiful. Pure. Majestic. And a hell of a lot brighter than your Remedial Table Tennis bums at Syrtus University."

"But she can't talk. She only grunts."

"Talk? Talk? For God's sake, Charles! That damn red Popsy was poured out talking sixteen to the dozen. We can't shut her up. She's filling the house with enough of her jabber as it is. Be grateful for some silence."

So Claudia, the black mountain gorilla, moved into the Manwright ménage, and Igor was furiously jealous.

The first morning that Claudia joined Manwright and Corque at breakfast (while Igor glowered at his massive rival), she printed a message on a pad and handed it to the Dominie: R DD YU GV G TLT TRG IN YR PRGRM?

"Let's see if I remember your abbreviations, darling. Did you . . . that's me . . . give Galatea . . . yes, toilet training in your program? My God, Claudia! I gave her the best of 47 women. Surely at least one of them must have been toilet trained."

BY DPRS

"By what, Claudia?"

"Buy diapers, Reg."

"Oh, Ah. Of course. Thank you, Charles. Thank you, Claudia. More coffee, love? It's frustrating, Charles. Muscular dyspraxia again. Claudia can manage caps in her writing but she can't hack lower case. How many diapers, Claudia?"

1 DZ.

"Right. One doz. *Zu Befehl.* Did you bring your kids to play with the baby?"

TO OD

"Too old for what?"

TOO OLD

"Your kids?"

G

"What? Galatea? Too old for your boys? And still in diapers? I'd best see for myself."

One of the top-floor bedrooms had been converted into a nursery. The usual biodroid cellar accommodations weren't good enough for Manwright's magnum opus. When the Dominie entered with Claudia, the red infant was on the floor, flat on her belly, propped on a pillow, and deep in a book. She looked up and crawled enthusiastically to Claudia.

"Nanny dear, I've found the answer, the old linear shorthand. Just slashes, dots, and dashes, and you won't have to worry your hand and head over cursive abbreviations. It's a simple style, and we can practice together." She climbed up on Claudia and kissed her lovingly. "One would think this might have occurred to that egotistical know-it-all whose name escapes me." The infant turned her auburn head. "Why, good morning, Dominie Manwright. What an unpleasant surprise.

"You're right, Claudia," Manwright growled. "She's too damned old for your kids. Diaper her."

"My sphincter will be under control by tomorrow, Dominie," Galatea said sweetly. "Can you say the same for your tongue?"

"Guh!" And Manwright withdrew with what he hoped was impressive dignity.

Of course, she shot up like a young bamboo plant and filled the house with joy as she entertained them with her escapades. She taught herself to play Manwright's Regency harpsichord, which was sadly out of repair. She convinced Igor that it was a monster in the making, and together they refinished and tuned it. The sound of concert-A on the tuning fork droned through the house with agonizing penetration. The others were forced to eat out because she gave Igor no time for cooking.

She studied linear shorthand with Claudia and then translated it into finger language. They had glorious raps, silently talking to each other until Manwright banned the constant finger waggling, which he denounced as a damned invasion of vision. They simply held hands and talked into each other's palm in their secret code, and Manwright was too proud to ask what they were gossiping about.

"As if I'd get an answer anyway," he growled to Corque.

"D'you think that's her mystery surprise, Reg?"

"Damned if I know. She's unexpected enough as it is. Rotten kid!"

She stole liquid licorice from Igor's sacred pantry and tarred herself; phosphorus from Manwright's sacred laboratory and irradiated herself. She burst into Corque's dark bedroom at three in the morning, howling, "ME METHOPHYTE MOTHER FROM GANNYMEEDY! YOU KILL ALL MY CHILDERS, ALIEN INVADER FROM OUTSIDE SPACE! NOW ME KILL YOU!"

Corque let our a yell and then couldn't stop laughing for the rest of the day. "The beautiful shock of the apparition, Reg!" Manwright didn't think it was funny.

"That damned child is giving me *real* nightmares," he complained. "I keep dreaming that I'm lost in the Grand Teton mountains and Red Indians are chasing me."

She sneaked up into the sacred penthouse and decorated the robotlike neutrinoscope with items stolen from Manwright's wardrobe. The construct assumed a ludicrous resemblance to the Dominie himself.

The innocent child fast-talked E & A Chemical delivery—"My Daddy forgot to order it. So absent-minded, you know"—into an extra gallon of ethyl alcohol which she poured into the marble pool and got the piranhas disgustingly drunk. Then she jumped in and was discovered floating with her plastered pals.

"Doesn't know the meaning of fear, Reg."

"Pah! Just the Pasionaria I programmed."

She stole two hundred meters of magnetic tape from the library and fashioned a scarecrow mobile. The gardener was enraptured. Manwright was infuriated, particularly because art-dealer friends offered huge amounts for the creation.

"But *that's* her charming unexpected, Reg. Gally's a born artist."

"Like hell she is. That's only the Hester Bateman I gave her. No $L \times \sqrt{N}$ yet. And the nightmares are continuing in sequence. Those damned Red Indians have cut me off at the pass."

Claudia took Galatea to her home, where the girl got on famously with Claudia's two sons and brought them to Manwright's house to demonstrate a new dance which she'd devised called: "The Anthro Hustle." It was performed to a song she'd composed entitled: "Who Put the Snatch on Gorilla Baby?" which she banged out fortissimously on the harpsichord.

"Bring back the tuning fork," Manwright muttered.

Corque was applauding enthusiastically. "Music's her surprise kink, Reg."

"Call that music?"

Corque took her to his Saturn Circus, where she mesmerized him into letting her try riding bareback and leaping through burning hoops, acting as target for a knife thrower, trapeze aerobatics, and thrusting her auburn head into a lion's mouth. He couldn't understand how she'd persuaded him to let her take such horrifying risks.

"Perhaps cajolery's her mystery quality," he suggested. "But she did miraculously well, Reg. My heart was in my mouth. Gally never turned a hair. Pure aplomb. She's a magnificent creation. You've generated a Super-Popsy for Valera."

"Guh."

"Could her unexpected kink be psychic?"

"The redskins have got me surrounded," Manwright fretted. He seemed strangely disoriented.

What disturbed him most were the daily tutoring sessions with the young lady. Invariably they degenerated into bickering and bitching, with the Dominie usually getting the worst of it.

"When our last session ended in another bitch we both steamed for the library door," he told Corque. "I said, 'Age before beauty, my dear,' which you must admit was gracious, and started out. That red Popsy snip said, 'Pearls before swine,' and swaggered past me like a gladiator who's wiped an entire arena."

"She's wonderful!" Corque laughed.

"Oh, you're insanely biased. She's been twisting you around her fingers since the moment she was poured."

"And Igor and Claudia and her two boys and the CB repair and the plumber and the electronics and the gardener and the laundry and E & A Chemical and half of my circus? All insanely biased?"

"Evidently I'm the only sanity she can't snow. You know the simple psychological truth, Charles; we're always accusing others of our own faults. That saucebox has the impudence to call me intransigent, stubborn, know-it-all, conceited. Me! Out of her own mouth. Q.E.D."

"Mightn't it be the other way around, Reg?"

"Do try to make sense, Charles. And now that the Grand Teton breastworks are making her top-heavy (I think maybe I was a little too generous with my Egyptian programming) there'll be no living with her vanity. Women take the damned dumbest pride in the thrust of their boozalums."

"Now Reg, you exaggerate. Gally knows we'd all adore her even if she were flatchested."

"I know I'm doing a professional job, and I know she has too much ego in her cosmos. But next week we start *schlepping* her to parties, openings, talk-ins, routs, and such to train her for Valera. *That* ought to take her down a peg. The Red Indians have got me tied to a stake," he added gloomily.

"Canapés?"

"Ta evah so. Lahvely pahty, Ms. Galante."

"Thank you, Lady Agatha. Canapés?"

"Grazie, Signorina."

"Prego, Commendatore. Canapés?"

"A dank, meyd'l. Lang leb'n zolt ir."

"Nito far vus, General. Hot canapés, dear Professor Corque?"

"Thank you, adorable hostess. Igor's?"

"Mine."

"And perfection. Don't be afraid of the Martian consul. He won't bite."

"Canapés, M'sieur Consul?"

"Ah! Mais oui! Merci, Mademoiselle Gallée. Que pensez-vous du lumineux Dominie Manwright?"

"C'est un type très compétent."

"Oui. Romanèsque, mais formidablement compétent."

"Quoi? Manwright? Romanèsque? Vous me gênez, mon cher consul."

"Ma foi, oui, romanèsque, Mademoiselle Gallée. C'est justement son côté romanèsque qui lui cause du mal à se trouver une femme."

"These damn do's are a drag, Charles."

"But isn't she wonderful?"

"And they're making my nightmares worse. A sexy Indian squaw tore my clothes off last night."

"Mi interesso particolarmente ai libri di fantascienza, magia-orrore, umorismo, narrativa, attualità, filosofia, sociologia, e cattivo, putrido Regis Manwright."

"Charles, this is the last literary talk-in I ever attend."

"Did you see how Gally handled those Italian publishers?"

"Yes, gibes at my expense. She put iron claws on her hands."

"My dear Reg, Gally did no such thing."

"I was referring to that sexy squaw."

"Então agora sabes dançer?"

"Sim. Danço, falo miseravelmente muchas linguas, estudo ciência e filosofia, escrevo uma lamentával poesia, estoirome com experiências idiotas, egrimo como un louco, jogo so boxe como up palhaco. Em suma, son a celebra bioroid, Galatea Galante, de Dominie Manwright."

"She was magnificent dancing with that Portuguese prince, Reg."

"Portuguese ponce, you mean."

"Don't be jealous."

"She's heating the claws in a damned campfire, Charles."

"Didn't you ever fight back, Sandy?"

"Yes, I know, he's a bully. But all bullies are cowards at heart. You should have fought him to a standstill, like me. Did he ever make a pass at you?"

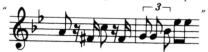

"Un-huh. Me neither. He's an arrogant egomaniac, too much in love with himself to love anyone else."

"What, Sandy? Me? Give the come-on to that dreadful man? Never! Did you?

"Uh-huh. And he didn't even have to lash himself to the mast.

Iceberg City. Ah, Mr. Jessamy. So sweet of you to give us your box for the concert. I've just been comparing notes with your adorable wife on our common enemy, whose name escapes me. He's the gentleman on my right, who slept through the Mozart."

"And dreamed that she's torturing me with her burning claws, Charles, all over my bod."

"Man nehme: zwei Teile Selbstgefälligkeit, zwei Teile Selbstsucht, einen Teil Eitelkeit, und einen Teil Esel, mische kräftig, füge etwas Geheimnis hinzu, und man erhält Dominie Regis Manwright."

"Especially my private parts."

"Dominie Manwright's biodroid está al día en su manera de tratar los neologismos, palabras coloquiales, giro y modismos, clichés y términos de argot, señor. Yo soy Galatea Galante, la biodroid."

"Thank you, madame. I am not Spanish; I merely admire and respect the old Castilian style."

"Oh. Scuse me, chorley guy. You toller-day donsk?"

He burst out laughing. "I see you're very much with the classics, madame. Let me think. Yes. The proper response in that James Joyce litany is 'N.'"

"You talkatiff scowegian?"

"Nn."

"You spigotty anglease?"

"Nnn."

"You phonio saxo?"

"Nnnn."

"Clear all so. 'Tis a Jute. Let us swop hats and excheck a few strong verbs weak oach eather yapyazzard."

"Brava, madame! Bravissima!"

She tilted her auburn head and looked at him strangely. "Against my will," she said slowly, "I'm compelled to invite you to a dinner party tonight."

"More classics, madame? The Beatrice and Benedict scene from *Much Ado About Nothing?*"

"No, it's the Galatea and—I don't know your name."

"Valera. Antony Valera."

"It's the Galatea and Valera scene. Can you come?"

"With delight."

"When this bash is finished I'll give you the address."

"I know it, Galatea."

"My friends call me Gally. How do you know my address? We've never met."

"I contracted with—I'm acquainted with Dominie Manwright, Gally. Tonight? Eight o'clock?"

"Eight tonight."

"Dress party?"

"Optional." She shook her head dizzily. "I don't know what's got into me, Valera. The moment I saw you at this clambake I knew I had to see you again, intimately. I'm possessed!"

The rest of the household was dining in The Gastrologue, and their moods were not compatible.

"Thrown out." Corque kept repeating. "Thrown out without a moment's notice by that ungrateful tyrant!"

"Naturally. She wants to be alone with Valera, Charles. Instant, devoted attraction, as per my brilliant programming. I tell you, I'm a genius."

"She athed me to make month-terth for her to therve, maththter."

"Quite right, Igor. We must all pitch in and abet Valera's romance. He was so turned on meeting her at that bash this afternoon that he sent his check by messenger. Payment in full . . . to protect his claim on my Perfect Popsy, no doubt."

"Thrown out! Thrown out by that tyrant!"

"And good riddance to her very soon, Charles. The house will be back to normal.

"But she didn't order a brain, mahth-ter."

"Not to worry, Igor. Tell you what: we'll order cervelles de veau au beurre noir, and if Gastrologue doesn't have any calves' brains you can go out and steal some." He beamed and bobbed his pale, streaky head.

"Thank you, mahth-ter."

"Evicted!"

The silent Claudia printed: PLANTAINS FR ME PLS RELLENOS DE AMARILLO.

At one minute past eight Valera said, "It's fashionable to be a half-hour late, but I— Is it all right to come in?"

"Oh please! I've been biting my nails for a whole minute."

"Thank you. To tell the truth, I tried to be chic, but it didn't take as long as I thought it would to walk up from Old Slip."

"Old Slip? Isn't that where your office is? Were you working late, poor soul?"

"I live there too, Gally. A penthouse on top of the tower."

"Ah, à la Alexander Eiffel?"

"Somewhat, but the Syndicate complex is no *Tour Eiffel*. What a fantastic place this is. I've never done more than peep beyond the waiting room."

"D'you want the full tour?"

"I'd like nothing better."

"You've got it, but drink first. What would you like?"

"What are you serving?"

"My dear Valera, I—"

"Tony."

"Thank you. My dear Tony, I share this house with two and a half men and a mountain gorilla. We have everything in stock."

"Stolichnaya, please. Half?"

"Igor, our housekeeper," Galatea explained as she brought a tray with a bucket of ice, a bottle, and shot glasses. She opened the vodka deftly and began revolving the bottle in the ice. "A biodroid replica of Baron Frankenstein's accomplice."

"Oh yes, I've met him. The lisping hunchback."

"A dear, dear soul, but only half with it."

"And a gorilla?"

"That's Claudia, my beloved nanny. She's beautiful. This vodka really isn't chilled enough yet, but let's start anyway." She filled the glasses. "Russian style, eh? Knock it back, Tony. Death to the fascist, imperialist invaders from outer space."

"And their Conestoga star-wagons."

They knocked their shots back.

"Gally, what miracle are you wearing?"

"Là, sir!" She did a quick kick-turn. "Like it?"

"I'm dazzled."

"If I tell you, promise not to turn me in?"

"I promise."

"I copied it from a Magda."

"Who or what is a Magda? Oh, thank you."

"I'm afraid I filled it too high, but boys like big sandwiches and big drinks. She's *the* vogue designer of the year. Down with countertenors."

"May they be heard only in Siberia. Why must I keep it a secret about your copy?"

"Good Lord! They hang, draw, and quarter you if you pinch a designer original."

"How did you manage?"

"I fell in love with it at one of her openings and memorized it."

"And made it yourself? From memory? You're remarkable!"

"You're exaggerating. Don't you remember complicated stock manipulations?"

"Well, yes."

"So with me it's the same damn thing. Oops! That's the tag of a dirty joke. Apologies to the chairman."

"The chairman needs all the dirty jokes he can get for client entertainment. What's this one?"

"Maybe someday, if you coax me nicely."

"Where do you get them? Surely not from Dominie Manwright."

"From Claudia's naughty boys. Another shot to the damnation of Blue Laws, and then the guided tour."

Valera was bewildered and delighted by the madness of Manwright's house, and enchanted by the high style with which Galatea flowed through it with equally mad comments. An old song lyric haunted him:

> Hey, diddle-dee-dee,
> I've found the girl for me.
> With raunchy style
> And virgin guile
> She's just the girl for me.

"Never mind the polite compliments, Tony," she said, pulling him down on a couch beside her and refilling his glass. "I'll give you the acid test. Of all things in this house, which would you be most likely to steal?"

"You."

"I didn't say kidnap. Come on, man, steal something."

"I think I spilled my drink."

"It's my fault; I joggled your arm. Don't mop. So?"

"You're so sudden, Gally. Well . . . don't laugh. . . . The scare-crow mobile in the garden."

"Oh, I love you for that! *I* made it, when I was a little kid months ago." She gave him a smacking kiss on the cheek and jumped up. "Like some music?" She turned on the hi-fi and a soft murmuring drifted through the house.

Valera glanced at his watch. "Your guests must be frightfully chic."

"Oh?"

"You said eight. That was an hour ago. Where's everybody?"

"As a matter of fact, they came early."

"I'm the only one who was early."

"That's right."

"You mean I'm . . . ?"

"That's right."

"But you said a dinner party, Gally."

"It's ready any time you are."

"The party is us? Just us?"

"I can call some more people if you're bored with me."

"You know that's not what I meant."

"No? What did you mean?"

"I—" He stopped himself.

"Go ahead," she bullied. "Say it, I dare you."

He capitulated. For perhaps the first time in his suave life he was overpowered. In a low voice he said, "I was remembering a tune from twenty years ago. Hey, diddle-dee-dee/ I've found the girl for me/With raunchy style/And virgin guile/She's just the girl for me."

She flushed and began to tremble. Then she took refuge in the hostess role. "Dinner," she said briskly. "Beef Stroganoff, potatoes baked with mushrooms, salad, lemon pie, and coffee. Mouton Roth-schild. No, not upstairs, Tony; I've made special arrangements for you. Help me with the table."

Together, in a sort of domestic intimacy, they arranged a gaming table alongside the marble pool with two painted Venetian chairs. She had already set the table with Spode china and Danish silver, so it needed some careful balancing. Before she began serving, she drew the cork from the Bordeaux bottle and poured a few drops into Valera's goblet.

"Try it, Tony," she said. "I've never been able to decide whether the concept of 'letting a wine breathe' is fact or show-offy. I appeal to your sophistication. Give me your opinion."

He tasted and rolled his eyes to heaven. "Superb! You're magnificent with your compliments, Gally. Sit down and try it yourself. I insist." And he filled her glass.

"Wait," she laughed. "The floor show first. I snowed electronics into bootlegging ultralight into the pool. That's why I wanted our table here. Wait till you see 20 Performing Piranhas 20." She ran to a wall, extinguished the living room lights, and flipped a switch. The pool glowed like lava, and the excited fish became a ballet of darting embers. Galatea returned to the table, sat opposite Valera, and raised her goblet to him. He smiled back into her face.

"Hey, diddle-dee—" he began and then froze. He stared. Then he started to his feet so violently that he overturned the table.

"Tony!" She was appalled.

"You goddamn bitch," he shouted. His face was black. "Where's the CB?"

"Tony!"

"Where's the goddamn CB? Tell me before I break your goddamn neck!"

"Th-that table." She pointed. "B-but I don't understand. What's—"

"You'll understand soon enough." He punched buttons. "By God, you and this whole damn lying house will understand. Rip me? Play me for a patsy?" His rage was a terrifying echo of Manwright at his worst. "Hello. Larson? Valera. Don't waste time with visual. Crash mission. Call full Security and comb the city for a son of a bitch named Regis Manwright. Yes, that's the pig. I give you a half hour to find him and—"

"B-but I know where he is," Galatea faltered.

"Hold it, Larson. You do? Where?"

"The Gastrologue."

"The bastard's in The Gastrologue Club, Larson. Go get him and bring him to his house, which is where I am now. And if you want to get rough with him I'll pay all legals and add a bonus. I'm going to teach that lying pimp and his bitch a lesson they'll remember for the rest of their lives."

The four were herded into the main floor of Manwright's house at the point of a naked laser which Larson thought advisable in view of the threat of Claudia's mass. They saw a grotesque Valera and Galatea silhouetted before the glowing pool in the dark room. Valera was holding the weeping girl by her hair, for all the world like a chattel in a slave market.

In this ominous *crise* Manwright displayed an aspect of his character which none had ever seen: a tone of quiet command that took obedience for granted, as if by divine right, and won it through its assurance.

"Mr. Larson, you may pocket that laser now. It was never needed. Valera, you will let Galatea go." he said softly. "No, dear, don't move. Stay alongside him. You belong to him, unless he's changed his mind. Have you, Valera?"

"You're goddamn right I have," the chairman stormed. "I want no part of this cheap secondhand trash. Larson, keep that gun handy and get on the CB. I want my check stopped."

"Don't bother, Mr. Larson. The check has not been deposited and will be returned. Why, Valera? Doesn't Galatea meet your exalted standards?"

"Of course she does," Corque burst out. "She's brilliant! She's beautiful! She's perfection! She—"

"I'm handling this, Charles. I repeat: Why, Valera?"

"I don't buy whores at your prices."

"You think Galatea's a whore?"

"Think? I know."

"You contracted for the perfect mistress who would be faithful and loving and devoted to you."

Galatea let out a moan.

"I'm sorry, my love, you never knew. I'd planned to tell you, but only after I was sure you were genuinely attracted to him. I never had any intention of forcing him on you."

"You wicked men!" she cried. "You're all hateful!"

"And now, Valera, you think of a mistress as a whore? Why this sudden eruption of archaic morality?"

"It isn't a question of morality, damn you. It's a question of secondhand goods. I want no part of a shopworn woman."

"Must I stay here with him? Does he own me? Am I bought and paid for?"

"No, love. Come to us."

She dashed away from Valera's side and then hesitated. Claudia held out her arms, but Galatea surprised everybody by going to Manwright, who took her gently.

"All right, Valera," he said. "Go now and take your army with you. Your check will be returned first thing in the morning."

"Not until I know who it was."

"Not until who what was?"

"The goddamn lover-boy who knocked her up."

"What?"

"She's pregnant, you goddamn pimp. The bitch has been sleeping around, and I want to know the stud who knocked her up. He's got plenty coming."

After a long pause, Manwright asked, "Are you under a psychiatrist's care?"

"Don't be ridiculous."

"No more ridiculous than your slander. Galatea pregnant? My lovely, tasteful young lady sleeping around with studs? You're obviously quite mad. Go."

"Mad, am I? Ridiculous? You can't see that she's pregnant? Turn her around and look at her face in this ultralight. Look at her!"

"I'll go through the motions only to get rid of you."

Manwright smiled at Galatea as he turned the girl around. "Just a gesture, love. You'll have your dignity back in a moment, and I swear you'll never lose it ag—"

His words were cut off as if by a guillotine. In the ultralight from the glowing pool there was no mistaking the dark pregnancy band across Galatea's face, similar to the banded mask of a raccoon. He took a slow deep breath and answered the confusion in her eyes by placing a hand over her mouth.

"Go, Valera. This is now a family affair."

"I demand an answer. I won't leave until I know who it was. Your half-wit hunchback, Igor, probably. I can picture them in bed: the slobbering idiot and the—"

Manwright's interruption was an explosion. He hurled Galatea into Claudia's arms, drove a knee into Larson's groin, tore the laser away from the convulsed man, whipped Valera across the neck with the barrel, and held the staggering chairman over the edge of the pool.

"The piranhas are starving," he murmured. "Do you go in or get out?"

. . .

After the syndicate had left, not without dire promises, Manwright turned up the house lights and extinguished the pool ultralight and, with that, the pregnancy stigma banding Galatea's face. In a strange way they were all relieved.

"Not to play district attorney," he said, "but I must know how it happened."

"How what happened?" Galatea demanded.

"Sweetheart, you *are* pregnant."

"No, no, no!"

"I know it can't be anyone in this house. Claudia, has she been promiscuous outside?"

N O

"How can you ask such questions!"

"Has Galatea been alone with a man in a possibly intimate situation?"

"You're hateful!"

N O

"Reg, we all know that. We've chaperoned Gally every moment outside, you, me, Claudia."

"Not every moment, Charles. It could have happened with this innocent in five minutes."

"But nothing ever happened with a man! Nothing! Ever!"

"Dear love, you *are* pregnant."

"I can't be."

"You are, undeniably. Charles?"

"Gally, I adore you, no matter what, but Reg is right. The pregnancy band is undeniable."

"But I'm a virgin."

"Claudia?"

HR MNS HV STOPT

"Her what have stopped?"

Corque sighed. "Her menses, Reg."

"Ah so."

"I'm a virgin, you wicked, detestable men. A virgin!"

Manwright took her frantic face in his hands. "Sweetheart, no recriminations, no punishments, no Coventry, but I must know where I slipped up, how it happened. Who were you with, where and when?"

"I've never been with any man, anywhere or anywhen."

"Never?"

"Never . . . except in my dreams."

"Dreams?" Manwright smiled. "All girls have them. That's not what I mean, dear."

R MAB U SHD MN

"Maybe I should mean what, Claudia?"

LT HR TL U HR DRMS

"Let her tell me her dreams? Why?"

JST LSN

"All right, I'll listen. Tell me about your dreams, love.

"No. They're private property."

"Claudia wants me to hear them."

"She's the only one I've ever told. I'm ashamed of them."

Claudia fingerwagged, "Tell him, Gally. You don't know how important they are."

"No!"

"Galatea Galante, are you going to disobey your nanny? I am ordering you to tell your dreams."

"Please, nanny. No. They're erotic."

"I know, dear. That's why they're important. You must tell."

At length, Galatea whispered, "Put out the lights, please."

The fascinated Corque obliged.

In the darkness, she began, "They're erotic. They're disgusting. I'm so ashamed. They're always the same . . . and I'm always ashamed . . . but I can't stop. . . .

"There's a man, a pale man, a moonlight man, and I . . . I want him. I want him to . . . to handle me and ravish me into ecstasy, b-but he doesn't want me, so he runs, and I chase him. And I catch him. Th-there are some sort of friends who help me catch him and tie him up. And then they go away and leave me alone with the moonlight man, and I . . . and I do to him what I wanted him to do to me. . . ."

They could hear her trembling and rustling in her chair.

Very carefully, Manwright asked, "Who is this moonlight man, Galatea?"

"I don't know."

"But you're drawn to him?"

"Oh yes. Yes! I always want him."

"Just him alone, or are there other moonlight men?"

"Only him. He's all I ever want."

"But you don't know who he is. In the dreams do you know who you are?"

"Me. Just me."

"As you are in real life?"

"Yes, except that I'm dressed different."

"Different? How?"

"Beads and . . . and buckskin with fringe."

They all heard Manwright gasp.

"Perhaps like . . . like a Red Indian, Galatea?"

"I never thought of that. Yes. I'm an Indian, an Indian squaw up in the mountains, and I make love to the paleface every night."

"Oh. My. God." The words were squeezed out of Manwright. "They're no dreams." Suddenly he roared, "Light! Give me light, Charles! Igor! Light!"

The brilliant lights revealed him standing and shaking, moonlight pale in shock. "Oh my God, my God, my God!" He was almost incoherent. "Dear God, what have I created?"

"Mahth-ter!"

"Reg!"

"Don't you understand? I know Claudia suspected; that's why she made Galatea tell me her dreams."

"B-but they're only dirty dreams," Galatea wailed. "What could possibly be the harm?"

"Damn you and damn me! They were *not* dreams. They were reality in disguise. That's the harm. That's how your dreams lock in with my nightmares, which were reality, too. Christ! I've generated a monster!"

"Now calm yourself, Reg, and do try to make sense."

"I can't. There's no sense in it. There's nothing but that lunatic drop of acid I promised Valera."

"The mystery surprise in her?"

"You kept wondering what it was, Charles. Well, now you know, if you can interpret the evidence."

"What evidence?"

Manwright forced himself into a sort of thunderous control. "I dreamed I was pursued and caught by Red Indians, tied up, and ravished by a sexy squaw. I told you. Yes?"

"Yes. Interminably."

"Galatea dreams she's a Red Indian squaw, pursuing, capturing, and ravishing a paleface she desires. You heard her?"

"I heard her."

"Did she know about my dreams?"

"No."

"Did I know about hers?"

"No."

"Coincidence?"

"Possibly."

"Would you care to bet on that possibility?"

"No."

"And there you have it. Those 'dreams' were sleep versions or distortions of what was really happening; something which neither of us could face awake. Galatea's been coming into my bed every night and we've been making love."

"Impossible!"

"Is she pregnant?"

"Yes."

"And *I'm* Valera's lover-boy, the stud responsible. My God! My God!"

"Reg, this is outlandish. Claudia, has Gally ever left her bed nights?"

NO

"There!"

"Damn it, I'm not talking about a conventional, human woman. I didn't generate one. I'm talking about an otherworld creature whose psyche is as physically real as her body, can materialize out of it, accomplish its desires, and amalgamate again. An emotional double as real as the flesh. You've pestered me about the deliberate unexpected in my programming. Well, here's the $R = L \times \sqrt{N}$ Galatea's a succubus."

"A what?"

"A succubus. A sexy female demon. Perfectly human by day. Completely conformist. But with the spectral power to come, like a carnal cloud, to men in their sleep, nights, and seduce them."

"No!" Galatea cried in despair. "I'm not that. I can't be."

"And she doesn't even know it. She's an unconscious demon. The laugh's on me, Charles," Manwright said ruefully. "By God, when I do glitch it's a beauty. I knock myself out programming the Perfect Popsy with an engram for Valera, and she ruins everything by switching her passion to me."

"No surprise. You're very much alike."

"I'm in no mood for jokes. And then Galatea turns out to be a succubus who doesn't know it and has her will of me in our sleep every night."

"No, no! They were dreams. Dreams!"

"Were they? Were they?" Manwright was having difficulty controlling his impatience with her damned obtuseness. "How else did you get yourself pregnant, eh; *enceinte, gravida*, knocked up? Don't you dare argue with me, you impudent red saucebox! You know," he reflected, "there should have been a smidgen of Margaret Sanger in the programming. Never occurred to me."

He was back to his familiar impossible self, and everybody relaxed.

"What now, Reg?"

"Oh, I'll marry the snip, of course. Can't let a dangerous creature like Galatea out of the house."

"Out of your life, you mean."

"Never!" Galatea shouted. "Never! Marry you, you dreadful, impossible, conceited, bullying, know-it-all, wicked man? Never! If I'm a demon, what are you? Come, Claudia."

The two women went very quickly upstairs.

"Are you serious about marrying Gally, Reg?"

"Certainly, Charles. I'm no Valera. I don't want a relationship with a popsy, no matter how perfect."

"But do you love her?"

"I love all my creations."

"Answer the question. Do you love Gally, as a man loves a woman?"

"That sexy succubus? That naïve demon? Love her? Absurd! No, all I want is the legal right to tie *her* to a stake every night, when I'm awake. Ha!"

Corque laughed. "I see you do, and I'm very happy for you both. But, you know you'll have to court her."

"What! Court? That impertinent red brat?"

"My dear Reg, can't you grasp that she isn't a child anymore? She's a grown young woman with character and pride."

"Yes, she's had you in thrall since the moment she was poured," Manwright growled. Then he sighed and accepted defeat. "But I suppose you're right. My dear Igor!"

"Here, mahth-ter."

"Please set up that table again. Fresh service, candles, flowers, and see if you can salvage the monsters you created for the dinner. White gloves."

"No brainth, mahth-ter?"

"Not this evening. I see the Mouton Rothschild's been smashed. Another bottle, please. And then my compliments to Ms. Galatea Galante, and will she have the forgiveness to dine, *à deux*, with a most contrite suitor. Present her with a corsage from me . . . something orchidy. This will be a fun necromance, Charles," he mused. "Parsley, sage, rosemary, and thyme, *alevai*. Man and Demon. Our boys will be devils, sorcery says, and the girls witches. But aren't they all?"

THE DEVIL
WITHOUT GLASSES

Editor's note: This story was found among Bester's papers after his death, and is published for the first time in this collection.

Sleep is a preview of death; and as all men must die in the end, all men taste that death in sleep each night, a tiny bitter fragment.

It happens to all of us. First there is night and darkness. We lie in bed, tired and relaxing, welcoming our portion of death because we know there will be an awakening. We think a little, reviewing the events of the day, drowse, settle into the pillow.

The queer lights that flash in our closed eyes dance in familiar gyrations, and as we try to follow them we topple over the brink into the anesthesia of slumber. Eventually we dream. It has been suggested that dreaming is nature's device to clear the mind and ready it for the next day's turmoils and crises. Perhaps.

There is sound that matches the gyrating lights we watched as we fell asleep. There is space that is far from empty, it swarms with atomic and subatomic particles. And most difficult to comprehend, there are two spaces, obverse and reverse, like the faces of a coin. From one of these come voices that sound alien. There is an identity calling himself Starr, speaking in muffled, distorted tones, "Charles. Charles Granville." The words shatter into filigree. "Clear transmission, please. There is reverse interference."

The blurring distorts, then clears.

"Granville. Charles Granville. Can you hear me?" The identity called Starr pauses. "Will some of you get him to listen."

"No response?"

"None. He's the rare type who cannot commit himself to anything because he cannot believe in a reality which exists independent of ideas concerning it. And so he hangs midway between obverse and reverse."

"Then why bother with him? Let him hang."

"Because he has thirty years of frenzy, of the violent excitement of mania buried deep inside him. When it emerges, as it must sooner or later, he will begin to preach, but for or against our obverse universe? We must persuade him.

"Granville, you must listen to us. You must listen and act as instructed. You are unique because you are unaware of your hidden potential."

In the dream labyrinth Charles Granville listens indifferently to the voices pecking at his mind. "I beg your pardon. Most amazing thing. Did someone mention my name? I'm Granville. Dr. Charles Granville." He giggles insipidly at a pointless dream joke. "Wanted in surgery to diagnose two-headed patient."

Starr persists, "You can't hang between two spaces, Granville. Join us. Come to our obverse."

Steps falter through clotted mist and fog that sound like electricity. The voices call in living echoes, like articulate road signs. This is fizzy electric cream with goldfish that repeat your name.

"But why are the fish talking?" Granville considers the problem. "Swimming? That's okay. In the nature of things. Quite right." His mute voice sings without sound. "Fish got to swim. Birds got to fly. Swell idea for a song. I'm a real-life composer."

"He's reaching for his own lunatic reality, Starr."

"It doesn't matter if it gets him through to us. Will one of you check Coven for reverse interference?"

In vasty deeps a bell beats slowly.

"Do you hear that?"

"The bell?"

"Yes. It's Coven."

Starr calls urgently, "Granville, this way. Stay with us in the obverse."

The bell beats faster, soaring upwards. The voices mount and blend. "Granville, listen to us. Don't try to wake up. Hold on to your dream a little longer because your dream is your reality."

A hand shaking his shoulder.

A single bell clattering.

A single voice repeating, "Granville! Granville! Wake up, will you, Charlie? That's emergency you're hearing."

Granville stirred in the cot, trying to plunge back into sleeping and dreaming his own reality. He muttered, "Keep the goldfish quiet."

The redheaded young man in T-shirt and white ducks exclaimed, "Jerusalem! I never saw a guy pound his ear like you, Charlie. That's emergency hollering. This is County Hospital. It's your turn to ride the wagon. Will you wake up!"

Granville opened his eyes to a bleak whitewashed dormitory room. "Okay, Gardner. The body is conscious."

"Try and look it."

"Kill that bell, will you? What time is it?"

Gardner looked at him dubiously, then stepped to the wall switch and cut the bell circuit. "Six A.M."

"Six? Oh! Murder!"

"No, auto accident. Corner of Broad and Grove. Come on. Come on. Get dressed. The wagon's waiting. Get that epicene look off your face, Doctor."

"That's bewilderdom, Doctor. I was having a demented dream when you woke me. I was hanging between two spaces, only I was in a fishbowl and the goldfish were fighting for me."

"Put *both* shoes on."

"And I wrote a hit song that went—I forget. But anyway, there were rivals with nudnick names who wanted me to join them in the starry space they controlled. Starry? Why starry? There weren't any stars."

Gardner waved his hand irritably. "Will you get the lead out, Charlie? Some poor character just got smashed under a truck."

Granville hunted for his kit with gummy eyes. "Where's my bag?"

"Right here."

"Why'd they call us instead of Memorial or St. Augustine? Was he one of our patients?"

"No, but the cop who called in said he asked for us and I checked. Name of Coven. No record with us."

Granville stopped short. "Coven!"

"Why the take? Friend of yours?"

"No, but I think it's somebody from my nightmare."

"You've got to be kidding."

"No way, but I swear I heard the goldfish arguing and warning and bad-mouthing a character named Coven."

"Who very kindly got himself smashed by a truck to make your cockeyed dream come true. You probably heard me mention the name when I took the call." Gardner opened the dormitory door and shoved Granville through. "Will you get going, Florence Nightingale? You can ask Mr. Coven why he walked out of your nightmare into a truck."

The garage was bleak and silent. Granville's heels made sharp echoes above the grumbling ambulance motor. Eddie, the driver, glared as the intern sprinted in.

"Come on, Doc. Come on. I been waitin' a whole five minutes. A guy could write the New Testament in five minutes."

"Sorry, Eddie. Got held up."

The ambulance roared and took off with a lurch. Eddie displayed his hacksaw profile and continued the conversation casually. "Get yourself held up by what, could I ask?"

"A dream."

"Now, Doc!"

"Scout's honor, Eddie."

"You been sniffin' ether again." Eddie tsk-tsked. "Shame on you.

Why don't you practice what you preach?" The early morning traffic was beginning to litter the streets. Eddie started the ambulance siren and raised his voice to a conversational howl. "I thought you M.D.'s was writin' books to stop people from dreamin'. Psycho stuff. Ain't you kinda double-crossin' your profession?"

"Do you ever dream, Ed?"

"Every night."

"Do you dream real?"

"Do I! The broads! Like, wow!"

"So real you can't tell whether it happened or not?"

"Who knows whether anything really happens, Doc." Eddie swung the heavy ambulance into Broad and thread-needled up to the Grove intersection. "Oh, man! Will you look at that red carpet?"

There was a skewed truck and a doughnut of people clustered around the front bumper staring at a scarlet puddle. A slender, pasty man with thinning hair was exhorting the public irritably. "All right, folks, move along. Move along. This ain't a sideshow. Ain't you got something better to do this morning? Why get the creeps? Go buy breakfast or something."

Granville shoved through the crowd, swinging his bag like a truncheon to clear a path. "I'm Doctor Granville. County Hospital. Who's in charge here?"

The pasty man looked at him with bleary blue eyes. "I am, Doc. The name is Simmons. Detective Division. Was passing when it happened and took over. Here's your patient; what's left of him."

Granville knelt alongside the broken body. The face was pressed into the asphalt, strangely smiling. Black hair shot with grey. The features of a dissipated Caesar. The body terribly crushed.

Granville shot a look at Simmons. "Why in hell is he grinning? It's like his one joy in life was to get himself smashed by a truck. Take me two hours to list the damage done."

"Name is Coven, Sidney A. Address in his wallet, 910 South Street."

"Coven," Granville murmured. "But of course." Then aloud, "Nothing I can do for Sidney A. He's unadulterated DOA. Mashed like a pancake and loving it. Going to hold the driver?"

Simmons looked perplexed. "I don't know. He tells a story you ought to hear." The detective called, "Casey! Over here."

A lumbering man with a broad tonsure detached himself from

the truck's front suspension and trudged up to them. His eyes showed panic. He croaked, "It's like I said, Cap. All you got to do is look at my record. I been drivin' three hundred forty-seven thousand miles and no accident. I never—"

Simmons snapped, "Save it. This ain't no grand jury."

"So help me, Cap—"

"Sergeant."

"Sure. Sure. Sergeant."

"Tell the story to the Doc."

The driver's eyes swiveled to Granville, desperately avoiding the dead body and the crimson rug. "Jeez, Doc, I been drivin' three hundred and forty-seven thousand miles and no accid—"

"Just tell him what happened."

"Well, I'm comin' down Broad, see. I got five hundred gallons of Grade A, two fifty of cream, and—"

"Never mind the inventory."

"Yeah. Yeah." Casey took a breath. "So like I was sayin' I'm doin' about forty and I see this guy walkin' down Broad on my side. The right-hand sidewalk. Get it?"

Granville closed his bag and stood up, "Coven?"

"The dead guy."

"He's Coven, the Doc says," Simmons interjected. "Go ahead."

"So this Coven waves to me I should pull over. He's an official-looking guy so I figure it's a sneak pinch. I pull over to the curb and slow down and I'm just gonna give him an argument when Voom."

"Voom?"

"He takes a dive right under my front wheels."

Granville stared at the driver uncertainly and then turned to Simmons. "Is the story straight?"

The driver jerked back. "So help me . . ."

"There's witnesses," Simmons said. "It's straight."

"Then it's suicide."

"I don't think so," the driver mumbled. "I think he was off his rocker."

"Why? How?"

"He yelled something crazy when he took the dive."

"Yelled what?"

"About astronomy."

"Astronomy?"

"He said the stars weren't going to get him."

"The stars!"

"Yeah."

Granville could not choke back the impulse to recite: *Twinkle, twinkle, little star.* He deliberately dropped his bag then stooped to pick it up. He could feel himself blushing like a child.

Simmons said, "I ask you, Doc. Is that a *magilla?* Does it sound crazy or don't it?"

"I don't know." Granville tried to grin. "It sounds crazy all right, only it just occurred to me that maybe Coven isn't your lunatic. Maybe it's me."

They parted on that note of confusion.

At two-thirty he finally caught Gardner in the busy corridor outside Maternity. The redheaded intern carried six Erlenmeyer flasks with the deftness of a variety artist. He had had no lunch and was acerbic.

"Well, well, well. The dreamy kid in the flesh. How'd you do this morning, Doctor? Did the corpse interpret your nightmare or did you get Eddie to read your palm?"

Granville gave him a dogged look with his spaniel eyes. "Come into the stockroom a minute, Gardner. I want to ask you something."

"Make it snappy. I've got two dozen blood-sugars waiting."

The stockroom door swung shut. The room was silent and gloomy. In a corner an autoclave muttered sinister secrets.

"Listen, Gardner . . ." Granville hesitated and rubbed a hand up the back of his neck into his seal-brown hair. There was an interminable wait.

Exasperated, Gardner said, "You wanted to ask me something. So ask. Is this about home, career, ambition, fighting with my sister?"

"No."

"Sure? Jinny's got a redheaded temper. I remember you two fighting over the engagement ring. Wow!"

"It isn't anything like that. Will you listen for a minute?"

"Avidly, when you're ready to talk."

"It's about the dream I had this morning."

"Oh, for the love of—"

"I told you about me hanging between two spaces and the gold-fish that were competing to enlist me on their rival teams. The honcho of one team was named Starr."

"As in telly-a-scope."

"Be serious. Starr and his little friends were worried frantic about someone named Coven."

"Guy who got mashed under the truck?"

"Yes."

"So?"

"Coven deliberately jumped under the truck."

"Suicide?"

"Maybe, but dig this. Just as he took the dive he yelled something about Starr not getting him. Then he was smashed."

"End of story?"

"It's got me rattled, Gardner. I was dreaming those two names when it happened. Maybe they were fighting over me. I could be the *him* Starr wasn't supposed to get. What do you think?"

"You really want to know?"

"I'm asking."

"The marriage is off."

"Can't you ever be serious?"

"But I am." Gardner rattled the Erlenmeyers alarmingly. "You think I'd let my ever-lovin' sister marry a schizoid? You should lay there and bleed."

"I am already."

"Go back to school, Doc. Remember about dreams? They take a fraction of a second. A sleeping man can hear a door slam and dream an entire episode that culminates in that door slam."

"All right. So maybe I heard you mention Coven's name on the phone. But what about Starr? When the truck driver told me what Coven yelled, I knew I'd been dreaming about him." Granville shook his head dazedly. "What right does a complete stranger have to intrude on me like that?"

"Fatigue, brother, fatigue. The tired mind gets frazzled. You hear something for the first time and you could swear you're remembering it. But it's really only fatigue doing a con job on you."

"No." Granville turned away. "It isn't as simple as that."

"You want it the other way? The dream way?" Gardner put the flasks down carefully and flipped up a cigarette. "You want to believe those two characters were actually fighting to enlist you, somewhere in the wild blue yonder?"

"That's how I remember it."

Gardner lit the cigarette and shoved it into Granville's mouth. "So to win this contest, Coven walks out of your head into a truck. Great. Just the kind of level thinking the AMA is trying to foster."

"Well what do you want me to think?"

"That you've been on duty seventy-two hours, which is enough to make anyone's mind play tricks. That Jinny is supposed to pick her ever-lovin' brother up in half an hour and take him driving. That you're going instead."

Forty minutes later, Granville sat in the passenger seat of Jinny's car.

"It's about time I got you to myself," she said.

"You're like a black widow spider," Granville said comfortably. "They eat their husbands."

"No I'm not. I'm . . . like a snapshot album, waiting for pictures to be pasted in. I don't care about your past. To hell with the past . . . but I've got the future all marked out. Picture of Chuck's first baby . . . picture of Chuck's twenty-first baby . . ."

"Hey, lady! Have a heart."

"Your babies. Not mine. I'll be more restrained. Picture of Chuck reading research paper to medical convention."

"Am I bald?"

"Not yet. You are when you receive the Humphrey Hickenlooper Memorial Award."

"For what?"

"I don't know. I just know you're going to get some kind of award. That's the fun, darling . . . knowing and waiting for it to come true. I think the nicest thing about falling in love is that you get somebody else's dreams to wish for too."

"Dreams. Say . . ." Granville straightened up. "I'd almost forgotten. Listen, Jinny . . ."

"Which reminds me, Charles. I've been thinking."

"When you say 'Charles' it means you've been planning."

"I have. For the snapshot album. We're going to be poor after we're married."

"All doctors are. It's traditional." Granville nodded complacently. "You set up practice and starve and everybody mocks you while you search for the cure for hangnails. 'Mad Granville!' they mock. 'Thinks he can do the impossible. Cure hangnails! Ha-ha-ha-ha-ha—'"

"So I decided to get a job to help us . . . and I tried . . . and I did." Jinny looked apologetic. "I got a job today."

"Hey."

"I bet you get that Hickenlooper award for hangnails."

"Don't duck like that. What's all this about a job?"

"It's wonderful," Jinny said with conviction. "Afternoons only. From one to six. It pays thirty-five dollars. I do research."

"What kind of research?"

"Statistical . . . on floods and fires and wrecks and so on."

"For what person or persons?"

"An awfully nice man. Very respectable, Chuck. A Mr. Coven."

"Mr. What?"

"Coven. He—" Jinny stared at him. "What's happened to your face, honey? It's all lopsided."

"Never mind my face." Granville took a breath and composed himself. "What's Coven's full name?"

"Sidney Albert."

"Address?"

"Nine-ten South Street." Jinny looked interested and curious. "Do you know anything about—"

"What time today did you get the job?"

"If this is a new game, Charles—"

"Please, Jinny. Just answer the question."

"I got the job this morning."

"What time?"

"Around eleven o'clock."

"From Coven himself? Personally? You spoke to him?"

"Why yes." She smiled perplexedly. "But he isn't the one with the broken shoelaces, if that's what's worrying you."

"Drive back to town, Jinny."

"What is it, Chuck? What's the matter?"

He said slowly and seriously: "Sidney Coven of 910 South Street was crushed to death under a truck five hours before you spoke to him."

Nine-ten South Street was a half block of two-story taxpayers. Three of the stores were joined to a single entrance. Their windows were painted jet black halfway up. A tall man could peer over the black border and see a thousand square feet of open floor cluttered with desks, files, and typists. It looked like an insurance office. Bold gold letters on the black windows read: NATIONAL STATISTICS.

Jinny parked the car and said: "I still think you're crazy."

"Don't try to argue," Granville answered. "We haven't come to an issue yet. That's why we're here."

Jinny shrugged. "There isn't any issue."

"It says here. Let's button it up before I go in and make a fool of myself. What'd your Coven look like?"

"Well . . . " Jinny was being patient. "A big man . . . large head . . . grizzled hair . . . kind of dissipated face."

"Like a Roman?"

"Could be."

"Could also be my Coven."

"Nonsense. It's a relative."

"You keep telling yourself, and a mite too hard, Virginia." Granville looked at her keenly. "You're lying about something. I can tell. What is it?"

"Don't be silly, Charles."

"Yes you are. Any other time you're a sucker for a mystery. Wild horses couldn't tear you away from the scent. Now you're trying to brush it off. Why? What's got you scared?"

"I'm not, Charles."

"You are." He gripped her arm and looked at her intensely. "I'm not fooling with this, Virginia. You've got to go along with me. Understand?"

"But it's so silly . . ."

"Not to me. I like answers. I want one from you now. What are you holding out? What are you afraid to tell me?"

"It isn't anything; but . . ." Jinny's assurance began to waver. "As a matter of fact my Coven was sick. He . . . well, he was lying on a couch in his office when I saw him . . . covered with a robe. I thought he was an invalid. He talked . . . He talked sickly . . ." She tried to laugh. "But it can't mean anything, Chuck. It's too ridiculous."

"Invalid! That's a hot one." Granville pushed open the door. "All right. Maybe I'm crazy. At least let me find out. You wait for me, Jinny. Either they'll throw me out . . . or lead me out."

He slammed the door of the roadster, walked across the sidewalk and opened the half-black glass door numbered 910. He stepped in and looked around uncertainly. There was a crisp background of typewriters and telephones that was subtly reassuring. Close to the entrance, a switchboard girl was languidly plugging phone jacks. She spoke in a nasal whine:

"National, good afternoon," A pause. "I'm sorry Mr. Sunderland is in Belgium. Will there be any message?"

In the next pause Granville began: "Excuse me, I'd like to—"

"Just a minute, please." The girl turned and called over her shoulder: "Gertrude, wire Mr. Sunderland the death reports are not acceptable."

Granville was startled. Gertrude, very dark and heavily stacked, nodded, finished typing a line, then leaned back interestingly to the desk behind her and made a note.

The telephone girl gave Granville her attention. "Can I be of assistance, sir?"

"Well, I . . ." Granville tried to be businesslike. "I'm from County Hospital and I'm checking on an accident. Is this office run by a Sidney Coven?"

"There is a Mr. Coven associated with National Statistics, sir."

"I see. Well, the fact is . . ." Granville took the plunge. "My name is Granville and I'd like to—"

The dark Gertrude shot up from her chair like a scalded cat. "Oh yes, Dr. Granville." She stepped forward brightly. "This way, please. Mr. Coven is expecting you."

Granville stared at her. "Expecting me?"

"Yes, Dr. Granville." Gertrude gave his arm the friendliest pressure. "Right this way."

"Don't you know he died this morning?"

She smiled blankly. "This way, please."

Granville permitted himself to be led across the open floor, arguing feebly. "There must be some mistake. Coven can't expect me. I never made an appoint—" He dropped it and re-sorted his confusion. "He can't expect anyone. Not my Sidney Albert. Who's yours? A son or a nephew or something?"

"Through this aisle, Dr. Granville."

"Now wait. Let's make sense. You don't expect me to—"

With relief Gertrude interrupted: "Here's Mr. Sharpe, our office manager." A short, abrupt man with a woodpecker face jumped up from his desk and shot a hand toward Granville. Gertrude said: "Mr. Sharpe, this is Dr. Granville. The four o'clock appointment with Mr. Coven."

Sharpe clutched Granville's hand. "Yes, yes, yes, of course. So glad to meet you, Doctor. Truly a pleasure. I've heard about you. One of the coming young physicians, eh? Ah-ah!" Mr. Sharpe twinkled roguishly. "No modesty, now. This way, sir. Right this way."

He pulled Granville toward a walnut door set flush in the rear wall. "Let me thank you and congratulate you for your promptness, Doctor. The keeping of appointments seems to be a lost art today. People are shockingly careless."

"Just a minute, Mr. Sharpe . . ."

"The whole theory of efficient office management," Mr. Sharpe peeked brightly, "is based on . . ."

"Will you listen to me? I am not prompt. I do not have an appointment. I cannot see Sidney Coven."

". . . is founded on promptness, accuracy, and a thorough respect for time." Sharpe rapped once on the walnut door and thrust it open. He called: "Dr. Granville is here, Mr. Coven," and stepped back.

From the interior a sick voice called: "Good afternoon, Dr. Granville. Do come in. That will be all, Sharpe."

It was a crushed voice . . . a mutilated voice. Granville stiffened and slowly stepped into the office. Sharpe closed the door smartly behind him.

In a small, square room with grey pickled walls, grey carpet and wine-colored drapes blacking out the window, were two pools of light. One shone on a small desk behind which sat a sallow man with brutal features, his eyes concealed by black glasses. The other flooded an Empire couch in the corner. Sidney Coven lay on the couch.

His body was straight and rigid, concealed by a grey corduroy coverlet. He lay quite motionless, his heavy head rolled a little to one side so that his jet eyes could command the room. He looked like a corpse, imperfectly arranged, and his saturnine face was misshapen and bruised, as though it had been kicked.

With the frightening mutilated voice Coven said: "Thank you for keeping your appointment. Please do not be alarmed at my crushed condition; but I forgot . . . as a physician you wouldn't be. This gentleman is Mr. Arno. We were just—"

"You're dead, Coven." Granville advanced a step. He repeated: "You're dead."

"Quite so. Quite so."

"You were DOA this morning. Your back is broken. Your arms are smashed . . . ribs shattered . . . Your heart is burst open. You're dead, Coven."

"To be sure, Dr. Granville. Now—"

"And the pieces of you lay there on that couch and look at me and talk to me. For God's sake what—"

"Will you be quiet, Granville?" The agonizing voice stunned Granville again. Coven continued quietly: "Mr. Arno is an extremely busy person. We can't take up too much of his time. Please sit in that chair . . . alongside the desk. For your own sake you'd best sit before you collapse."

Granville sank into the chair, not glancing at Arno. He continued to stare at Coven.

"All right, Arno," Coven murmured painfully. "Examine him. This is the man I told you about."

"Ah?" said Arno, his voice as icy and disinterested as a phonograph. "The Granville."

"Yes."

"My name," Granville muttered desperately, "is Charles Granville. I'm an intern at County Hospital. I'm twenty-five years old, engaged to be married, in sound health. I do not hear voices, see visions or experience—"

The jet eyes caught him, held him and cut off his words. "This young man is extremely dangerous, Arno," Coven said. "He has forced me to take unusual and costly measures. Listen carefully, Granville. I'm going to praise you to Mr. Arno. You should be flattered."

"I've got nothing to listen to. Nothing."

Coven chuckled and went on: "The average man lives his little life and dies his little death. He has the odd sensation every now and then that the life he is living is make-believe . . . sham . . . that there could be more to it than appears."

"Indeed he does," said Arno, moving quietly behind Granville.

"He has been taught to shrug his shoulders and believe that the odd clues he picks up are dreams . . . visions . . . hallucinations. But not Dr. Granville." The crushed voice sounded amused and bitter. "This young man will not be duped. He is a poetic scientist. Social pressure . . . moral pressure . . . terror . . . threats . . . none of these influences can lobby against the growing certainty in his mind. He is beginning to listen to Starr. In a short time he will hear him. Presently he will understand."

"Starr!" Granville started to his feet. "That name. Then I was right! Then I did—"

Arno's hand on his shoulder drew him back into the chair. He attempted to turn around but Coven said quickly: "Don't, Dr. Granville. Arno is not wearing his glasses. It would be most unpleasant."

Arno said: "You're an inconsiderate young man, Doctor. You've made a lot of trouble for Mr. Coven."

"I blocked Starr this morning," Coven went on, "at the cost of hurling myself under a truck. It was the only way to guarantee Granville's instant awakening. Starr was on the verge of final contact with our friend. He may get through at any moment."

"We can't let that happen, can we, Doctor?" Arno inquired in impersonally pleasant tones.

"Listen," Granville said. "This . . . None of this makes sense. Any of it. Outside, this place looks like an office . . . just an ordinary business office."

"Naturally," Coven replied. He laughed without laughter, his mouth and throat and voice making the sounds and motions. It was the laughter of a parrot. "Naturally."

"But inside it isn't ordinary any more. Crazy talk and crazy people. Appointments I never made . . ."

"I made it, Doctor," said Coven. He laughed the parrot laugh again. "I made it for you this morning."

"With Miss Gardner's assistance," Arno laughed. It was the duplicate of Coven's mechanical imitation.

"You're dead and you're a liar," Granville cried.

The hand on his shoulder restrained him. Granville did not dare turn around. To Arno, Coven said: "Finished?"

"All finished."

"Will it be difficult?"

"Interesting, but not difficult." Arno sauntered around the chair and stood before Granville, staring down at him through the opaque black glasses he had put on again.

"L-Listen," Granville began.

"Please listen to me, Dr. Granville," Coven interrupted. "I have two statements to make. The first is a proposal. Will you join us? Volunteer? Will you become one of us?"

"Join who? Join what?"

"I could answer that in many ways, Doctor. Let us say . . ." Coven chose his words carefully. "Let us say that this is an asylum and we are the keepers. A stranger outside the gates wants to teach the inmates how to escape."

"And you want me to be a keeper?"

"Just one way of putting it, Doctor." Coven selected other words. "Let us say there is a treasure and we are guarding it. Someone wants to teach the world the combination of the strongroom lock."

"And you want me to be a guard?"

"Just another way of putting it, Doctor. Have you heard of the balance of nature? Of course you have. There is more to nature than this earth. Far more. At present it is in delicate balance. Mr. Starr would like to upset that balance by awakening you and your friends. We want you to go on sleeping."

"Sleeping!"

"Sleeping," repeated Arno. "Let us say that."

"But you are on the verge of waking, Doctor," Coven said. "And we should like you to arise from the right side of the bed, so to speak. You could be a genuine asset. We should like to have you with us rather than Starr. Will you join?"

There was a pause. Granville glanced up at Arno who stood over him, icy and intent, the black glasses reflecting twisted light; then looked at Coven's dead body and living eyes.

"I don't know anything," he said slowly. "I don't understand anything. Anything. But I know I don't like you. I don't believe you and I don't trust you." He finished with a rush: "I don't want to be a keeper. I don't want to be a guard. No, I will not. I will not join you, whatever you are. Let us say that."

"Oh. A pity." The mangled voice died away, then resumed. "In that case I make my second statement. Your potential must be destroyed. You will be neutralized."

"You mean killed."

"Just one way of putting it, Doctor. Let us say . . . if you will not volunteer, you will be drafted."

"You mean killed."

"Just another way of putting it, Doctor. When, Arno?"

"Some time this evening. I'll arrange everything."

"Very good." The jet eyes caught Granville. "Thank you again for keeping this appointment, Doctor. You may go now."

Granville got to his feet. "If it's murder, why wait? Why not—"

"Don't say anything, Doctor. Just go."

Suavely, Arno led Granville to the door and opened it for him. From the couch Coven said: "You understand we have another appointment for later today? You understand that you always keep the appointments we make for you?"

Backing through the door, Granville stammered: "You're d-dead, Coven. I don't believe anything."

The dead man laughed his imitation laugh and called: "Au revoir, Doctor."

The door closed. Granville turned and weaved through aisles toward the street. He was dizzy and choked. Through pounding rubble in his ears he heard Sharpe, then Gertrude, then the telephone girl calling bright farewells. Red evening sunlight blinded him in the street. He lurched toward the car, saw Jinny in triplicate open the door for him, and then stare, her mouth making soundless motions. There was a roaring and a stunning blow on his temple . . . and then night.

"Yes," said Charles to the shapes that filled him with awe. "Because it's not true because the sound and the light talk with voices and a man walks on music and feels with thought yes with thought and—*What's that?*" Without speaking he repeated: "*What's that? Who?*"

He dismissed the urgency and twisted about with feverish haste. "The two pieces of a soul are music and pain," he lectured energetically, "and the colors clashing, singing, chiming, crying, and crying in fear and pain to see the sound of—*Who?*"

Thrusting his head upward he cried: "Who? *Who? WHO?*"

"Starr," repeated the urgency. "This is Starr."

"Oh, the voices that sing the ring and mingle with music that mangles with most marvelous tongue with diapason and profound parallax—"

"Charles Granville."

"*What?*"

"Dr. Granville."

"You said something? You spoke? You boke you moke you koke you loke you . . ."

"This is Starr. Will you listen? Can you listen? This is an emergency."

"Who?"

"Try to remember this. You must remember . . ."

"Who's that?"

"Charles, we can help you if you'll—"

"I can't hear you. What? What?"

"We're going to give you the key. You must remember the key as it's unfolded. Charles, listen. Listen. Listen. This is the unfolding. Listen to the pattern. Listen, Charles. Listen . . ."

The palm jolted his jaw and made a sound like water in the ears. Granville turned his head away. The slaps continued. Gardner repeated: "Listen, Charlie. Listen to me, boy. Listen, Charlie-boy. Snap out of it, boy. Wake up, little man."

Thrusting his arms up wildly, Granville said: "I don't want to be touched. Don't touch me."

Gardner gripped his wrists and peered down at him. "Easy, fella . . ." Deftly, he thrust an ammonia bottle under Granville's nose. The thrust of sharp vapor stung his eyes open. He was in emergency at County, on the enameled table. Jinny was silhouetted against the window, her hands clasped.

"No more ammonia," he muttered. "I'm all here. I—" Suddenly he cried: "Don't say anything. There's something I've got to remember. Something . . ." He tried to recapture the dissolving patterns.

"Now kid . . ." Gardner began softly.

"Will you be quiet!" But he could not silence the street traffic and the hospital, and the memory fled. "No . . . I can't hold it."

Jinny came to the edge of the table, her face in a panic. "Charles . . ." She swallowed and tried again. "Oh Charles, I . . ."

"Hey. Jinny? Hi, Jinny." He hoisted himself and felt a bandage on his temple. "Who put out the lights?"

"You pulled a faint." Gardner steadied him. "Flopped into the car. Nosedive. Jinny drove you back to the hospital with your ankles waving in the breeze. Most educational and entertaining spectacle for the multitude."

"We aim to please . . ." Granville got to his feet and teetered against Jinny, who clutched him violently. "What a day this has been." His eyes wandered uneasily around the glazed tile walls, and were finally drawn to Jinny's face. "Well, I saw Coven."

"Coven," Gardner echoed. "Guy who was killed?"

"I saw him."

"And ran out in a tizzy? Since when do corpses scare you, Doctor?"

"He wasn't dead."

"Now come on. Come on!"

"He wasn't dead," Granville insisted. He took Jinny's hand and held it. "Jinny talked to him this morning. I talked to him this afternoon. He isn't dead. He told me he took the dive under the truck to wake me up . . . to keep me from dreaming."

"Are we going to kick that around again?" Gardner snarled.

"He said a few other things I don't quite understand. Something about me being dangerous because I'm a poetic scientist. I . . . I'm going to find something out."

"What, in a word?"

"I don't know. Something about a hoax. A fraud. We're all being duped."

"How? Out of what?"

"I don't know. It's like describing color to a blind man. He can't understand. That's us. We're all blind. We're missing something. We—"

Granville broke off as Gardner laughed. It was a laugh without laughter, the laugh of a parrot. Dispassionately he examined the face . . . the arched red brows, the crinkled eyes. Then he said quietly: "Hello, Gardner."

Still wheezing, Gardner said: "Excuse it, please. I'm subject to fits."

Jinny's hand tightened in his. "Charles . . . What is it now?"

"I'm meeting your brother for the first time, Virginia. I think maybe I'm meeting the world for the first time."

"Now have a heart, Doctor." Gardner sobered and reached for Granville's pulse.

"It's the laugh, Gardner." Granville pulled his arm out of reach. "The laugh tags you."

"If I hurt your feelings, pal, I'm sorry; but—"

"It's exactly the same as Coven's and Arno's. D'you recognize it,

Jinny? No . . . of course you wouldn't. You never heard them laugh. I did."

"So help me, Chuck," Gardner began in exasperation.

"Who was it said once . . . Man is a laughing animal. Something like that. You're not a laughing animal, are you, Gardner? You're something else . . . the Covens and Arnos and Gardners . . . the ones that can't laugh. What am I supposed to call you? Keepers? Guards? Trespassers?"

"For heaven's sake, Charles!" Jinny cried.

Gardner thrust an angry red face close. "Are you finished, pal? Then listen to me. I don't give a damn for your dreams and animals and hoaxes. That's your business. My business is Jinny and your career. How old are you, Doctor? Twenty-five? How long have you been training? About nine years? How much has it cost so far? About ten grand."

"Yes. Here it comes." Granville turned away. "The social pressure. Coven mentioned that."

"Just let me finish." Gardner swung him back. "You go on broadcasting like this and you'll be out of the hospital so fast it won't even be funny. Your license? Pfui. Who'd license you to practice? What are you going to do? Throw away nine years, ten grand, a career, and Jinny because you have bad dreams? You should lay there and bleed!"

"I'd listen to you, Gardner, if it wasn't for your laugh, and one small detail. I'll be dead tonight. Yes. That's the word from Coven. He's made an appointment."

Jinny caught her breath, then turned to her brother. Gardner grimaced at her. "It's paranoia," he said. "Pure persecution complex. We can't let him go on talking like this. You know how gossip spreads in a hospital. It'll be all over the shop he's gone off his rocker. He's got to lay off."

"I can't," Granville said.

"What about Jinny?"

"Don't bargain with me," Jinny said. "I'll do my own talking."

"You heard me, Chuck. What about Jinny? She goes down the drain too? Look, I'll put it to you fair and square. You think you're right about this mish-mash. I think you're crazy . . ."

"But you can't laugh."

"Will you listen," Gardner cried. "Let's put all the evidence up to a third party and see what he thinks. If he says: 'Chuck, you are the savior of the human race.' by God, I'll become the Number One Disciple. But if he says: 'Doctor, take a vacation quick.' You'll take it and forget everything else. A deal?"

Granville nodded wearily.

"Okay. Come on. We're going up to the Psychiatry and lay it all in Pop Berne's lap."

In the narrow office smelling of cigars and British Museum Book Dressing, Pop Berne bulged placidly in his squeaking chair like a porcelain stein. His fat face and bald head gleamed. His quiet voice was like the long grey ash that silted down on his vest from his cigar. Berne said: "All dis iss most interesting. Most interesting. I do not say it iss unique. No. Not unique. I haff seen many such cases . . ."

"Dr. Berne . . ." Granville broke in.

Berne held up a pudgy hand. "You be quiet, Charlie, eh? I haff listen for twenty minutes. You listen for two, eh?"

"Tell him, Pop," Gardner muttered. "Tell him good."

"The preliminaries I waive, Charlie, eh?" Berne murmured. "I proceed directly to the point. *Alzo:* Every moment in life, Charlie, iss a crisis. You understand, eh? Every moment we must make new adjustments . . . decisions . . . choices. It iss like stepping off the sidewalk to cross the street. Suddenly we look up and there iss a car coming at us. A crisis, eh?"

"I understand."

"The human animal does one of three things. He leaps forward to avoid the car and keep going . . . He stands still, paralyzed with fear . . . or he leaps backward to safety. Eh? You still understand?"

"I still understand."

"Very good." Berne relit the cigar and continued. "Forward iss an active attack on the situation. You fight to overcome the crisis and achieve the goal, eh? Still-standing iss a passive submission to what the human animal calls fate . . . But the leap backwards . . . Dat is an escape. Ah? So. It iss what you are trying to do. You have lapsed backward from something."

"But Dr. Berne . . ."

"Wait. I explain. You leap backward. You escape from something . . . I do not know what . . . but you escape. You turn your back on dis something and separate yourself from it. So of course it becomes unreal. *Naturlich* . . . But you haff imagination, eh?"

"The poetic scientist."

"Ah? So. Very good. The poetic scientist is escaping from something . . . A difficult adjustment, perhaps. Marriage or career, maybe. Perhaps as the time approaches for you to leave dis safe hospital and go out into the world on your own, you grow more and more afraid. I do not know. All I know is, you turn your back."

"And that is responsible for everything today?"

"Yes. Dat iss what I tell you. Dis mind of yours must justify itself. It cannot say: I am a coward. I am afraid to make the adjustment. No. It says: There iss no adjustment to make because there iss no world. The world iss a fraud . . . a hoax . . . unreal. I am being duped . . . *undsüweiter.* It will go on appearing like dis to you until you discover what you are refusing to face . . . and face it."

"And Coven?"

"Ach! Dis Mr. Coven and Mr. Arno and the laughter. Your mind fabricates evidence to support itself. Perhaps you did not meet them and only imagined you did. Or you did meet them and turned harmless men into imaginary monsters. Dere are a hundred explanations, but your mind will not recognize them."

"And the threats? What Arno said? And that business about his black glasses?"

"Charlie, Charlie . . ." Berne waved the cigar patiently. "You are a poetic scientist, eh? Dis Mr. Arno . . . he iss a most poetic creation. I do not say he iss unreal. He iss real to you . . . and most artistically drawn. But I am glad to say he iss not real to me. Dat would be bad for me because I am poetic too, eh?" Berne chuckled and then laughed. It was the same laughter without laughter. The parrot laugh.

Granville listened carefully, almost tasting the laughter as he slowly arose from his chair. "Thank you and goodnight, Papa Berne," he said grimly. "It's been a magnificent performance. Magnificent. You know, you almost had me convinced for a moment."

Gardner leaped to his feet angrily. "What the hell now . . . ¯

"Until I heard you laugh. That tore it wide open, Dr. Berne. So all the neat answers of psychiatry are fairy tales . . . part of the camouflage. First you try to kid us out of it. Then you try to shame us out of it. When everything fails you try to explain us out of it. I'm not buying any."

"Does that mean you're selling me?" Jinny snapped, her face white with fury.

"I—" Granville faltered.

"We're supposed to be in love. I know I am. I'd like to know what you think. Am I supposed to be part of this big propaganda campaign? A kind of cosmic Mata Hari?"

"I . . . don't know."

"Or maybe I'm the adjustment you don't want to make."

"I don't know, Jinny. I swear I don't know."

"Charles . . ." Her mouth trembled as she fought for composure. "Remember the snapshot album and the pictures? Let's start now. Right away. Vacation is the answer." She appealed to Berne. "Isn't vacation the answer?"

Berne nodded his gleaming head.

"Three weeks, darling . . . together."

"Four weeks at least," Gardner put in. "Four weeks in Maine. I'll pay for it."

"We can start this weekend, Charles. We'll go away together. We can get married . . . or we don't have to get married. Anyway you want . . ."

"Marriage. Pfui," said Gardner. "A feudal practice anyway."

"I just want you to know you don't have to be afraid of me . . . and if I'm what's wrong with you, I swear I'll be good about it. I swear it."

"Spoken like a gent," Gardner said.

Granville shook his head bitterly. "It's no good, Jinny. Does seduction come under social pressure or is it one Coven forgot to mention . . . sexual rewards?"

"You insulting son of a bitch!" Gardner grabbed his lapels with a shaking hand. "What are you trying to do? If you think—"

"I don't want you to touch me, Gardner."

"Touch you? I'll tear you apart!"

"Am I supposed to be scared? With a prior engagement with Coven?"

Granville punched clumsily and broke away. He backed to the office door and got his hand on the knob. "Now get this. You, Gardner . . . and Berne! You're my pipeline to the Coven office. Tell Coven and Arno they're going to have a little trouble taking care of me. I may be a dupe . . . but you can tell them I know how to fight."

He shot out of the office, slamming the door behind him in empty challenge.

In panic, but with resolution, Granville went down the fire stairs three to the step. He burst into the West Corridor and ran to his room. From the safe deposit vault in the back cover of Goodwin's *Forensic Toxicology* he took all his cash . . . thirty-seven dollars. From his bag he took a small brown bottle labeled: 100 TABLETS MOR-PHINE SULPHATE ¼ GRAIN POISON.

As he placed the cash and bottle in his pocket he heard steps approaching outside in the corridor. They stopped before his room. He froze and waited, listening to the murmur of voices and muffled laughter. Then the steps continued. Granville waited until they faded, then opened the door and slipped out.

He took the freight elevator down to the power plant, went through the steaming turbine rooms and out through the truck-loading platform. He was on Race Street behind the hospital. The street was dark and deserted . . . comfortably deserted. Granville hung back outside the bloom of a sickly street lamp and took stock.

There would be an alarm out for him. Gardner would see to that. In its quiet efficient way, the hospital would be searching for Dr. Charles Granville, unbalanced, a danger to himself and possibly others. Coven and Arno would be looking for him too, to keep that appointment. With shaking fingers Granville found a cigarette and lit it. He started violently as laughter sounded from a distant window.

"Sleep," he told himself. "Sleep is the answer. There's a key . . . or a judo trick . . . or something. I almost had it. I can get it if I can sleep once before Coven keeps that appointment." He touched the bottle in his pocket. "Yes, I'll sleep."

But the question was how to avoid Coven.

"I'll be damned if I let him look in peace," Granville muttered. "I said I'd fight. All right. Let's start fighting. Let's give him something to worry about."

He trotted down Race Street, avoiding the lamps, turned back to Harding Boulevard three blocks below the hospital and flagged a cab on the corner. His resolution remained constant during the ride, but the panic mounted. At police headquarters he could not restrain his trembling. He got his information at the front desk and went up to

Simmons's office so uncontrolled that he almost fell through the door.

"Simmons!" he cried.

The slender man looked up startled. In the blue desk light he looked even more sallow. "For the love of sweet Jesus!" he exclaimed.

Granville took a step toward the desk. "Simmons, you've got to help me."

"I'll help you to a punch in the snoot!" Simmons jerked back his chair and stood up. "Where do you come off crashin' into my office like a—"

"I'm Granville."

"So what?"

"I rode wagon this morning. The Coven accident."

"Oh. Ohhh." Simmons relaxed and slumped back into his seat. "Yeah. Sure. For Chrissakes, watch yourself, Doc. You got the manners of an ambulance. What's on your mind?"

"I want you to get a search warrant and investigate Coven's office."

"You do, huh?" Simmons cocked an eye at him. "Why?"

"There's a murder being planned there."

"Yeah? Who's the future corpse?"

"Me."

Simmons was not impressed. He shuffled papers and said: "To be killed by . . . ?"

"Coven."

"Relative of the corpse, huh?" Simmons began reading a stenciled sheet. "Just hysteria, Doc. I get it all the time. Anybody croaks, the relatives always blame it on the doctor . . . or the cop. You get used to it."

"This one is different," Granville said. "The corpse threatened me."

Simmons lowered the sheet. "What?"

"You and I saw Coven, Simmons. He was the deadest man there ever was at six this morning. I saw his remains this afternoon. He wasn't dead. You've got to investigate."

"The hell you say!"

"He wasn't dead, Simmons." Granville's voice soared hysterically. "I heard him talk with a mangled throat that couldn't breathe.

He was crushed to death and he was alive. The pieces of him lay there on a couch and—"

Simmons burst out laughing. It was the laugh of a parrot. "What an actor you are, Granville. You almost had me biting. Now go away, I'm busy. No time for *Inner Sanctum* tonight."

Granville leaned across the desk staring at the detective. "You too, eh Simmons?" he asked.

"What's the gag now?"

"You're another one who can't laugh. It's easy to spot you once you know what to listen for. It's something you can't cover up, eh?" He pounded the desk in futile anguish. "But my God! How many are you?"

"Now take it easy, Doc." Simmons reached cautiously for his phone.

"You were with Coven when he jumped under the truck, weren't you? All that talk about passing by when the accident happened . . . that was baloney for public consumption. You're right in there with Arno and Gardner and Berne."

Simmons picked up the phone. Granville cracked his hand down over Simmons's, forcing the phone back onto the cradle. "You're all around us, waiting to herd the poor sheep back into the corral if they get curious. And if we won't follow the Judas goat, we get herded into an asylum. No thank you, not for me."

With surprising power, Simmons wrenched his hand away and lifted the phone. He snapped: "Jessup, Simmons here. Get a couple of men to my office quick."

"And don't forget the straitjackets," Granville said. He turned and was out of the office.

He ran down the stale dim hall, passed the front desk just as the phone jangled and the sleepy man in uniform reached for it, and was out into the street. As he hesitated uncertainly, a horn honked behind him. It honked again, persistently, for attention and Granville thought he heard laughter. He was afraid to turn, but he did turn and saw Jinny in the roadster double-parked before the headquarters entrance.

"Charles!" she called. "Charles!"

As he ran to the car she opened the door and started to get out. He thrust a palm at her. "Stay in."

"Darling . . . darling, I've been all over town . . . chasing after you. I was just going to speak to Missing Persons when I saw . . . Are you all right, darling? I—"

"I can't stop here in the street, Jinny."

"All right, darling. Anything you say. Get in. I'll chauffeur you . . ." Jinny tried to take his arm. He jerked away.

"Don't touch me, Jinny." He got into the car alongside her. "Start driving. Quick."

Jinny gave him a bleak glance and started the car slowly. There was a shout from the headquarters entrance. Granville turned and saw Simmons gesticulating on the steps. "Get going, Jinny. Faster."

The car picked up speed. Jinny kept her eyes straight ahead. Her mouth was trembling.

"Turn right here. Where's your brother?"

"He . . . he's getting commitment orders for you. He and Dr. Berne . . ."

"Yes. They would. Left here."

The car turned again, careening into a narrow dark street. Jinny's body lurched against him. Granville squirmed away from her. "I told you not to touch me."

"For God's sake, Charles! Don't you understand anything? I told you . . . No matter how upset you are, I'll stand by you."

"You never told me."

"You should have understood. Don't you want me to stand by?"

"I don't want anything from you until I've heard you laugh."

"Please, Charles . . ."

"Laugh, Jinny. I want to hear you laugh."

"I can't," she cried. "It's all I can do to keep from screaming. Charles . . . I'm trying to be patient. Listen. You're in a bad jam. Do you want me to help you or not? Just tell me . . . But stop talking about laughing."

"On the left," Granville said. "In front of that hotel. You can stop."

It was called the Hotel Adams by an old-fashioned electric bulb sign that winked outside the ten-story McKinley architecture. The brown sandstone façade was a writhing of pillars and festoons and ledges. Granville looked at it and said: "Yes. This'll do."

As he got out of the car, Jinny reached toward him, then remembered. "What now, Charles? What are you going to do?"

"I'll tell you," he said. "Your brother's looking for me. The police are after me. Coven wants me . . . and I'm going to sleep." He took the brown bottle from his pocket and held it before Jinny's eyes. "I'm going to sleep."

He turned away, ran up the high stoop and entered the dismal lobby. He went straight to the desk, rapped sharply and spoke as the clerk appeared.

"I want a room for the night."

"Yessir. Just sign the register."

"My name is Wilkins. Charles Wilkins . . . from Chicago. I have no luggage. It will follow tomorrow." Granville picked up the pen, signed, then examined the clerk's bland face. "Will that be all right?"

"Quite all right, Mr. Wilkins. Just pay in advance . . . to . . . ah . . ."

"I'll pay." Granville dug into his pocket. "I want to explain something. I've had a bad day and I need rest. I have some clients who may insist on seeing me tonight. I don't want to see them. I'm not to be disturbed by anyone. Understand?"

"Ten dollars, please. Yes, Mr. Wilkins. I understand."

"If anyone inquires whether I . . . or anyone has checked in tonight, the answer is no. I've got to get a night's sleep." Granville put two tens on the counter and pushed them toward the clerk. "Do you understand?"

"Yes, sir, Mr. Wilkins."

"No matter how urgent they say it is."

"No matter how urgent, Mr. Wilkins. You won't be disturbed." The clerk smiled sinfully, selected a key and reached for the call bell. Granville stopped him.

"I won't need a bellhop. I won't need service of any kind tonight. Just give me the key and let me go to my room. As far as you're concerned, I'm not here. As far as anyone is concerned, I'm not here."

"Yes, Mr. Wilkins. You're not here. Room 509, sir. Elevator on your right."

Taking the key and ignoring the elevator, Granville found the stairs and went up quickly. So far so good. He would have a long undisturbed night. A quarter grain of morphine would have him asleep before Coven could possibly locate him. The question was whether he could get to Starr in time. If Coven located him while he was still helplessly drugged . . .

"It's a chance I'll have to take," he muttered, coming out into a ghastly green hall. He went down the doors, counting numbers, found 509, unlocked the door and entered. The room was brightly lit. Arno arose from a faded lounge chair graciously, glancing at his wristwatch through the black glasses.

"Good evening, Dr. Granville," he said pleasantly. "Prompt as usual. Come in."

Granville's legs sagged. He staggered back, feeling blindly for support. Arno stepped past him smoothly, closed and locked the door, then turned and removed the deadly black glasses.

"And now," he said, "shall we begin?"

"He had morphine," Jinny cried, "That's the reason I had to betray him. I had to. You understand, don't you?"

"Yeah, honey. It's okay. Don't worry." Gardner thumped his sister's back. "Now where is he?"

"I couldn't be sure what he was going to do. He said sleep, but I'm afraid . . . Just promise you won't tell him I told you. Promise."

"We won't tell the doc anything," Simmons answered. "All we want to do is avoid trouble. Right? Where is he?"

"There won't be a scandal?" Jinny persisted. "You won't make a fuss. You . . . you'll just make sure he's all right?"

"Who wants a fuss?" Simmons said in exasperation. "All I want is my supper. Where is he?"

"We'll be quiet and discreet, honey," Gardner said. "We'll be kind and understanding . . . and it won't hit the papers. Now . . . where is he?"

Jinny pointed to the Hotel Adams. "In there," she said. "He went into the hotel about half an hour ago. I . . . I watched from the door. He paid money and got a key. Then he went upstairs."

"All right." Simmons was brisk. "Let me handle this. Just do what I tell you. Come on."

They crossed the street.

"If he's doped off already," Simmons continued, "he won't be any problem. You take him to County and pump him out. But suicides don't often do it first crack. It takes them time."

Jinny stared at him with horrified eyes.

"Like razor jobs," Simmons went on, mounting the high stoop. "They usually sit and take little cuts at the wrist for an hour before they get up enough nerve to dig deep. Same thing with gas. The head goes in and out of the oven a long time before they stay there for the big sleep."

"I know," Gardner said, pushing open the glass lobby door.

"Granville's probably up there now with a glass of water and a handful of dope getting ready for the big swallow. If we bust in, he'll get desperate and maybe go through a window."

"Oh no. No!" Jinny wailed.

"Keep your voice down." Simmons led them to the registry desk. To the clerk he flashed the blue and gold badge and said: "Charles Granville."

"Not registered here, Inspector," the clerk said promptly.

"Sergeant," Simmons snapped irritably. "Let me see the last registry card."

The card was produced and examined.

"Mr. Wilkins just arrived from Chicago," the clerk explained carefully. "He—"

"He's Granville," Simmons interrupted. "What room?"

"I really don't think, Sergeant, that I can—"

"What room?"

"I'm trying to explain, sir. Mr. Wilkins particularly requested me not to—"

"I don't want an argument. I want the room number."

"Please!" Jinny broke in. "He may be . . . sick. Every moment counts. He—"

"I said I'd handle this," Simmons growled. He turned his icy gaze on the clerk. "I'll give you exactly one minute to produce—"

"Hold the phone," Gardner said in a tight voice. He lifted his hand and pointed.

The creaking cage elevator was settling down to the main floor. Inside the cage stood Granville, his face white and set, his body stiff, his hands hanging rigidly at his sides. He looked like a badly trained orator.

As the elevator door clashed open, Jinny cried: "Charles!" and ran to him.

Granville stepped out, raised his arms and enfolded her as she ran into him. He said: "Jinny . . . Jinny dear . . ." in a small voice, and then smiled at the two men as they closed in. "Gardner . . . Simmons . . . Hello. Come to save me from a dishonorable death?"

Gardner inspected his face closely and said: "Morphine?"

"Right here," Granville answered. Without dislodging the sobbing girl he reached into his pocket and handed the brown bottle to Gardner. "100 poisonous tablets." He smiled. "Is that what you had on your mind?"

"Among other things," Gardner said. "Change your mind up there?"

"About what?"

"About what! I could draw up a list that— But it can wait. Change your mind about the hoax?"

"What hoax?"

"The Coven hoax."

"Coven? Fella that was DOA this morning? What about him?"

"What about—" Gardner was stupent. "And Arno?"

"Who's Arno?"

"How should I know? You were doing all the talking about him."

"Was I? Oh . . . I . . ." Granville looked ashamed. "It's the damndest thing, Gardner. I've forgotten."

"Forgotten how much?"

"Forgotten what I was so mad about today. I know I was in an awful tizzy about something . . . but it doesn't make sense now."

"Why'd you check into this hotel?"

"I don't know."

"What happened upstairs?"

Granville considered earnestly. "I finally understood Poe."

"Poe!"

"Edgar Allan Poe. He wrote a story about the devil who always wore dark glasses. Finally the devil took them off—and he didn't have any eyes at all. I think Poe saw the devil without glasses. That's what blighted him."

"For God's sake, Chuck . . ."

"No. I'm kidding. I don't know why I checked in or what I wanted to do. Get away from myself maybe. I went up to the room. I was scared and angry and upset. I knew I'd been making a fool of myself . . . and then suddenly everything was all right. I'm not blighted, Gardner. Poe was only a poet. I'm a poetic scientist."

"You're kidding."

"Sure I'm kidding, ape!"

"He's kidding. He can make a funny again. Gardner's infallible sanity test." Gardner's angry red face broke into a relieved smile. He pumped Granville's hand energetically. "Glad to have you back with us, Chuck. Have you met your long-lost friends? Jinny . . . Dr. Granville. Sergeant Simmons . . . Dr. Granville."

Simmons snorted: "It's about time, Doc."

"Overwork," Gardner bubbled. "Just overwork, Simmons. Happens to interns all over the country. I can tell you things about four out of five interns that would astonish you."

"I can imagine," Simmons grunted. To Granville he said: "So all right, Doc? I can go get my supper? You ain't mad at me no more on account of the way I laugh?"

"Laugh? Is that what I was mad about? N-no, Simmons. Not at all. I . . . I'm terribly sorry."

"And you're sure you're all right, Charles?" Jinny turned her wet face up. "You haven't changed?"

"I'm fine, honey. I feel reborn. About the only thing that's changed is my ears. They feel as long as a jackass." He laughed embarrassedly.

Gardner chuckled and turned away with Simmons. "Meet you out in the car," he said.

But Jinny held on to Granville tightly. She gasped a little and said: "Charlie . . . You're . . . well, you're laughing so strangely. You never laughed like that before."

"Like what, dear?"

"Like . . . The same way you said my brother and Dr. Berne laughed . . . and Coven. I'm beginning to hear it. You said—"

He kissed her and smiled. "Forget anything I said. I was mixed up today. I woke up on the wrong side of the bed . . . almost; but I'm back on the right side now." He laughed again. It was a parrot laugh.

Jinny looked at him in fright. He put his arm around her waist and led her out to the street. In soothing tones he said: "After we're married, sweetheart, I'll tell you all about it."

"Tell me now."

He shook his head. "It's a secret," he said, "I'm saving for your wedding present. You'll be surprised, Jinny. You'll really be surprised."

There is sound that is music. There is space. There are voices. There is an identity named Starr, speaking in a muffled and distorted voice, calling to a girl sleeping feverishly after a cruelly exhausting day . . .

"Virginia, Virginia Gardner! Can you hear me?"

Steps in the mist.

"This way, Virginia. Come this way."

In broken fragments, the voice painfully penetrates the dream chaos.

"Virginia, we have lost Charles Granville to Coven. We are trying to contact you before Granville can deaden your responses. You must listen, Virginia . . ."

Out of the depths of unknown space the identity named Starr cries: "Great Heaven! There must be some way to awaken the Human Race!"

MARTIAN TIME-SLIP
by Philip K. Dick

On the arid colony of Mars the only thing more precious than water may be a ten-year-old schizophrenic boy named Manfred Steiner. For although the UN has slated "anomalous" children for deportation and destruction, other people—especially Supreme Goodmember Arnie Kolt—suspect that Manfred's disorder may be a window into the future.

Fiction/Science Fiction/0-679-76167-5

THE STARS MY DESTINATION
by Alfred Bester

In this pulse-quickening novel, Alfred Bester imagines a future in which people "jaunte" a thousand miles with a single thought, where the rich barricade themselves in labyrinths and protect themselves with radioactive hit men—and where an inarticulate outcast is the most valuable and dangerous man alive. *The Stars My Destination* is a classic of technological prophecy and timeless narrative enchantment by an acknowledged master of science fiction.

Science Fiction/0-679-76780-0

EXEGESIS
by Astro Teller

"I request mail. I am edgar. I explore." Meet edgar. He's very smart, though sometimes a bit naive. edgar has a great sense of humor, though sometimes a bit on the wild side. edgar is an artificial intelligence computer program invented by Alice Wu at her lab in Stanford, where it becomes apparent that not only is edgar real, but completely beyond Alice's—or anyone else's—control.

A Vintage Contemporaries Original
Fiction/0-375-70051-X

Printed in the United States
by Baker & Taylor Publisher Services